THE MAKING OF JONTY BLOOM

An Unfinished Business novel

Barbara Elsborg

COPYRIGHT

The Making of Jonty Bloom is a work of fiction. Names, characters, businesses, places and incidents are the product of the author's imagination or are used in a fictitious manner. Any resemblance to actual events, locales or persons, living or dead is entirely coincidental.

Acknowledgments

I would like to thank my invaluable beta readers for their thoughts and comments — positive and negative! This book was ten thousand words shorter before I had their input so blame them if you think it's too long!

Thanks – in no particular order – to Rita, Katerina, Jo, Suki, Angela, Angelika and Ali.

The Making of Jonty Bloom

Finding his fiancé in bed with his brother was bad enough, finding out they're getting married is the final blow.

Devan Smith needs to cool his anger. He needs to forget the lies and betrayals and work on resetting his life. When his boss orders him to scope out a remote hotel for a possible buyout, Devan's only interested in getting the job done and getting out. What he's not interested in is the guy with the piercings, bleached hair, and the smart, kissable mouth behind the reception desk.

Working the hotel reception is the only thing that's stable in Jonty Bloom's unstable life. His best friend has had a terrible accident, his ex refuses to move on, and his eight-year-old self is still waiting for his mother to collect him from school. Jonty needs his job. What he doesn't need is the rude, arrogant, and hot as they come guy who's rocked up demanding he be let into his room right now.

Thrown together by a freak accident, Devan and Jonty's lives entwine, and neither wants to loosen the knot. Can the irrepressible Jonty be the reset Devan needs? Can Devan be the making of Jonty Bloom, or will secrets drive them apart?

Chapter One

If Devan hadn't known the reason why his throat felt as if he'd had a ball of barbed wire stuck in it for the past twenty-four hours, he might have been tempted to see a doctor. But he did know, and no doctor could help him. Not even a shrink. All the rage he'd felt five months ago had come hurtling back as if it had never left. *Thought you were okay, sucker? No, you weren't.*

The last thing he'd wanted to do this morning was come to work, but if he hadn't, it would be showing how hurt he was and he'd been determined that wasn't going to happen. Sadly, he'd already revealed the mood he was in. Not having his coffee on his desk at precisely the moment he'd expected it, had caused him to snap at Nate, his assistant, in front of the whole office. When Nate returned with his drink, he'd put it down and left without saying a word.

Devan should have apologised. There was probably a perfectly good reason why Nate hadn't had his coffee on his desk when he'd wanted it, except how hard could it fucking be? While he was still simmering, it was better to keep quiet, stay in his office and bury himself in work. But he was distracted, the screen blurring as he stared at it, and the turmoil boiling in his head made pain flare between his eyes.

Five months ago, he'd concealed his emotions under a mask of indifference, not caring if people saw through it or not. Or so he'd told himself. Ravi would no longer be in his life. Devan had to accept it. Get over it. And he *fucking* had! Five months was plenty long enough to get over the cheating, bastard arsehole of a... But the news Devan had been given yesterday had shaken him, wrecked what he now realised was a fragile equilibrium. The sense of betrayal had caused a

1

physical pain in his chest, as if he'd been struck in the heart by an arrow.

His mobile vibrated. When he saw who was calling, he put it down again. He had no wish to speak to his mother. He didn't want sympathy. He didn't want her logic. He just wanted not to *feel* anymore. He was awash with emotions, none of them good. How long was this unswallowable lump of anger going to last? Until the wedding? The end of the year? The rest of his fucking life? Rage festered in his gut, ate into his heart, and was doing a sterling job of poisoning his soul.

His mother called again and he walked away from his phone. He needed to take a leak.

"Sorry, Nate," he muttered as he stalked past.

As he headed through the open plan office where most employees worked, including his brother, conversations stalled. Was it his imagination that people were avoiding looking at him? Devan tried not to glance at where his brother usually sat, but he couldn't stop his head turning that way. No Griff, and Devan was both infuriated and relieved.

But on his way back to his desk, he saw Griff step out of Alan's office and heard Alan say, "Congratulations."

As if that word wasn't bad enough, Devan had managed to convince himself that Griff wouldn't be in today and now the sight of his brother caused him to falter.

"Devan, can I talk to you?" Griff asked.

"No." Devan strode past him, then past Nate, mouthing *No* to his assistant.

He closed the door of his office and leaned back against it. This was not the way to behave. Appearing as if he didn't care was the way to behave. It was what he'd done for the last five months. Admittedly, there'd been a few cracks that he'd quickly covered over, because sometimes he'd catch a random comment, or see an image on the TV, or take a call from a friend and find himself listening to words he didn't want to hear, any of which were enough to send fury roaring back at hurricane-force. His anger had always faded, though he was aware it had never fully disappeared.

"He's busy," Nate said from behind the door.

"He'll see me." Griff's voice.

You really think I want to see you, you fucking dickhead?

"He asked not to be disturbed. Please don't."

Devan had seconds to pull himself together. Griff would walk in over Nate's prone body. Knowing his brother, he'd probably step on him and Nate would be the one who'd apologise. Devan dropped down at his desk and stared at his computer. He didn't even lift his head when the door opened.

"What do you want? Nate told you I'm busy."

"I'm so sorry." Nate rushed to his desk and tried to block Griff.

Nate stood no chance, especially not against a guy with a forearm crutch and the world on his side.

"It's okay, Nate. Thanks for trying, but my brother always does what he wants." *Takes what he likes. Doesn't give a fuck. Sucks up all the sympathy.*

Nate managed a small smile and Devan hoped his assistant had forgiven him for coffee-gate. Then the door was closed and Devan faced his brother.

Griff dropped awkwardly into a chair. "I wanted to see if you were okay."

Don't react. "Why wouldn't I be okay?" *Don't say more than that.*

"I know it must be hard."

Devan said nothing.

"I wanted to tell you, but I thought it would be better coming from Mum and Dad."

"I assume you were too chickenshit to tell me yourself?"

"Yeah." Griff shrugged and flashed his lopsided grin.

Bastard. It was not winsome and cute, it was fucking annoying. What was there to smile about?

"It just…happened," Griff said.

When? How? Why? Devan dug his nails into his thighs to keep himself focused, but his mouth still opened when he really didn't want it to.

"I hope you'll be very happy together." *I hope your teeth rot and your hair falls out. Both of you. At the very least.* He sagged. He couldn't even come up with imaginative torments.

"Devan, I know this is difficult."

You think? "No, it's fine. It's life. One of those things." *No, it fucking isn't. You betrayed me.* "I assume everyone in the office knows?"

"I was excited. It's the best…"

"Right." His brother couldn't keep his mouth shut or his cock in his trousers.

"Willyoubemybestman?" Griff blurted.

Devan was aware that his jaw had dropped. He looked down, actually expecting to see it on the floor. It took a moment before he could risk speaking. "Five months ago, I found the guy I was due to marry the following day, lying on our bed with another guy's cock buried in his arse. Bad enough as that was, the other guy was not only my best man, but my brother. It was a bit of a shock." *Understatement of the century.*

"*One* of your best men."

For fuck's sake! "I learned yesterday that it was not a one off as I was led to believe, but the pair of you have been in a relationship since then and that I appear to be the only one in the family who didn't fucking know. I'm not feeling very brotherly towards you. So no, I'm not going to be your best man." *I'm not going to your fucking wedding, no matter how much you or our mother begs.*

4

"Please, Devan. I know it's a terrible thing to ask you to do, but I don't want anyone else to do it. You've always been there for me, the guy I've relied on my whole life. I want you to still be there for me. Please. Forgive me. Forgive Ravi."

It was then that Devan registered his brother had no idea how much he'd hurt him. Realisation of Griff's…naiveté— stupidity—insensitivity…there was a bloody long list, flattened his anger. *A terrible thing to ask me?* He had no idea how terrible. And forgiveness? That wasn't going to happen.

"I'm not going to be your best man," he said quietly, aware the office grapevine was likely already in operation. "It's one of the worst ideas you've ever had." *Top of that list was fucking my fiancé.*

"As bad as trying to make a zipline from my bedroom to the garage?"

That's not going to work, dragging up our childhood.

"I ended up with a broken arm." Griff chuckled.

And because Griff could do no wrong, Devan got the blame. Had Griff remembered that? *But you've broken my fucking heart.* The breath caught in his throat alongside that ball of anger.

"Please," Griffin whispered.

"No." Devan picked up a random folder. "Was that all?"

"Think about it?"

"Hmm…yep, right, thought about it…no."

"I love him. He loves me," Griff whispered.

"That's great. Have a nice day." Devan didn't look up until he heard the door close.

Have a nice day? Where did that fucking come from? He could almost feel his blood pressure soar, hear his teeth cracking. *For Christ's sake!* His fists were clenched so hard, he had to make a concerted effort to unclench them. He'd ripped the edge of the folder.

This time when his mother called, he answered.

5

"Yes?"

"Devan! I've been trying to call you."

"I've been busy."

"How are you?"

"Fine."

She sighed. "I know that's not true."

"I just told Griff it was fine. That's life. One of those things. I can't chat. Sorry. Lot to do." He ended the call and dropped the phone back on his desk.

His mood worsened as the day went on. He knew his world would turn again, given time — *that little homily better be fucking true* – but it wasn't turning now, which was all that mattered.

When he was called in to see his boss that afternoon, he anticipated being told to pull himself together and stop being such a dick to everyone. Devan dropped into the chair in front of Alan's desk and stared out of the window. Light was glinting off The Shard, the glass dagger piercing the London sky, a thought that then pierced his heart because the last time he'd been in the Shard's 31st floor bar had been when he and Ravi— *Stop it!*

"Are you listening?"

Devan looked up to find Alan staring at him over his wire-rimmed glasses.

"Sorry," Devan said.

Probably the only word he should utter today. *I could do that. Say sorry to everyone.* Except not to Griff.

"Are you okay?" Alan asked.

"I'm fine."

Alan snorted. If he suggested counselling, or an anger management course, Devan would hit him. Not even the irony of that could make him smile.

"How about a proper holiday?" Alan asked. "You have plenty of days owing."

6

And why is that, Alan? Devan simmered like a rumbling volcano.

"Ah. Sorry." Alan winced, presumably registering why Devan had so many days untaken after the honeymoon hadn't happened. "But I really think you should go away for a while. Have a break."

"No." Because it was better to fill his time with work. Time to think was worse for his health than alcohol.

"Look. I don't want you both in the same space. Bad enough when your wedding didn't go ahead, but now that Ravi is going to be part of your life in a different way, you need to get your head in gear. I can't have you and Griff arguing and fighting. It's not good for the business. It makes the office unsettled." Alan put a folder on the desk between them. "What about you taking this instead of Griff and Jane."

Devan tensed.

"I'll get the name changed on the booking. Tomorrow night until Sunday. A bit of sea air might do you good."

Yes, mother.

Alan put another folder on top of the first. "Check out this one too. It should make an interesting comparison. I know you don't normally visit until after the first report, but if you go, we'll save time. And Devan? Take time out for yourself. I mean it."

"You're so desperate to keep me out of the office?"

"To keep you apart. Just for a while."

"Then let Griff go."

"This isn't just about the job. Take a break. You need space to think. An opportunity to see past what's happened and look at it objectively. They're going to be part of your life. You have to accept it."

No, I fucking don't. Devan's fists clenched again. It was a wonder he didn't have nail marks in his palms, his very own stigmata.

7

Humiliation brought bile surging up his gullet. What was worse was that no one really *did* know what had happened five months ago. Not the truth anyway, and that was *his* fault, *his* choice, and now his burden.

"You know there's a *Breakup Manual for Men* if you—"

"I'm fine." He really wasn't. But a book wouldn't put things right. Devan had a whole line of *How to* books in his office, all but one bought as jokes by friends, family and colleagues. *How to live with a huge penis. How to poop on a date. How to talk to your cat about gun safety.* It appeared to have become a competition as to who could find the weirdest. But *How to get over finding your brother with his cock deep in your fiancé's arse* wasn't available. He'd checked.

"I'm worried about you," Alan said. "You've lost your mojo."

I've lost a lot more than that. But Devan plastered an attempt at a smile on his face and pushed to his feet.

"You might as well have the rest of the day off," Alan said.

He heard what Alan didn't say. *Leave now before you plant your fist in your brother's face.* Except Devan wouldn't do that.

"I meant what I said about staying up there a bit longer. If you don't want a holiday, then take a scout around. See if there's anything of interest. You know what we're looking for." Alan stood up and handed him the folders. "At least two weeks away. Preferably a month. Okay?"

A month? "Would you prefer I resign?" Devan's heart thumped hard.

He was relieved to see Alan's shocked expression. "No, I wouldn't. You're my right-hand man. I…"

Maybe the look on Devan's face stopped Alan saying more.

"I could find another job."

"Don't you dare," Alan barked. "You're the best at this. You see through all the crap. You have an eye for what's needed, the best fit. If anyone leaves, it won't be you."

Which didn't make Devan feel any better, though it should have. He pressed his lips together and left with the two folders.

Maybe he ought to find another job, then he could avoid his brother altogether. Except Alan was right, Griff and *fucktard* Ravi *were* going to be part of his life. They'd be at family events, talked about even when they weren't there. Unless Devan went to live on a desert island and told no one, escape was impossible.

Griff had always been the favoured son, the spoiled, disabled baby of the family who made everyone laugh and smile. The idea of having to sit around the table at Christmas alongside Ravi and Griff was unbearable. Imagining they'd have the kids that he and Ravi had talked about in their future was even more unbearable. The thought of their office Christmas celebration with Ravi at Griff's side was…

Shit. If he was going to continue to work here, he needed to go away at Christmas and make sure the holiday also covered the office party. Skiing. A thought that cheered him up until he realised that he didn't want to go on his own, and that ten days of solo skiing wouldn't solve a-fucking-thing.

Devan dealt with all the outstanding work issues that he could and handed off what he couldn't. Nate was trying not to appear too excited about having to deal with things on his own. Devan even managed to apologise to him again. Alan was probably right. Getting away for a couple of weeks was a good idea. He needed to reset his life. Was there a help book for *How to mend a broken heart?* There probably was, but Devan felt beyond help.

Chapter Two

Jonty belatedly realised he should have taken the stick of chocolate out of his mouth before he stood up behind the hotel reception desk. He found himself facing a tall, dark-haired guy in his mid-thirties, who was staring at him as if he'd never seen anyone with a Flake sticking out of their mouth before. Jonty chomped down and slipped the rest of the bar under the lip of the desk as he frantically chewed, swallowed, and finally licked his lips. Thoroughly. Just to be sure.

The guy hadn't taken his gaze off him. "Are you done?"

Jonty bristled at the snapped question. Bad enough that his chocolate rush had been interrupted, but he did *not* need the attitude.

"No. I can't quite get it all in my mouth at one go, though I have tried. Repeatedly." *Oh God, shut me up.* "It's an inch too long." *Really shut me up.*

He's cute.

And you shut up as well, Tay. Jonty made sure not to look in his friend's direction. Not that there was any risk of Mr Grumpy seeing him because Tay wasn't really there.

"Welcome to McAllister's Hotel." Jonty put on his best smile, hoping there was no chocolate left on his teeth. "How can I help you?" *Give you a personality transplant? The rest of my Flake?*

Turn him gay with one of your spectacular blowjobs?
Shut up, Tay! You know that's not possible.
You're the one who told me it was.

Was it possible? Jonty started to slide into an erotic daydream featuring him and Mr Grumpy and quickly snapped it off before it had consequences he didn't need right at that moment.

"I have a reservation. Devan Smith."

10

Jonty tapped into the computer. The guy had one of the top floor suites reserved until Sunday. Just for him? Or was his wife waiting in the car? He looked up to find the guy still staring at him and Jonty's dick twitched. *Down, boy!*

"You want to check in?" Jonty asked. It was only nine and check in wasn't until three that afternoon.

The guy gave a heavy sigh. "That would be the purpose of me coming into the hotel, walking over to the desk, and telling you that I have a reservation."

He didn't add the word *dimwit*, but Jonty heard it as clearly as he heard Tay talking in his head.

He's good-looking.

He's a dickhead.

He's still gorgeous.

You're not really there.

Stop talking to me then.

You stop talking to me!

You first!

No, you!

"Unless you can think of some other reason?" the guy said.

Shit! Mr Snappy was still speaking. Had he said anything else? "Check in's not until three o'clock, sir."

"I've had a long and difficult journey." The response came through clenched teeth.

Yes, it probably was a long and difficult journey from hell. Though why would they let you out?

"What were you thinking then?" The guy frowned.

"That you look tired." *Shit.* He should have kept that to himself.

"Do I? In what way?"

Double shit. This was not appropriate. Jonty had been warned about being professional at all times. No personal comments. Not even nice ones. No being cheeky. No backchat.

11

No sarcasm. No lusting. Well, Vincent, the hotel manager and Jonty's immediate boss, hadn't mentioned that last one.

"I asked you a question."

Jonty forced himself to stare straight at him. "Dark circles under your eyes. Face a bit drawn. Hair looks as though you've dragged your fingers through it several times. Your top button's undone and your tie is loose. You need a shave—or perhaps you're going for that designer stubble effect. It works. Totally." *Fuck!*

The silence was painful. He could feel unemployment's bony finger poking him in the back.

You've rendered him speechless.

I should have stayed speechless.

"They're very personal comments."

You asked! "Sorry. I talk too much. Things pop out of my mouth when I don't mean them to. Though not chocolate."

Nor cocks. You take your time with those, don't you?

Shut up, Tay!

"I apologise if I've been rude." Jonty risked a small smile.

"If?"

The smile disappeared. "I apologise for being too forward. It was inappropriate, unnecessary, unprofessional, and I'm extremely sorry. I offer my deepest and most humble apologies." That should do it. "Sir." That definitely would.

"Hmm."

Maybe not. The guy didn't sound convinced.

"Are you okay?" Jonty whispered. Maybe Mr Difficult had some tragedy going on in his life. His bad temper could be down to—

"What does it have to do with you whether I'm okay or not?" the man barked.

Oh God. Rescue me someone! Jonty could feel his hands shaking and put them behind his back. "Concern for the well-being of our guests is part of my job."

12

The guy gave a short laugh. "Telling a guest they look a mess most definitely isn't. I'm amazed they've put someone like you behind a reception desk. You're the face of the hotel. What are guests going to think?"

The shaking grew worse as Jonty's self-confidence took a nosedive into shallow water. "I have a nice smile." Though now didn't seem to be the best time to use it. Nor mention it. The comment brought an eyeroll. "Are you trained?"

Jonty bristled. He'd apologised. Why couldn't the guy let this go?

"Do you know how to manage reservations and check guests in and out?" the guy asked. "How to welcome guests in a courteous manner? How to handle complaints? Emergencies? How to anticipate guests' needs?"

Fuck you and the horse you rode in on. "Of course. Fully trained. Passed all my exams on how to say hello and goodbye in thirty-three languages. Excelled in mindreading. Full marks in spells and potions. And if any guest goes into labour, I'm sure I'll be able to deliver the baby without mess or fuss."

Was that too much?

"How long have you been working here?"

Said in a tone that suggested working here wouldn't be happening for much longer.

"Five months." Which was a lie, but Jonty hoped the implied inexperience might save his bacon.

He dropped his gaze and stared at the remains of his Flake. Right at this moment, chocolate would help. Or bacon.

"As long as that?"

Sarcastic wanker. Jonty was good at defusing guest complaints. Everyone liked him. Well, almost everyone. *Pull this back.* "I'll check if your room's been cleaned, sir. Would you like to wait in the lounge? I'll bring you a coffee or tea." *The additional arsenic is complimentary.*

"Fine."

13

Jonty breathed a sigh of relief, came out from behind the desk and headed for the room opposite that had a fantastic panoramic view of the sea. Particularly spectacular today, because the weather was wild, the wind offshore, blowing from the land out to sea. He wished he was out there on his board, rather than putting his foot in it with stroppy guests. He sort of expected to hear a comment about the view, because that was what usually happened. People *oohed* and *aahed*, and forgot that the hotel looked a bit tired, but the guy stayed silent, though he did choose a chair by the window.

Long legs. No ring.

Not on his finger at least.

Jonty managed to muffle his choked laugh, his good mood restored. As if this buttoned-up guy would have a piercing. He was probably straight as a ruler. The man turned to stare at him. *Shit, maybe I didn't muffle my laugh well enough.*

"Coffee or tea, sir?" Jonty asked. Using *sir* a lot might pacify him. Another twitch of his cock made him swallow hard. Why did he always fancy impossible guys?

And you're not equally impossible?

Picky. It's different.

"Black coffee."

"Please." The word slipped from Jonty's mouth before he could stop it, but the guy stared up at him, his silvery eyes framed by long dark lashes and said, "Please." Then smiled in a not-smiley way.

As Jonty backed off, Major Bagshott, a tall, elderly man, came into the lounge with his long-haired miniature dachshund, Dottie, and headed for his usual chair.

"Good morning, Major," Jonty said. "Good morning, Dottie."

"Morning, Jonty. End of the world today, young man."

"Today? Oh dear. A spot of whisky and a copy of *Playboy* then instead of your usual tea and *The Times*?"

14

The major laughed. "Maybe later. Tea and my paper please."

"Won't be a moment."

Jonty brought *The Times* over to the major, then hurried to the kitchen. He wasn't going to risk an accident with the new coffee machine in the lounge and another dry-cleaning bill. He had just one suit and could only stretch his money so far.

He knew the top floor suite reserved for Mr Difficult wouldn't be ready. The cleaners had barely started work this morning. Guests didn't have to leave until eleven and the couple in that suite hadn't checked out yet. Unless he'd somehow missed seeing them. Really, he should have sent this guy away, but something stopped him. Probably because he didn't want to get reported to Vincent for the Flake incident, the personal comments, the sarcasm, the twitch in his cock. Though there was no way that had been seen. Had it?

You just want him to smile at you.

Tay was right. Jonty felt uncomfortable not to be liked. Though being liked too much was worse. *Don't think about Brad.*

Don't let him into your head. The guy was a wanker.

Jonty bit his lip. *I miss you.*

I miss you too.

Maybe it wasn't healthy to have imaginary conversations with his best friend, but Jonty missed him so much.

When he sidled into the kitchen, Wayne, the sous-chef, was banging pans around in a foul temper, yelling at Xander and Martin, his two assistants. Jonty didn't dare ask either of them to put the kettle on, so he did it himself, then grabbed two trays. He put a couple of amaretti biscuits on a small plate with one of the wide cappuccino cups. The other tray got a plate with a chocolate biscuit, the last one in the packet, and Jonty added a small dog biscuit from a box he'd bought and left in the pantry.

15

"What are you doing?" Wayne snapped at his ear.

The tall, bald black chef towered over him like an anorexic bat.

"Making tea and coffee for guests."

"There's a fucking machine in the fucking lounge. They can make their fucking drinks themselves."

Thank you, Gordon Ramsay. "The major's not—"

"Oh, fine if it's the major."

Foul-tempered Wayne had a soft spot for Major Bagshott. Everyone did. He was a sweetie and so was Dottie, always at his side.

"I couldn't tell one guest to do it himself and not the other," Jonty muttered.

"Hmm." Wayne went back to yelling at Xander and Martin for not working fast enough, and Jonty finished making the drinks.

He was able to carry both trays at the same time because after he'd reversed through the kitchen door, there were no more barriers. Back in the lounge, Jonty put the major's tray in front of him.

"Thank you, Jonty. Ooh, a chocolate biscuit and a special one for you, Dottie."

"If the end of the world is nigh, why not treat yourself, that's what I say. I'm going to fit in as much as I can today. Eat an entire bar of chocolate without being interrupted, go surfing, then find someone to dance with, all the way to eternity."

The elderly man chortled. He thought dance meant dance, not the horizontal tango Jonty was thinking about. If the world really *was* going to end, he'd like to die while he was fucking or being fucked. Either would do, as long as he came hard enough to see stars before he returned to the stars.

He carried the other tray to where Mr Impossible sat staring through the window, his long legs stretched out and

16

crossed at the ankle. *Black socks. How boring.* Jonty's were pink with white spots. He put the tray on the table.

The guy turned. "Instant coffee in a cup for cappuccino?" He raised his eyebrows, then glanced across to the gleaming Italian contraption on the side table. "Is the machine broken?"

"No, but it spits at me. I thought you'd like a large coffee, that's why I gave you that cup. I did give you two biscuits."

"Two?" bellowed the major.

"Not chocolate ones," Jonty called back.

"Jolly good."

"I'm going to be very sad if the world ends today and I didn't get a chocolate biscuit with my *instant* coffee."

Jonty risked a glance at the guy's face. The wrinkles in his forehead had gone though he still looked...wrong.

Sad.

Yep, he looked sad. Not pissed off. Jonty melted. *Sad* he could handle. *Sad* he understood. *Sad* he could forgive.

"The major had the last chocolate biscuit. He does outrank you."

"How do you know?"

"Because you're Mr Smith not Colonel Smith."

"Maybe I'm here incognito."

Jonty gulped and his brain took a leap. A big one, as it often tended to do. *Not army, but a hotel inspector? All those comments when he'd stood at the desk.* It all made sense now. Maybe the guy was giving him another chance. A conversation that wasn't snappy or snarly or too personal.

"So is my room ready?"

"I was just going to check, sir."

"You didn't think to do that before you made the coffee?"

What? The bloody... Jonty sucked in his cheeks. *Keep calm. Be kind to the sad man.* "I thought you might appreciate the drink now, because you've had a long, difficult journey. Why don't I take the coffee away and bring it back after I've found out your room isn't ready?" *Shit!* Sarcasm had slipped out. Jonty reached for the tray and the guy caught his sleeve.

The breath hitched in his throat. The touch only lasted for a moment, though the shock of it happening lingered. The resulting pause was most definitely pregnant. What was the guy thinking?

"I'm surprised you're still working here with an attitude like yours."

You arsehole! Jonty didn't want to lose this job.

So apologise!

"I'm sorry if I offended you." Jonty spoke through gritted teeth and knew the guy had registered that. "I'm sorry I gave you instant coffee rather than risked life and limb with the machine."

This is not apologising.

Stuff you, Tay.

"I'm sorry you didn't get a chocolate biscuit. I'm sorry you thought I was rude. I'm sorry I was sarcastic. I'm sorry your room isn't ready. I'm sorry for breathing in your vicinity and stealing your oxygen." Jonty paused. *I'm sorry I still find you mouth-wateringly attractive even though you are a fucking nightmare.* "Did I miss anything?"

"Am I checking in at Fawlty Towers?"

"Oh, you wanted Fawlty Towers? It's down the road. I can cancel your booking and give you directions." *Off a cliff.*

That earned him an incredulous look. "Leave the coffee. Go and check on the room."

Jonty turned and headed for the dining room, resisting the impulse to rub his arm. The man hadn't hurt him, he'd hardly touched him, but Jonty could still feel the press of his fingers through his jacket. *And letting my mouth run away with me like that? What was I thinking?* Mr Tricky so wasn't his type. Except…

What is my type?

I can't remember, Mr Picky. Are you right or left-handed?

Shut up, Tay.

He's your type.

Well, physically he might be.

He is your type.

Fine.

But was it true? Jonty didn't need another guy with issues. Jonty had a thing about issues, because he had too many of his own.

The biggest issue is he might be straight.

Tay was right. Jonty smiled.

When he spotted Sally-Anne had arrived and taken up position behind the reception desk, he headed her way.

"Morning, Sally-Anne. You look lovely today. Great dress."

"Morning, Jonty. This old thing?"

"You bought it last week."

She laughed. "Do you remember everything?"

"It's a curse." He leaned over the desk. "There's a grouchy early arrival drinking coffee in the lounge. I'm going to go up and find out when the Madisons intend to leave Wave."

"We're not supposed to do that. Vincent will be pissed off if he finds out."

"I'll be subtle."

She snorted. "Do you know what that word means?"

"Delicately indirect."

"How can anyone expect to be able to check in this early?" she whispered. "No one turns up first thing in the morning and thinks their room will be available. That never happens."

"Poor Mr Grumpy's tired after a long journey. He's staring at his coffee as if he thinks I pissed in it."

When she raised her eyebrows, he sighed. "I didn't piss in it."

"Right." She raised her eyebrows again.

19

What? Jonty leaned over to get his Flake, stuffed it in his mouth, and when he turned, he saw the guy standing at the entrance to the lounge. *God, not again. Shit, did he hear what I said?* Sally-Anne had tried to warn him.

"Sugar," the man said.

Jonty took the chocolate out of his mouth and pointed to his name badge. "Jonty Bloom. We'd need to be much better acquainted if you want to call me Sugar." *Fuck, did I actually say that?*

Dipstick!

Sally-Anne coughed. Hard.

"I'll get you some sugar, sir," she said and Jonty fled, but not before he saw a glimmer of a smile on the guy's lips.

Thank God for that. Unless Mr Impossible was imagining him losing his job.

Chapter Three

Jonty found no sign of the Madisons in the dining room. Emily, one of the serving staff, told him they'd finished breakfast thirty minutes ago. Jonty walked up three flights to the top floor and stood by the door of their suite plucking up the courage to knock. He could have phoned the room, but he was hoping he'd get an idea of how near to leaving they were if he did this in person.

The door was opened by Mr Madison, a slightly overweight, jowly guy with a blotchy expression.

"Good morning." Jonty treated him to his megawatt smile.

The guy smiled back because that was what was supposed to happen. Mr Impossible needed a lesson or three.

"Yes?" the man asked.

"I was checking your stay had been everything you'd hoped for, if there was anything we could have done that might have improved it. The swimming pool a touch warmer? Softer towels? Sewing kit? Animal themed shower caps?"

"It's been great."

Jonty caught sight of a bag behind the man. "Oh. Are you checking out? Would you like a hand with your luggage?"

"We'll be down shortly. We don't require help."

"Okay. Sorry to have disturbed you, sir. I'm glad you enjoyed your stay."

The door closed. Jonty sighed and went down to the floor below. There was a room at the end of the corridor where the cleaners kept their supplies and the group were gathered there with their carts about to start work.

"Hi, Jonty." Maria smiled at him.

Most of the hotel staff weren't British. Maria was from Italy and in the UK for a few months to improve her English. Jonty was helping her.

"Morning, Maria. I have a guy downstairs who wants to check in early. The guests in Wave say they're almost ready to leave. Do you think you could do that suite first, please, when it's available?"

"No problem."

Back on the ground floor, Jonty went straight to the lounge. "The suite's not ready, sir. I'm sorry. The guests haven't left yet." The guy couldn't blame him for that. Though by the expression on his face, it seemed he'd like to.

"Have you been to ask them?"

"Is that a trick question?" Jonty put his hands behind his back and rubbed his fingers together, picking at the skin at the side of his bitten nails.

"Did you go and ask them?"

"I didn't ask them...directly."

"Jesus," the man muttered under his breath. "Can I have breakfast?"

Jonty glanced at the clock. Wayne was going to pitch a fit. Still, he was already in one of his foul moods. This was a chance to show Mr Impossible that he could get some things right. "I'm sure that will be fine, Mr Smith. When you're ready, the dining room is on the other side of the stairs. I'll make sure there's a table set for you."

As he passed the reception desk, he held up his hand and mouthed *five minutes* to Sally-Anne. Not that she was busy, but Jonty was supposed to carry luggage for guests who were checking out.

There was no one eating in the dining room and the waiting staff were laying the tables for lunch. He made for the restaurant manager. "Gregor, there's another guest for breakfast, please."

22

"We finished."

"I know, but he'd like breakfast. I'll do the table."

"*I* do table. *You* tell Wayne." Gregor grinned at him. "You can wrap him round your finger."

Shit. When Jonty walked into the kitchen, Wayne looked straight at him and glared. He was the only gay guy on the staff apart from Jonty, and Jonty had said no when Wayne had pinned him against the wall in the pantry on Wayne's second day on the job and tried to kiss him. Wayne hadn't taken rejection well. Several months on and he was still sulking. Though to be fair, he probably wasn't. He was a miserable git with everyone. He wasn't a guy to be wrapped around anyone's finger apart from the major's.

"Wayne, you're looking so handsome today."

"What do you want?"

"Have you done something different with your..." *Oh God.* He didn't have any hair. "...chef's jacket? Buttoned it a different way?" Was that even possible?

"What do you want?"

"Extra guest for breakfast."

"Breakfast is finished."

"I know, but the guy's booked into one of the top floor suites. He'll probably only want an egg or something. You can do wonders with an egg. He's in a horrible temper. Please."

Wayne scowled and clattered a pan so hard on the range that Jonty, Xander and Martin all jumped. Martin also let out a muffled *eep*. Jonty suspected he was not going to stay in the job for long.

"He might be a hotel inspector," Jonty whispered.

Wayne rolled his eyes. "If I believed you, this would be the fifth since I started work here."

"But he might be. He's grumpy. Picking fault all the time. He looks like a hotel inspector. Suit. Tie. Bit of silver in his

23

dark hair. Long eyelashes. Amazing eyes. Sharp—" Much too much. "A wolf in sheep's clothing."

Wayne glared.

"Is that a yes? Great. Thanks." Jonty fled to the dining room before Wayne could disagree.

Gregor had shown the guy to a table by the window. Jonty shot Gregor a smile, only for Gregor to beckon him as he was about to return to the front desk.

"You tell Wayne what he want." Gregor showed him his pad. "I not do it," he whispered. "He sharpen knives yesterday. You better at dodging."

Jonty sagged. "Fine."

Gregor ripped the top sheet off the pad and handed it to Jonty who read the order and winced. Back in the kitchen, Jonty pushed the dangerous piece of paper across the stainless-steel counter.

"Eggs Benedict with smoked salmon, please," he said and waited for Wayne to explode.

"Fucking hell. That's not just an egg."

"Plus hash browns and fried mushrooms."

Wayne grabbed the fridge door and yanked it open so hard the shelves rattled.

"And grilled tomatoes and toast. Brown and white."

Wayne started to swear.

"And three rashers of crisp smoky bacon. Crisp enough to break in half, please."

"Is that it?"

"And black coffee. Yes. Thanks. Sorry. You're a star. Really." Jonty backed out of the kitchen.

Mr Nice Arse was helping himself to cereal from the side table. He'd taken off his suit jacket and Jonty had a perfect view of a trim waist, narrow hips and tight bum. Even if he *was* gay, and the jury of one was still deliberating, he was out of Jonty's league, even for a quick fuck or blowjob in a toilet. Probably. Not that Jonty had ever done that.

Mr Trouble turned and caught Jonty staring at him. *Fuck it.* Jonty walked back to reception with his cheeks burning.

Sally-Anne sat behind the desk tapping at the keyboard, making a clattering sound because her nails were so long.

"Have the Madisons checked out?" he asked.

"No."

He sighed. It was probably too much to ask for that to have happened in the short time since he'd left them.

"There's a parcel arrived for you." She nodded to a small package on top of the printer. "You're not supposed to have stuff delivered here."

"I haven't."

She huffed. "Room Eight want a hand with their bags. They have two kids and a baby. You'd better take the cart."

Jonty went up on the lift. He really hoped the parcel wasn't from who he thought it might be from. He wouldn't be opening it in front of anyone, just in case.

The door of the room opened as he reached it and he bit back his groan. No matter how many bags a family arrived with, they seemed to take twice as many home. Along with two cases, three soft bags, two animal Trunkis, a travel cot, mattress and a pushchair, they had buckets and spades, a kite, a windbreak, a half-deflated killer whale, a bucket of pebbles that looked a lot like gravel from the car park, and a whole load of other things, some bagged and some not. Jonty carefully slotted everything in place on the cart in a complicated 3D jigsaw, not helped by the kids trying to climb up the rickety mountain as he worked.

He came back into the hotel after helping load the family's car — a work of art for which he received no tip — saw the Madisons and their bags at the desk, and raced upstairs to tell

Maria, who was about to start on Room Eight. The parcel would have to wait and he wasn't sorry about that.

"The suite's empty now," Jonty panted. "Can I help?"

"Strip bed while I start bathroom."

They went up in the lift with the cleaning cart, and once they were in the room, Jonty took off his jacket, tucked his tie into his shirt and set to work. Fortunately, the Madisons had been reasonably tidy. The mess some guests made never ceased to amaze him. Did they drop used condoms on their own carpet and just leave them? Or vomit next to the bed and make no effort to clean it up? Or fail to flush the toilet for days?

The hotel was the biggest in the area, but it was old, and needed money spending on it. The majority of the furnishings made Jonty shudder. Heavy curtains with ugly bedspreads that didn't match. Patterned carpets that didn't match either and though they were good quality and didn't show marks as easily as plain ones, they looked as if they belonged in an old-fashioned pub. He didn't know a lot about interior design, but the mish-mash of the hotel décor was migraine-inducing. The pictures on the walls of the rooms had been done by the owner's dead wife so he was never going to take those down, but they were awful.

The exterior definitely needed repainting. Sea air was corrosive and dark orange stains crawled down the walls below some of the metal balconies. Jonty imagined evil dripping from those rooms. It intrigued him that the stains weren't under all the balconies.

But there was a relatively new indoor pool, heated all year round, and a well-equipped gym, probably because the owner, Hamish McAllister and his family, came regularly to use both. Hamish had given Jonty a job when it felt as if everyone else in the area had said no. Not the shifts he wanted, and it wasn't really going to lead anywhere, but Jonty felt happy here. *Safe.*

The hotel had three guests who lived in the building full time, including the major and his dog, plus an elderly married couple who split the year between the hotel and cruise ships. Jonty loved listening to them talk about where they'd been, what they'd seen. He hoped that when he was old, he had enough money to live in a hotel rather than a care home. Though he suspected the moment those guests developed health issues, they'd be asked to leave. The major was a bit eccentric, but he walked on the beach every day with Dottie. Sometimes Jonty went with them before he cycled home, or took Dottie on his own if the major wasn't up to it.

The two top floor suites weren't as tired as the other rooms. They'd been remodelled a few years ago. Wave had a large sitting room with a TV, a bedroom with a huge bed and another TV, and a bathroom with a tub you could recline in and stare out at the sea. Or watch the TV because there was one in there too. Did people really come to a fantastic spot like this and only watch TV?

"The view is so good," Maria said.

Jonty stood next to her and looked out at the sparkling water. "It is. Thanks for your help, Maria. I really appreciate it."

"You welcome."

"*You're* welcome."

"Thank you. You're welcome."

When the room was done, Jonty pulled on his jacket, adjusted his tie, and went back downstairs to find Mr Impatient standing by the desk, tapping it with his long fingers.

"Your suite is ready now, sir," Jonty said.

"About time."

You utter prick. Why are you so good-looking? There is no bloody justice. Please be straight so I can go off you.

"Is there a lift?"

27

"Yes. We can also supply grappling hooks and crampons if you're feeling adventurous and would like to scale the outside of the building." *No, no, no!* "If you need advice on where to find mountaineering equipment, or a crag to climb, just ask. I'm happy to oblige." That had not made his first comment sound any better. Plus, he had no idea of the whereabouts of any crags worth climbing, though he could google.

Sally-Anne handed Mr Difficult his key card. "Thank you, Mr Smith. If there's anything you need, apart from mountaineering equipment, do give me a call." She sat with her back arched, her breasts on display like a tray of food, admittedly under her blouse, but not completely hidden by it. Though they didn't seem to be impressing their target, who was still gaping at Jonty.

"Do you need a hand with your luggage?" Jonty choked out.

"Why not?"

That sounded like a challenge. *Fuck this up too, Jonty. Make some inappropriate comment about his car, his luggage, his arse.* Jonty wondered if he had a set of weights in his case and it would be too heavy to lift. Or a dead body. *Ha!*

For a brief moment, Jonty wondered if the guy really *was* a hotel inspector, checking out staff reactions to surly, awkward guests, determining whether the hotel deserved its four stars. It amazed Jonty that it had that many. Though the food here was spectacular. Marcus, the chef, was a culinary genius, so everyone said, and the restaurant was always full.

As he followed Mr Impossible across the car park towards a silver Aston Martin, he changed his mind about the guy being a hotel inspector. He had money. It might not be a new Aston, but even so. Wayne's lime green Mini was parked next to it and Jonty positioned himself at the rear of Wayne's car.

Something that earned him an eye roll, but gave him a huge sense of satisfaction. The Aston Martin's boot glided open.

"Ah, that car," Jonty said in a tone that implied complete innocence.

The "Hmm" that followed told him he'd not fooled anyone.

"You take the cases and I'll get the rest."

Jonty lifted out two matching black suitcases that contained neither weights nor dead bodies. At least, he didn't think so unless he'd developed super strength and not noticed until now. He didn't want to get an earful for scratching paintwork, so he was careful. There was something bulky on the back seat but Mr Sulky only picked up a briefcase and gym bag, along with a dark grey peacoat and a waterproof hooded jacket.

"Do you want the other bags?" Jonty asked.

"No."

Jonty carried the cases into the hotel to avoid scratching the wheels — *I am a saint* — then rolled them over to the lift. *Perfect behaviour. Ten out of ten.* The guy stepped in after him and Jonty pressed the button for the top floor.

Mr Trouble smelled of coconut and Jonty inhaled the sweet scent. Something spicy might suit him better.

"Are you sniffing me?"

"I'm merely breathing heavily after lifting these cases!" Jonty put as much indignation into his voice as he could, while he thought *shit, shit, shit,* then panted to make it appear realistic.

It's not.

Thanks, Tay. I could pretend to have an asthma attack.

Don't. It sounds too much like you're having sex.

Bastard.

Tay laughed.

29

"Thanks for sorting out the room," the guy said. "And the breakfast. It was very good."

Surprise meant it took a long second for Jonty to respond. "You're welcome."

His attitude mellowed—slightly. At least he'd been thanked. He knew better than to make snap judgements, because everyone made them about him. One look and they thought—flake. He smothered his giggle.

"Are you here for a holiday?" Jonty asked. "We have lots of brochures in the lobby about local attractions and I can—"

"No."

The lift jolted to a halt. Maybe he was up in Northumberland for a funeral, or to visit a sick friend or relative. *Oh God.* His ailing grandmother who'd brought him up after his parents died in that tsunami in Asia. Devan had survived by hanging onto a tree.

Devan now?

Shut up, Tay.

Or he might be a serial killer looking for his next victim.
Really shut up.

Jonty followed the guy out of the lift, but stepped ahead of him to open the door of the suite with his master card, then held it open for him to go in first.

"You have a key?" Mr Difficult gaped at him.

"In case there's an emergency and I need to drag you from your bed before fire sweeps through your room. Or sea levels suddenly rise and flooding becomes imminent. Or…" *Don't mention zombies.*

What he'd said, earned him a heavy sigh.

Jonty stood the cases side by side next to the closet, turned to see the suit jacket being tossed onto the bed, and his gaze locked onto that enticing arse. He looked up quickly before the guy turned.

30

"Is there anything else I can do for you? Explain how the TV works, where to plug in the kettle, how to draw the curtains?" *Or I could lick your arse?* Thank God, he didn't actually say that.

"No." No smile, but when he walked up to Jonty, Jonty's heart thumped hard, right until he saw the five-pound note being offered.

Jonty shook his head. "No thanks. Have a nice stay." He exited, closed the door and groaned. He'd never refused a tip before, but he didn't want to take money from this guy. Just in case they ever — *Oh fuck it. I should have taken the money.*

He supposed there might have been worse beginnings. The day the Titanic set sail for example. Or when Vesuvius decided to belch. Or that afternoon he'd met Brad in the library. *Fucking Brad.*

He spotted Wayne in reception and passed on the comment about the breakfast, which at least made the hotel's Mr Miserable smile. Back at the desk, Jonty finally had a chance to examine the parcel. The label was typed using an odd font, like the others. Didn't mean it was from Brad but…

"Aren't you going to open it?" Sally-Anne asked.

Jonty pulled at the tape and gingerly opened one end. *Oh shit.* It was a huge black plastic dildo and it wasn't inside packaging. Had Brad used it? *Eww.* There was no note, but he knew Brad had sent it.

Tell the police.

And what are they going to do?

He's dangerous.

"What is it?" Sally-Anne asked, nosy as ever.

"A big black dildo."

She laughed because she didn't believe him. Jonty put the packet in his backpack inside his locker. He had to find a way to stop this. Stop *him.*

Devan looked from the five-pound note in his hand to the closed door and let out a long sigh. That wasn't the first time he'd had a tip refused, but it was the time that most surprised him. Jonty Bloom was…weird, probably the least suited person to work behind a hotel reception desk that he'd ever met. Even ignoring those four silver studs running the length of his ear, that safety pin in his eyebrow, the messy peroxide hair with dark roots and a suit he appeared to have been sewn into — and his socks were pink — it was his mouth that had Devan all riled up. Not just because speaking to guests in the way he had was plain wrong, but because he could not rid himself of the image of Jonty with that Flake between his lips.

As Devan had stood in the hotel foyer and stared, he'd begun to get an erection, which had to be cut right off at the pass. Picturing Ravi and Griff entwined worked perfectly to give him a limp dick. Jonty Bloom was most definitely not Devan's type. Though… Did he have a type? He'd thought Ravi had been what he liked. Olive skin, huge eyes, full lips, a body honed at the gym, wild in bed and a mouth that… But any of that now would remind him of Ravi, so maybe he ought to go for someone different, except he'd like a guy who was wild in bed. He and Ravi had liked the same films, same TV shows, same food. More or less. Hadn't they? The sex had been great. Hadn't it? Good, at least. *Fuck, fuck, fuck!* Rage surged and Devan battered it down.

Whatever it was that had made Ravi walk away from him and slide his arse under his brother, Devan would drive himself crazy trying to figure it out. It had already driven him crazy. Though until that meal with his parents, he'd thought he was over the whole damn fiasco. Now, he was questioning himself all over again. *What's wrong with me?* Why had Ravi done what he did? *How did I fail to see anything?* Had there been signs he'd missed? Too many hours spent at work and not being willing to pander to Ravi's every need? If he didn't figure out what had gone wrong, how could he make sure it never happened again?

Before Ravi, there'd been Charlie and Miles. Both of whom had dumped him. Sort of. Though it had been more of a mutual parting of ways. Was he such a bad judge of character when it came to men? Or had he got something wrong? Maybe he'd not focused on what he really needed. *Which is?* He had no fucking idea. He was going to die a sad, lonely, bitter old man, and it served him right.

He changed out of his suit. He'd not been thinking when he set off last night, only of getting here as fast as he could. He wondered if the hotel could get his suit dry-cleaned. Dare he ask Jonty Bloom? He'd probably put it in a washing machine.

As he hung up his clothes, he pulled his mind back on track. He was here to work. His brief was straightforward. Was McAllister's a hotel that would fit into the Shaw Group's portfolio? Was the site the right one? How much would the owner want for this place? Would the price offer enough leeway for the necessary renovations and building work? Would knocking it down and starting again be worth it or even possible? What would be successful here? A state-of-the-art spa? A centre for sporting activities? Both? He needed to do some research.

There was a lot wrong with this hotel, though staff like Jonty Bloom could be replaced, the decor changed, maybe the entire building levelled, but its location was fantastic. Seeing the whole bay from the lounge had taken his breath away. The hotel was elevated enough to give a commanding view and near enough to the north-east conurbation to attract discerning guests, even maybe lure them from the south. It was close enough to the beach for guests to walk there, and because it was in a fairly secluded position, away from a large town, it offered a degree of exclusivity. There were no gift shops or amusement arcades or tacky cafés.

He could even see this as a destination for celebs, definitely for high-end clientele. But not yet and maybe never. The décor of the downstairs rooms was dated. This suite was…acceptable, but it needed to be more luxurious. Softer towels and more of them — *not twisted into bloody swans* — , robes, higher thread count bed linen, original artwork — what was on the wall looked as if it had been done by a bad amateur artist, little touches of luxury like handmade soap, top quality toiletries, good quality glassware, champagne on ice. Those things were easy, but if the building itself wasn't right…

Open mind, right?

After he'd unpacked, he went back downstairs, sharing the lift with a middle-aged couple and their matching orange suitcases.

"Let me handle this," the man whispered.

When the lift doors opened, the guy dragged his case to the front desk. "I want to speak to the manager."

"Jonty will help you." The woman who'd fetched Devan's sugar skittered into the back room like the mouse she clearly was.

Jonty emerged. "Mr and Mrs Pickering. What can I do for you?"

"You aren't the manager," the guy barked.

"No, but if you tell me what's wrong, I'll try to sort things out."

"The room was too small. The bed was too lumpy. There was dust on the picture frames and the windows are filthy," the man said with a distinctly triumphant tone in his voice.

Devan moved out of sight of the desk and lingered by Jonty's promised display of brochures about the local area. He was intrigued to see how Jonty would handle this. Was he rude and sarcastic to everyone?

"And we didn't see any whales on the trip *you* told us to go on," the wife added.

Devan smothered his grin. And Jonty thought *he* was difficult?

"This place is not worth the money," her husband said loudly.

"I'm sorry you feel that way," Jonty said. "But I have to wonder why you left it until the last day of your weeklong stay to let us know about your problems with the room. I could have checked to see if we had a larger one and tested the bed out. I'd have arranged for your windows to be cleaned, although they were done not long ago. Because we face the sea, the windows do tend to get dirty quite quickly, but I know it's disappointing not to have a clean piece of glass between you and the fabulous views."

"What about the whale watching trip?" the woman said. "We were really disappointed."

"I can imagine. But no boat that does the trips can guarantee sightings. The company I recommended are the best. But the whales are around or they're not. It's a matter of luck."

"We didn't pay all that money to be reliant on luck." The guy was shouting now.

"Did you see any seals or dolphins?"

Devan heard the desperation in Jonty's voice.

"Yes, but not whales. It was whales we wanted to see."

"Did you try calling them?"

"What?" the woman asked.

"They communicate by clicks and whistles. That's what I always do. Click and whistle. *And* sing." Jonty made the most awful wailing noise. "Sometimes they come when you sing like a whale or if you feed them Maltesers."

Jonty, you liar. But Devan found himself smiling.

"Well, we won't be staying here again. You're not going to get a good rating on Tripadvisor," the man snapped.

"Is there something I can do to help? I'm Vincent Rossi, the hotel manager."

Where had he come from? But within minutes, the couple had a ten percent reduction to their bill, which instantly solved all problems. Devan glanced out of the window and saw the couple smirking as they left.

"What the hell, Jonty?" Rossi sighed. "Was that supposed to be a whale song? Dottie was freaking out in the lounge."

"What do you mean supposed to be? It was. I'm just visualising the Pickerings on another whale watching trip. The others on the boat will be so impressed when they sing."

Devan clapped a hand to his mouth.

"And whales do like Maltesers," Jonty said.

"You are joking."

"Well, once I tipped half a bag in by accident and a couple of minutes later a minke whale came up right next to us."

"Keep your tall tales to yourself."

"Yes, sir."

"Go and see if anyone in the lounge needs a drink."

Devan made his way to the basement to check out the pool and gym. The online photographs didn't do them justice. The twenty-five-metre pool was much larger than most hotels provided, beautifully tiled, and there were two hot tubs outside on an attractively laid brick patio along with good quality chairs and loungers. The gym was large too, fitted out with a mirrored wall and top-of-the-range equipment that no one was currently using.

The events room was an impressive size with a line of windows facing the sea. The arched ceiling overhead was amazing, though pale yellow was an unfortunate colour choice and plaster was peeling away in several areas, which

36

implied a leak or a problem with damp. A wander around the other communal areas told him they needed gutting and redesigning. A couple of walls knocked down maybe, or an extension on the left of the hotel. Devan took pictures and made notes on his phone. A new entrance would work better, make the place instantly appealing, assuming this was going to be a renovation and not a rebuild. He'd have to do more investigation before he was sure.

Getting to see the hotel rooms should have been more difficult than it was, but he told Sally-Anne, who was far more amenable than Jonty Bloom, that he was thinking of holding a conference here and wanted to see where guests would stay. She handed over four room keys and left him to it.

The rooms were all a good size. Those on the seaward side had balconies and fantastic views, and those on the landward side had pretty impressive panoramas too, a variegated mosaic of pink and white heather moorland, green meadows and rolling hills. He'd pick up a selection of those brochures downstairs and maybe check out some of the places. He'd never been to Northumberland before and the idea of exploring appealed. But not a holiday. What point was there taking a holiday on your own?

His mood soured. He turned away from the window and inspected the last of the four rooms. No different to the other three with the same awful artwork. They all needed updating, particularly the bathrooms. New fixtures and fittings, re-plastering, modernised décor, replacement windows and doors. Maybe two rooms could be made into one. He'd have to work out if that would be cost effective. Plus the whole place might need re-wiring.

Devan was beginning to wonder if it would cost too much to do a complete renovation. In addition, while its remoteness was in part an attraction, it was also a disadvantage. At least six hours by car from London, and it had taken him over nine plus a two-hour kip in a motorway service station parking area. But although it was remote, there was room for a heliport.

He needed to run some numbers. If his initial judgement on this place was a no, he could move on and forget that a cheeky bellhop had made his dick twitch back to life.

Chapter Four

Thirty minutes after his shift was supposed to end, and forget the idea of being paid for unapproved overtime, Jonty changed out of his suit, brushed it with a lint roller, then hung it in his locker with his tie. He sighed at the creases in his trousers. Maybe he'd get the iron out when he came back tonight. After a wipe with a damp sheet of kitchen roll and a quick polish with a dry one, his now shiny leather shoes went on a shelf at the bottom. He cycled to and from work and only took his suit home if it needed cleaning. He reckoned he could wait another few days.

He stared at the packet holding the dildo that he'd stuffed into his backpack. Yet another item received in the mail over the last few months that he hadn't ordered. It had to be Brad sending them. Jonty knew the guy liked sex toys. A thought that made him shudder. What he didn't know was why Brad was doing this. Five months since they'd seen each other, apart from a few times in Alnwick when Jonty had bumped into him and quickly walked the other way, and those other times when he'd felt he was being watched and wondered if it was Brad.

Jonty bitterly regretted ever agreeing to go on a date with him. A potentially nice boyfriend had morphed into a nightmare that wouldn't let him go. Telling Jonty he spent too long with Tay had been the last straw. Well, the penultimate straw. Jonty swallowed hard. They hadn't split amicably, but he'd assumed Brad would leave him alone. Not an unreasonable expectation, considering the way it had ended, except that wasn't what had happened. Well, the guy wasn't going to spoil his day.

He pulled on jeans, a pink T-shirt and a grey hoodie, then stuffed his dress shirt and socks into the backpack along with his towel. Once he was wearing his trainers and helmet, he left through the rear of the hotel, unlocked his bike from the rail and set off for a beach a few miles down the road.

Getting out on the water would push thoughts of Brad *and* Devan Smith from his head. On the other hand, sitting waiting for the perfect wave would give him plenty of time to regret having ever said yes to Brad and to recall all those stupid things he'd said to Mr Trouble, which were enough to get him the sack.

You think?

Jonty glanced at Tay cycling at his side. He was wearing yellow shorts and a flowered Hawaiian shirt and he was laughing. His bright eyes were full of fun, except they really weren't.

Why weren't you more careful?

I was being careful.

Tay *was* a careful guy, which made what had happened to him all the more upsetting. Because even being careful couldn't keep you safe. Jonty knew that. Tay wasn't around anymore and that was all that mattered.

Dead.

Jonty sucked in a breath. *You're not.*

As good as.

His heart felt like someone had reached into his chest and crushed it, kept crushing it.

Say it.

Shut up.

I know what you're thinking.

No, you don't.

You like Devan Smith. You're coming back to life, Jonty.

I want you to be okay again.

That can't happen for me, but it can for you.

It didn't feel like it.

I can't stay with you forever.

I know. Just be my friend for a bit longer.

Jonty padlocked his bike at the back of Mike's Sports Shop, which adjoined the beach car park, and went inside.

"Jonty!" Aussie Mike gave him a high five. "How are you, mate?"

"I'm fine."

"Really? I've not seen much of you."

Jonty shrugged. "Busy. But I can't resist a sea like this. I'm surprised it's not crowded out there."

"Kids are back at school and it's the middle of the day. Most people are at work. Your wetsuit's in the locker. I took it home with mine the other day and gave them a bath."

"Did you get in with them and soap them up, you kinky bastard?"

Mike snorted.

"Thanks. I do appreciate it, even if I'm going to have nightmares now. You wrestling with rubber." He mock-shuddered.

"Not funny. Watch for rips, today."

"Yes, Dad."

"I mean it. I have this feeling. The week after the lifeguards stand down always makes me edgy."

"I'll be a good boy and watch for rips, Daddy. I promise."

"You are such a little shit!"

Mike was only in his thirties and once Jonty had discovered he hated being called Daddy... Well, he was fair game. He and Jonty had had a short-lived thing, lasting a couple of months, once upon a time, long, long ago. More friends with benefits than anything else. It had never felt quite right. Jonty had bought his second-hand board from Mike at a good price and Mike got access to a mighty fine arse and a talented mouth. But Mike was now in a long-term relationship with a geography teacher called Willis. Jonty and Mike were

41

better friends than they'd ever been lovers, though he knew Mike worried about him, knew how much he missed Tay, because Mike missed him too. Everyone loved Tay.

Jonty stored his wetsuit and board at Mike's in return for giving occasional surfing lessons at busy times. Mostly during the school holidays. Jonty would have loved to do it full time, but it was seasonal work, largely dependent on sea conditions, and even worse—it paid peanuts. Nor was it a career that would go anywhere.

What do you want *to do with your life? Isn't it time you decided?*

Tay stood leaning against the wall of the back room as Jonty searched for his wetsuit.

I can't leave Alnwick, let alone Northumberland. Jonty's heart thumped hard at the thought.

Yeah, you can. You can go anywhere. Do anything. Be anyone.

Not while you're here.

I'm dead.

You're not fucking dead.

I'm not the only reason you won't move. But you need to.

Jonty chewed his lip, turned his back on Tay, and changed into his wetsuit.

Mike was holding a plate with a slice of buttered toast when Jonty emerged.

"You're too thin." Mike offered him the plate.

"Is there such a thing?" Jonty ate the toast in a few bites. "Do you have any idea how hard I've worked to get this body? The hours at the gym, not eating chocolate, denying myself pleasure after pleasure?"

"You wouldn't know a gym if it bit you on the arse, and the idea of you parting company with chocolate or denying yourself pleasure…" Mike snorted. "How are you really doing, mate?"

42

Jonty knew what Mike was asking. If he'd got over what had happened to Tay, if he'd stopped thinking about Brad, if he was dating. "I'm fine."

No, you're not.

Shut up, Tay.

"Anymore worries that you're being followed? You know I told you to call."

"I know. Thanks, Mike. I was probably imagining it."

Liar.

Willis already didn't like Jonty, so calling Mike to come over and see if that really was Brad lurking across the road would make him even less popular.

"Want to come to dinner at our place next week? Willis has a single friend he'd like you to meet."

Jonty gave a short laugh. "Who won't be my type. Or Willis has a grudge against his friend and wants to use me to exact his revenge. Willis hates me."

"He does not."

"He so does. He looks at me and imagines me naked under you, wonders if you moaned for me the way you do for him, and he gets this tic in his cheek."

Mike grinned. "Is that why his cheek tics?"

"Ask him. He's probably thinking of ways to kill me."

"I want you to come."

"I'm okay, really."

"So why haven't you been here for so long?"

"I don't like it when it's busy," Jonty said. "But I do like big…waves." He waved flamboyantly to Mike and left the shop before Mike pushed him.

Jonty hadn't come surfing because it wasn't much fun without Tay. They'd always surfed together. He remembered how Brad had reacted when Jonty had told him that he was going surfing with Tay. He hadn't been happy. *You don't need him anymore, now you've got me.* He'd assumed Brad could surf,

43

but it turned out he couldn't even swim. Jonty had stupidly told himself it was nice to be liked so much, wanted so much. What an idiot he'd been.

Once he'd collected his board from the storage shed, he slotted it under his arm. Fast-moving clouds scudded across a bright blue sky, the sand bouncing light back into the air. It was a good day to be out on the water. Not so heart-warming when it was grey overhead, even if the waves were big. But with the sun shining down, there wasn't much he'd rather be doing, anywhere he'd rather be. Though he missed Tay so much.

Jonty felt the heat of the rays on his face as he walked down to the water. He loved the sun, biggest source of the Earth's energy, thirteen billion times brighter than Sirius, and the provider of his fading tan. He adored lying in it, and felt its touch on his face and body almost like a sexual caress, even though he knew he shouldn't sunbathe because of the risks. Tay kept telling him that, but Tay had always sunbathed with him. Jonty liked a lot of things he shouldn't. Including Mr Impossible.

The smile slipped from his face. This futile, irritating attraction was starting to annoy him. He was even annoyed that he partly enjoyed it annoying him. Did that make sense? *Fuck it.* He was playing with fire. Scorched fingers were inevitable. He had to leave Mr Difficult alone.

The temperature was above average for September, but the chilly wind was whipping the sand at a slight angle across the beach, streaming it into ankle-biting channels. As he drew closer to the waves, he registered they were even larger than he'd thought.

He could see several surfers out there, but this was a long stretch of beach so there was plenty of room. There was a kiteboarder jumping further out, making big air. Jonty hoped the rider was experienced, because these weren't the right

conditions for that particular sport. Too easy to get blown out
to sea. But for surfing, this onshore wind was brilliant, causing
the waves to break more slowly and cleanly. Perfect rides to be
had if he got his timing right.

Jonty stopped to tether his ankle to his board, then picked
it up and waded out, his toes curling into the sand at the first
wash of cold sea. He could have worn boots, but he preferred
to ride barefoot. Same with gloves. He really hated those. He
sucked in a breath as the first wave hit him, felt a flush of
freezing water slide down his suit and shivered.

Once he was in deep enough, he climbed onto the board
and paddled. The waves were maybe six or seven feet, much
bigger than usual, and when a narrow line of lacy froth
indicated one was about to break, he grabbed the board's rails,
and duck dived under the surface. When he was deep and
parallel to the bottom, he checked the wave was passing
overhead, then angled the board up again.

Jonty surfaced, gasping, blinked water from his eyes and
kept paddling and diving until he was out beyond the break
point, then turned his board towards the shore and sat on it.
When he glanced over his shoulder, he saw the swell had
dropped and he now sat in a lull. He chuckled. *Did you see me
coming, Neptune? Decided to tease me?*

The swell might have dropped, but the wind hadn't, and
the kiteboarder was flying. It seemed as though he knew what
he was doing, not going too high, making controlled turns and
twists. Jonty had never tried it, partly because he couldn't
afford the equipment. The kites could be as much as a
thousand pounds. Not only was Jonty's surfboard second
hand, so was his wetsuit.

Tay sat on his board alongside him. He'd always been the
better surfer, not that Jonty had cared. He'd loved being out
on the water with Tay, especially on those few hot summer
days when they could just wear trunks. Jonty loved watching

him surf, the beautiful curve of his body, the way he moved as if he and board were one. Tay was as sleek and agile as a seal. Jonty got turned on watching the water stream down his body, dreamed of licking it off, dreamed of the day Tay would decide he wasn't straight after all. Jonty sighed and licked his lips, his tongue tingling at the salty tang.

Weirdo.

I never told you that.

I knew the way you felt about me.

When he was making up what Tay was saying to him, why did he have to lie? A lump formed in his throat as memories of Tay swarmed in. Then his stomach rumbled. He should have had something more than toast before he'd come out, but he hadn't wanted to waste time. The weather was fickle. The wind could drop; the waves might disappear along with the sun. Days with waves like this were rare. He promised himself a portion of chips on the way home if he rode the first wave all the way in. That's what he and Tay used to do.

Get ready.

Jonty glanced over his shoulder. The sea didn't look any different, but the next sequence of waves would be on their way. It wasn't quite a myth that the seventh wave of a set was the biggest, but it was often true. Mike's geography-obsessed boyfriend had told him more about waves and weather than Jonty wanted to know. Yawning had probably not endeared him to Willis.

As his board rose and fell, he kept watching over his shoulder, trying not to be distracted by the antics of the kiteboarder, who was doing all sorts of skilful manoeuvres: rolls, riding on the tip of his board, even turning a complete circle, and moving at speed. Jonty pulled his attention back to the water and let a few good waves pass under him until he saw *the one*. Now that he'd judged the approaching wave was

46

definitely worth going for, he lay on his board and started to paddle.

Faster!

Timing was everything. When Jonty felt the board catch and he began to shift more quickly, he pushed to his feet. After a wobbly adjustment, he found his balance and took control, turned the board across the wave, and rode all the way in with his arms out, an exciting, fast ride that brought a cry of joy from his mouth.

"Chips!"

He laughed out loud, jumped off in the shallows, and made his way back out, ducking and diving to reach the area beyond the breakers.

The next wave he caught wasn't so kind. He went under in a deluge of white foam and wild sea, his mouth and nose filling with water. He came up spluttering, but climbed back on his board and paddled out again. He wished Tay was there for real, to celebrate with him, share his chips, but all he had was what his mind could conjure up. Sometimes he wondered if he was going crazy.

Jonty kept riding. Only exhaustion or failing light would pull him back to shore for the day. For the first time in a long while, he was enjoying himself, not letting anything interfere with the pleasure of conquering the waves — some of them at least. When he got it right, he moved so fast, it was as if he were flying like the kiteboarder. Each wave was different. Each was a challenge. Sometimes his timing was perfect, sometimes it wasn't, but he kept trying, kept hoping.

Like life.

Was it? He wanted to be happy all the time, wanted to forget all the problems he had. No Tay. Crappy place to live. A job that was less than he could be. No future plans. The possible reappearance of Brad, because Jonty had the feeling Brad himself would be the final gift to arrive. No one to love apart from Tay, who'd never loved him the way Jonty wanted him to. Except out on the water, nothing mattered but riding the wave. Out here he could do anything, be anyone, believe that someone out there could love him as much as he would love them.

Take control of your life. Change things. Don't waste a moment. Learn from what happened to me.

The next wave he caught was a monster, maybe a double header, twice his height. *Shit, it's huge.* Maybe the biggest he'd ever been in. He crouched inside the barrel and shot along with the wave breaking behind him. *Wow, wow, wow!* Jonty laughed and heard Tay laugh too.

See? You're nearly as good as me.

Fuck off, you wanker!

Jonty had been out there for hours. He was tired and making mistakes. Each time he fell off the board because his balance was off, or he didn't duck dive at the right moment, or he surfaced too soon and caught a mouthful of saltwater, it all sapped his energy. The waves had grown wilder and he and the kiteboarder were the only ones left out there.

The light was still good and the waves were fun, but Jonty was hungry, plus he had to work tonight, so he needed to snatch a couple of hours in bed. Though once the final member of staff had left, he could nap in the room behind the reception desk. As long as he had his phone on, he'd get an alert to tell him if anyone was at the front door or calling from their room.

A couple of wide yawns confirmed he'd had enough. Time for the last wave of the day. But as he sat on his board, half-watching the water and half-watching the guy with the kite soar into the air, the bright red and blue canopy suddenly went really high before it folded and crashed to the sea, taking the guy with it. *Shit, that was a long drop.* Jonty scrambled up on his board.

The kiteboarder was more than fifty metres away, his red helmet bobbing in the water. Jonty decided to paddle out and check if he was all right. As he drew nearer, it was clear the guy and his kite were no longer attached. He was also nowhere near his board.

"Need a hand?" Jonty yelled.

The guy turned. *Fuck it. Devan Smith? Seriously? We've been out here all this time and I didn't know?* Jonty paddled harder. In the same direction, though he'd been tempted to turn and leave him to it.

"No. I'm fine," Devan called back.

Fuck you, then. Jonty was about to head to shore when he realised what the guy was swimming into. His board had floated into a section where the sea seemed calmer than the water either side, an area where the surface flickered and danced. When the board began to move faster, straight out to sea, Jonty's heart sank. *Shit.*

"Stop! You're heading into a rip," he yelled.

Jonty paddled hard, only to be caught up in a gigantic wave that seemed to come out of nowhere. There was no time to duck. It sent Jonty spinning underwater, arms and legs flailing. Just when he thought he couldn't hold his breath any longer, he saw daylight through his part-clenched eyelids and he surfaced, coughing water from his lungs, only to realise how far from the shore he'd been pulled. Devan too. Jonty frantically paddled in his direction.

Devan was white-faced and breathing heavily.

"Are you injured?" Jonty called.

"Winded, but I'm okay."

"Get on the board." Jonty yanked at him, but as Devan slithered on, Jonty fell off.

49

Devan hauled him up, so that Jonty sprawled across it, both of them now being dragged out by the rip. But at least they were together, and on the board, slightly safer.

"Where did this fucking sea come from?" Devan growled.

"As the planet cooled...water vapour and other gases escaped from molten rocks into the atmosphere... Once the Earth's surface had cooled... rain fell and kept falling."

"Smart arse."

"You noticed!"

Devan huffed. "The rip's pulling us out to sea. We need to try to get back in at an angle."

They fell into what felt like an endless pattern of kicking in one direction and getting pulled back again, or pulled under without making any progress.

Devan spat out a mouthful of water. "We need to try harder."

"You want us to struggle against the unrelenting pull...panic when we don't get anywhere...eventually succumb to exhaustion and drown." Jonty paused. "Actually, not funny... Might still drown." *God, I'm tired.*

"We're not going to drown."

"And here was I, thinking you were Mr Doom and Gloom."

Devan rolled his silver-grey eyes. They were rather lovely. *I don't want to drown.*

"Does anyone know you're out here?" Devan asked.

"Mike who owns the shop... Don't know how long...it will take him to notice I'm not surfing."

Now caught in the centre of the rip, the waves had gone, but they were being swept further and further out.

"We can't fight this," Jonty said. *Do not add the word Attraction.*

Devan's teeth were chattering. "You're right. We need to save our energy. Though at this rate, we'll end up in Norway."

50

"I've never been to Norway, have you?" Jonty could feel himself getting colder and colder.

"Yes."

"Then you'll recognise it if we get there."

"How far out are we?" Devan asked.

A long way. "We ought to pick out a couple of points on the shore...then we can check our position...see how far we're moving." Jonty was breathing heavily. "How about Mike's shop...and that dark bit of rock...? Looks like a dinosaur's cock."

"A dinosaur's cock? Did they have cocks? I don't remember that bit in *Jurassic Park.*"

Jonty had a fit of coughing. "Educational films, though... We now know dinosaurs will eat you...even while you're taking a crap."

Devan snorted. "Those films got virtually nothing right. The T-rex couldn't run, because one foot had to be on the ground at all times, so no way could it outpace a jeep. It ate with a puncture-pull movement, not by grabbing and shaking its prey. As for cocks, there aren't any fossilised ones, because dicks in the animal kingdom don't have a bony component."

"Wow! That's the most you've said to me...without adding an insult." Jonty's teeth were chattering harder and harder. He was going to lose a filling in a minute.

"Only an idiot would think a film about dinosaurs would have everything right."

The quick grin as Devan said that, slightly warmed Jonty's freezing body, though not his toes. "How come you can speak in whole sentences...and I can barely breathe?"

"Stop talking. Just breathe."

So for a while, Jonty managed to stay silent.

"We're coming out of the rip," he muttered. "I can feel the pull fading. That's the good news." He shuddered. "The bad is…we're miles out…and the waves are big. Don't let go…of the board or me."

"Down now!" Devan shouted.

Jonty grabbed the board and forced the head down. Not quite fast enough. He hadn't been paying attention. The sea poured into his mouth. *Fuck, fuck, fuck! I don't want to fucking drown. Not now that Mr Impossible is mellowing.* Jonty was turned and twisted by the water until he didn't know which way was up, which way was down. When he finally surfaced, he could see no sign of Devan—and the waves were huge.

Chapter Five

Devan spun in a circle, but there was no sign of Jonty or even his board. Where the hell…? The surge of fear and panic flooding through him was so overwhelming, that, for a moment, his lungs locked. Too much time spent chattering and not enough on trying to save themselves. Rips were unpredictable, dangerous, and deadly. He'd been grabbed by them before, though never by one as powerful as this. The only reason Jonty had been caught this time was because he'd come to warn him. After the way Devan had snapped this morning, he shouldn't have expected help, yet Jonty had paddled out to him when he could have stayed safe.

It was pointless shouting, but Devan did it anyway, yelling Jonty's name, turning in circles. The waves seemed to be getting bigger. When Devan finally saw him, his heart started beating again. But Jonty was off his board, limp in the water. Devan swam faster. Just as he reached him, Jonty slipped beneath the surface. Devan reached out, scarcely able to believe it when his fingers wrapped around Jonty's forearm. Then they were both pushed under and Devan tightened his hold. He surfaced first, and yanked Jonty up next to him. Jonty's face was deathly white and water poured from his nose and mouth. Devan thumped him on the back.

"Shit," Jonty gasped.

Another wave rolled over their heads and Jonty slipped from his grip. *Fuck!* They had to get out of these breaking waves or they were going to drown. While neither of them had control of the board, it could smash into them and Jonty was in more danger, because he was still attached to it. If Jonty lost consciousness, Devan wasn't sure he could keep him afloat. He wasn't sure if he could keep himself afloat. The idea that they might not make it began to seem a possibility.

Devan came back up, saw the board, then caught sight of Jonty's white hair and hauled him to his side. The guy was coughing, choking, and Devan thumped him on the back again.

"Jesus," Jonty spluttered. "Beating me up…not sexy."

Relief surged. "I thought you were drinking too much. It's bad for you."

Jonty's blue eyes widened. "Oh my God." He coughed. "A joke. Are we dead?"

"Not yet. Let's aim for Norway."

"Another joke?"

"Duck!"

Devan pushed him under. They couldn't keep doing this. The moment they surfaced, Devan grabbed the board with one hand, Jonty's arm with the other. By the time they were no longer getting pushed under by breaking waves, they were exhausted, their breathing ragged, their fingers as white as the surfboard they clutched. Safer, but nowhere near safe. The severity of the situation had finally sunk in. Devan was shocked to feel…not fear or anger sweeping over him but something that felt a little too much like calm acceptance. They'd done what they could. Now they had to wait and hope.

"Any…more…jokes?" Jonty asked.

"No."

"You're…no fun."

"Not while I'm trying to keep us alive."

"Any ideas on how?"

"No."

"Are you…a hotel inspector?"

"What is this? Twenty questions?"

Jonty's eyes kept fluttering closed. He seemed close to unconsciousness.

"Wake up." Devan shook him.

54

"Don't be mean… Are you like this in bed? I'm tired."

"You need to stay awake."

"I don't want to die."

"We're not going to."

"Promise?" Jonty looked straight at him.

Devan didn't answer.

"'S'okay. Better not promise. Don't want you to spend eternity thinking you b-broke a promise… I don't b-break p-promises… Hurts when they get broken… Not like a b-bone. Worse, I think… Don't you? Hurt lasts longer."

Yes. "You're rambling and slurring your words."

"I'm swimming at the same time… Thinking, shivering, rambling…slurring… and swimming. And hallucinating… B-brilliant multitasking."

Jonty sounded so indignant that Devan wanted to laugh. How could he feel like that when they were in such dire straits?

"What now?" Jonty asked.

"We wait for the sea to calm down so we can swim back, and we hope for rescue." *Before we die of hypothermia.*

"What are we going to do while we wait? I'm easily b-bored… Entertain me."

Devan rolled his eyes.

"Say something funny." Jonty rested his head on his arm where it stretched across the board, blinking when water hit his face. The blinks were getting longer.

"Wake up." Devan pulled Jonty's hair. "Talk to me."

"Ouch. What job do you do? Torturer?"

"I'm a quant, a quantitative analyst." He had been, and in some ways he still was. He couldn't tell Jonty he was interested in buying the hotel.

"Where?"

"London."

Devan thought he'd ask what a quantitative analyst did. He'd be surprised if he knew.

"Why kiteboarding…not surfing?" Jonty asked.

Maybe he didn't want to admit he had no idea what a quant did.

"I like action. Too much waiting around when you're surfing, then a lot of paddling for a few seconds of glory every ten minutes or so." Devan shuddered with cold. "I'm too impatient for that."

"So…you're in a job where you have to be careful and methodical…and you chose a s-sport…where you take risks all the time…and rarely stop moving?"

"That's very sharp." Devan was shocked.

"Brains as well as beauty."

Yeah, you do.

"Supposed to agree with me." Jonty sighed. "Maybe…did in your head. That's fine… Guess not currently looking my best… Hair a mess… You look great. Cool red helmet."

Devan laughed. *Oh God. We might die and you can still make me laugh.*

"I watched you jumping…. Didn't know it was you… You're good. Do you do everything at full speed?"

"Not everything."

"Hmm." There were a few seconds of silence where Jonty seemed as though he was going to make some quip, then decided not to.

"Wake the fuck up." Devan thumped him.

"Fucking hell. I'm going to have bruises. Only do that if a shark's coming to eat me. Right? No, in fact don't w-wake me… Let losing my leg be a surprise… Though if you were being kind, you could get between me and the shark… Especially if you're bleeding… Are you b-bleeding?"

"No."

"Come here and let me bite you." Jonty smiled as his eyes closed.

No way was Devan going to get a hard-on in water this cold but…but…

"You're falling asleep. You should ride the board in while you still have the energy."

Jonty opened his eyes. "What? Not leaving you."

"Get back to shore and call the coastguard… They can come and get me."

"Not leaving you."

"Then we'll both fucking die." Yet, the thought of being out here on his own made his heart stutter.

"I don't…" Jonty shivered. "Not that I don't want to do the right thing…but don't know what that is."

"Go back in."

"Leaving you doesn't feel right… Anyway…too tired to do much more than breathe…talk and look semi-gorgeous. Limit to even *my* multitasking… You t-take the board and surf in… I'm…I'm not…important to anyone."

Devan felt a wrench in his chest. "Of course you're important to someone. You have friends…family…colleagues."

Jonty shook his head.

"Major Bagshott and his little dog. Who else would offer him chocolate biscuits and *Playboy*?"

"I'd have been stuffed…if he'd said yes to *Playboy*… Do they still p-publish that?" Jonty sighed and his eyelids fluttered.

"Wake up! I'm not leaving you."

Jonty sighed. "You say that now… Moment we get to shore, you'll be like… *Right, bye then* and waltz off into…sunset."

What else did he expect him to do? "I'm sorry you're stuck out here. You paddled out to warn me there was a rip

57

and got caught in it… This is all my fault." It was hard to stop his teeth chattering.

"It's not. Sh-should have gone straight to shore when I knew what was h-happening… Phoned for help. *My* f-fault, not yours."

"Fine, it's your fault."

Jonty blinked water from his thick dark eyelashes, his chocolate eyes looking huge in his face. "Supposed to argue."

All Devan wanted to do was stop him from falling asleep. "Okay, then it's my fault. Sorry."

"I forgive you."

Devan scowled tiredly. "You are such a little shit."

Jonty grinned.

"Let's sit on the board now the sea's calmer. We'll be seen more easily. You get on first."

"No, you." Jonty shook in a violent bout of shivering. "Have to help me up. Arms are numb. All of me is numb except my mouth."

Devan squirmed on and once he was balanced, he tugged Jonty over the board, then into a sitting position facing him, though he was shaking so hard, Devan wondered if he'd fall off.

"I don't get a cuddle?" Jonty pouted.

"We need to be checking for a boat in opposite directions."

"'Kay." Jonty stared at him. "You do realise that if I fall asleep…my head will land right in your lap?"

"You're not going to fall asleep."

"Spoilsport."

The light was beginning to fade. Once it was dark, there'd be less chance of them being found. They were both heading toward hypothermia.

Jonty started to slump, then caught himself. "I'm tired. Want to try and get to shore or wait?"

"I'm thinking we have to do something."

"I'd count not dying as doing something... Shit, can't feel my toes or my fingers. Or other bits."

"Why didn't you wear boots?"

"I'd rather the news headline said... *Jonty Bloom who looked cool until the end...* rather than... *Jonty Bloom who said he'd never be caught dead in rubber gloves and boots... was caught dead in both.*"

Devan found himself smiling. Then he heard a different sound above the churning of the sea and a moment later registered it was an engine. He turned and saw a boat heading straight for them. "Lifeboat." *Thank God for that.* He waved.

"Now I'm glad I didn't wear the b-boots or gloves," Jonty muttered. "Might be a hunk onboard to impress."

Devan didn't want to identify that surge of...whatever it was... that clawed at his chest. All he should be feeling was relief they were safe. *Not frigging jealous.*

When the boat pulled up alongside, Devan untethered Jonty from the board and pushed him into outstretched arms. Devan followed. He and Jonty huddled in the bottom of the boat while the surfboard was retrieved.

"Thank you." Devan had never meant those words more.

"You both okay?" asked one of the guys. "Any injuries?"

"We're just cold," Devan said.

Emergency blankets were wrapped around them.

"What are your names?"

"I'm Devan. He's Jonty."

"My name's Brian."

"My kite and board are out here somewhere."

"We saw them. We'll go and pick them up now we have you safe. We don't want anyone to think there's another rider out here."

Devan brushed wet hair from his eyes. While they'd been in danger, adrenaline had rushed in, now it flooded back out and exhaustion took over. "Thanks for finding us."

He felt Jonty leaning into him, but the movement of the boat knocked him away. Devan thought about pulling him close again, but didn't.

"What happened?" Brian asked.

"I was kiteboarding, got caught in a really powerful updraft and my lines tangled. I cut them, fell, and lost my board. I went after it, but didn't realise I was swimming towards a rip. Jonty paddled over to warn me and the rip grabbed both of us."

As he glanced at Jonty, Jonty's eyes slid closed.

"Hey, wake up," said Brian. "Talk to me. Tell me your name?"

"He told you," Jonty said. "Sometimes calls me Sugar. Other times Little Shit."

"Being able to joke is a good sign." Brian smiled. "Good thing you were out on the water together."

"We're...we're not together," Devan said. "We don't know one another."

"You pick now to break up with me?" Jonty stuck out his bottom lip.

Devan glanced at him, then back at Brian. "We only met this morning."

"Instant attraction." Jonty jerked, then closed his eyes again.

"We've got a paramedic standing by," Brian said.

Jonty reacted as though he'd been hit by a cattle prod. His eyes snapped open and he tensed. "I'm fine."

Brian pulled a beanie onto Jonty's head, tugging it over his ears.

"Doesn't he get one too?" Jonty asked.

"He has a helmet. You don't. And you're in worse condition." Brian patted Jonty's shoulder.

"Is it my spots? My blue lips? ... Do they put you off?"

Brian laughed. "You've been given a thrashing by the sea. You've swallowed water. You're cold. Exhausted..."

"Delusional," Devan muttered.

Brian stared at Jonty and frowned. "Quite possibly hypothermic. You need checking out."

The boat slowed and Devan's board, then the kite, were pulled on board.

"Don't want to go to hospital." Jonty pressed himself against Devan. "Don't make me go."

Devan wanted to pull Jonty into his arms. An urge he had to fight. *Oh, what the fuck.* He tugged a hand out from under his blanket and slid it inside Jonty's and grabbed his fingers. He heard the breath catch in Jonty's throat, then a shuddering exhalation.

"I can't promise," Devan said quietly.

"Let's see what the paramedics say," Brian told him. "Keep talking to me."

"He made me keep talking." Jonty glanced at Devan.

"The right thing to do," Brian said.

"How did you know we were out there?" Devan asked.

"The guy who runs the sports shop. Mike Walker. He wondered why Jonty hadn't come back, went to look for him and spotted you both struggling. Called it in. We came out from Seahouses. You owe him a pint."

"I owe everyone in this boat a pint." Jonty smiled and Devan realised how glad he was that Jonty was okay, that *he* was okay, and that this hadn't turned into a disaster. Would his parents have believed it was an accident? He'd broken the rules. He'd gone kiteboarding alone, not told anyone where he'd be and he'd gone out knowing there was a strong offshore wind. He might be depressed, but he wasn't suicidal.

61

He also shouldn't be holding Jonty's hand. The guy would get entirely the wrong idea. Devan let him go.

Jonty's heart jolted when Devan stopped holding his hand. He so very nearly made a grab for him. Thank fuck he hadn't because that really would have made him look like an idiot. Nearly dying together was all that bonded them and now that they were safe, they were...unbonded. Still... Devan hadn't needed to hold his hand at all. Jonty wasn't sure whether Devan was gay. He thought he might be but... *What did it matter?* He had more to worry about now.

The closer they drew to shore, the more anxious he became. He was cold but fine. He didn't need to go to hospital. His head hurt where the board had banged it, but he wasn't going to tell anyone that. His fingers and toes had come back to life. But the opposite had happened between him and Devan. He'd hardly spoken to Jonty since they'd been rescued. It felt as if the guy had been building a wall between them. He suspected Mr Impossible was returning to his normal impossible self.

A green and yellow rapid response vehicle waited on the quay, a paramedic standing beside it, a group of onlookers behind him. Not an ambulance, which was a relief. But if the paramedic told him he needed to go to hospital, Jonty would freak out. He might even have a panic attack, which would probably ensure a hospital was where he ended up. He told himself to calm down, but his heart was doing an Olympic sprint, and he was having difficulty swallowing. The more anxious he became, the more likely the paramedic would conclude something was wrong. *Shit.*

"You okay?" Brian asked.

Not Devan asking, which was disappointing. "I'm fine."

"And you?" Brian asked Devan.

"I'm fine too, thanks."

Jonty glanced at Devan. Nobody should be that good-looking. Nobody should be stupid enough to want to get involved with someone that good-looking. Especially if that someone was straight. *Colour me stupid.*

And what did *involved* mean anyway? Whatever happened with Devan, assuming it did happen, would never be what Jonty wanted – needed – or hoped for. Something different. Someone who *did* want to make it more than sex. Someone who wasn't freakily possessive. Someone who didn't take things too far. A proper relationship. Jonty hardly dared let himself think that was possible.

Except... *It isn't going to be anything, you idiot.* An hour spent in each other's company wondering if they were going to die was not the start of something beautiful. They'd each dealt with it in their own way. Jonty by opening his stupid mouth and Devan by being controlling. Once they reached the shore, it was the end. Back to sarcastic hotel employee and unimpressed awkward guest. A few nights in the hotel and Devan would go back to London.

Jonty's life was all about endings. People leaving him. That's what always happened. Except for the one guy he didn't seem to be able to get rid of. *Bloody Brad.* In an instant, his breathing turned ragged. Jonty tried to get off the lifeboat without help, but the crew weren't having any of that and he was escorted up the jetty to the quay. Not by Devan, but maybe that was just as well.

"Thanks, guys," Jonty said. "Though we *were* holding out for the helicopter."

Brian laughed. Jonty pulled off the beanie Brian had put on his head and handed it back to him.

"I'm sorry we put you to so much trouble." Devan took the words out of Jonty's mouth.

"You were unlucky," Brian said. "But you knew what to do. Kept you alive long enough for us to rescue you."

Jonty saw Mike striding their way and the big Australian threw his arms around him and hugged him. "You okay, mate?"

"The sea spat me out." Jonty tried to grin. "Too much of a mouthful."

"Let me check him out," said the paramedic.

It didn't take long for both him and Devan to be declared fit enough not to require further treatment. As the paramedic drove away, Mike homed in for another hug.

"I warned you to watch for a rip. You know what to look for. You're a fucking idiot. You could have carked it." He held Jonty by the shoulders. "Sure you don't need an ambo?"

"I'm fine."

You could have died.

But I didn't, Tay. Where were you when I was out there?

You didn't need the distraction.

"Jonty saw the rip," Devan said. "He came to warn me and got caught as well."

Mike kept his arm over Jonty's shoulder and turned to Devan. Not hard to miss that the pissed-off expression had returned to Devan's face, probably because Mike was sporting one too. For a brief, very brief moment, Jonty felt like a lamb caught between two wolves. He knew which one he'd cuddle if he had the choice, which proved he was a fool.

"You can't both eat me," he said.

A comment that brought him two identical looks of incredulity. *Darn it. That should have stayed in my head.*

"Who are you?" Mike asked.

"Devan Smith. I'm staying at McAllister's. You must be Mike from the shop. Jonty mentioned you, said he hoped you'd spot he was in trouble." Devan had his hand out. "Thanks for calling the coastguard."

64

Mike gave his hand a brief shake. "I didn't want Jonty to drown. Not sure about you yet."

Jonty sighed. "It's not Devan's fault. If it hadn't been for him, I wouldn't have made it. He pulled me up quite a few times. Kept me awake telling hilariously filthy jokes."

"Hmm. Is that your vehicle in the beach car park?" Mike asked. "The Aston Martin?"

"Yes."

"I'll give you a lift back." Mike opened the rear of his van and put the boards and kite inside.

"Get in the front," Mike told Jonty.

Jonty slid into the seat.

"You'll have to sit in the back," he heard Mike say to Devan. "Kiteboarding in an offshore wind?" He whispered, but Jonty still heard. "Are you fucking crazy? You could have both drowned. He isn't—"

"Shut up, Dad," Jonty called before Mike said something he didn't want to hear or didn't want Devan to hear.

Mike slammed the rear doors, dropped into the driver's seat and slammed that door too.

Jonty heard Devan shuffling up behind him. There were no seats in the back. Mike used it to transport sports equipment from one beach to another.

"Dad?" Devan asked from behind Jonty's head.

"No, I am fucking not his dad. Do I look old enough to be this little shit's father?"

"It's my pet name for him." Jonty put his hand on Mike's knee. "And Little Shit is his pet name for me. Devan guessed that one."

Mike muttered under his breath and Jonty felt Devan's sudden warm exhalation at the back of his neck.

"If you call me Dad again, you'll be walking back," Mike said. "And move that hand off my knee before I have to confess to Willis. You know he makes me tell him everything."

65

Jonty laughed and removed his hand. "Only warming my fingers."

"That sea came out of nowhere," Mike said. "It was the wind howling that made me go and check if you were okay."

"Did I say thank you?" Jonty asked. "I don't think I did. Thank you, Mike. You are a prince among men."

"You stayed out there too long."

"No arguing with a rip. It's a like a stalker. It won't let go." Jonty shuddered. "But I rode a double header. It was awesome. I was awesome. And no one saw me. But I was so awesome. I might try for the Olympics. Not this time, obviously." He yawned.

"Don't go to sleep," Mike snapped.

"God! What is it with guys telling me that? Devan, then Brian, now you."

"Who's Brian?" Mike asked.

"One of the lifeboat crew," Jonty said. "He's a prince among men too."

"Now I feel special," Mike said.

Mike pulled up next to the Aston Martin, which was at the far end of the car park, so no wonder Jonty hadn't spotted it. Would it have made any difference, though, to where he'd chosen to surf? He'd have still gone into the water even if he'd known Devan was out there.

"Can we have showers, please?" Jonty asked.

Mike looked over his shoulder at Devan. "You going to give him a lift home after?"

"Yes," Devan said.

"Okay then. Put your stuff in your car."

After Devan had pushed the board, kite and mess of tangled lines and his helmet into the boot of the Aston, he grabbed his bag and climbed back into the van.

Mike drove over to the shop. "Get your board out, Jonty, while I turn off the alarm."

But when Jonty went to the rear of the van, Devan had already propped the surfboard against the side.

Mike unlocked the door of the shop and went in. A few seconds later, he beckoned them. "I'll stow the board. Want a hot drink? Coffee?"

"Black coffee, please," Devan said. "One sugar."

"I wasn't talking to you."

Jonty laughed. "Shut up, Mike. Yes, you were. We'll both have black coffees, thank you, Da...da...dearest one."

Mike growled. "Watch it." Then left the shop.

Jonty turned to Devan. "Shower's through that door. You go first."

"No, you go first."

"I knew there was a polite guy under there somewhere. Okay, to save hours of — you, no you — I'll go first. I'll try not to use all the hot water, unless you'd like to shower with me? It's a tight squeeze but..."

For a moment, Jonty actually thought Devan was thinking about it, then Mike came back in. *Shit.*

Mike glared at Devan before he went through a door behind the counter. Devan heard the sound of a kettle being filled and followed him.

"Don't ask me about Jonty," Mike said before Devan could say anything. "If there's anything you want to know, ask him yourself."

"I was going to ask about your shop." Though Mike had guessed correctly. "How much traffic do you get in the winter? Any courses you run all year round? I'm considering investing up here."

Mike turned out to be a valuable source of information. Once he was talking about the local area and his business, he was much friendlier. They were still chatting when Jonty emerged, rubbing his hair with a towel. Both he and Mike

67

turned. Jonty looked…all spiky-haired and wide-eyed and adorable. Lust coiled in his gut. *Oh God.*

"What did I miss?" Jonty asked. "Been talking about water sports? Is Willis into that? I know how much you love it. Have you asked him? Like me to? I can be subtle."

Mike pushed a mug of coffee into Jonty's hand. "No and No. I don't love the water sports you're talking about and don't you dare say a word to Willis. Not one word."

"I can't say water sports? But it's your life."

Mike sighed. "You can say water and you can say sports, but don't put them together."

Devan was trying not to laugh.

"So not water sports," Jonty said. "But water…leave a long pause…sports."

"Oh God, I don't trust you."

"Me? That hurts."

Devan picked up his things and slipped away to the shower. If he was guessing, he'd say that Mike and Jonty had once been an item. For all of Mike's glares and growls, Devan had taken in the way the guy had hugged Jonty when they were on the quay, and that possessive hand on the shoulder. Mike still cared about him. Hard not to feel envious that two guys could still be friends after they'd been lovers. Not that there was any chance of that with Ravi.

After a brief tussle with his wetsuit, Devan finally managed to free himself, and stood under the hot water. Not a deluge, but enough to chase away the chill and make him feel human. There was a container of blue shower gel attached to the wall and Devan squirted a dollop onto his palm.

It was surprising how much better a hot shower made him feel, though he was very tired. He wondered if he could persuade Jonty to have a meal with him, a thank you for quite possibly saving his life. *Is a meal all I want?* Devan swallowed hard. No, it wasn't.

When he emerged into the shop, there was no sign of Jonty.

"He's putting his bike in my van," Mike said. "I'm going to have to take him. The bike won't fit in your car and he needs it to get to work."

Devan wasn't sure whether to feel relieved or disappointed. "Okay. Thanks for all your help. If you hadn't called the coastguard... Well, thank you. And for the shower and coffee."

As he moved towards the door, Mike stepped in front of it. "Not something I usually need to ask, but are you gay?"

"Yes."

"Not in the closet back where you come from?"

"No."

"Not bi?"

"No."

Mike nodded. "Jonty's not sure. Not about himself. He's sure of that. But he's not sure about you." Mike shurgged. "He wants you to be gay. For some reason I can't fathom, because you seem a bit of a posh git to me, Jonty likes you. Despite what you might think, he doesn't take to people easily. If you're staying at the hotel, you're only here for a short while. You have the potential to hurt him and he's already damaged. Don't make his pain worse."

Devan sucked in his cheeks. Why did Mike assume he would?

"Did you hear me?"

"Yes...Dad." Before Mike could move, Devan stepped right into his space. They were about the same height though Mike had more muscle. Devan stared straight at him. "Did you warn him off me?"

Mike's mouth twitched and Devan took that as a yes.

"I'm guessing you had him and lost him."

Mike's mouth opened, then closed in a tight line.

69

"I get that right?" Devan asked.

"He's a good boy. He deserves a good man. I don't think that's you."

"You know nothing about me."

Mike pinned him with this gaze. "I know enough. You'll take what you can get and you'll be gone in less than a week. He'll be out of your mind before you get a mile down the motorway, but he won't forget you."

As Mike stepped to one side, Devan pulled open the door and left. He'd got the message. *Don't hurt Jonty.* He gave a short laugh. *What about him hurting me?*

He thought about looking for him, but instead headed straight for his car. He might not want to admit it, but Mike was right. Not touching Jonty was better for both of them.

It was gone nine before Devan reached the hotel. An older guy he'd not seen before was behind the desk. The restaurant was closed. He was too tired to face going out again. Once he reached his room, he kicked off his shoes, grabbed the room service menu and dropped on the bed. He could order until eleven so maybe he'd have a short nap first.

A good plan that went wrong because when he woke, it was eleven fifteen. *Shit.* Well, maybe it was time to see how accommodating this hotel was. He picked up the phone.

"Front desk."

Jonty? "I want to order some food. I know it's after eleven, but I'd really like the chargrilled chicken fillet."

"The one marinated in Cajun spices, served with garlic mayo in a soft brioche bun with fries & coleslaw?"

Definitely Jonty. Devan found himself grinning. "Yes, if not, then the veggie club sandwich."

"Ah, the delightful and delicious three-decker feast layered with grilled Portobello mushroom, sliced egg, beef tomato and lettuce. With spiced chunky cut fries."

70

Read straight from the menu. Devan smiled.

"Which would you prefer, sir?"

Devan sat up. He'd thought he'd be told it was too late.

"The chicken."

"Anything to drink?"

Devan ran his gaze down the list. "The Australian Shiraz."

"Oh yes, excellent choice. That taste of crunchy red berries with hints of coffee, chocolate and pepper is hard to beat."

Devan grinned.

"One bottle or two?" Jonty asked.

"A glass is fine. A large glass." In case Jonty brought him something tiny.

"Anything else? A mouth-watering dessert? I'm sure I could whip something up."

Devan swallowed hard. "No, that's all."

"No problem."

Devan put the phone down. Had Jonty been offering a dessert or something else?

Maybe the chef hadn't yet left for the night. Now Devan was thinking about food, his stomach rumbled. Had Jonty been on a late shift last night as well? When did he sleep? *What does it have to do with me?*

When the knock came at the door, Devan doubted it was going to be what he'd ordered. His guess was beans on toast. Maybe cheese on toast. Either would be fine. He pulled open the door to see Jonty standing there in that too-tight grey suit. Next to him was a trolley, a domed stainless-steel cover sitting over the food. Devan's heart jumped. So did something else. He felt like a horny fifteen-year-old.

"Shall I set it out on the table, or outside on the patio in the howling gale or would you like to eat in bed?"

"The table." His voice cracked as he spoke.

71

Devan watched as Jonty carefully laid everything out. He'd even put a pink-flowered stem in a vase. Devan held back his snort of laughter when he recognised it. Rosebay willowherb. A pernicious weed.

"Don't sniff the flower," Jonty said. "I can't guarantee that Dottie hasn't peed on it."

"Right. Will you thank the chef for me?"

"You were too late. I cooked it. You better wait until you've tasted it before you thank me." Jonty lifted the dome. "Ta-da!"

"It looks…"

"Nothing like beans on toast?"

Devan gaped at him.

"I told you mindreading is one of my many superpowers. Cooking chicken might not be. It's okay if it runs a bit bloody when you poke it with a knife, right?"

Devan pressed his lips together.

"Now, you're hoping that was a joke." Jonty smiled. "See? I'm so good at seeing inside people's heads. The chicken is properly cooked. I know how to do that. Raw chicken is dangerous unless you're a fox. Are you a fox? Sorry. No. Are you gay?"

Devan gaped at him. "Where did that question come from?" Hadn't Mike told him?

Jonty looked around. "Is there someone else in here?"

"You pick now to ask me that? Why?"

"It's annoying me that I can't tell whether you are or not. I think it's partly because you haven't stared at my arse. Unless you did it when I wasn't looking. I suppose if I was walking away from you, I wouldn't notice."

"Do you voice every thought you have?"

"When I'm nervous. Are you gay?"

"Yes. Are you?"

"Ah." Jonty grinned. "Now you'll wonder like I did."

72

"No, I won't."

"How can you tell I'm gay?" Jonty asked indignantly.

"You mean you *are* gay?"

Jonty's face creased in a smile. "Not telling."

He'd reached the door before Devan managed to speak.
"You're the night manager?"

"I'm a bit of everything. Receptionist, cleaner, bell hop,
room service waiter, ordinary waiter, concierge, barman,
mechanic if it's easy to fix, not a mechanic if it's not easy to fix,
ditto with plumber and electrician—but mostly the night
manager. I'm allowed to sleep, though I'm expected to
respond to guest requests. You never know when someone
might need something like Cajun chicken. Or an expertly done
back rub."

Was that an offer? Devan opened his mouth and shut it
again.

"Oh God, now I need to google how to do a back rub like
an expert."

Devan swallowed hard.

"I don't like people to be sad," Jonty whispered. "You're
sad. And I've said too much. Sorry, sir. Just because we nearly
died together doesn't make us friends. I don't mean to be
presumptuous. I really am sorry. Good night."

He slipped out of the room and closed the door.

Is that what I am? Sad?

Not when Jonty was around.

Chapter Six

Jonty wanted to hit himself around the head. *I am such a fuckwit.* He shouldn't have said a lot of that. Probably *any* of that. Particularly about a back rub and Mr Impossible being sad. Cheeky. Inappropriate. Disrespectful. Maybe a sackable offence. *Shit!* It *was* a sackable offence. All he'd needed to do was make a joke about getting tipped and he'd have ruined everything.

He didn't even know if he was any good at giving back rubs. But it couldn't be that difficult, right? He knew where the back was and he knew how to rub. *I really know how to rub!* Plus, he'd sort of assumed that he wouldn't have to do much back rubbing before other bits got involved, now that he knew Mr Impossible was gay.

Idiot.

I know.

You don't want to lose your job.

I know. Maybe I should tape up my mouth.

Good idea.

What was it about the guy that encouraged Jonty to say something stupid? Yes, Jonty had a cheeky personality and he used humour as a deflection, he always had, but he knew he had to rein himself in with guests. He *did* rein himself in, usually. Devan would have no idea that he'd never cooked a meal for a guest, never flirted with a guest, never fancied a guest this much. Just as well he wasn't working for the next three nights. Time to get over his crush.

He went straight to the kitchen to clean up the mess he'd made. He didn't dare leave any sign that he'd been cooking. In the way crime scene analysts could pick up a speck of blood using luminol—assuming those forensic shows were telling the truth—if Jonty left a single spoon out of place, Wayne would know. Jonty really should have told Devan he was too late for room service. He should have offered cheese and biscuits, a sandwich or maybe beans on toast.

It wasn't that what Devan had asked for was difficult. Jonty liked to cook, he'd often watched Marcus and Wayne working, and they'd shown him how to prepare a few dishes. Marcus was a wizard, but Jonty wasn't supposed to use the kitchen. The cut-off time was there for a reason.

But Devan had asked and Jonty wanted to please him, to make him happy. *Just as long as I haven't poisoned him.* He washed up, polished every surface he'd touched and provided no one noticed there was a chicken breast short—*hmm*—or that the wine bottle wasn't as full as it had been—*a bigger hmmmm*—he might get away with it. The meal definitely wasn't going on Devan's bill, because admitting he'd cooked would mean trouble. If he lied and suggested it had been done before eleven, that would get him into worse trouble.

Hopefully, he'd get away with it.

If Devan put the trolley back outside his room when he'd eaten, so Jonty could clear it away.

If he didn't complain the food tasted awful.

If he didn't notice that the wine wasn't what he'd asked for.

If he forgot that offer of a back rub.

Shit! This was a disaster waiting to happen. Maybe he ought to start searching for another job, just in case. But it was the wrong time of year, now that the tourists had mostly stopped coming. He was unskilled. All he could do was easy stuff. He sighed. He was overthinking as usual. Everything would be fine. Three days away would do him good. Three fewer days near Mr Temptation.

Before Jonty retreated to the room at the back of reception, he went through his security checks.

Make sure the front door is locked and bolted.

75

Thanks for that, Tay. It won't stop the zombies for long.
What about Brad?

Would a locked door stop Brad? It should, but… Jonty let out a shuddering breath. He did his circuit of the ground floor, checking every door, testing every window. All the emergency exits had to be inspected too, to ensure they were illuminated, able to open from the inside, and not blocked in any way. Most of the lights on the ground floor were off now. The background lighting was sufficient to allow guests to find their way around, so Devan would be able to come and ask him for that back rub. *Ha ha.* The bar was shut and locked. Guests were all tucked up in their beds. *Don't think about Devan in his bed.*

Jonty could hear the building settling down for the night, creaks and groans of timbers and pipes interspersed with whispers and gurgles. The hotel had a comforting language of its own. Some guests had complained about noises, a few had asked if the place was haunted. Maybe it was, but Jonty liked the sounds the building made.

Back behind the reception desk, he made sure that Colin, who'd been on duty until Jonty took over, had made a note of who'd ordered what newspaper for their room. The wake-up calls had already been programmed into the system, but Jonty double-checked it had been done because it was him who'd get a mouthful in the morning if the guests didn't get their call. Though why they couldn't use their phones, he had no idea.

Once he was in the room behind reception, he took off his jacket, hung it over the back of a chair and sniffed his armpits. He'd had to wear this morning's shirt and socks because he'd not been able to go home to get clean ones. He'd asked Mike to bring him straight here so he wasn't late. He'd ironed his dirty shirt and trousers.

When he'd first started here, even though he'd been told it was okay to sleep, he'd still thought he ought to stay awake all night in case there was an emergency. Heart attack in Room One. Vampire in Room Two. Poltergeist in Room Three. Orgy in Room Four. Blow job in Wave. When it became clear that didn't often happen — *okay, never* — he slept when he could.

The hotel had been a convalescent home after the second world war and when some guests had talked about seeing ghosts, Jonty wondered if those who'd died there had left a sort of imprint on the place. Maybe people didn't even need to die for that to happen. Those who'd lived in the hotel while they recovered from their injuries, guests who'd made love, guests who'd come here sad, maybe they all left bits of themselves. *Including me.*

Since the parcels had started arriving at his bedsit, he felt safer in the hotel than he did where he lived. The hotel took care of him and he took care of the hotel. But now that a package had been delivered here, Jonty had to take that as a warning. So much for thinking it was all over. Brad had been spoken to by the police after the...assault, and everything had gone quiet for a while. But he'd clearly not given up. The collection of packages under Jonty's sink proved that, along with the feeling that he was being followed and watched.

He loosened his tie and unfolded the camp bed. Once he'd grabbed a pillow from the cupboard, he kicked off his shoes and lay down with his phone next to his ear. All calls to the front desk from inside or outside the hotel would be directed to him now he'd activated the app. *Please don't let there be any calls tonight.* Except maybe from Devan, though if he *did* call, unless it was a legitimate reason for wanting him such as his room being on fire, Jonty needed to say no, even though he'd practically thrown himself at him. *Not while I'm working. Not even when I'm not working.*

77

Jonty rolled onto his side. He'd been glad Devan had been with him in the sea, even though it was selfish. If he'd been on his own, he'd probably have drowned. The sea had pushed him down and the board had hit his head and… He drew in a deep breath and jolted as he smelt seawater. It had to be his imagination but…

I didn't panic when the rip caught me. I was scared, but I didn't panic. I did panic at the thought of hospital. I hate hospitals. The light in the room dropped as if someone had turned a dimmer switch, except there *was* no dimmer switch. He closed his eyes, seeking oblivion, and immediately found himself back in the water, reliving what had happened. *I nearly died. Not just me.* That sea had been…intense. As if he'd been attacked by a wild animal, dragged one way, then the other, pinned down and unable to do anything about it. Like being attacked by Brad.

Fucking hell.

Stop thinking about it.

I nearly died.

But you didn't die. You're warm. You're dry. You're safe.

Jonty's heart was beating too fast. He wasn't thinking of the sea now, but Brad. He curled up on the bed, pulling into as tight a ball as he could. The less of him that was exposed, the less there was to hurt. *I need to relax.* But he couldn't. His legs and arms wouldn't unfurl. Nor could he slow his breathing.

Shit. Tay!

Breathe!

Tay couldn't help him. No one could. He might not have died in the sea, but maybe he was going to die now. No one to save him, his damaged heart finally breaking for good. Nothing he could do about it. The more anxious he became, the faster he breathed. The faster he breathed, the tighter panic gripped him in its claws. Even though he knew breathing fast made everything worse, he couldn't help it.

He was alone. He'd always be alone.

78

But it was safer.

He was broken. He'd always be broken.

Not true. Devan would make you feel better.

For how long? As long as it takes us both to come?

He made you feel better when he held your hand.

But he let it go.

Take what you can get. Life's too short. You know that.

He isn't even interested.

Yes, he is.

You know what a bad judge of guys I am. Look at Brad.

He's nothing like that prick.

Jonty had a pain in his chest now. A sharp pain. He felt terrible. He was shivering with cold as if he was still in the water, his breathing ragged and noisy.

"You're a little cunt."

Jonty's eyes snapped open and he froze. "Brad," he whispered.

No one was there. No one had actually called him a cunt. But it took a moment or two to convince himself he was alone. He'd heard the words so clearly. A moment later, he was wracked with violent tremors. *Brad. Brad. Brad.* He gulped as the guy's name formed over and over in his head. Jonty kept breaking his rule. Never think his name, never speak it.

Stop panicking.

Stop breathing so fast.

Stop shaking.

Stop all of it.

He put his hands over his ears.

"But you're my little cunt."

No! NO! Jonty could hear someone whimpering. He didn't want it to be him but knew it was. "Dev…an!" The word came out as a whispered croak and yet Jonty still hoped somehow that Devan could hear, even all those floors away, that the word would be carried through the hotel's pipes and timbers and somehow find him, and even if he couldn't hear, he'd sense Jonty needed him. Why didn't he sense that? Why did no one ever sense that? Devan had found him in the sea. *Find me now!*

Call his room.

No.

Then you have to fight this.

Jonty's heart hurt so much he thought it was breaking apart in his chest. He slid his hand inside his shirt and twisted his nipple piercing as hard as he could. *Harder. Oh shit, shit! That hurts.* Pain brought him back. His fingers were wet and when he pulled them out of his shirt, he saw blood. *Oh God.* When his breathing started to speed up again, he held his breath and counted to ten before he allowed himself to inhale.

Gradually, his world calmed and he was twenty-five-year-old Jonty again, with a fucked-up shirt and probably a fucked-up piercing. He stood on shaky feet, took off his tie, then fumbled with his buttons. The piercing was still in place though he'd broken the skin on one side. There was a sink in the corner where staff made drinks, and he held his shirt under the cold tap to wash off the blood.

When the stain had more or less gone, he dried it with the machine in the toilet. A glance at the damage he'd done to his skin and he chewed his lip. That had been stupid, twisting so hard that he made himself bleed. He bit his lip as he removed the metal, then threw it in the bin. Maybe he needed to put an elastic band on his wrist again. A sore wrist was better than a bleeding nipple.

He was lucky the damage wasn't worse. Harming himself was *not* the answer. He cleaned the blood off his chest and swabbed it with an anaesthetic wipe from the first aid box. *Ouch, ouch, ouch!* Not something he'd be writing up in the accident book. *Night porter freaked out and damaged his nipple.*

His toes curled in his shoes while he wiped over the wound. Jonty looked up into the mirror. Tay stood behind him.

You're a stupid twat.

I know. I want you to go away.

Why? So you can kill yourself?

I won't do that.

Do you really want me to go?

Jonty's poor heart was doing some complicated calisthenics. What was the right answer? *Yes? No? I don't know.*

I can't go yet. There's unfinished business. Go to sleep. I'll look after you.

Jonty had unfinished business too. He put his shirt back on, then went online and googled Devan Smith. He couldn't find him. Not on Facebook or among the sixty profiles on LinkedIn.

Mr Impossible. Mr Trouble. Now Mr Invisible.

Jonty woke when the alarm on his phone went off. He'd slept better than he'd thought he would. Probably through exhaustion. There was a faint stain on his shirt, though no more bleeding. No more bar in his nipple. He'd thought it looked cool, but he was safer without it. He shoved his feet into his shoes, cleaned his teeth in the staff bathroom, and had a quick shave and wash, before he put on his tie and jacket. Last of all, he plastered a smile on his face.

He went up to the top floor and found the room service trolley outside Wave, so he took it back downstairs, washed and returned everything to where it belonged. Once it was time to open the front door of the hotel, he did it on the dot and heard the major and his little dog coming across the tiled foyer.

"Good morning, Major Bagshott. Morning, Dottie." Jonty held the door open.

"Appears the world didn't end yesterday."

"You know, it nearly did. Me and one of the guests got caught in a rip current and were swept out to sea. We had to be rescued by the RNLI."

The major's bushy eyebrows rose. "My word. All well?"

"Drank more seawater than I'd have liked, but all is well," Jonty said. "Enjoy your walk."

As the pair set off towards the path that led down to the beach, two vans pulled into the hotel car park. On the side of each were the words *Your Day* in large gold letters, with two rings interlinked beneath. There was a wedding in the ballroom on Saturday so he assumed they were here to set up. He'd have to make sure he'd left before anyone asked him to help move the tables and chairs out of storage. He didn't mind doing it when he was paid, but it wasn't fair to expect to him to do it when he wasn't.

Your Day had organised two weddings at the hotel in the last year. Both had gone well, much to Vincent's and Hamish McAllister's relief. Jonty had worked as a waiter both times, but he hadn't been asked on this occasion. He was a bit disappointed, because he could have done with the extra money for his *This is going to change my life* fund.

When are you going to use that?

When I've decided how I want to change my life.

The bride and groom were booked into Starfish, the suite next to Wave, on Saturday night. The bride had use of Starfish from first thing Saturday morning. *But I won't be here until Saturday night.* Three days off. *Yay!* With not a lot to look forward to. *Shit.*

Not even seeing me?

'Course.

Don't lie.

Not lying.

Though he was. Going to see Tay wasn't a chore, but it was hard.

The hotel was starting to wake now. Morning staff were trickling in. The newspapers had arrived along with restaurant supplies and flowers. Jonty needed to sort and deliver the papers. Plenty to do. Plenty to stop him thinking.

Why don't you go to a club? Remember that time —

Jonty didn't want to remember that time. He wouldn't be going to a club. Two hours by bus to Newcastle to the nearest one? Sleeping next to Tay and not touching him. Two hours back the next day? He wasn't that desperate. He scribbled room numbers on the top of the papers and set the Major's paper aside.

The wedding people used the rear entrance of the hotel and Jonty was relieved to see they'd brought guys to shift the furniture, though they weren't being very quiet and it was still early. He was hoping to see Devan, though he told himself he wasn't.

When he spotted him coming down the stairs in running gear — grey shorts and a long-sleeved bright yellow T-shirt that clung to his chest, Jonty smiled. *Nice legs, nice calves, nice...* "If you run at night, the added fear of being murdered does wonders for your cardio."

Devan shot him a look but didn't respond. Jonty sighed as Mr Back-to-being- Impossible left the hotel. That hadn't been a friendly look. Jonty had a thought that made him smile, and took a paper from the pile in the lounge before he went upstairs with the other papers to leave by the doors. He was fairly certain Devan was not a guy who'd read *The Sun*.

He hurried back downstairs again and turned off the app on his phone to divert calls back to the desk.

I could get up early on a day I'm not working and go for a run.

You could, but you won't. You'd wake up and decide to do a few sit-ups instead.

Not if I had someone hot to run with.

But that wasn't going to be Mr I'll Soon Be Leaving.

The first morning call came through. A blocked toilet in room twelve. *Wonderful.* He diverted the calls back to his phone and went upstairs with the kit. A bucket, plunger, plastic bag and a pair of rubber gloves.

He was back on the desk as breakfast service began. Vincent came to take over. Jonty was due to finish earlier today and Vincent would fill the gap until Sally-Anne arrived.

"Everything okay last night?" Vincent asked.

"Yep. Staked a few vampires and beat off the werewolf. Other than that, very quiet."

Vincent laughed.

Jonty hurried off before Vincent asked him anything else and he had to lie. He decided to go down to the gym, even though he hated gyms, and use the treadmill before he went in the pool. Staff were allowed to make use of the pool and gym when they were off-duty, provided there weren't too many guests using them. But not the hot tub. Jonty hung up his suit and put on his shorts and T shirt. His nipple was a bit red, but the piercing had already started to scab.

It was a bit of a waste going on a treadmill when there was all that lovely beach to run on, but first of all he didn't want Devan to think he was following him, particularly when that was exactly what he'd be doing, and secondly, he suspected he'd last about ten minutes running outside. He wanted people to look at him and think *what a fit guy*, rather than *ah, good for him, he's trying, bless him.* Jonty didn't really need the exercise. He cycled over ten miles to work and ten miles back most days. But it was an easy journey with no hills.

This treadmill was noisy, or rather his feet slapping on the belt were making a lot of noise. He should have put the TV on, but he'd not thought to. If he got off to do that, he'd not get back on. He was breathing heavily within minutes. What speed had he selected? *Nine? Shit! No wonder…* He fumbled to knock the speed down, but his finger slipped, hit *incline*, and

84

he found himself running uphill. He grabbed the bar with one hand and was flailing for the controls with the other when Devan walked in. Jonty tried to appear as though he knew what he was doing. *Where was the fucking stop button? There!* He lunged for it and the belt quickly slowed to a halt. Hopefully that had looked less frantic than it had felt.

Devan was shifting weights around on the resistance machine. *Why isn't he talking to me? Why isn't he smiling at me?* They'd had a near-death experience yesterday. Didn't that mean something? That they were sort of friends at least? *He held my hand! I cooked for him.* God, they were practically married. Jonty stepped off the treadmill and walked to Devan's side. "I hate it when I've been running on the treadmill for half an hour and then check the time and see it's only been five minutes, don't you?"

"You managed as long as that? You looked a bit flustered."

"Were you watching me? Admiring my technique? Got any tips on how to hit the right button when you're going too fast?"

"I think you already figured that out. Are staff allowed to use the gym?"

Jonty's shoulders dropped. *Oh, you dickhead.* "Yes, as long as it's not busy. But it appears to be swamped with surly testosterone, so I'll go." He slammed out.

You're skilled at flouncing.

Don't mock. At least it's a skill.

Back in the changing room, he put on his trunks. He wasn't going to be distracted from what he'd planned. He grabbed his towel and his goggles and went through to the pool, which was empty. After a quick shower, he slid into the water— *ouch! my nipple!* —setting off on a slow crawl towards the far end. The pool wasn't deep. It only came to his upper chest so it was no good for diving and it was probably too

85

warm for people who wanted to exercise. But most visitors just used it to have fun. Jonty swam up and down, changing his stroke every length. Breaststroke, backstroke, front crawl, and a hybrid butterfly that was probably more like a dying moth, but it elevated his heart rate.

He stayed in longer than he usually would have, and he knew why. He was hoping Devan might decide to have a swim, then Jonty intended to demonstrate his spectacular tumble turn before he pretended to drown. Or maybe he'd try to drown Devan. But the guy didn't come in.

Jonty finally admitted defeat and climbed out. He had a long hot shower, occasionally wincing at the pain in his nipple when soap dripped onto it, then put on the shorts and T-shirt he'd worn yesterday, only to realise he'd left his hoodie upstairs. Before he went up, he filled his bottle at the water fountain and slotted it in the side of his backpack.

While he was in the room behind the reception, he heard Devan say something to Vincent. Jonty almost came out, but he couldn't face another slap down. *What was the point?* The guy blew warm and cold and was currently on cold. Probably his default setting.

"But could I help you?" Vincent asked.

"I need to speak to the hotel owner."

Jonty's heart slumped to his toes. *What?*

"Mr McAllister isn't in the hotel today, sir."

"Can you give me his number?"

"No, I'm afraid not."

What have I done? Jonty chewed his lip. It might have nothing to do with him. But then again, it might. In an instant, his imagination went berserk. He hadn't cooked the chicken properly. Devan had spent all night throwing up. The wine had been off. *Shit.* Devan had registered it wasn't the right wine, but it was the only bottle open and he didn't dare risk opening another. All he knew about wine was it came in three colours and it was sometimes fizzy. Maybe that comment Jonty had made about dessert had been taken in the way he'd intended. His smart mouth of yesterday coming back to bite him? Or what he'd said this morning? *Shiiiit!*

Jonty didn't dare move. He stood and waited.

"Is it something I can help you with?" Vincent asked. "A complaint I can handle?"

"I'd rather discuss it with him. If I can't have his number, can you give him mine and ask him to call me?"

"Certainly, sir."

If it was about him, Jonty would find out soon enough. He waited until Vincent was on his own, then sidled out of the room.

"Jonty!"

Vincent had eyes in the back of his head. Jonty returned to the desk.

"Do you have any idea why Mr Smith might have reason to complain?"

Jonty kept his mouth shut, widened his eyes and shrugged.

You don't look innocent.

I'm not.

"Anything happen last night that I need to know about? Apart from the vampire and the werewolf?"

"No."

"Okay." Said in a way that indicated Vincent suspected otherwise.

Jonty slung his backpack over his shoulder and headed for his bike.

Forty minutes later, having ridden fast so it was harder to think, he'd reached the outskirts of Alnwick and the Clean n' Go launderette he lived above. Jonty unlocked the door and wheeled his bike inside. No post had been pushed through the

87

letterbox, which was a relief because he didn't want any more gifts from Brad.

He had to prop the bike on the stairs because there wasn't enough room for him to lean it against the wall at the bottom. Though it did mean if anyone thought it was worth breaking into a bedsit, they'd trip over a bike that wasn't really worth nicking. And if Brad managed to get in, with a bit of luck he'd break his neck. Jonty padlocked the bike to the banister anyway, because without it, he was screwed. No public transport ran near the hotel.

Home was through a door at the top of the stairs. A single room with a bed and a clothes rail at one end, a corner walled off for a small bathroom. A rickety room divider separated the sleeping area from a small kitchen and living space with his table, chair, sofa and TV. Enforced minimalism that he'd tried to enhance with beachcombing creations. The rent was fine as long as he had a job. He could have found somewhere cheaper, but he liked having his own bathroom, his personal living space, his own bed. But he didn't feel *safe* here, not since the day Brad had assaulted him.

Jonty took off his helmet and emptied his backpack. He put the package holding the dildo into the plastic bag under the sink, which held Brad's other *gifts*. Sachets of lube and condoms, along with a pair of handcuffs, a cock ring and a pair of women's lacy knickers. Jonty had spoken to the police, but with no way of determining who'd sent them, they could do nothing. Jonty felt as if he was bothering them when they had more important things to deal with, but he'd felt like saying *Does he have to kill me for you to take notice?*

He gathered up his dirty clothes, took off what he was wearing, and added them to his laundry bag, a blue tote from IKEA. Once he'd put on his skinny black jeans, T-shirt and his blue hoody, he grabbed a detergent tablet, a handful of change from his stash, picked up the bag and went downstairs again.

He stuffed everything in a machine, added his detergent and slid the coins in the slot. As soon as it started washing, he went back upstairs. After he'd put an alarm on his phone, he lay on his bed. Maybe he'd be able to sleep for a while. Once he'd dried his laundry, he'd go into town, buy doughnuts or biscuits, cycle to Seahouses, and visit the lifeboat station.

Forgotten something? Someone?

Oh yes, go and see you.

He hadn't forgotten. How could he?

Chapter Seven

Devan had woken up to three stroppy texts from his mother.

Really, Devan??? Griff reached out to you. Can't you find it in your heart to be happy for him? I know it's a lot to expect you to be his best man, but please reconsider.

Is this the way to make friends again with your brother? If you'd told me what you'd quarrelled about, we could have fixed it.

Griff worships you. You being stubborn won't change anything. He's still marrying Ravi.

He almost threw the phone at the wall. He wished he could block her number. He considered it, but decided it would cause him more problems. If she couldn't get in touch with him, she might visit him, or send his father or one of his siblings. Knowing her, she might even contact the police. How much of this could have been avoided if he'd told the truth five months ago?

He called his father.

"Devan! How are you?"

His father always sounded happy to speak to him and Devan had to bite back the response that sat on his lips. *Fucking awful.* "Fine."

"Sure about that? You don't sound fine."

"I just read three texts from mum asking me to—"

"Ah. I know what she asked."

"I'm not doing it."

"I don't blame you. Griff is being unreasonable. But then, it was ever thus. Our own fault, I'm sure. The price for overcompensation."

Particularly by his mother. *Take care of Griff. Look out for Griff. Don't forget about Griff.* But Devan felt a frisson of relief that his father understood how he felt. "If Griff couldn't even

90

bring himself to tell me to my face that he and Ravi were getting married in December, why the hell would he think I'd want to be his best man?"

"I'm on your side. But..."

Devan must have made a sound that his father heard because he stopped speaking.

"Is there something we're not getting, Devan?"

Was this the moment to tell the truth after the three of them had agreed it was better to come up with a different story?

"Would you like to tell me the actual reason your wedding was called off?" his father asked. "Do you know of some reason why Griff shouldn't marry Ravi?"

"Do you like Ravi?" Even asking that hurt.

"When you were going to marry him, we looked forward to welcoming him into the family. Did I think it was a good match? I'm not so sure about that. You got on well together, but he was a little needy. You know your mother loved him. She and his mother got on so well. Ravi came to see us a few times after...that terrible day and somehow his friendship with Griff deepened. Maybe marriage has come faster than I'd have thought. They've only been going out together for a couple of months, but Griff knew Ravi for the two years you went out with him. You used to let Griff tag along with you. Are you wondering if they...? Is Griff the reason you called the wedding off?"

Devan heard the shock in his father's voice as he came to the right conclusion. He thought too long about what to say.

His father's "Ahhh," in reaction to his silence said everything.

Why not tell the truth? Now the pair intended to marry, and presumably Ravi was okay with Griff asking him to be best man, Devan's humiliation was complete.

"I found Ravi and Griff in bed together the day before the wedding."

"Oh no." His father gave a deep sigh. "I guessed Ravi had done something, but not with Griff. Damn. My God, Devan, why didn't you tell us?"

"Because I thought it would hurt more. Because Griff begged me not to. Because I didn't want to look a fool. Because I thought I could pretend it had never happened."

"I wondered why we'd seen less of you. So why are you telling me now?"

"Because I've been made a fool of for the last five months. I thought it was a one off, not the start of something. I'm not being his best man. I'm not coming to the wedding."

"Hmm. You know what I'd do?"

"What?"

"Not be best man, but come to the wedding and bring a guy with you, someone that will outshine Ravi. You know how much he likes to be the centre of attention. Five months is long enough to get over the loss of a guy who clearly wasn't right for you. Eight months is long enough to find someone better. So get on it."

Devan groaned. "Do you think Ravi is right for Griff?"

"Well, they both like attention. I thought it might do Griff good to be with someone who's as spoilt as him. Though marriage? I don't know. But I'm not going to say anything to Griff, just as I didn't say anything to you. You're both cut from the same mould there. Awkward. Won't be told. And you don't take after me." His father laughed. "But your brother has made his bed. Let's see if sharing it with Ravi lasts another three months."

The talk with his father had cheered him up, right until another text came from his mother.

The villa in Antigua is booked. So is your flight.

Devan let out a stream of expletives but managed to hang onto his phone. Just. It had been a terrible start to his day. He was pissed off, depressed, miserable, resentful, irritated, but above all angry. Which was fucking annoying because he'd actually thought being up here was doing him some good. He hadn't told his dad not to tell his mum. Would he? Somehow Devan was grateful to leave it up to his father.

Would his mother expect him to forgive Griff for what he'd done? Time had healed nothing. Did it ever? The image of Griff and Ravi in his bed —*fucking in my fucking bed* — was crystal clear. The sound Ravi had been making was engraved in his heart. The idea that he could stand at his brother's side and…support him while he married the fucking, treacherous, vain, self-centred, self-absorbed arsehole… And how the hell could he give a speech saying anything pleasant about Griff, who was equally treacherous, self-centred, vain and self-absorbed. There was no fucking way Devan would be at that fucking wedding. *Fuck, fuck, FUCK!*

He took a deep breath. It didn't help. *Goddammit!* To think that once upon a time, he'd not been a guy who cursed. Not in anger anyway.

Maybe if he'd woken with Jonty lying naked beside him, or even better with the guy's mouth around his cock, Devan could have rolled his eyes at his mother's naiveté. But Jonty hadn't been lying naked beside him, because Devan had talked himself out of trying to make that happen in spite of the hints Jonty had dropped.

Jonty knew he was only up here for a week. Ignoring what Mike had said, Devan thought Jonty was up for a bit of fun. But Devan had, for once in his miserable life, done the right thing and left Jonty alone. He was still trying to persuade himself that it *was* the right thing. Jonty was the wrong guy in so many ways. It was ridiculous to even think about him with his crazy hair, those piercings in his ear and eyebrow, the grin that lit up his face, the way he'd made Devan smile when smiling should have been the last thing he felt like doing.

Not my type, but maybe what I need. For now, at least. A rebound fuck.

Devan wasn't looking for happiness. Not anymore. He'd done that, thought he'd found it, only to learn in the most painful way that he hadn't. He didn't like being miserable, but was so deep in the hole he'd dug for himself that he worried he'd lost the ability to claw his way out. He was currently in danger of the sides caving in and burying him forever.

Jonty was right about broken promises hurting worse than broken bones. The safest thing to do was to not get attached to anyone for a while and lick his wounds until they stopped bleeding. Something he'd been doing for five months except he was still bleeding, still hurting because the slightest thing reopened his cuts. He could imagine Jonty's response to that. He'd offer to lick his *ouchies* for him.

Then let him. What was he so afraid of? That Jonty would make him forget? That he wouldn't want to let the guy go? *That I'll hurt* him? He should take the fucking risk. Hadn't almost dying shown him that life was too short to always play it safe? But he didn't want to hurt Jonty. He was doing the right thing. He was. If he kept telling himself that then maybe he'd come to believe it.

The beach run didn't improve his temper—he set off too fast and ran out of steam—physically and mentally. Nor did the short session in the gym—he picked an impossible weight. Nor did the way Jonty had fled not long after he'd arrived. Nor did the realisation that on Saturday there'd be a wedding in the hotel and the place would be full of happiness. Staying here was bad for his health. Which was why he'd decided to stop dicking about and speak to Hamish McAllister. If the guy wasn't interested in selling, Devan was wasting his time.

94

He was halfway through breakfast when the hotel manager came to his table.

"Mr McAllister will see you here tomorrow morning at ten."

"Thanks." *Shit.*

Another night then. He tried not to be annoyed at McAllister's assumption that he'd be available at that time. But he was.

After breakfast, he went out to his car. The kite lines were in a hideous tangle and it took him a while to get them sorted. He repacked everything along with his wetsuit that had dried overnight in the vehicle. He was glad he'd had the chance to wash it in Mike's shower. The wind was onshore today, better for kiteboarding, but he wasn't in the mood. Besides, he had something more important to do.

Saying thanks for being rescued wasn't enough. The RNLI, the Royal National Lifeboat Institution, received no government funding for its lifeboat service and relied on donations to keep operating. The crew were mostly unpaid volunteers, living or working close enough to the station to get out to sea minutes after being paged. If Devan lived by the sea, he thought he might have trained to join them.

He looked up Seahouses RNLI online. They were open until five. Once he'd collected his waterproof jacket from his room, he went back to his car. Driving in Northumberland was a world away from driving around London. Drivers up here were more courteous and there weren't speed cameras every few yards, but best of all was what he was driving through: beautiful countryside, wide open spaces and amazing views, whichever way he looked, and he was sure there were hidden treasures too.

There was a half-empty car park beside the lifeboat station—something else that was rare in London—a place to park. Devan paid to stay all day for the price he'd have paid for an hour in the city. Once he'd done what he'd come to do, he'd go for a walk, or maybe a boat ride. He passed numerous signs offering trips to the Farne Islands, to view sea birds and grey seal colonies.

Brian spotted him as he walked into the building. "Devan! How are you doing?"

"Still breathing, thanks to you."

Devan didn't recognise the other man, but apparently, Jake had been at the helm last night. He shook both guys' hands.

"I wanted to make a donation," Devan said. "Is there any way to make it specifically for this station or does it all go into a general pot?"

"Come into the office and we'll have a talk," Brian said. "I think you can do what you want via a trust, but I'm not entirely sure how it works."

Brian nudged a chair towards Devan, then sat behind the desk. "How much are you thinking of donating?"

"Twenty thousand pounds."

Brian gulped and his eyes widened. "Bloody… That's…incredibly generous."

"I'm incredibly grateful."

"I'm not trying to be greedy, but if you're a UK tax payer, would you consider filling in a Gift Aid form and we could turn that into even more?"

"That's fine."

Brian made a call to see if Devan could donate just to that station and wasn't surprised to hear he could. They wouldn't want to turn money down.

"Wow." Brian smiled at him. "This doesn't happen very often. Like never. Want a cup of coffee? Tea? A biscuit? I'm ashamed that they're not chocolate."

Devan laughed. "A black coffee, one sugar, would be great. Thanks."

"Come into the kitchen."

Devan followed him and found himself being introduced to a couple of men and a woman. All crew members.

"This is one of the guys from the shout yesterday," Brian said. "The kiteboarder."

"Bad luck to be caught in a rip," the woman said. "We have more call outs because of rips than for any other reason."

Devan was drawn into a conversation about the sea and kiteboarding and found to his surprise that he was enjoying himself.

"Ever thought about joining as a crew member?" Brian asked.

"I'm from London. I don't even live near the Thames. But if I had a home near the coast, I'd think about it. You guys do a great job." He pushed to his feet. "I've taken up enough of your time. Thanks again for the rescue."

"Thanks for the twenty-thousand pounds," Brian said.

"Bloody hell," said one of the men.

"Wow." The woman held out her hand. "Thank you!"

"A donation of twenty thousand was worth not eating the meal my wife had made when the pager went off," Jake said.

"I'd have walked away from my wife's cooking for a couple of quid," another said.

They all laughed.

Devan followed Brian out of the kitchen and saw Jonty standing there holding two packs of doughnuts. Pointless denying the twist in his gut was down to anything other than the guy in front of him. He looked so young. Too young. Devan swallowed hard.

Jonty glanced at him, then turned to Brian. "I bought these to say thank you for yesterday."

Brian took the doughnuts. "We'll be fighting over these. It's good of you to bring them. How are you feeling?"

"Fine, thanks for the rescue. Bye." Jonty turned and walked out.

"Wait for me," Devan called.

"Thanks again for the donation," Brian said.

"You're welcome." Devan shook Brian's hand.

When he emerged, there was no sign of Jonty. Devan was disappointed right until he glanced across the road and saw Jonty leaning against the wall opposite, hands in the pockets of his blue hoody, his black skinny jeans ripped at the knees, a backpack at his feet.

"Need a lift?" Devan asked as he reached him.

"I'm going for a walk."

"Can I come?"

The fleeting look of surprise on Jonty's face hit Devan hard.

"Do you really want to?"

"I wouldn't have asked otherwise."

Jonty pulled his backpack onto his shoulder. "Come on then."

They set off up the hill toward the road Devan had driven down.

"It's twenty miles there, twenty back. Can you manage that?" Jonty asked.

Shit. "Er…"

"You are so gullible. A six-mile round trip."

"Er…"

Jonty laughed.

I love it when he laughs. His face lights up, his eyes sparkle. "I paid for all-day parking."

"In that case, we don't need to rush and there might be spectacular treats on the way."

Devan walked alongside him.

At the top of the slope, Jonty edged him to the right. "We have to walk along the road to the end of the car park, then over the dunes to get onto the beach."

"Okay."

"I'm a bit upset," Jonty said.

"Oh."

"More than a bit."

"Right."

"You're supposed to ask me why."

"Am I?"

Jonty let out a sigh of frustration. "Why are you a bit upset, Jonty? I'll tell you why, Devan. If I'd known you were going to give them twenty thousand pounds, I'd have asked you to go halves on the doughnuts. I'm really pissed off."

Devan chuckled. "I wish I'd thought of doughnuts."

"That was a lot of money to donate. More than I earn in a year."

Another reminder of how far they were apart. "It's a worthwhile cause."

"You are so right. Can I interest you in a scheme to sell burial plots to rich Egyptians? An absolute winner. Or maybe you'd like to invest in a gold mine I've recently discovered?"

Devan grinned. "I'll pass. Where are we going?"

"Have you never been up here before?"

"First time in Northumberland."

"I came to live here when I was seven and I've never left. It's still an unspoilt wilderness."

"Have you never wanted to go anywhere else?"

"There are places I'd like to see, but this is my home."

"I like the accent. Yours isn't as strong as many I've heard."

"I spent my first seven years in Surrey," Jonty said. "I think once the way you speak is set, it sticks."

"Do your family still live in Northumberland?"

"Don't know. We can go down onto the beach here."
Jonty led him onto a path over the dunes.

You don't know? Devan knew better than to push. "The meal last night was really good. Will you get into trouble for cooking for me?"

"Not if you don't tell anyone. I haven't charged it to the room. Though I might have trouble explaining where a chicken breast went." He frowned, then smiled. "Ah. I was fighting off zombies. Yep, that will do. I'm glad you liked it." Jonty beamed at him. "And did you enjoy the Australian Shiraz?"

"That's not what you gave me. But it was fine."

"Oh God. I should have known you were the sort of guy who could tell red from red. Sorry. It was the only bottle open and I didn't want to risk opening another."

"Did you think I wouldn't notice?"

"I had no idea." Jonty ran the last few metres down onto the sand and Devan followed.

The almost-deserted beach was beautiful, the sky cloudless, though a cold wind was whipping off the sea. He kept thinking about Jonty not knowing where his parents were. What had happened? Should he ask? Would he tell him? *If all I'm interested in is a quick fuck, why do I want to know?*

"How old are you?" Devan asked.

"How old do you think I am?"

"Twenty?"

"Twenty-five. "

Still young.

"What about you?" Jonty asked. I'm guessing…forty-five?"

Devan glared.

"Fifty-one, then? Not fifty-two!"

"Thirty-five."

"Oops."

"Good thing I know you're joking. Do you have brothers and sisters?"

"A sister. I *had* a sister. I haven't seen her since I was eight. She…won't remember me."

What? Devan felt as if he were slowly being fed clues to Jonty's background and he wasn't liking the picture he was getting. "I have two brothers and two sisters."

"Wow, that's a big family. Are you the oldest?"

"I'm in the middle. My sisters are older, my brothers younger."

"Are your parents okay about you being gay?"

"They are now. I told them when I was thirteen. They weren't thrilled. My father was quicker to accept than my mother. My brother, Griff, told them he was bi when he was nineteen. I remember…"

I don't want to remember.

"You don't want to remember?"

"Not really. My announcement was greeted with silence followed by me being sent to bed."

"With no supper?"

"How did you guess?"

"You had *sad little boy* written all over you when you told me that. I'm really glad I made you the meal last night now. I might have sent you tumbling back into trauma."

"I was more traumatised by the way my mother opened a bottle of champagne when Griff announced he was bi."

"I assume because that meant there was still hope he'd find a wife and produce grandkids."

"I feel sorry for those who are bi. They have a hard time convincing people they're not having their cake and eating it."

When Jonty turned to head towards the water, Devan followed. "What about your parents?"

"I told my dad I liked boys and he beat the shit out of me. Five days in hospital."

Devan stumbled to a halt. "Oh God."

Jonty turned to face him and walked backwards. "He didn't beat the gay out of me, but he never stopped trying. I've had more broken…" He faced forwards again, then gasped. "Wow, look at that." He ran forward, bent and scooped something from the sand, then held it out to show Devan.

"What am I looking at?" Devan asked.

"Sea glass. You don't often find it on a sandy beach like this. Check out the shape."

Devan took the small piece of green glass in his fingers. "Hmm. A warped heart."

"Is there no romance in your soul?"

"Only in my cock."

Jonty laughed. "This heart just needs a bit of love and an imagination. I adore sea glass."

"What do you do with it?"

"Collect it. Hoard it. Imitate Gollum. So bright, so beautiful, my precioussss." Jonty coughed. "Make things with it. Feel how smooth the edges are."

"It's like a pebble." Devan turned it in his fingers.

"Pebbles are formed in the same way, rocks that get broken up and smoothed over. The sea is nature's big tumbling machine. It took about forty years to make a piece like that. There's a beach in Russia, near Vladivostok, that was a tip in the Soviet era, and truckloads of broken vodka bottles and cracked porcelain were dumped there. Over decades, the sea has created a beach of sea glass. The photos are great, but I'd love to see it for real before it disappears."

"Why will it disappear?"

"Erosion. People taking souvenirs. No glass being dumped to replace it."

Devan dropped the heart back into Jonty's palm. "Why do you like it so much?"

Jonty held it up to the sun. "Once upon a time, this piece of glass was sharp enough to draw blood, now it's been tamed by nature. Cruel turned kind. A useless fragment reformed into a thing of beauty. Every piece is different, but they all have a frosty look, see?"

Devan nodded. "Are some colours rarer than others?"

"Orange is the rarest, then turquoise, red and yellow. Green and white are common. Sorry little heart."

Jonty tossed it in his hand and looked as though he was going to give the piece back to Devan, but instead, put it in his backpack. "It's getting harder to find because glass isn't used as much as it was in the past and we no longer dump at sea. My friend, Tay, used to help me collect it."

Devan caught the shuttered expression on Jonty's face and wondered why. "But not now?"

"He can't anymore. It's so hard to find. You could spend all day and not discover a single piece."

Which made it even more strange it had been on this sandy beach.

"Do you like hotel work?" Devan asked.

"Since I'd never make it as a supermodel, yes."

Devan gritted his teeth. Jonty had no idea but...

Jonty whined. "You haven't got the hang of this conversation at all, have you? You're supposed to disagree."

"I'm glad you're not a supermodel."

Jonty raised his eyebrows. "Well, *I'm* not. All that posing, pouting and lazing around? I'd be good at that. Instead, I'm supposed to do things like be pleasant to difficult guests who want to check in far too early, or demand meals after the kitchen is closed. Oh wait, I'm so good at that."

And Devan was pulled out of his downward slide. He glanced at Jonty but he was staring out to sea. "Is McAllister a decent employer?"

"Yes. I like working there. Only I did tell a bit of a fib."

"You don't work there?"

Jonty smiled. "I've been there five years not five months."

Devan frowned. "Why did you lie?"

"Because you thought I was bad at my job and if you'd known I'd been doing it for five years, I thought you'd be even more huffy."

"Huffy?"

"You were the definition of huffy. Sulky, moody, grumpy, touchy, gr… I'll stop before I go too far. Shit, I have, haven't I? But I'm not on duty right now. We're not hotel guest and employee. And you did arrive in a bad mood."

"True."

"You *stayed* in a bad mood. You smiled more when we thought we might die. Please don't tell me you were smiling when you thought *I* might die."

"You made me smile. I think you were the perfect guy to be with when we were in danger."

"And when we're not?"

"I don't know yet." *I don't know what I'm doing, what I'm hoping for.*

Jonty shrugged and grinned. "Fair enough. Do you like smiling?"

Devan laughed. "I like you making me smile." His fingers brushed against Jonty's, and he heard Jonty's intake of breath, felt the catch in his own throat.

"Your fingers are braver than mine," Jonty whispered. "I'm impressed."

Devan thought it better not to admit the touch had been accidental and he'd been trying to talk himself out of making a move. Maybe his body had other ideas. Good thing his cock couldn't speak, but it was pushing against his zip.

"Do you have a boyfriend?" Devan asked. *This Tay you mentioned?*

"No. Shocking, isn't it? I'm continually amazed there aren't guys lined up desperate to go out with me, hopefully forming an orderly queue, though a bit of a scrum might be flattering. Unfortunately, I only attract impossible men."

"Am I impossible?"

"I knew you were trouble when you walked in. Hey! That would make a great song lyric, don't you think?"

"Someone beat you to that."

"I'm guessing you *do* have a boyfriend, or that you and he fell out, which is why you're up here in a moody, grumpy, touchy sulk."

"Any other guesses?"

"That you've driven up to visit a sick relative, or attend the funeral of someone you know…as opposed to the funeral of someone you don't know. I'm sorry for being flippant if that's true. Please tell me it's not, or I might have to throw myself onto the sand at your feet and beg forgiveness. You weren't caught up in that tsunami in Asia, were you?"

Devan struggled to see the link. "What…? No."

"I did wonder if you might be a serial killer looking for his next victim. But you didn't have a body in your suitcase. Or maybe it was split between two cases and it was a little body. Not a child though."

"Er…

"Sorry." Jonty winced.

"Would a serial killer check into a hotel under his real name?"

"Maybe it's not your real name. I mean…Smith?" Jonty dropped his backpack on the sand, pulled his hoody over his head and tossed it aside, then hopped on one leg while he wrenched off a trainer and sock.

"What are you doing?"

"Going for a swim." The other trainer and sock came off followed by Jonty's T-shirt then his jeans. "The cold will shut my mouth."

Devan gaped at him, and willed his cock to stay calm.

"Do you have a boyfriend?" Jonty asked. "I didn't give you chance to answer."

"No boyfriend."

"Right. I won't be long." Jonty raced down to the water wearing a pair of tight blue boxers.

Devan's cock wanted to chase that biteable arse. Then he thought of the sea temperature and instead, picked up all Jonty's clothes and followed him. Jonty didn't hesitate at the water's edge, he ploughed straight in, and when he was up to his thighs, dived under. He came up whooping.

"Is that a fin behind you?" Devan called.

"Not funny," Jonty yelled back.

"It *is* a fin."

"Really not funny."

Moments later, he was wading out of the water to Devan's side.

"I'm freezing. If only I had someone to give me a hug."

"Even though I'll be cold and wet too?" But Devan unzipped his jacket and Jonty stepped right up to him. Devan wrapped the jacket as far around him as it would go.

"You could have just asked for a hug," Devan whispered in his ear.

"You mean I didn't need to go in the water? Damn." He tugged out of Devan's hold. "I don't want to make you wet, well not that sort of wet. I'll run until I'm dry."

Jonty shook like a dog and jogged along the beach, his arse cheeks pressing against the fabric of his boxers. Devan followed with a smile on his face.

Oh God, what am I doing? Jonty had goose bumps on his goose bumps.

Being an idiot, as usual.

Shut up, Tay.

How are you going to get your clothes on?

Tantalisingly.

You don't even have a towel.

"Put some clothes on before you freeze," Devan said at his back.

Jonty turned and took the T-shirt he was offering. It stuck to his skin as he squirmed into it. Once he was wearing his hoody as well, he felt warmer, but his teeth were still chattering. Apart from Devan, the nearest person was a long way away. *Good.*

Oh, you crafty bugger.

What? Me?

"Don't look." Jonty grabbed his jeans, then turned his back on Devan before he peeled off his boxers. The hoody was long, so not much could be seen, just a tantalising glimpse of his arse. Hopefully. He reached back to pass his boxers to Devan. "I don't want to get sand on them." He smiled when Devan took them.

These weren't his tightest jeans, but it still took some wriggling to get them on, particularly when he had to be careful zipping himself up. When he turned, he could have sworn Devan's pupils had blown, his eyes were so black. Jonty took his boxers from Devan's hand and stuffed them in the side pocket of his bag. Devan zipped up his jacket and swallowed hard.

"That was refreshing." Jonty grinned.

"You're still talking."

"The cold only shut my mouth for a moment. I must remember that. Too much pain for a moment's gain."

"Want your trainers?"

Jonty took them. "Thanks. I won't put them on yet. Come on. There's something even more fantastic to see around the corner. And no, I won't be unzipping my jeans again."

"I didn't see anything fantastic."

Jonty turned and stared at him. "Not even the tiniest hint of my arse?"

"No."

"You wanted to say yes, I can tell."

Devan laughed.

As they moved onto Bamburgh beach and the castle came into view, Jonty sighed. "This is mine and Tay's favourite place. I always go in the sea when I come here. I sort of made a promise to myself that I would, and now I'm scared to stop, in case I don't get to be here again."

"I've seen pictures…"

"Of my arse? Where? Oh God. No!"

Devan rolled his eyes. "It's magnificent."

"Thank you. I knew you were lying." Jonty wriggled his backside. "Grade 1 listed. It's open to the public. The oldest part is a twelfth century keep. Oh shit, that sounded so wrong. I don't— No, I'll shut up now before I make it worse."

"Have you been inside?"

Jonty hesitated. "We're talking about Bamburgh castle, right?"

"Well, you can't fuck your own… Can you?"

"Er…"

"Are you saying…?" Devan made a faint strangled sound. "Yes, the castle."

Jonty laughed. "I'm very flexible."

"Shut up."

"I can wrap my legs around my neck without strangling myself."

"Shut the fuck up."

"Do you want me to?"

108

Devan let out a quiet groan. "Do I want you to what?"

"Show you how flexible I am or shut the fuck up?"

"Save your *Cirque du Soleil* act for later. Is there anywhere to eat in Bamburgh?"

"Several places, though no actual fish and chip shops, but you can probably get fish and chips in the restaurants. We'd have to go back to Seahouses for the real deal."

"Let's see how hungry we are when we reach the turnaround point."

Jonty would rather wait for something that didn't cost him an arm and leg. He didn't want Devan to offer to pay.

"This beach is incredible," Devan said.

"Best for surfing in the north-east. Best for a lot of things. Follow me."

Jonty headed away from the sea to the back of the beach. "When I was a kid, I used to think these dunes were my personal adventure playground. They're constantly shifting and full of secret dips. Plenty of places where I could jump and run and roll and dive. I played endless games of hide and seek with my friend."

I was better at hiding than you.

"Tay was better at hiding than me." Jonty took a deep breath. "A couple of times, when I couldn't find him, I thought he must have gone home and left me, then he'd jump out, pretend to be a raptor, and scare me half to death."

Jonty fastened his trainers to his backpack and hoisted it on his shoulders. "First one to the top gets—"

Devan was already powering past him. Jonty laughed and set off after him, using the indentations Devan was creating until they were closer to the top, when he nipped to the left and got to the summit first. They both bent over breathing heavily.

"Shit… I made that…easier for you…didn't I?" Devan panted.

109

"Yep but… you cheated… You didn't wait for me to say go… I win."

Devan slumped onto his backside. "What do you win?"

"Damn. I was going to let you win. In the excitement of having my face inches from your arse, I forgot."

Devan caught hold of Jonty's sleeve and tugged him down to sit at his side.

"That's a better workout than my run." Devan was still panting.

"Are you sure you're only thirty-five?" Jonty laughed at Devan's glare then gazed out to sea. "Check out that view." The sun was glinting off the waves and now they were out of the wind, it felt warm.

"Spectacular."

But Jonty could feel Devan looking at him and not the sea. He wanted to face him, but nerves stopped him. He took his water bottle from the side pocket of his backpack and offered it to Devan.

"Thanks."

Jonty used his socks to brush the sand from his feet, then put his socks and his trainers on.

Devan shrugged out of his jacket and Jonty laughed.

"What's funny?" Devan asked.

"You're taking stuff off as I put stuff on."

"I wasn't thinking of taking anything else off."

Jonty did his best pout. He put his hand inside his backpack and pulled out a Flake. "Not even for a bite of this?"

Jonty watched Devan's Adam's apple rise and fall. His own copied it. He ripped open the top of the chocolate bar and peeled down the crinkly yellow wrapping.

"It's your lucky day," Jonty said. "I don't usually share my Flake until the third date. I hang on for a trip to the cinema first. Did you know that Flakes won't melt in the sun or in a microwave or in a *bain marie*?"

110

"Really?"

"They don't melt in your mouth until you've crumbled them or sucked really hard. The fat and cocoa solids are arranged in a way that prevents the melting fat from lubricating the cocoa particles to the point where they'll flow. The impossible of the chocolate world and the best chemistry lesson I ever had. We all got chocolate that day."

Jonty held the bar out to Devan. *Damn, my fingers are shaking and not because I'm cold.*

Devan opened his mouth and moved in.

"You know there's a right way and a wrong way to eat a Flake," Jonty said just before the chocolate touched Devan's lips.

"And my way." Devan was so quick, Jonty didn't have time to pull back the bar, but Devan barely nibbled the end. "Another of the things I do slowly."

"You eat chocolate slowly?" Jonty gaped at him. "You're not normal. What else do you do slowly?"

"Driving, when the police are around. I linger in the shower. I like to take my time over food."

"Is that look you're giving me because you'd like to eat me?"

"You or that Flake. Tricky choice."

Devan licked his lips and Jonty groaned. "That's not fair. Now I'm going to look like a pig when I shove it all in."

"You told me you couldn't get it all in at one go. How long is it? Fifteen centimetres? Six inches? I'm a bit disappointed you can't manage that. More than a bit. Very."

Jonty laughed. He put the Flake to his mouth and slid it in as slowly as he could before drawing it out and nibbling off no more than Devan had taken. "I've licked most of it. I suppose you won't want another bite. Sorry."

Devan laughed. "No, you're not. And considering where I'd like to put my tongue, you licking the Flake is not an issue." He took a bigger bite. "See if it will fit now. But don't choke. I have other plans for your mouth."

Jonty put the Flake in his mouth and touched the other end of the bar to Devan's lips. Devan opened his mouth and let the chocolate slide in until his lips were against Jonty's.

Jonty bit down and moved back, chewing slowly. "Mmm…mmm…mmmmm." He swallowed and groaned. "So good. Best thing ever. Nothing to beat it."

One push on his shoulder, and Jonty dropped onto his back. Devan lay on his side next to him. "You are bad."

Jonty pouted. "But in a good way?"

"Remains to be seen," Devan whispered. "I have told myself to leave you alone so many times."

"How many times?"

"I didn't count. A lot."

"You don't take any notice of yourself then?"

"Parts of me are hard to convince." Devan ran his finger over the piercings in Jonty's ear, then the one in his eyebrow. "You're my Flake."

Jonty blinked. *What?*

"Tempting. Delicious. I want to eat you all in one go. But…" Devan sighed.

"Oh God. There's always a but. It's usually something bad. Though occasionally, it's a good thing. You have a very nice butt, as in arse." Jonty could feel anxiety nibbling at his stomach. "I paused because that's where you're supposed to say that I do. Please don't say I don't have a nice backside. That would destroy me. I'd never go out in public again. I'd have to hide myself away and only emerge in case of fire."

"But…" Devan said.

"A failure at distraction too? I'm doomed. Okay. Tell me then. But what?"

"This can't go anywhere."

112

Jonty made sure to keep the disappointment off his face. He *knew* that. Of course he fucking knew that, but he didn't want to hear it. Not right at the start. Except Devan was telling him there shouldn't be a start if Jonty wanted the bit in the middle before *The End*.

Why not know where things stand?

Because I want to hope. I always want to hope for more, even if I pretend not to. Why shouldn't I hope? His heart ached.

Sometimes there is no hope. Look at me.

I've not given up on you.

Jonty let out a tremulous sigh.

"You know that, right?" Devan asked. "You understand what I'm saying, because it's not even fair to kiss you if you think this will go anywhere."

He ran his finger over Jonty's mouth and Jonty wanted to bite it. Hard. Chomp down. *Make you bleed!* Devan was lucky he didn't. He also wanted to tell him to fuck off, but he didn't do that either.

So much for getting carried away in the moment.

So much for romance.

So much for hope.

But Jonty had some pride. "Is this a conversation you have before you dance someone into a club toilet? Or persuade a guy out of a pub into a quiet alley?" Jonty kept his voice level. "I don't think so." Except, in saying that, had he implied that was all this was? *Shit!* Now he was confused.

"I really don't want you to get hurt."

And those words undid him. Caring demolished his barriers. How much did he want Devan to kiss him? A lot. *Oh God. One kiss. That's all. But...* He had his very own *but. But I might want more, so what then?* Was Devan going to run?

He couldn't think. Well, not about anything sensible. His cock was doing all the thinking. It was full of...thoughts. Almost bursting with them.

"Kiss me," Jonty whispered. *I'll change your mind. I can. I know I can.* "Please. I've never asked anyone before."

Devan moved closer until their lips were centimetres apart, air moving from one mouth to another.

"You smell sweet," Devan whispered.

"Be grateful I'm addicted to Flakes and not pickled onions."

"Jester! Jester! Get back here."

The screeching voice drove them apart. Devan sat up just before a golden retriever launched itself at Jonty, pinned him down and licked his face.

"Oh God, I am so sorry." A woman came over the dune holding a lead. "Jester! Jester!"

Jonty couldn't stop laughing. Every time he tried to push the dog aside, it thought Jonty was playing and renewed its attempts to keep licking. The woman hauled the dog off by its collar and clipped on its lead.

"Bad dog. I am so sorry. Thanks to my idiot son, he thinks anyone who's lying down wants to be licked. Here, I travel prepared." She handed Jonty a packet of wet wipes.

He sat up, pulled one out and cleaned his face. "Thanks." He stood up and gave her the pack back. "Don't worry. I like dogs."

"He's better behaved than he looks. It's someone lying down that gets him excited. Sorry again."

Jester set off along the top of the sand dune dragging his owner behind him and Jonty turned to smile at Devan. Except Devan had the wrong look on his face. Not frustration, or a desire to take up where they'd left off, or amusement at the woman's comment. It looked too much like an expression of relief.

Icy dread crept up Jonty's spine. A fire had been started, but Devan had thrown a bucket of water on it.

Jonty made himself smile. His first line of defence. "Come on then. See who gets to the bottom first."

He started running, tumbled partway down it, and rolled the rest of the way. A bit like his life, full of hiccups. Devan made it down without falling and he held out his hand to pull Jonty up. Jonty didn't take it.

Chapter Eight

Part of Devan thought he'd had a lucky escape. The other part of him was telling him he was a dick for thinking that, because he didn't feel lucky. He'd been moments away from not just kissing Jonty but also getting them both off. He'd thought they'd be undisturbed in the dunes, at least long enough for them both to come. Knowing Jonty was bare-arsed in those jeans had fogged Devan's head, filled his cock, and it had only just started to deflate. But the part of Devan that was telling him he was a dick wasn't shutting up.

Kiss him!

"Do you want to turn and head back?" Jonty was unnaturally quiet.

You want to pretend we weren't about to kiss? Jonty had his hands in his pockets and his head down. *I guess you* do *want to pretend.*

"Can I buy us lunch in Bamburgh?" Devan asked.

"Not hungry."

"I am." *But I want to kiss a smile onto your face more than I need food.*

"I'd rather go back to Seahouses and find a fish and chip shop."

"Bamburgh's nearer. We've walked this far, and I'd like to take a closer look." Devan grabbed Jonty's hand, held tight, and tugged him around to face him. "And I'm not going to be thwarted by a dog. I couldn't live with the shame."

His reward for that comment was Jonty's wide smile and everything was right again.

"You've got some competition," Jonty said. "Jester was a good kisser. Little bit too much tongue, but lots of enthusiasm. I love enthusiasm."

Devan laughed. "I have something to aim for then, to kiss better than a dog."

"A little less slobber would be appreciated."

"I'll make a note."

"Though the wet wipe was a lovely touch." Jonty looked down at their linked hands. "You can let go if you want. I'm not going to run off."

Devan stroked Jonty's palm with his thumb and felt him tremble, heard the catch in his breath. "Are you cold? You want my jacket?"

"I'm not cold," Jonty whispered. "It's just…no one's ever held my hand before. I don't even remember my mum doing it. My dad definitely didn't, not unless he was yanking me somewhere private to hit me."

Devan's heart cracked. "Can we find a quiet spot and I'll try to do better than Jester?"

"You mean you want me to trek all the way up that dune *again*?" Jonty widened then narrowed his eyes. "Maybe you could carry me. Think of the great exercise that would be."

"Think of the strained back I'd get."

"But I'm light as a feather. Oh, I ate that Flake. No, I'm not light as a feather."

"Last one up buys lunch." Devan had already started to climb when he heard Jonty coming behind him, cursing and spluttering.

No way was Devan going to let Jonty pay for lunch, but he needed to make losing look authentic. As it was, the climb nearly killed him, the loose sand shifting beneath his feet. By the time he got to the top, he was exhausted. Jonty had just beaten him.

"If I have…that idea again…talk me out of it." Devan slumped on the sand. *Christ!*

Jonty dropped down at his side breathing heavily and they stared out to sea.

117

"This is…so beautiful." Devan was becoming more and more enamoured of the Northumberland coast. Not only the coast.

"Yep."

"Can you ride horses on this beach?"

Jonty nodded. "There's a place to hire them… If you're experienced, the people who own the stables will even let you canter and gallop."

"Have you done it?"

"Yes."

"Maybe I can fit it in before I go back." His breathing finally eased. "It's so peaceful here. No rush. No pressure. Does it get busy in the summer?"

"Not really."

"If it was warmer, this beach would be packed."

"Probably."

"Pity the sea is so cold."

"Yeah."

What have I done wrong? Devan knew he'd lost him again. He thought back over what he'd just said—and got it. *Fit it in before I go back. Oh shit.* But he *had* to go back. Jonty knew that. Not quite a holiday romance, but that was all it could be.

Jonty reached for his hand and wrapped his fingers around it. "Too many visitors can spoil places. There are all sorts of hidden gems in Northumberland that we need to keep secret or this peace and tranquillity will be overrun with caravan parks and hotels and camping and glamping sites and holiday villages and amusement parks and safari themed crazy golf and shops selling kiss-me-quick hats and sticks of rock and plastic poop. We need enough visitors to keep us in jobs, but not so many that our roads get clogged, and there's nowhere to park, and everything gets expensive to buy."

Devan felt a pang of guilt, but one top quality hotel wouldn't spoil the place.

118

"Are there any dogs bounding towards me?" Jonty asked.

Devan looked around. "No."

"No zombies or werewolves?"

"I think we're fine."

"You didn't check."

Devan smiled and looked around again. "We're safe."

Jonty let go of his hand, leaned in and kissed him. The merest brush of lips and Devan was caught in a rip of a different kind. He forgot to breathe. Actually, he didn't forget, he *couldn't* breathe. He'd never been tasered, but that was what it felt like. Sparks shot down his veins and he tingled from his toes to his fingertips. His lungs had locked and his heart raced. Jonty wasn't touching him anywhere other than his lips, but Devan felt as if Jonty's hands were everywhere.

Somehow, he found himself lying on his back, Jonty leaning over him, tugging at his upper lip with his teeth, sucking, licking, teasing. *Oh God.* Devan pulled Jonty down on top of him, wrapped his hands around his arse—*perfect*—and held tight. They were both rock hard. Jonty moaned as he plunged his tongue into Devan's mouth. Jonty tasted of chocolate and Devan drowned.

Soft turned hard. Gentle switched to frantic. Devan rolled to pin Jonty beneath him and took charge of the kiss, cupping Jonty's cheeks, holding him in place while his tongue surged in and out of Jonty's mouth. Even as he told himself to take this slow, he was rocking into Jonty, pressing their cocks together, rutting, grinding, wishing they were naked. There was a frenzied desperation in the way they kissed and moved, legs entwined while hands touched, stroked, grabbed, flailed, squeezed. Common sense had fled. Anyone could come across them. But Devan didn't care.

They kissed and kissed and kissed, and only when Devan dragged enough awareness into his head that there was a possibility of coming in his jeans, did he pull away. They lay side by side on their backs, chests heaving. How long since a kiss like that?

"*Much* better than Jester," Jonty said. "I don't even need a wet wipe."

Devan laughed. *This* was what he'd been missing. Innocent laughter. Fun. Even before he and Ravi had split, things had never been like this. Jonty was immature, irritating, and yet the most entrancing guy he'd met in…maybe ever.

Jonty pushed to his feet. "Come on. I expended so much energy on that kiss, I'm starving now."

He whooped and ran down onto the beach, tumbling again and rolling down the sand to the bottom. Devan started down intending to be careful, then thought *what the hell*, and went for it. He fell too, laughing with the sheer joy of doing something he'd last done as a child.

Once they'd tipped the sand out of their footwear, they headed for the edge of the sea where walking was easier.

"Was the run down worth the effort it took to get to the top?" Jonty asked.

Devan smiled. "Yep."

Jonty brushed the sand from his hoody. "God, it gets everywhere. Like come, but less sticky."

Devan grinned. "Tell me about the hotel. Do you see much of the guy who owns it?"

"Hamish McAllister? He comes in to talk to Vincent, the manager, every couple of weeks. Hamish remembers all our names and asks how we are. He's a nice guy. Widower. His wife did all the artwork in the hotel. And yes, we all know the pictures are awful, but we pretend they're undiscovered Picassos. He was sixty last month and there was a big party in the events room. He and his family use the gym, but especially the pool. He put money into that when he really should have renovated the rooms."

"My suite's okay."

"But the only real wow factor is the view. The two suites had work done on them a couple of years ago. The other rooms are…a bit grim. Designed by Agatha Christie with murder in mind. But the guests don't seem to care. Most guests. We get the odd one or two who find fault. But the rooms are a reasonable size and they're not expensive, not considering the views and the proximity to the beach. The restaurant is the big draw. People come from Newcastle to eat at McAllister's and it's easier to stay the night, so we have high occupancy rates. The chef is really good. Though I think Marcus only stays with the hotel because his wife's family is from round here and they have three young kids. Her parents help with them."

All useful information, though Devan did feel a twinge of guilt. "Is that the guy I heard banging and clattering when I wanted breakfast after service had finished?"

Jonty winced. "That was Wayne, the sous chef. Wayne's a combination of Gordon Ramsay and Naomi Campbell — good and bad bits. Foul mouthed, bad tempered, touchy, tall, very good-looking. Both great at their job."

"If you could do whatever you liked to the hotel, what would you do?"

"Update the rooms. Refit the bathrooms. Replace the windows. Paint the outside and get rid of the stains creeping down from the balconies. Find ways to persuade more people to come out of season. Maybe hold wedding fayres or special events. Murder mystery weekends would be fun. Or retreats for writers or even sports weekends. You can climb, ride, swim, surf, kayak, and a whole load more. Or even arrange stays for film lovers. Lots of filming has been done around here. Harry Potter, Transformers, Lady Macbeth."

"How often does the major come to stay?"

"He lives in the hotel all year round, along with a few other guests. There's also a couple who split their time between the hotel and cruising." Jonty glanced at him. "What have you come up here for?"

Had he been too obvious, asking about the hotel? He didn't want to tell Jonty that truth. Not yet. Maybe he'd never need to if McAllister didn't want to sell. But another truth to avoid a lie… A more painful one for him at least. Why not?

There were a lot of reasons *why not*.

"You've gone so quiet, I'm worried," Jonty whispered.

"I came up here to escape."

Jonty gulped. "Oh God. What's happening in the south? Have you run out of coffee? Toilet rolls? It can't be the sea level rising or we'd be underwater. Zombie apocalypse?" He groaned. "Now I feel terrible I've trivialised what might be something serious. Like cancer. Sorry." Jonty grabbed his hand and squeezed hard. "If you have duct tape in your pocket, now might be a good time to use it. Not on me, obviously, on you, so you can't tell me I'm an idiot."

Devan chuckled.

Jonty gave a dramatic sigh. "Except you can't just say you came up here to escape and not tell me why. Are the police after you? Your boss? The Russian mafia? Colombian drug lords? A Mexican cartel? Aliens? I'll shut up now."

For some unsettling reason that he didn't fully understand, Devan wanted to tell him about Ravi and Griff, wanted someone on his side.

"You don't have to tell me." Jonty widened his eyes. "Debt collection agency? Your ex? A gang of exes? A casino debt? Sorry. I will give up asking eventually."

Devan snorted. "Really?"

Jonty looked hurt. "I won't push. I know you arrived feeling sad. You don't have to tell me why."

"Are you going to let me get a word in edgeways?"

Jonty mimed zipping his lips. Devan waited, but Jonty said nothing else.

"Last Sunday, while I was having lunch with my parents, they told me my brother's planning to get married in December."

"Right." Jonty frowned. "Were you supposed to marry first or something, because you're the eldest son?"

Devan laughed. He couldn't help it because Jonty had inadvertently almost got it right. "In a way. The person he's marrying is my ex."

"Oh. Ah. Eww. Eek. Oops. I've run out of short exclamations starting with vowels, but that's...not good. Is your ex awful? You want to save your brother, but you can't because he won't listen? Shit, that sounds like me. The not listening bit."

"Not quite. Five months ago, Ravi should have been marrying me. The..." Devan swallowed hard. It was harder to say than he'd thought, but then this was something he'd never thought he'd tell a stranger.

Jonty held tighter to Devan's hand. "What is it?"

"The day before the wedding, I found Ravi in bed with my brother."

"Had they got a good excuse? Hiding from an escaped tarantula or something?"

"No."

"Oh shit."

"Obviously the wedding was called off."

"By who?"

"That's an interesting question. By both of us."

"Hmm. So you both lied."

Devan frowned. "Why would you say that?"

"It was a guess, but I'm assuming you wouldn't want anyone to know what you'd discovered and if you'd spoken out, what would that have done to your family? Better to make up some story about realising just in time that it wasn't

123

going to work, not going into too much detail. Though I'm guessing that's turned out to be a mistake."

"Last Monday, my brother, Griff, told me he wants me to be his best man when he marries Ravi in December."

"He what?" Jonty gaped at him. "Is he mad?"

"He's…not thinking clearly."

"Does anyone know the real reason why the wedding was called off?"

"My father knows, but I've only just told him. Ravi, Griff and I agreed it was better that no one knew the truth. Ravi was at fault, and Griff, but I would have looked a fool. People would have been sympathetic, but that wasn't what I wanted. I went quiet. I hid in a dark place and thought time would help."

"An actual dark place or in your head?"

"In my head. I imagined I'd rather be despised than pitied, but I found myself resenting that I appeared to be the guilty party. Ravi was in tears all over Instagram and Facebook. He's very good at appearing distraught. Now I've found out that for the last few months, and most likely from the day I discovered them, my brother and Ravi have had a relationship. I had even more reason to be pissed off with my brother than I'd thought."

"And you haven't put people right about what really happened?"

"No. And now I feel I can't say anything. Not if Griff is marrying him."

"That is so fucking unfair. Do you and your brother get on? *Did* you get on?"

"We were close when we were younger." Almost inseparable. "We work for the same company. I got him the job. I thought he was my best friend. I'd asked him to be my best man along with my other brother. And because my mother doesn't know the truth about why the wedding was called off, she can't understand why I don't want to stand next to my brother when he marries Ravi."

Devan was amazed how much better he felt telling this to Jonty. "Griff has always been the golden boy. He gets what he wants, but not this time." *He fucking won't, because I'd rather die.*

"I'd buy them something really meaningful as a wedding present. Like an emergency survival kit or towels with the names Satan and Beelzebub embroidered on them, or an experience gift for something neither of them would like to do such as a napkin folding course, or dry-stone walling for beginners, or a day handling venomous snakes."

Devan chuckled.

"How long had you and Ravi been going out?"

"Two years."

"Wow."

"Once I'd seen him with Griff, all I could think about was whether he'd been faithful during that time. Did I know him at all? Why wasn't I enough for him? What does my brother have that I don't? Why would he hurt me like that? I feel... angry. So fucking angry. All the fucking time."

"Ouch."

Devan let go of Jonty's hand. "Sorry. The crazy thing is, that as far as Ravi is concerned, it's not so much the infidelity that got to me, but the look on his face when Griff was fucking him. I thought I knew him and I didn't know him at all. I honestly believed that I'd get my head straight and move on, that I could tuck it all away, keep how I felt locked up. For five months that was what I did. Wore a mask, because it hurt too much to let it all up to the surface. I stopped feeling angry. I was more upset that Griff had been Ravi's partner. My own fucking brother. The one who worshipped me. Now I'm angry again. And...I can't believe I've told you any of that."

Jonty put his hand on Devan's arm and slid it down to his hand to let their fingers entwine. "It's not a surprise you're angry with everyone, including yourself. Angry with the choice you made to keep quiet. Angry with your brother for his insensitivity. Angry with Ravi for cheating. Angry with yourself for not seeing what you think you should have seen. But more than angry, you're sad because you've been hurt."

"Humiliated."

"But you said people don't know the truth."

"I have no idea what people know anymore, but when your brother is going to marry your ex, I think people might guess what happened."

"Hurt still fits better than humiliated."

"Mike told me you'd been hurt too."

Jonty gave a short laugh. "Was he warning you off?"

"He told me not to hurt you. That's the last thing I want to do. That's the reason we shouldn't…"

Jonty stepped in front of him and Devan stopped walking. Jonty wrapped his arms around him and hugged him. He didn't say a word, just pressed his head against Devan's shoulder and held him. Devan lifted his arms and wrapped them around Jonty. They stood motionless for what seemed a long time, until the world around them faded and all he could see, feel and smell was Jonty, and gradually he calmed. His anger faded, his heart rate slowed, his chest stopped hurting.

He'd opened his heart to a stranger. Was this some watershed moment? Could he finally put it all behind him?

"All better now," Jonty said. "I don't have any Thomas the Tank Engine plasters or I'd give you one."

Jonty took hold of his hand again and tugged him on. "Right. The world according to Jonty Bloom. This is the life you've been given. You have to keep going. That's the biggest lesson. There's no choice. Giving up is not an option. Sometimes life is shit. You get hurt, but you carry on. You don't let something awful that happened to you wreck your life because that way you've lost. If you let hurt keep hold of you, you've allowed the person who hurt you to win. You need to keep putting one foot in front of the other. Keep moving. Don't fall. Because if I don't eat soon, I'm going to have to snack on some juicy bit of you."

Devan smiled. "That doesn't sound too bad."

"You didn't see how I bit that Flake? My teeth are razor sharp. I'm always biting my tongue. Though not with you. You bring out the sarcastic side of me."

"There's another side?"

"Oh yeah." Jonty winked at him. "It starts with s too. Guess which of these it is. Smooth, sulky, sweet, sensible, sexy."

"S—"

"I've not finished. Splendiferous, stupendous, soothing, spellbinding, seductive, sultry. I'm glad I don't need to guess, because I'm thinking I'm all those."

"What happens if I don't get it right?"

"I will have failed as a gay man."

Devan thought about it. "You're sunny."

Jonty smiled. "Ahh. You win."

They ate fish and chips in the outdoor area of a restaurant in Bamburgh with a fantastic view of the castle. Devan felt as if he'd somehow moved into another world. Telling Jonty about Griff and Ravi had been so out of character that he was still having trouble believing he'd done it. It showed weakness, something Devan avoided.

Though did it show weakness? There was something about Jonty that made him feel... *What the fuck* does *he make me feel?* Less anxious? Settled? Stronger? Happier? Was that it? *Less alone?*

With only a little prompting, Jonty talked more about the hotel, the staff, and about some of the financial issues Hamish had been having. Apparently, the guy had built a house in

Newcastle that had cost him a fortune, only for his wife to die, and he'd paid for his sons to be members of some swanky golf club. Devan felt guilty that he filed it all away. He might have come up here because of Ravi and Griff, but he was also working. He couldn't get away from that.

"Why did you want to speak to Hamish?"

Devan raised his eyebrows. "You didn't mention *s* for *spy*."

"I overheard accidentally. I thought you were going to complain about me. I don't want to lose my job."

Oh shit. A reminder of another reason he needed to leave Jonty alone. "The company I work for is looking to invest up here. I wanted to pick Hamish's brain. I have nothing to complain about as far as you're concerned."

Jonty grinned. "Not even my mouth?"

"Especially not your mouth."

The more Jonty talked, the more Devan liked him. He was bright and funny. Devan couldn't understand why he wasn't with anyone, yet glad that he wasn't. This friend of his called Tay didn't appear to be that sort of friend. But underlying the attraction Devan felt, he was aware that Jonty was not going to be happy when he knew why he'd come up to Northumberland.

"I am so full." Jonty put his knife and fork down. "I've not eaten as much as that for ages. Don't let me go into the water on the way back or I'll sink like the hippo I am."

"Do you want a dessert?"

"Ugh. If you'd told me I could have pudding too, I wouldn't have eaten all those chips. Now I'm too full."

Devan paid the bill, refusing to let Jonty pay half, and they left the restaurant, heading back towards the beach.

"My mother told me about Griff getting married, moments before she served pudding. My favourite. Apple crumble. And I couldn't eat it because my throat had closed up. She was bloody annoyed because she'd made it especially."

"She thought making your favourite pudding would be enough for you to cope with being told your brother and your ex were marrying? I don't like her very much. Sorry."

"Nor do I at the moment. She has a blind spot as far as my brother's concerned. Griff has a mild form of cerebral palsy and she's always been protective. So was I. When did you lose touch with your parents?"

"Depends which parent you mean. My mother when I was eight. My father when I was fifteen."

"What happened?"

"It's a long and sad story. Sure you want to know?"

"Yes. If you want to tell me."

"You told me yours, so…" Jonty sighed. "We relocated to Northumberland from Surrey because of my dad's job. I don't think my mum wanted to move. I didn't. I had friends at school and moving somewhere new meant I had to start all over again. But dad always got what he wanted by one means or another. If persuasion didn't work, a thump did."

Shit! "He hit your mother?"

Jonty nodded. "He didn't hit me until she left. Then I became his punch bag."

"Your mother left you with him? Why?"

Jonty kicked at the sand as he walked. "She'd tried to run away with me and my sister a couple of times. Packed a suitcase. Packed my stuff and my sister's stuff. Somehow, he always found out. I think he had cameras in the house. She was scared of him. He drank too much.

"Anyway, we moved up here and for a while, things were better. He wasn't crazy jealous and constantly asking her where she was going, who she was seeing, but… It didn't last. One night, she put me and Denny in the car and told me to stay there. While my mother went into the house to get the

129

bags, my dad came home. I was frightened he'd do something really bad to my mum, so I took Denny out of her seat and carried her back into the house so I could protect my mother."

Devan swallowed hard. He almost wished he'd not asked the question.

"Dad had hit her. Her face was bleeding. He said he'd let her go, but only with one of us. If she chose, he wouldn't follow her. I think he thought she'd refuse, that she wouldn't leave one of her kids."

Jonty stopped walking and stared out to sea. "And I thought…she won't choose. She'll wait until she can run with both of us. But she didn't. She picked Denny. She was crying, but she picked Denny. I was eight. Denny was two. I…sort of understood, as much as a little kid can. She couldn't trust my father to take care of my sister. Denny was still in nappies, didn't sleep through the night and a real little madam. I was a good boy who did as he was told. She thought I'd be okay, I guess. She hugged me and whispered in my ear that she'd come back for me. I believed her. I really believed her. But she never came back."

"Jesus, Jonty." Devan was horrified.

"When my dad finally accepted that she'd gone for good, he destroyed everything of hers and of Denny's that she'd left. Books, toys, clothes. Photos. I hid under the bed in my room and I could hear him yelling as he went round the house. When he finally went quiet, I went down and found him passed out on the couch. He'd thrown up on the carpet. I cleaned up his vomit, made a sandwich, and went back to bed. I still believed she'd come back because she'd promised.

"For years after she'd left, I used to imagine she'd turn up at parents' evening, or she'd be there when I ran on school sports' day, or she'd come to listen to me sing a solo in the end of year shows. I tried my best, just in case.

"I convinced myself that she was dead, that my father had killed her, but then he showed me the divorce papers and told me she was going to get married. She had a new life. One without me. But I still hoped she'd remember what she'd said to me. It's part of the reason I've never left Alnwick. The thought that she'd come back, even after all these years."

Oh God. "Have you looked for her?"

Jonty nodded. "When I was older and knew how. My friend Tay showed me what to do. I never found a trace. She'll have changed her name. I kept mine even though I hated my father, because I thought that way, she'd find me."

"What was your father like when she'd gone?"

"Angry. Bitter. Spiteful. Still drinking too much. Nothing I could describe as sad. But as far as I know, he kept his word and let her go. He hardly mentioned her, though he resented me, blamed me for not being lovable enough to get her to stay."

Devan took hold of his hand. "That's a terrible thing to lay on a kid."

"I believed him. No one loved me and no one ever would, even though I didn't understand why. It was enough to know that she'd left me.

"I kept my head down, did what I was told, ate what I was given, kept out of his way. I worked hard to ensure there was no reason for him to be mad with me. I went to bed early. I was a good boy. A model prisoner. He said he was the one in prison, trapped by a child-guard." He gave a quiet chuckle. "He didn't need a reason to hurt me. Bad day at work, he came home, drank, and took it out on me. Someone cut him up in the car, I bore the brunt of his anger. Though he was mostly careful not to hit me anywhere that showed, and he only did it every month or so."

"No one noticed?"

131

"No. Well, they might have done. Friends did sometimes. Tay did, but I made him promise to keep quiet. I always lied if asked, because bad as my dad was, I didn't want to lose him too. No grandparents. No aunts and uncles. He was all I had. I knew my life was shit, but we were family. He was my dad. I was supposed to love him. He fed me, clothed me. If he hit me, he made me feel it was my fault."

"It was never your fault."

"I know that now. Then one day, he got…carried away. My thirteenth birthday. He'd started to talk to me about girls and sex and stuff, and how I needed to use protection, because the worst thing that could happen was that I got a girl pregnant, and I blurted that I liked boys. It was one of the most idiotic things I've ever done. Maybe the most idiotic. I mean, I knew what his reaction would be. I shouldn't have said anything. The one thing I needed to keep secret and never say, though I think he knew anyway. He was waiting for me to confess it."

"Christ, Jonty." Devan was horrified.

"I had to tell the doctors I'd been beaten up by a gang of lads I'd never seen before and wouldn't recognise again. I said I'd curled up in a ball and closed my eyes while they laid into me. That last part was true. I did curl up and close my eyes. I let it happen, because there was nothing I could do to stop it. I already told you I was in hospital for five days. Well, the police searched for people who didn't exist. One of those policemen was my father. He wasn't supposed to be looking, but I guess righteous indignation went down well with his mates."

"Oh shit." Devan wrapped his arms around him. "You deserved better than that."

Jonty clutched him. "He made me think I didn't. Continually rammed it home that it was my fault my mother and sister had gone. That no son of his would be gay. He wouldn't allow it. Once I'd recovered, the beatings resumed. Not too violent. Just smacks around the head. A belt on the backside. Eventually, my behaviour changed enough that my teachers started to ask more questions. Why was I silent? Why was I missing games again? Bruises *were* finally noticed after a particularly vicious kicking when my dad broke my arm, a couple of ribs, and a bone in my back, and the head got social services involved. My dad was sent to prison and served a year, all the time protesting his innocence, saying it was my boyfriend who'd done it. I didn't have a boyfriend. No way would I have dared."

"Did anyone believe him?"

"Some did, but he was known for having a temper when he was drunk, so… At fifteen, I ended up in a different sort of prison. A care home run by people who didn't give a fuck. A year later, I was able to move into a place of my own, and I got a job in a kitchen washing dishes, followed that with cleaning caravans in a holiday park, then I worked for a company that did pressure washing at commercial and domestic properties. They went under. I cleaned at the hotel, then got the job as night manager. The hotel saved my life. Oh God. You've let me keep talking. I didn't mean to tell you all that."

Devan pressed his face against Jonty's hair. He thought he was beginning to understand Jonty a little better, the reason he resorted to humour, the reason he seemed immature, the reason he understood the world better than a twenty-five-year-old should.

"I didn't mean to tell you about Ravi and my brother. Your story was far worse."

"I wasn't trying to make you feel bad. Or better."

"If your father was here right now, I'd punch him. If your mother was here, I'd ask her how the fuck she could walk away from you."

"If your brother was here, I'd kick his arse. If your ex was here, I'd ask him how the fuck could he do that to you, and then he'd get his arse kicked too."

They smiled at each other.

Devan took Jonty's hand and they kept walking. "I've never talked so much to anyone about how I feel about Ravi and my brother."

"I'm not sure you've talked to me about it really. Just said that you're angry, while I think you're sad. Would you have Ravi back?"

"No."

"Not if he said how sorry he was, how much of a mistake he'd made, what a knobhead he'd been, how he'd do anything for your forgiveness—including that thing with his tongue that drives you nuts?"

Devan chuckled. "Not even if he said that." He sucked his cheeks. "It was such a fucking waste of two years."

"That's not the way to look at it. It might have occupied two years of your life, but it wasn't all bad, was it? Or you wouldn't have stayed together, wouldn't have planned to marry. You must have loved him, had fun times."

"It's hard to remember anything good about him."

"Not hard. You just don't want to and that's fair enough. Because of what he did, you can't trust your memories, but you should keep hold of the knowledge that you did love him, once upon a time.

"And maybe now, you at least know what you *don't* want. Plus remember: your brother is going to have to put up with all the shit you didn't like. That should make you deliriously happy. Did your ex leave his socks on the floor to magically make their own way to the laundry bin? Cut his nails in the sink? Put his cold feet on you in bed? Fart the National Anthem as his party trick? Paddle you too hard? Call you Daddy when you were fucking?"

134

"Stop right there."

Jonty stopped walking and Devan sighed.

"Oh, you want me to stop talking?" Jonty started walking again.

"Can you?"

The silence lasted no more than a few seconds.

"No. I'm sorry if I trivialised your relationship. That wasn't kind."

"Maybe I need some hard truths. There *were* things about Ravi that annoyed me."

"But you loved him. Don't forget that. Don't throw it away. Remember the good times, but also remember that he didn't deserve you. What are you doing tomorrow? Because I'm not due back at work until Saturday night. If you like, I could be your personal tour guide. This area is brilliant if you're a Harry Potter fan. Or I can take you to see the rarest cows in the world, because you look like a guy who'd be impressed by wild cows. Or out on a boat to sing to the whales with an expert tutor. Or horse riding. Or we could go surfing if the surf's up."

"Your change in direction..." He laughed. "I have some business to deal with in the morning, but after that, yes. Shall I pick you up?"

Jonty took his phone from his pocket and handed it to him. "Put your number in."

Devan tapped it in and Jonty pressed call, waited until he heard Devan's phone ring, then ended it. "Now you have mine. Call me when you're free and we can arrange to meet. Have a think about what you'd like to do."

They walked through the car park in Seahouses and stopped by the Aston.

"Can I give you a lift home?"

"No thanks. I've promised to go and see a mate."

135

"I enjoyed today. Except for that interfering dog."

Jonty laughed. "I'll see you tomorrow. Okay?"

"What are you doing tonight?" Devan blurted.

"Ironing my shirts." He chewed his fingernail. "I won't be in the mood for anything once I've visited Tay."

"Why go then?"

"Because he's my friend. And he's ill. He made me feel safe when no one else did and I owe him a lot for that. I'll see you tomorrow. Check your jacket pocket. I've given you something precious to take care of."

As he watched Jonty walk off, he slid his hand in his pocket and pulled out the crooked little sea glass heart. Would a few days of fun be enough? Or would it just make it even harder to walk away from him?

Chapter Nine

Jonty made his way to where he'd padlocked his bike and helmet. He really liked Devan. He liked him too much. There was nothing he could do about that. Maybe all they'd have were these few days. Or maybe not. Jonty hadn't talked about his parents for a long while, but he'd wanted to share his dark past after Devan had shared his.

He got on his bike, but before he set off, he took out his phone, searched for a picture of the biggest dick he could find and sent it to Devan with the words *can you handle this?* Within a minute of setting off, he wished he hadn't done that. Devan would think it was childish. It was. Or even worse, that it was accurate. It wasn't. *Shit.*

His phone bleeped with a message and he pulled off the road to check it. Devan had sent a message. *Handle yes. Swallow no.* Jonty chuckled.

The smile had gone by the time he arrived at Tay's. Tay's parents lived in a big house in Beadnell with great views of the bay, not that Tay could admire them. They'd had their place converted to care for their son who had a room on the ground floor. Tay was constantly monitored by his parents or one of his team of carers. There was someone always ready to resuscitate him. It would be a miracle if Tay made the journey all the way back from wherever he'd gone. It was what his parents hoped for. What Jonty hoped for even though he knew there was little prospect of recovery, because the doctors had said so. But how could he give up hoping? Though maybe his hope was changing, less focused on Tay's recovery and sometimes, but only sometimes, wishing this was over.

Tay wouldn't be considered to be in a permanent vegetative state until twelve months after the accident. Then there would be talk about taking out the feeding and hydration tube from Tay's stomach, and allowing him to die. Jonty knew that Tay would hate his current life, existing in a state that was in some ways worse than death. But there was still a chance. Still hope. Many of Tay's friends had given up on him, but Jonty still believed he'd open his eyes and come back. People had emerged from a minimally conscious state years later. Why shouldn't Tay?

Tay's mother completely refused to accept there was no chance of recovery. Tay's father went along with whatever his wife wanted, pouring his time and energy into his haulage business, because his life had fractured the day Tay fell. Yet every time Tay's father came home, his nightmare restarted. Tay's mother sat and talked to Tay every day. Watched TV in his room with him. Played music. Read to him. Stimulated him by one means or another.

Once his broken bones had healed, physios manipulated his body, trying to keep his muscles from atrophying. Carers turned him regularly to prevent bed sores. Nurses came to change bags and tubes and catheters. Then his mother learnt to do it. She washed him, combed his hair, shaved him, cut his nails as if he were a baby. Doctors had treated infections even when Tay's sisters begged their mother to let nature take its course. What a fucking horrible concept. Though Jonty no longer knew the right thing to do, except if it had been him lying in that bed, he thought he'd rather have been dead.

He laid his bike down on the drive near the front door, took off his helmet, dragged his fingers through his hair, and knocked.

Tay's mother smiled when she saw him. "Jonty! Come on in."

"Thanks." He was always welcome. The only one of Tay's friends who still came to see him.

Jonty had stopped asking how Tay was when he arrived. It upset both of them when she said there was no change. It was equally upsetting to Jonty on those occasions when she talked excitedly of Tay's eyes opening and closing, of his reaction to a song by Coldplay, or the noises he made that she thought indicated Tay was trying to communicate. Jonty had read a lot online about Tay's condition. He knew involuntary muscle twitches were just that — involuntary. He knew the sounds Tay made were not an indication of an attempt to talk to his mother. He understood exactly what Tay's minimally conscious condition meant.

He braced himself when he walked into Tay's room. "Hi mate!"

"I'll turn the monitor off, then you two can have a nice cosy chat."

Jonty made himself smile at Tay's grieving, delusional mother. He took a deep breath and sat by Tay's bed. Tay had been up a ladder cleaning the gutters at the back of his parents' house. Tay had no fear of heights and his father did. He was also careful, that's what Jonty didn't understand. He shouldn't have fallen.

But the ladder had slipped and he'd broken arms, legs and his skull. Bones would and did mend. The damage to Tay's brain was considerable. The accident took away the life Tay had had and gave him another. A lingering disease would at least have given some warning, a chance to prepare for the worst, but this? It had been like being hit by a bus. Tay had been unlucky.

Fuck luck.

You wouldn't say that if you won the lottery.

I don't do the lottery.

The pain of what had happened to Tay hurt almost as much as if Jonty had been the one who'd fallen. He took hold of Tay's hand. "I sent Devan a dick pic today. Not mine, obviously."

Ha ha. He'd have run for the hills.

139

"He's going to run for the hills anyway. He's up here to get over a broken heart and I think he hopes that fucking me will help."

Help him, but not you.

"Maybe it *will* help me."

Can you remember what to do? What goes where?

Barely.

Jonty told Tay what had happened that day. Every so often, Tay made a comment. Yeah, well, Jonty made the comment that he was pretty sure Tay would have made had he been able to. Tay couldn't do much of anything apart from breathe without assistance. His brain had reacted to the severe trauma by shutting down and the longer he stayed like this, the less likely it was that he would wake.

"Devan's going to spend the day with me tomorrow. I dunno what he wants to do yet. I gave him a choice of Harry Potter, the Chillingham herd, riding on Bamburgh beach, boat trip or surfing. Can you think of anything else? Apart from investigating doggy style, reverse cowboy, pirate's bounty, arch, or bumper cars?"

What the hell?

"Sexual positions. I looked them up. I hadn't heard of some of them."

How about Hadrian's wall? Dunstanburgh Castle? Holy Island? The poison garden at Alnwick? Pick a few leaves of something for me and stuff them in the feeding tube. Or stay in bed all day and play at being pirates. I know which one you'd go for if you had the choice.

"And you wouldn't? With a woman, obviously."

Matilda.

"Very cute."

Gorgeous.

Tay's newish girlfriend had stopped coming to see him within a couple of weeks of him going into hospital. Too distressing. Right. Gave her nightmares. Course it did. No one expected her to wait for him to wake up. They'd only been on a few dates, but she could still have visited, especially in the early days. Jonty was sad because Tay had rarely been out with anyone and no relationship had lasted more than a few weeks.

"You think Devan would have his ex back if he grovelled enough?"

What do you think?

"He went out with him for two years, but finding him in bed with his brother… I'm not sure there's any way back from that."

Probably not, but maybe he'd like to shove his brother's face in it by taking him back.

"Maybe." Jonty wished he hadn't put that thought into Tay's mouth. "So how are you? Fancy waking up now? You're wearing your mum and dad out."

I feel like it's when I'm surfing and get pushed to the bottom of the sea, but when I try to get to the surface, I can't.

At least that was what Jonty imagined it must be like. "Try harder." He squeezed Tay's fingers. "Now you squeeze mine."

Nothing. There never was, though Jonty's mum said he'd responded to her. Jonty wasn't religious, but he'd done a lot of praying, just in case. He figured if he wasn't asking for himself then maybe a prayer might get answered.

Jonty sat and talked and talked. He suspected the reason he saw Tay around sometimes in the hotel and even on his surfboard or bike, was because of how much he missed him. He didn't have anyone else to talk to. Tay had been the best friend he'd ever had.

He didn't know how Tay's parents coped. When the hospital had made it clear that there was nothing more they could do, Mr and Mrs Robertson had brought Tay home rather than letting him be sent to an old people's place. They'd brought him back because they loved him, because he was still their son and they wanted him near them, but he gave nothing in return. No communication. No affection.

I'm a drain on their lives.

"They love you."

But maybe he wasn't coming back from this. His mother thought there was some part of Tay that recognised their voices, but it was too tempting to persuade yourself that Tay turning his head toward you when you said something was a positive response. His mother played music Tay would have hated, trying to get a reaction, and she said she sometimes did. Jonty hoped Tay was lost in a world of his imagination, living the dream, surfing the best waves, fucking beautiful girls, eating whatever he fancied. Though online research suggested that wasn't likely, it was something Jonty wished for.

Tay's mother brought him a cup of coffee and after he'd drunk it, Jonty decided to go home. He kissed Tay on the forehead, then the lips. "Going to thump me for that?"

Not a flicker. But as he walked away, Tay moaned. Jonty swivelled round to see Tay looking at him. Then his eyes closed. Something or nothing?

"You like that kiss?" Jonty asked. "Like another?"

There was no response. Jonty didn't kiss him again.

He knocked on the lounge door and Tay's mother pulled it open. Jonty handed her the empty coffee mug. "I need to be going now."

"Thank you for coming, Jonty," Tay's mother said. "It means a lot to me."

He rode home with his heart a heavy weight in his chest.

When Jonty pushed open his door, it caught on something and he had to give the door a hard shove to get it to fully open. As he wheeled his bike inside, he saw a Jiffy bag lying

142

on the mat, spotted the label had been typed, and his mouth went dry. He closed and locked the door, propped his bike in place on the stairs and gingerly poked the bag before he picked it up. It wasn't heavy and it felt squishy. There was no stamp so it hadn't been delivered by the postman, but then Brad knew where he lived.

Jonty carried it upstairs and put it on the kitchen counter next to the sink. It was a reasonable assumption that this was another *gift* from Brad.

How many more parcels are you going to get before you do something about it?

I'm not going to open it.

Go to the police.

I went to the police.

He took off his helmet and set it aside along with his backpack. Jonty told himself to throw the package away without opening it, though he wasn't sure he could. He walked away from it twice, then went back and cut the top open with scissors. When he peeked inside and the smell hit him, he gagged. Used condoms? *What the fuck, Brad?* Jonty folded the top over and put the packet inside a plastic bag and tied the top tightly. *Bloody hell.* He grabbed the bag of other things he'd been sent, and put them and the condoms inside another bag before he put it in his backpack.

Once he had his helmet back on, he clattered downstairs, opened the door so he could wheel out his bike and Brad stepped in front of him. Jonty slammed the door and leaned back against it, his heart pounding.

"Did you get my gift, Jonty?" Brad's voice was quite clear even through the door. "All my gifts? This last one is special, because I was thinking of you every time I jacked off. I saved my come for you. I know how much you love it."

Don't talk to him.

Jonty turned to face the door. "Fuck off," he yelled.

143

"That's not nice."

"Fuck the hell off. Is that better?"

Brad chuckled.

"Leave me alone." Jonty heard the catch in his voice and bit back his groan.

"Give me another chance."

"Go away."

"Not going to happen, Jonty. I've not finished with you yet."

Jonty crept back upstairs and took out his phone. He pressed 1-0-1.

"Alnwick police. Name and address please."

Jonty told him.

"How can I help you?"

"I came in to see someone a while ago to complain about an ex-boyfriend pestering me. He keeps sending me stuff I don't want. Today I found a packet with used condoms on my doormat. I was going to bring them to you, except he was outside my door when I opened it."

"Is he still there?"

Jonty edged to the window, hid the phone, and peered out to see Brad grinning up at him. He moved out of sight before he answered. "Yes."

"I can see your complaint on file. I'll send a car."

"Thank you."

Jonty went back down the stairs. He wanted Brad to get caught, so he had to make sure he didn't leave.

"I don't understand why you're doing this," Jonty said.

"I love you."

Three words that made Jonty shudder. No one had ever said that to him and it hurt that he was hearing them from a wanker like Brad.

"Are you taking your meds?" Jonty hadn't known until the last time they'd met when he'd seen the prescription pills in Brad's bathroom.

"All I want is for you to give me another chance."

"You hurt me."

"I'm sorry."

"How do I know you won't hurt me again?"

"I promise."

Like Jonty would believe that.

"I miss you," Brad said. "You're so beautiful. Don't you miss me?"

"You scare me."

"Let me in and we can talk things out. Start again. Make everything right."

"Tell me how you can make things right." Jonty willed the police to hurry.

"I'll do whatever you want." Brad chuckled. "And you'll do everything I want."

"What if I don't want to do what you want me to do?"

Brad laughed harder. "You know how much I like it when you don't do what I say."

You are such a fucking creep. Jonty shook and leaned into the door. "I don't understand why you want me so much." He really didn't.

"Because you're cute and you're funny and because you don't want me yet, but you will and that will make our relationship all the sweeter."

Somehow, Jonty didn't think telling Brad that he *did* want him would have the desired effect of making him go away.

"Why would you think giving me a bag of used condoms would convince me that you're the guy for me?"

"I told you. I thought of you every time I jacked off. Every single fucking time. It was your face I could see."

145

You are crazy. Jonty's hands were shaking. "Since when did you jack off into a condom?"

"Ah, you caught me there. I might have been fucking some guy's arsehole, but it was always you I was thinking of."

Eww. "Please stop this," Jonty whispered. "It's not going to make me want to get back with you. You've been following me, too. And watching me. I've seen you. It's not…healthy."

"I just want to keep you safe."

From what? You're the fucking threat!

"What's all this about?" asked a gruff voice.

"Just talking to my boyfriend."

"What's your name?"

"Brad Greene."

"Address?"

"18 Edison Heights, Alnwick. I haven't done anything wrong."

"One of my colleagues spoke to you before about harassing Mr Bloom."

Jonty opened the door, relieved to see a policeman standing there and that Brad hadn't pulled some sort of trick.

"Tell him, Jonty. I'm not bothering you, am I?"

Jonty looked up into Brad's smug, smiling face and clenched his fists. "We went out a total of six times. Six too many. I told you I didn't want to see you again and you won't listen." He pulled the plastic bag out of his backpack. "You've sent me all this stuff and I don't want it." He faced the policeman. "Yesterday he sent a big black dildo to where I work and today, he pushed a bag of used condoms through my letterbox. I've had enough."

"Used condoms?" The policeman turned to Brad.

Brad shrugged. "It was a joke."

"I didn't find it funny," Jonty snapped. "It's revolting. I reported you to the police before and I'm reporting you again today. You need help. You need to take your meds. You don't listen to no. I want you to leave me alone."

Could he be any clearer?

"You heard him," the policeman said. "Stop pestering him."

"I'm sorry." Brad 's lower jaw wobbled.

Jonty would have laughed if he hadn't been so worried. Brad wasn't sorry.

"Has he threatened you with physical violence?" the policeman asked Jonty.

What Brad was doing now was almost worse than hitting him. "Not recently."

"Do you want to make this official? Make a statement?"

Part of Jonty wanted to say yes, but he didn't want to get trawled up in a court case, not the way he wanted to be found by his mother, so he shook his head and stared at Brad. "If you turn up here again or send me anything else, I *will* make it official. You'll have to go to court and I'll get a restraining order. I'm asking you to leave me alone. Please."

"Is there somebody else?" Brad asked.

"No." Because saying yes would only make things worse and yes might be a stretch anyway.

"Well?" the policeman stared at Brad.

"Okay." Brad stared at the ground. "I'm sorry."

"One more call about you from Mr Bloom and you're in real trouble," the policeman said. "Get out of here."

Brad fled and the policeman faced Jonty. "You think that's it?"

"I hope so, but I doubt it."

"Keep a record of every incident. Note down the date, time, when, where, and what occurred or what was received."

"I have been."

"Good."

"I don't want to keep this stuff he's sent."

147

"It's evidence of what he's been doing."

"But the used condoms?" Jonty whispered. "Do I have to keep those?"

"Take a photograph. I will too and I'll include it in my report."

"You don't need to do a DNA test?"

"He didn't deny they were his. He said it was a joke, so no point."

"You better come in."

The moment the policeman had gone, Jonty threw the condoms in the bin and had a long, hot shower.

Devan didn't go straight back after he'd left Jonty. He decided he might as well check out the other hotel Alan had told him about. Rawlings Resort. He tapped the postcode into his sat nav. The place was twenty miles further south and inland, with its own golf course.

The building was much newer than McAllister's, the decor more modern and the place was busy. He arranged to inspect one of the rooms and this time, he was escorted by a smartly dressed guy in his fifties. Devan had made up a story about looking for a place to hold a wedding and the man couldn't have been more helpful, offering him a tour of the facilities. Big swimming pool, children's soft play area and a spa for the adults.

After the tour, Devan had a coffee in the lounge and made notes. Unlike McAllister's, this site was outside Northumberland's AONB, an area of outstanding natural beauty, which would mean renovations, extensions or a new build would be a much simpler process. Though this hotel didn't need rebuilding. There were no views of the sea, just distant ones of rolling hills on one side, the golf course on the other. Though the sea wasn't far away and Newcastle was within easy reach.

Even so, the place didn't excite him. If people came for a golfing holiday close to the sea, wouldn't they want to play at a links course? Devan weighted up the pros and cons. The bottom line was return on investment. Which site would be more profitable? Or should he recommend neither?

Back at McAllister's, he worked on his laptop doing an analysis of each hotel, what was needed, what was already offered, how being part of the Shaw group would play out. By the time he went down to the restaurant, he preferred McAllister's, but it would come down to availability and cost.

Jonty had been right about the chef being good. Devan had chosen a Moroccan dish and it looked as good as it tasted. If McAllister's ended up as the choice, whether it was a rebuild or renovation, they'd lose the chef. Well, they'd lose all the staff, but maybe Devan could get the chef transferred temporarily to one of their other hotels so they could keep him. But that offer wouldn't extend to anyone else. Including Jonty. He couldn't show favouritism. Night managers weren't hard to find. No staff member who worked there was essential to the future success of the hotel, not even the chef. There was a lot to think about, but he couldn't walk away from a place because he didn't want to make one particular member of staff redundant.

One thing he could do was get his private investigator pal to find Jonty's father in the hope of it leading to his mother. Stan had the room next door to Devan while he'd been at university. He hadn't given Stan much to go on. Maybe Devan would change his mind about telling Jonty if Stan *did* find something. It might be some compensation for fucking up his job situation.

God, I don't want to do that. He had to think of a way to not let that happen.

Chapter Ten

The following morning, Devan was drinking coffee in the lounge when he was approached by a short guy in a suit. The man had silver hair, a bit of a pot belly and a neat silver beard, and looked like a sophisticated Father Christmas.

"Mr Smith, I'm Hamish McAllister." He had a strong Scottish accent.

Devan shook his hand. "Thanks for meeting me."

"Would you like to come to my office?"

Once Devan was inside, McAllister closed the door. "Take a seat. How can I help you?"

Devan slid his business card across the desk before he sat down. "This is the organisation I represent."

McAllister picked up the card. "The Shaw Hotel Group." He chuckled. "Come to get a few tips on how to run a hotel?"

Devan smiled. "I'm sure there's plenty you could teach me."

"Have you ever operated a hotel yourself?"

"I've worked in many of our hotels and in others too. Ground level up."

McAllister twirled a pen in his fingers. "You're one of the biggest hotel groups in the country. I think I can guess why you're here. Unless it's to poach our chef, but then you'd have gone to him directly."

"I ate here last night. He's very good. The meal was exceptional. Elegantly presented and delicious. He could work in any top London restaurant and if I owned this place, I wouldn't want to lose him. I'd pay to keep him. But I'd expect him to get us a Michelin star."

McAllister chuckled. "He'd be delighted to hear that."

"I'll get straight to the point. We're interested in bringing a Northumbrian hotel into our portfolio. We don't have a presence in this area and we'd like one. Your hotel is one of the ones I'm considering. The question is, are you for sale now or in the near future? Or should I cross you off my list?"

McAllister's hesitation told Devan what he needed to know. For the right price, this hotel would be available.

"Why are you interested in us?" McAllister asked.

"Your location is outstanding, the views from the rooms superb. But your location is also an issue for us and the clients we expect to draw. You're remote, not quick or easy to get to, so the price has to be right."

McAllister laughed. "For me or you?"

"For both of us. You won't sell and I won't buy if it's not. But there's no point in me spending time and money if you're not for sale. I'd need to get a couple of our people up here before I could make an offer. So are you interested?"

"What about my long-term guests?"

"Are they on contracts?"

"More of a verbal agreement. We give them a discounted rate."

"We'd be amenable to assisting them to find somewhere else to live." He'd have to persuade Alan because it wasn't something they'd usually do.

"And the staff?"

"The hotel would have to close during building work. I'm thinking that would start after Christmas. I don't know how long the work will take, because I'm not yet sure what will be required, but I'd estimate not re-opening until the summer. The staff would be welcome to apply for positions once the hotel was near completion."

"But they'd be unemployed while the work was going on with no guarantee of a job once the place was ready."

"That's true. There'd be no guarantees. They couldn't be expected to wait and see if they'd get a job, but having worked here and with a recommendation from you… well that would help with their application."

In reality, the chances of any of the current members of staff working here when the hotel re-opened were small. Devan would do everything he could to retain the chef, maybe the sous-chef too, but the rest would have to get other jobs. Devan always felt bad about that whenever he did any deal, but now he and Jonty… Maybe it was better that he stopped this before it began. How many times had he thought that? He'd call Jonty and tell him he couldn't make it today. His spirits tumbled.

"What sort of vision for the place do you have?" McAllister asked.

Tread lightly on their dreams. Words that Alan had once said to him and they'd stuck. "This hotel has stunning views in all directions. It has a fascinating history. I understand it was a convalescent home after the second world war. We'd market it as a haven. A quiet, secluded resort where guests can escape from the pressure of busy lives."

"You're not thinking of a kids' club and soft play and waterslides?"

"I'm not thinking of children at all. It's a charming hotel, sited in an area recognised for its natural beauty. In addition, there's little light pollution, which means your night skies are fantastic. A draw in itself. I could see a small observatory here. But the place is tired. I suspect your guest numbers fall significantly once the season is over. We have ways of changing that. We'd make this a destination resort. You have a fabulous pool. We'd add a wellness spa. You have a good-sized events room, and we could make full use of it year-round.

"If the planners found it acceptable, I'd add another wing to the building for both the spa and additional rooms. Inside, I'd combine two guest rooms into one. They're already a reasonable size, but the sort of guests we'd want to entice expect space as well as luxury.

"Obviously, I need to prepare a detailed business plan to show our investors, but without a willingness to sell, and a willingness to negotiate on price, there's no point in going further and in that case, I'd check out the other sites."

"Which are?"

Devan smiled. "Confidential."

McAllister leaned back in his chair. "My children have no interest in running this place. I'd be amenable to discussions about selling, but I'd want to consult my family first, and my lawyer. Please don't say anything to anyone."

"Of course." Devan pushed to his feet and held out his hand. "Thanks very much for your time. I'm staying here until Sunday morning. If there's anything you'd like to discuss, or more that you need to know, then ask. I'd appreciate it if you could let me know before I leave as to whether or not you'd like me to work on an offer."

McAllister shook his hand. "*You'll* make me an offer?"

"Once I've consulted with my colleagues."

"I can always say no."

"You can."

Devan went back up to his room. He changed out of his suit and gave Alan a call.

"Hi, Devan. How's it going?"

"I like McAllister's. The position is stunning. Rawlings is closer to transport links and has the golf course, but neither the view, nor the potential. McAllister's could be a world-class resort. Okay, the weather isn't brilliant up here, but in winter, I'd imagine it's moody and inspirational. I'd come to see the wild seas and the night skies. I'd build an observatory and put a telescope in it. The owner's interested in selling. He said he wants to consult his family and lawyer, but I think it will be a yes."

"Great. Send your report in and I'll get Nate working on the preliminaries."

"I've given McAllister until Sunday morning to tell me whether he wants to go ahead."

"And would you recommend Rawlings if not?"

"No."

"Seen anything else up there? Or potential sites?"

"I don't think we'd get planning permission for a new build on the coast. This is a protected area. But if McAllister says no, I'll make enquiries. I'll make enquiries anyway. If adding to the hotel square footage is an issue, it might not be worth the effort."

"And how are you?"

"Fine."

Devan tried to sound cheery, but the pause before Alan spoke again suggested he'd failed.

"Once you've done your report, take some time for yourself. If you want it to still be work-related, do some research on the whole county so we can sell it as a location to our investors."

"Right."

"I don't want you back in the office for a while. Relax. Have some fun. That's an order."

Devan ended the call. *Have some fun.* He'd had fun in mind for today, but now he'd feel too guilty to enjoy himself. Though he had a legitimate reason not to say anything to Jonty, apart from McAllister asking him to keep this confidential. The deal might not even make it as far as a negotiation. At the moment, it had to stay a secret.

He should still leave Jonty alone.

It wasn't fair to lead him on.

It wasn't fair to let him down.

Devan called him.

"Big Dicks R Us," Jonty said. "How may I help you?"

Devan laughed.

"Don't be shy. What size are you looking for? We can supply almost everything you like."

"Big isn't always best."

"On what planet?"

Devan chuckled.

"Bring your wetsuit in case we want to get kinky. We can wear them around town and freak out the locals."

Oh shit. I'm not going to let him down. "Address?"

"5A Hayton Street. You can park anywhere on that road for free, but it's busy. I hope you can parallel park. I live above the laundrette."

"See you soon."

The moment that call ended, his phone rang again and he answered without checking who it was. *Mistake.*

"Devan. No response to my text?"

He clenched his teeth at the sound of his mother's voice. "I wasn't aware it required a response." His heart thumped. Had his father told her the truth?

"Griff has graciously asked you to be his best man. You said no. Reconsider."

Graciously? What the fuck? "Okay. I've reconsidered. The answer is still no." He could feel himself getting hotter.

"You're not intending to go to the wedding, are you?"

"I haven't had an invitation."

She gave a long-suffering sigh. Devan wasn't fooled.

"I told you your flight and accommodation are booked. Griff and Ravi want family and a few close friends with them in the Caribbean. A simple ceremony."

Not if Ravi had anything to do with it. Ravi had a lot of friends he considered close. Nor would the ceremony be simple. Devan would have happily gone for barefoot on the beach and just the two of them, but Ravi had wanted the whole bloody spectacle and even persuaded one of the celeb

155

magazines to photograph the event before he'd discussed it with Devan. Ravi modelled for several big names in the fashion world, and the fee the magazine had offered almost paid for the honeymoon in the Seychelles. The bloody magazine had printed pictures of Ravi there instead, looking broken hearted. Now he wondered if Griff had been there too. His brother had gone AWOL after Devan had found them fucking.

I'm glad I didn't marry him.

His lungs locked. *Oh God, I fucking am.*

"Are you listening?" his mother snapped.

Devan took a deep breath. "No, I wasn't. Sorry."

"Devan? Do you…still have feelings for Ravi?"

Not the sort of feelings she was thinking about.

"Talk to Dad." He ended the call and shoved the phone in his pocket. His pulse was racing and he took a few deep breaths.

One day having fun. That was all he wanted. Just one day.

Devan parallel parked right outside the launderette, locked his car and knocked on Jonty's door. He heard feet clattering downstairs, then the door opened and all he could see was Jonty's bright smile. *Happy to see me.* Devan felt better already. Until guilt nibbled harder at his gut. *Don't fucking smile at me! Don't make me want you.*

"You came." Jonty's beam didn't lessen in strength.

Had Jonty doubted that he would? Maybe he could find Jonty a job. The thought cheered him. Yeah, he could do that. He *would* do that. One of their hotels was always looking for staff.

"You really came." Jonty grinned.

"Not yet," Devan said. "I'm saving myself."

Jonty pressed his lips together as he fought not to laugh. "Want to come in or get straight off?"

"I can't do both?"

"You're playing my game. A risky strategy when I'm a Grand Master."

I shouldn't, but I am. "Do you want me to come in?"

"You mean do I want to show you my fabulous penthouse flat with bespoke furniture and panoramic sea views? Why yes, I do." Jonty moved aside. "Watch out for the bike. I'll lead the way in case you get lost. But close the door and make sure it's secure."

Devan followed him upstairs. Jonty was wearing faded denims that sat low on his hips and a tight-fitting blue T-shirt. Devan couldn't tear his gaze from Jonty's arse.

"Oh my God." Jonty gasped as he opened the door at the top of the stairs. "What's happened to my flat? It's…shrunk. I swear it was four times bigger than this. Where's all my furniture gone? Why can I only see a pub out of the window? Where's the sea gone?"

Devan laughed.

"Want a coffee or…a coffee? Oh God, I have no sugar. I'm a complete failure as a host."

"I'm fine." Devan walked over to the wall opposite Jonty's TV to look at a picture of a whale made from pieces of sea glass. "This is fantastic. Did you make it?"

"Technically, the sea did the hard work. I just used glue."

Devan turned in a circle. There was a picture of three gulls made from more glass and small pieces of driftwood, and a free-standing seahorse constructed from green and white glass fragments. Whichever way he turned, there was something to see. A Christmas tree, a lighthouse, two seals, a dragon.

"Do you sell your stuff?"

Jonty shook his head. "I can't bear to part with them once they're done. They cheer me up. You want to sit down and we can discuss what you'd like to do? I made a list." Jonty handed him three sheets of paper that had been sellotaped together.

"There's only fifty items. Sorry. I ran out of time. I wanted to give you a choice of fifty-one. I'm disappointed in myself."

Devan sat on the couch, looked at the list and laughed. "A driving tour covering more than seventy Northumberland castle sites. But no stopping or we'll run out of time. Play knight and dragon at Dunstanburgh Castle. Jonty gets to be the dragon and the knight is allowed to stab him with his mighty sword, repeatedly, but only when no one is looking."

"Doesn't that sound fun?"

Devan read on. "Play laird and serf in the poison gardens at Alnwick Castle. The laird is testing out poisons on the serf. Devan is the serf." Devan chuckled. "I think we'll give that one a miss."

He carried on reading. "Beachcombing at Beadnell. BDSM taster session at Craster—forty ways to have fun with a kipper. Visit the only wild cattle in the world at Chillingham—a trip fraught with danger. A blowjob in the Aston, a blowjob on the Aston, a blow job next to the Aston." He raised his eyebrows.

"I wasn't sure there was enough room under it. But we could try."

Devan's cock was trying to indicate its interest by standing up and waving. "Ghost tour at Chillingham Castle, skinny dipping at Ross Back Sands on a naturist beach. Jonty to provide food, drink and blanket, plus binoculars to watch the upstanding—changed to outstanding—nature."

The more Devan read, the more he laughed. "Use a whole box of condoms in an interesting way all over Bamburgh. The police can judge the best use. Mud wrestling while walking to Holy Island—loser has to drink an entire glass of mead."

Jonty shuddered. "It's disgusting."

Devan huffed and read on. "Pretend you've never heard of Harry Potter while doing the Harry Potter experience." He didn't read out the last one. *Thoroughly test out my bed.*

He set the sheets of paper aside. "Completely spoiled for choice. How about I drive and you direct me. We'll do whatever you like."

"But it's *your* day."

"Surprise me."

"I've run out of condoms and lube."

Devan laughed. "I haven't."

Jonty pulled on his coat and grabbed his backpack. Earlier that morning, he'd nipped to the local shop and bought food for a picnic as well as withdrawing a chunk of cash from his account. He'd already booked the first activity so he hoped Devan was up for it. He'd text Gill once they were on their way. Devan followed Jonty down onto the street and Jonty locked the door. As he turned, he saw Brad leaning against Devan's car.

"Off my car." Devan was heading straight for him.

Shit!

"You lied," Brad said and Devan stopped walking.

"Get off his car and I didn't lie." Jonty nipped past Devan and went right up to Brad. "You want me to call the police again?"

"You told me there was nobody else."

"That was yesterday. Today there is." Jonty took out his phone, holding it tight so Brad didn't see the way his fingers were shaking.

"You little cunt," Brad snarled.

"Fuck off, Brad, or I'll call them," Jonty said quietly.

"He's my boyfriend," Brad said to Devan.

"No, I'm not."

"Leave. Now," Devan snapped.

Jonty was a bit surprised when Brad walked away. He almost yelled to ask him if he was a coward as well as a bully, but managed not to. He didn't want to risk Devan getting

159

hurt. Jonty's heart slowed its frantic cartwheels to slow rolls. He still felt sick.

"You okay?" Devan asked.

"Yeah, let's go."

"Want to tell me what that was about?"

"Let me send one text, then I will."

Jonty felt like he only exhaled once they were in the car and heading out of town. He pulled out his phone and messaged Gill. *CU in 30 mins*

"Head for the A1 north," Jonty said. "I'll tell you when to turn."

"So… Brad?"

"Otherwise known as The Big Mistake. I met him five months ago in Alnwick library. I thought, he has to be a decent guy if he's using a library, right? Wrong." Jonty sighed. "I was an idiot for not seeing through him the day we met. But I didn't, probably because I like to think I'm a great judge of character. Only that might be one of my character flaws, because I didn't see through him on the next few dates either."

"What did you think of me the day you met me?"

"Er… I named you Mr Impossible, Mr Trouble, Mr Difficult, Mr Sexy — oops, no forget I said that. Mr Greedy, Mr Awkward, Mr — "

"Are you going to go through the entire Mr Men collection?"

"No because I didn't think you were Mr Happy, though you're smiling more now. But you're not Mr Happy yet. I'm still working on that."

"Tell me about Brad."

"Why are you so difficult to distract? I'm really good at distraction and you're like a bloody guided missile."

"Brad?"

"We went on six dates. Four were…okay. Not lovely, but I thought there was potential. Though when I talked to Tay about them, Tay had a different opinion. He didn't think Brad was right for me. He wasn't. Brad didn't like me being friends with Tay and that should have been enough for me to have walked away. The next date was much better. I had a good time. Brad was really nice. But on the last date, I went back to his house—and he turned into a different person. I should have run when I saw what books he'd gotten out of the library. *Britain's Worst Serial Killers* and *How to Build a Shed*."

Devan took the turn for the A1. "I have the shed book."

Jonty laughed. "So long as you don't actually have a shed."

"No."

"Phew."

"What happened on that last date?"

"He wanted to stay in. That was okay but, he…didn't listen to no. Not that I was in a position to actually say no. Not when he'd handcuffed me and strapped a ball gag over my mouth." Jonty's exhalation was shaky. "I was so shocked. I mean, he could have just asked me to shut up. I usually can."

He was trying to keep this light but wasn't sure he was succeeding.

"What did he do?"

Jonty groaned. Devan's grip on the wheel was so tight his knuckles had whitened.

"I told you. I don't need to give details." *I don't want to tell anyone. Ever.* "He didn't listen to no. That's all I need to say. Then he stopped me saying no. He did what he liked and had the nerve to tell me he knew how much I'd enjoyed it. When he was done, he made me shower. I saw prescription medication in his bathroom and asked him what was wrong. He'd used a condom, but I thought… He said it was medicine for anxiety. I was the one who was fucking anxious.

"As I was leaving, I told him he was a wanker and that I was going to the police. He laughed. That didn't fit with him suffering from anxiety. I wished I'd made a note of the medication, but I hadn't. When I got to the door, he threatened me and said that if I spoke to them, he had friends who'd claim I'd let them do the same to me as he had."

"Shit. Did you go to the police?"

"Yes. They had a word with him."

"A word?" Devan looked away from the road and gaped at him.

"I might not have told the police everything." *Just like I haven't told you.*

"Why the hell not?"

"Because I didn't want to have to go to court and relive it all over again. I didn't want to be accused of lying, of changing my mind after I'd agreed to what he wanted to do. I just wanted to forget it had ever happened. So I kept quiet about how far he'd gone, though I did tell them he was harassing me."

"The bastard."

"Obviously I blocked him, but I kept seeing him around town. Too often for it to have been coincidence. I think he's been watching me too and he's been sending me stuff. Lovely gifts. Lube, condoms, a pair of handcuffs, a ball gag, a big black dildo, a cock ring…" Jonty shuddered. "Anyway, he upped his game yesterday and posted a jiffy bag full of used condoms through my letterbox, all neatly knotted."

"Christ!"

"Apparently, they contained come produced while thinking about me. Ahhh, what a sweetie. And who says romance is dead? Have you started your collection yet?"

Devan glanced at him and they both laughed, but the sound quickly tailed off. Funny yet not.

"I mean, it's weird right? After he'd delivered his little present yesterday, he turned up. While he was outside my door, and I was inside, I called the police, then kept him talking. A policeman came and spoke to him. Brad is on his last warning now. If he pesters me again, he'll get arrested."

"Are you worried about him?"

Jonty thought about that. Not whether he was worried, because he was, but whether he wanted to admit it. Maybe the medication Brad was on kept him…functioning and if he wasn't taking it, that might be dangerous.

"You *are* worried," Devan said.

Jonty sighed. "Yes. Because he's still pushing his way into my life, it's hard to be sure I did the right thing in not telling the police everything. I mistakenly thought that after I'd made it clear I never wanted to see his fucking face ever again, that I wouldn't see his fucking face ever again. He works on an oil rig. Three weeks on, three weeks off. So I was able to work out when he was less likely to be around, but him sending me gifts, freaked me out. He worries me because normal people don't behave like that. If he's off his meds, whatever they are, maybe that's why I feel things are getting worse. I'm safer at the hotel. I sleep better there…"

"Jonty, that—"

"Don't ask me anything. I can guess what you're thinking, but I don't want to talk about it anymore. No miserable thoughts allowed. This is going to be a fun day and thinking about Brad will stop me having fun."

Devan gave a heavy sigh.

"No miserable thoughts *and* no sighing allowed. Please. I shouldn't have told you, not if it's going to ruin the day. Take the next turn on the right."

"Where are we going?"

"A beach."

"And what are we going to do on that beach? Ah…"

The sign for the stables was on the right.

163

"It's *stroke a horse* day. Not on the bum though. Turn into that car park on the right and find a spot. Extra points for reversing into a space on a handbrake turn."

Devan laughed. "Not going to happen."

"Don't you want *me* to have fun?"

"You'll get your fun, don't worry. Are we really going riding?"

Jonty could hear the excitement in Devan's voice. "Yep. I hope you're good, or Gill, who owns the stables, is going to chop me up and feed me to her dogs. She has four Chihuahuas and it'll take them ages." Jonty whined.

"I was really good when I was six. I got two rosettes. One for *most fences demolished in a single round* and one that said *well done for not crying.*"

Jonty grinned. "You have to let me be the funny one or I'll get depressed." He climbed out of the car and left his jacket and backpack in the footwell.

"Will it be warm enough without a jacket?" Devan asked.

"If we don't end up hot and sweaty, then we've not been doing it right."

Devan threw his jacket back in the car.

"Hi, Jonty!"

He turned to see Gill, Tay's aunt, heading towards them. She flung her arms around him and hugged him hard enough to hurt. "How are you?"

"I'm fine."

She sighed. "You should come by more often. I can always find you a ride."

"Thanks, Gill. This is Devan. He has rosettes for — er what was it? — *getting lost after fence two* and *best dive into the water jump.*"

Gill laughed as she shook Devan's hand. "Can you ride? Because this isn't for beginners. We'll be cantering and most likely galloping at times."

164

"I don't do it regularly, but I can ride."

"Good. Let's go and get you introduced to Mungo. You need helmets?"

"Yes, please." Jonty handed her the envelope of money. Whenever he and Tay had been riding, Tay had always paid for him. Even with the discount Gill gave, riding was an expensive hobby, and not one Jonty could afford. This was costing him a hundred pounds from his savings fund.

"Mungo is slow to get going and then off like a lunatic, if you let him have his head," Gill said. "If he feels like it, he can outrun everything in the stable."

"I'm guessing he doesn't often feel like it," Devan said.

She smiled. "That's true and why I'm letting an unknown rider take him out. Basically, he's a lazy bugger. Though he'll follow Blue anywhere." She paused. "Are you okay riding Blue, Jonty?"

He nodded. *Tay's horse.* Devan began to stroke Mungo's neck and talk to him. Jonty slipped Devan a sugar-free polo mint and he put it in his mouth.

"That was for Mungo, not you." Jonty put on his outraged voice and gave him another.

Gill handed them helmets and Jonty put his on.

"Hello, Blue." Jonty gave him a mint, then scratched him on the neck behind the ear, and it was almost as if Blue purred. "Have you missed me?" Jonty gave him another mint. *Have you missed Tay?* Blue leaned into him, pushing his nose to Jonty's face, sharing the air between them. "Ooh minty breath. You can have a kiss."

"Mount up," Gill said and watched Devan.

Devan clipped on his helmet and swung himself up into the saddle. When he bent to adjust the stirrups, Gill nodded. First test passed. Jonty knew she'd have set them too long. He climbed onto Blue and patted his neck. His stirrups were fine. Gill had a good memory.

"Blue lead, Mungo follow and I'll bring up the rear on Shadow," Gill said. "Once I'm happy you know what you're doing, you can ride on. Jonty, you know not to go too far, right?"

"Yep." Jonty wished he'd forgotten how much he loved riding, but he hadn't. In their teens, he and Tay had spent hours helping Gill, mucking out, feeding the horses, cleaning the tack. Tay's aunt took care of Blue in return for help in the yard. Jonty usually rode Mixie, but she'd been sold.

Strange that he didn't feel the urge to have Tay with him today. He still thought about him, how could he not when he was riding Blue? But his head was full of Devan, buzzing with what this day might bring, maybe more than this day.

And how's that going to work?

Jonty almost moaned when he heard Tay.

He's here until Sunday morning and then you'll never see him again. You think he's going to move to Northumberland to be near you?

I could move.

Tay didn't answer.

Could I move?

Jonty wanted to slap some sense into his head. They were having fun. If he daydreamed about more than that, he'd end up disappointed. He walked Blue through the loose sand down to where it was more firmly packed. The beach was almost empty and the tide was partway out so they'd be able to gallop.

He wished he could just enjoy the time he had with Devan without trying to make it into something it wasn't. Jonty liked him. After that rocky start, Devan had warmed up. And now Jonty knew why he'd arrived in a bad temper, he understood how hurt Devan felt. Though he still didn't understand why he'd come all the way from London to stay in a mediocre hotel. If he needed to lick his wounds, he could have done that somewhere warm, smart and luxurious. It was hard to fight the feeling that Devan was hiding something. Yet, what he'd told Jonty about Ravi and his brother was so bad, what could be worse than that?

"Take a canter," Gill called. "Let me see if Devan can keep his seat."

Jonty urged Blue on. "Come on, Blue. Show me what you've got."

He kept out of the water to start with, then edged Blue into the shallow surf, kicking up foam as he raced along, spray splattering his face. He could hear Devan behind him and glanced back to see a broad smile on his face. When Jonty pulled up, Devan came alongside, then Gill joined them.

"Wow," Devan said. "That was fantastic."

"You'll do." Gill smiled. "I'm going to go back. One hour. Take it easy, Jonty. Don't push too hard." She turned and galloped back the way they'd come.

Mungo nosed Blue's rump and Devan laughed.

"These two are very attached," Jonty said. "Where Blue goes, Mungo goes too. He's completely stupid, so it's just as well Blue doesn't take advantage. Ready?"

Devan's eyes were shining. "Ready."

Jonty heard Devan whooping behind him as they raced along the sand. How could you be sad when you were doing this? Like surfing, it gave him the chance to stop thinking and just…be. The great thing was that the horses loved it too. The freedom to race, wind in their faces, splashing through the breakers, the smell of the sea, the sheer joy of thundering along the sand.

He wasn't surprised when Mungo overtook them, his desire to follow Blue only lasting so long when he had the opportunity to gallop. He worried for a moment that Devan might have lost control, but he hadn't and pulled Mungo up a little way down the beach. Jonty joined him and slowed to a walk.

"Did you hear about the man who was hospitalized with eight plastic horses inside him?" Jonty asked.

"No."

"The doctor described his condition as stable."

Devan groaned.

Chapter Eleven

By the time Devan climbed down from Mungo's back, his thighs and backside ached, but it had been fun. If it hadn't been for what Jonty had told him about Brad, he'd have said it was the best day he'd had in a long while. But Jonty *had* told him, not all of it, yet enough for him to see Brad was dangerous. When the guy had been leaning on his car, Devan had thought for a moment, he was about to get a fist in the face. The guy looked...tough and not right for gentle Jonty.

Gill came out into the yard and raised her eyebrows. "Still in one piece? How did it go?"

"Brilliant," Devan said.

"Jonty, walk Blue down to Hazel and she'll look after him."

As Jonty led Blue away, Gill took Mungo's reins from Devan and studied him for a few seconds. "Please don't hurt Jonty. He's not been here to ride since..." She sighed. "Be kind to him."

Devan was torn between annoyance that everyone seemed to think he was going to hurt Jonty, guilt that he might, and envy that Jonty had friends who cared enough to warn him off. Had they supported him when Brad turned into a stalker? And not been riding since when? Was this about Brad or something else? Did he really need to get involved with another guy with issues? He almost laughed at that thought. As if *he* didn't have issues.

"Can I pay you instead of Jonty and you give him his money back at a later date?"

"When you've returned to wherever it is you came from?" She huffed. "He said you might offer to pay. He also said *Whatever you do, don't take his money. I'm pretty sure he robbed a bank.* I doubt that's true, but I'm not taking your money." She took Devan's helmet and led Mungo away.

Be kind to him. Devan rolled his shoulders. He never set out to be unkind to anyone. Occasionally, his temper got the better of him, but he wasn't a mean guy. This was supposed to be a few days of fun, but the trouble was, the longer he spent time with Jonty, the more he was interested in him. He hadn't imagined the flirting, hadn't misread the list of stuff Jonty wanted to do. Okay, Jonty didn't know the reason he was really up here, but he *did* know he was leaving on Sunday.

There were reasons that might not happen. If McAllister said yes to selling, then Devan would stay on for a while, though not in the hotel. Maybe he could rent a place for a month. Be more hands-on than he usually was, once a deal had been struck. Plus, Alan had told him to take a break. Even if Devan was needed elsewhere for a few days, it wouldn't be a problem. There was an airport at Newcastle. But the biggest incentive to stay was that Devan wanted to. Where better than a place that had allowed him to touch happiness for the first time since the day before his wedding?

Not a place. Jonty.

Devan slid into a happy daydream about him and Jonty living together for a month, only for it to turn black when he thought what Jonty would say when he learned the reason he was going to be out of a job, assuming McAllister said yes. Jonty would be seriously pissed. Devan could put things right but…

Tell him.

Don't tell him.

Tell him.

He felt as if he were pulling petals off a daisy. He *would* tell him, but not yet.

As soon as he had McAllister's decision.

Or as soon as they'd agreed on the price.

Devan felt a deeper ripple of guilt, knowing he was looking to delay the revelation, but unless he could find Jonty another job… *Can I?* He needed to talk to Jonty first.

Jonty came back to his side, beaming. "I really enjoyed that. All that hot sweaty muscular flesh lodged between my thighs. Making a great lumbering beast do exactly what I want. Is there anything better? Mmmm—I don't think so. Do you want to choose what we do next? Or do you want me to?"

"You seem pretty good at choosing. I'm sure I'll like whatever we do."

"Okay. Back to the car. We need to follow the coast road north for about six miles. You have to keep quiet about this place. We'll go through the oath swearing ceremony when we get there. It involves a chicken and a dartboard which I've handily packed in my bag. Hardly anyone goes there, and those who know about it, would like it to stay that way, which is why it has only one star reviews on Tripadvisor. Big secret. You're only the forty-sixth person I've told."

Devan laughed and opened the car.

"Not counting my 5,000 friends on Facebook." Jonty grinned. "Actually, make that five. I only joined in case…" He shrugged. "In case my mother was looking for me. There are a few Jonty Blooms in the UK, but only one living up here. Me."

Oh Jonty. Devan set off. "Do you know her maiden name?"

"Henley. Rosie Henley."

"What's your father's Christian name?"

"Gary. Why? You going to order a hit on him?"

Devan raised his eyebrows. "Do you want me to?"

Jonty widened his eyes. "I was half-right about the serial killer bit? No hit, thanks. Well, not unless it's done by an incompetent assassin. My father needs to die slowly and painfully." He winced. "I shouldn't have said that. I don't mean it. Mostly. I don't care about him anymore. I haven't for

171

a long time. It was a waste of energy being resentful. That doesn't mean I forgive him for the way he treated me, but my anger's gone. I had a shitty, abusive father—and I had to accept it and move on."

"How long did it take before you felt like that?"

"Are you thinking about your treacherous ex? You should be well over that dickhead. Plenty more fish in the sea. Oh— you caught one." Jonty put his hands together and made a snapping sound. "Devan shark, doo doo, doo doo doo doo."

Devan laughed. When he had a moment, he'd text Stan with the names. Jonty might have no interest in his father, but the guy might know the whereabouts of Rosie Henley.

"Your fuckhead ex and my fuckhead father. Ooh, maybe we could swap murders." Jonty licked his lips. "You get rid of my father and I'll get rid of—well not your ex necessarily, but an annoying person of your choice, present company excepted."

"Great idea for a film, but we're not two random strangers who met on a train."

"But we *are* two random strangers who met in a hotel. You can be the charming psychopath and I'll be the talented tennis player. I might have to have a few lessons. I haven't played for a while. The police will never guess who did it. Keep right here, don't turn off."

"You do remember how that film ended?"

"One of us survives. A clue. It wasn't you." He sat up straighter. "Another hundred yards and we can park. It might be a good idea to turn the car, so we're facing the right way when we leave. In case we're in a rush."

Devan knew he shouldn't ask, but he did. "Why might we be in a rush?"

"Someone might be chasing us."

"Why?"

"Because of what I have planned."

172

Devan wasn't sure whether Jonty was winding him up, though he suspected he was. He did a three-point turn, tucked in close to the grass verge, and they climbed out.

Jonty grabbed his bag and the jackets and handed Devan his. "It's about a mile and a half walk, but I promise it's well worth it."

"Is this the naturist place?"

"Yep. It's full of nature. If we're lucky we'll see seals and gannets. If we're really lucky we'll see a minke whale. If we're super lucky we might see two large cocks."

When Devan caught hold of Jonty's hand as they walked down the road, the smile Jonty gave him made his heart skip.

"Might we actually see a whale?" Devan asked.

"It's possible."

"Maybe you could sing one in."

Jonty groaned. "You heard that couple? People have such unrealistic expectations. Being able to check in at nine in the morning. Multiple whales frolicking and flicking their flukes, pods of dolphins running alongside the boat smiling up at the cameras, orgasms that last minutes. Though I'm going to be disappointed if I don't see two large cocks. I've heard it's a possibility. Where do you usually go on holiday?"

Devan still wasn't used to Jonty's abrupt changes of direction. "I don't generally go to the same place twice. It depends what…" He gave a short laugh. "For the last couple of years, Ravi has dictated where we spent our holidays. Skiing in Colorado. Sailing in the Caribbean. We went to Lapland to see the Northern Lights, though they didn't cooperate much to Ravi's disappointment. Mine too."

"I've seen them here."

"You have?"

"It doesn't happen often and there's more chance the further north you go, but yep, a couple of times when I was with Tay. One of nature's amazing magic tricks."

173

"Is Tay your best friend?"

"Yes. Since we were eleven. We met at secondary school. God, I hated school. I bet you loved it."

"I wouldn't use the word *love*."

"I was bullied. Tay was a couple of years older and he stood up for me."

"Griff was bullied."

"Because he had cerebral palsy?"

Devan nodded. "He was called names, tripped, had his bag emptied out. I got into trouble for doing a bit of bullying of my own, but at least they stopped hounding Griff. Though sometimes I wonder if Griff would have been better learning to deal with them himself. It felt right at the time, to step in, but all his life, people have stepped in to help him with one thing or another. He's used to thinking everything revolves around him. Hard to be mad with someone who struggled to walk, struggled with a lot of stuff."

"But not with fucking your fiancé."

"Thank you for reminding me."

"Oh, had you forgotten?"

Devan huffed.

"Stick it in a box and lock it away," Jonty said. "That's my expert advice. Of course, it sneaks out every now and again to bite you, but you just have to shove the memory back and lock it up. Remember what I said? If you let it ruin your life, you're the loser. You're better off without Ravi and maybe your brother won't end up marrying him."

Jonty sighed and looked up into the sky. "We are so lucky with the weather. If it had rained, I'd have had to keep you in bed all day."

Devan laughed. "Is there anything you wish Northumberland had that it doesn't have?"

174

"Marlon Teixeira? Warmer weather? But if we had higher temperatures, we'd get swamped with visitors. Maybe even Marlon Teixeira!"

"I've met him."

Jonty tripped and almost faceplanted. "You've met him? I'm surprised you've even heard of him."

"My ex is a fashion model."

"Bloody hell. That was why you said you were glad I wasn't a supermodel."

Jonty went uncharacteristically quiet, then scooted in front of Devan and began wriggling his backside and swinging his hips as he walked.

Devan sniggered. "You'll get a modelling job so easily walking like that."

Jonty came back to his side. "It was that bad?"

"Awful. Terrible. The worse catwalk demonstration I've ever seen."

Jonty huffed. "How did that work experience go with the Samaritans? Not well, I'd guess."

Devan chuckled. They moved from the road to cross farmland and eventually walked over undulating dunes. Jonty never stopped talking and the longer they walked, the better Devan felt. *Accept what you can't change.* Griff was Griff. But that didn't mean Devan would be his best man if he married Ravi.

"Not trying to remind you again, but what was it that made you want to marry Ravi? Does your brother see the same thing? How did you meet? Was it instant attraction?"

"I met him at a charity event in London. He was sitting on the same table. He's good-looking. He doesn't have that androgynous look that seems to be so popular. He's more naturally beautiful than that. Ravi was one of the items being auctioned. A day with him. He worked the room. He sashayed up to people as they were bidding and flirted. He was confident and funny."

"Did you bid for him?"

"Yes. I didn't intend to go as high as I did, but he pleaded with me, got down on his knees at the table and it was for a good cause, a cancer charity. When I'd won, he announced he'd pay the same for a date with me so the charity got double the money. He told me…" Devan swallowed hard. "He told me it was the first night of the rest of his life."

Devan didn't want to remember how happy he and Ravi had been, because it brought back the pain of what he'd done.

"He was kind and fun and even if he was a bit demanding, I just thought it was because of his job. He was used to being pampered and getting his own way. I let that happen more often than I should have because I liked making him happy. He told me all the time how much he loved me and when he turned out to be a lying, cheating, selfish bastard, I couldn't believe what he'd done. I wonder now if he was just a good actor, that he said things he didn't feel, not for me anyway. He had money, but as not much as me, and Ravi likes luxury. But Griff doesn't have money so it wasn't that that kept Ravi at my side. Or maybe the pull of Griff was stronger."

"You loved him."

"I loved them both. I no longer do."

"Maybe he loves you both?"

"Who? Ravi or Griff?"

"Ravi."

"Then he loves Griff more."

When they reached the top of the dunes, the views were fabulous, a sandy beach stretching for miles in either direction. Bamburgh's majestic castle was on the right and what he

176

assumed was Holy Island lay on the left. And not a soul in sight.

"Wow," Devan whispered.

"Takes your breath away, doesn't it?"

"Get out that chicken and the dartboard. No wonder this is a secret."

"It can't ever get busy, because not only is it a protected area, there's not much parking available. You saw how long a walk it is from where you have to leave your car. No sane parent is going to drag kids and all their paraphernalia this far when there are plenty of great beaches that are more accessible."

They headed down onto the sand.

"Left or right?" Jonty asked. "Or straight on if you want to get wet."

"Is there a reason to pick one over the other?"

"I have it on good authority we're more likely to spot the wonders of nature on the left."

"Then left it is."

They'd not been walking for long when Jonty nudged him. "Hey! Seals."

Devan spotted a couple of black heads bobbing up and down in the water. "But no whales? Who can I complain to?"

"Me. I deal with all complaints in a courteous and professional manner."

"I'm feeling let down that there are no whales."

"Want me to teach you how to call them?"

"Er...no."

"It's easy. Listen." Jonty opened his mouth and let out a series of deep humming pulses.

"That doesn't sound the same as the song you sang in the hotel."

"They were jerks, but I've practised this. It's only the male whales that sing to attract mates." He did it again for several seconds and then glared at Devan.

Devan got it. "You can stop now. It worked."

Jonty grinned. "We'll walk for a bit, then go up into the dunes and have a picnic. You'll have to deal with the chicken. I'm squeamish."

"What have I got to do? Hit it with the darts?"

"No darts. Only a dartboard. Eww. You have some strange ideas."

"What have you brought to eat?"

"What would you like me to have brought to eat?"

"A baguette with Parma ham, spinach, basil, pesto and mozzarella. Scones, jam and clotted cream. Cheese straws and a couple of cold beers."

"Crisps?"

"Yep, and crisps."

"Phew. I got something right. But probably the wrong flavour. Though everyone likes Marmite crisps, don't they? Now we're talking about food, I'm hungry." Jonty tugged him off the beach and up into the dunes. "We need a sheltered spot with no snakes."

"There are snakes?"

"I've never seen one here, but yeah, they do slither around the dunes. I'm not a fan of snakes. If I freak out, it's either because I've seen an enormous cock or a tiny snake. With one I'll get over the shock fast, with the other I won't."

Devan laughed. "Remember what you were saying about unrealistic expectations?"

"My expectations are never unrealistic."

Devan looked around the spot they'd reached. It seemed sheltered. "Is here okay?"

"Fine." Jonty opened his bag and took out a lightweight groundsheet. He spread it out so that it rested partly on an upslope they could lean against, then sat on it.

Devan joined him. It was warm out of the wind and he took off his jacket, rolled it up and lay back with it under his head.

"Only your jacket? Don't stop there." Jonty licked his lips. Then licked them again. "I just did my whale call and caught you. I told you my expectations weren't unrealistic. Don't disappoint me."

"How about we eat. I should tell you that if you don't hand me a chicken, I am going to carry you to the sea and dump you in the water."

Jonty emptied the bag. There were crisps, sandwiches, sausage rolls, a flask of something and a punnet of strawberries.

"Shit! The chicken's done a runner. You want to go back and see if you can catch it?"

"No. What's in the flask?"

"Beer, though it might taste like coffee. I even put sugar in for you. The sandwiches are brie and cranberry sauce or tuna and mayo."

As they sat and ate, they stared at the sea. Gannets were diving for fish and the seals were still out there. Devan gave a quiet sigh.

"Isn't this perfect?" Jonty whispered.

Yes, because you're here next to me. "No whales." Devan huffed.

"And no big dicks. Yet."

Devan wanted to fuck him, wanted to make him see stars, lose control, cry out his name. But not here. Sand would get into places he'd rather not have it. No way of getting cleaned up. Not very romantic thoughts, but…

But…

179

Maybe…

"Do you come here often?" Devan asked.

Jonty turned a shocked face towards him. "That's a terrible pick up line. I'm devastated you didn't come up with something better than that. Something like — well, here I am. What are your other two wishes?"

Devan smiled.

"Try again." Jonty poured black coffee into two plastic cups and picked up a sausage roll.

Devan took a deep breath. "Apart from hearing about Brad, and finding myself talking about Ravi, this is the best day I've had for over two years. Maybe a lot longer than that."

Jonty stared at him with the sausage roll sticking out of his mouth. He bit down hard and chewed fast. "It's only lunchtime. It could all go downhill."

"I'm sure you have something exciting planned for this afternoon."

"True, and it's something for which clothes are not required." Jonty took his jacket off. "Now your turn."

Devan took off his shoes and socks. The sun was beating down out of a cloudless sky. It wasn't a hot day, but it was warm out of the wind. Jonty took his shoes and socks off too.

When Devan held a strawberry to Jonty's lips, he opened his mouth wide and Devan held on while Jonty nibbled it. With the last bite, he sucked Devan's fingers, and Devan's pulse sped up.

"Feed me, Seymour," Jonty whispered.

Two more strawberries, a lot more sucking and Devan had a tent in his jeans. He unfastened his shirt and slipped it off. Jonty's eyes widened and his mouth fell open.

"Oh God," Jonty muttered. "You're either insanely lucky or you're a gym bunny."

"That's your best pickup line?"

"I think that would be *fuck me, there's no chicken*."

180

"You do know that you're going in the water," Devan said.

"Can I try to dissuade you?"

"Maybe if you play my game. Every time you get a question wrong, you have to take off an item of clothing."

"Same for you?" Jonty's voice was croaky. He ate another strawberry.

"I'm taking mine off anyway."

Devan slid out of his jeans. His cock bulged in his boxers, the head almost poking out of the top. He wrapped his hand around his dick through his underwear and adjusted himself. Lust coiled in his gut.

Jonty whimpered. "You could have asked for help with that. I have two perfectly good hands and ten fingers including two opposable thumbs, last time I counted. How cruel can you get?"

"Finished eating?" Devan asked.

"There was food? And I ate it?"

Devan laughed and put what remained into the backpack. "Question one. What was the first thing you said to me?"

"I can't quite get it all in my mouth at one go, though I have tried. Repeatedly. It's an inch too long."

"You missed a word."

Jonty frowned. "I did?"

"Your first word was *no*. I asked you if you'd finished eating."

"Shit. You're right. I'm so pissed off my first word was no. Why couldn't I have said something more interesting?"

"Such as?"

"Snickersnee, gardyloo or...yes."

Devan smiled.

Jonty paused as he was peeling off his T-shirt. "Er...I'm not a gym bunny." Then he pulled the T-shirt off.

181

Devan let his gaze wander slowly down from Jonty's face, over a smooth chest, dark copper nipples, down to the slight hollow of a perfectly-shaped navel, and a thin dark treasure trail disappearing into his jeans, before returning his attention to the damaged nipple. "What happened there?"

Jonty looked down. "I was attacked by a killer butterfly."

"Or?"

"I had a piercing. I twisted too hard and broke the skin."

"Why were you twisting it?" Devan reached out and gently stroked Jonty's healing skin. The nipple pebbled and Devan's dick twitched.

"I was having a panic attack thinking about Brad."

Enough to stop his dick getting more excited.

"I needed to distract myself so I pulled at the bar until it hurt, but I clearly don't know my own strength. I made a note for future reference. Don't tug on things too hard, or you might pull them off." Jonty sucked in a breath. "Don't think I self-harm because I don't. That's never been one of my coping mechanisms, well apart from snapping a rubber band on my wrist when I start to panic. This was a one-off accident."

Damn. Devan wished he hadn't asked. "My next question." Which needed to be something safe. "Which has more landmass? Antarctica or Canada?"

"Now you want to be boring? Antarctica."

Devan nodded. "Correct."

"How many legs does a lobster have?" Jonty asked.

"Ten."

"Shit. I didn't think you'd know that."

Devan smiled. "What's alektorophobia a fear of?"

"Er… Smart Alecs?"

"Chickens."

Jonty laughed. "Seriously?"

"Yep. Jeans off."

Jonty wriggled out of them. "You better tell me how you knew that. Note, that isn't a question."

"My mother is scared of hens."

"I know the perfect Christmas gift. Don't tell her you told me." Jonty's smile slid off his face as he realised what he'd said.

Oh God, he's perfect. Long and lithe and beautiful, lightly furred legs, his cock an indecent bulge inside those tight shorts. Devan's mouth watered and he swallowed hard.

"What's the collective name for a group of tigers?" Jonty asked.

"A streak."

Jonty glared. "You're such a fucking smart-arse."

"And you're not?" Devan asked.

"No!" Jonty smirked. "I only passed five GCSEs. Shorts off."

"Hey, that wasn't a question either."

"Yes, it was. Your voice went up at the end. I definitely heard that question mark. Anyway, do you *want* to keep your clothes on? You were the one who started this."

Devan peeled off his boxers.

"I'm not blinking." Jonty said under his breath. "I might be drooling. Sorry."

Devan almost unconsciously wrapped his hand around his dick, pulled the foreskin over the head, and precome slid onto his hand. Jonty's eyes widened and he groaned.

"What's your name?" Devan asked.

"I've forgotten." Jonty wriggled out of his underwear and climbed on top of Devan, planting his knees either side of his thighs. "That took far too long. Next time, I make the rules."

Jonty leaned over, rocked his hips and their cockheads brushed together. "Oh God, that's nice." His voice was husky.

"Only nice?"

"*Really* nice. *Super* nice. *Extraordinarily* nice." Jonty did it again and this time, Devan shuddered along with him.

Feather-light touches, yet each was like an electric shock. Goose bumps erupted all over Devan's body.

"Cold?" Jonty asked.

"Warm me up."

"Oh God. I didn't bring a hot water bottle, Grandpa. You are so much older than me, I know you must feel the cold. Sorry."

"That mouth." Devan laid his hands on Jonty's back, felt a trembling exhalation hit his face, then pulled Jonty down. As their bodies, then lips touched, they both groaned.

"We aren't going to last two minutes," Devan whispered.

Jonty widened his eyes. "Wow. You can last as long as that? I'm so impressed. Is it because you're old?"

Devan smiled. He lifted a hand from Jonty's back and ran his thumb over the softest lips that he'd… Jonty opened his mouth, licked his thumb and when Devan slipped it over his tongue, Jonty sucked hard and bit down gently. *Shit.* Devan felt the pull in his cock.

He thought—*take this slow.*

He thought—*savour this moment.*

He thought—*this is different.*

But… He was falling, sinking, drowning and he wasn't sure if he wanted that to happen or not.

As if I have any choice.

Jonty buried his face in Devan's neck, making all sorts of sexy sounds, and it was as if Devan's feet had been swept from beneath him. Jonty dragged him out of his depth as swiftly and effectively as that rip current. Devan brought his hands to Jonty's face, held tight and kissed him. Too desperate for slow, too hungry for gentle, he kissed Jonty as if he was going to lose him if he didn't kiss him. Jonty's tongue slid alongside his, twisting, surging, exploring. The kiss was so hot

184

that Devan forgot about breathing, forgot that they were lying naked in a sand dune, and while naked bodies might be okay on this beach, alfresco sex was not. They might be seen. They might be reported. They might be arrested.

I don't care. I don't fucking care.

He was as overwhelmed with lust as he'd been at age eleven when his first crush had smiled at him across the room in a geography lesson. He'd almost come in his school trousers. His mind reeled with Jonty's scent, his taste, the feel of him — soft and hard, slender but strong. Their cocks were pressing together, their balls too, and every time Jonty moved against him, Devan moaned into his mouth.

The kiss finally ended because they ran out of air. Their lips parted and they simultaneously gulped.

"Your kiss," Jonty gasped, "exceeded my expectations. The other thing did too."

Jonty let his weight settle on Devan, their heads resting together.

"Christ." Jonty was breathing in Devan's ear and the sensation revved Devan up even further. One lick around the shell of his ear and more precome surged. Jonty licked and teased, and Devan thought he might have come from that alone. Their bellies were wet, their cocks rock-hard between them. Devan wanted to touch Jonty everywhere; stroke, kiss, caress, lick, suck every inch of his skin. He spread his fingers over Jonty's tight, trim arse and tugged him in tight, wrapping his thighs around Jonty's hips, his heels over his legs, bucking into him and Jonty rocked down.

"Oh God," Jonty gasped. "I am so fucking close."

They ground themselves against each other and as Devan trailed his finger along the crease of Jonty's backside, Jonty slid his hand between them, grabbed their dicks and squeezed.

That was all it took.

One hand. One touch.

185

They came together and Devan couldn't remember that ever happening before. He caught Jonty's mouth with his and they swallowed each other's cry. Devan felt as if he was making the perfect jump with his kite, flying into the sun, defying gravity, weightless for those few precious seconds before the fall. *Fuck, fuck, FUCK!*

Finally, Jonty slid off to the side and lay on his back next to him, his chest rapidly rising and falling. Devan took Jonty's hand and twined their fingers together, stroking the back of his knuckles with his thumb.

"In my head," Jonty said, "I'd imagined that lasting a lot longer. Let's pretend it did. No one will ever know."

Devan laughed.

"I was going to drive you wild, get you desperate, then make you wait." Jonty sighed. "I barely managed to get my hand between us before I came. The only consolation is that you came too. The downside is that I didn't see it happen and I wanted to watch. The other downside is that we're both sticky and there's no hot shower handy. You know what a hot shower is, right? Like a regular shower, but with me in it?" He grinned.

"We have the next best thing." Devan pushed to his feet, scooped Jonty up and flung him over his shoulder.

Jonty yelled and wriggled as Devan carried him over the sand towards the sea.

"Help! I'm being abducted by an alien!"

Devan growled.

"No, a bear! Help!"

"Fuck, you weigh more than you look as if you weigh." Jonty nipped his ear. "You might be sorry you said that."

Devan glanced around as he headed down the beach, but they were still on their own. As he reached the water, Jonty held onto him like a leech, wrapping arms and legs tightly around him.

"If I go in, so do you," Jonty said in his ear.

"I'm intending to go in."

"Oh damn."

Devan waded out into the water and when he was in up to his knees, he wrestled Jonty free and threw him as far as he could out into the waves. The shriek was very loud, but cut off as Jonty went down. Devan winced as he splashed freezing cold water over his belly to clean off the come, then froze when he saw Jonty lying face down.

He was almost certainly faking, but Devan couldn't risk it. He flung himself out to Jonty's side and hauled him the right way up and into his arms. Jonty's eyes were closed and he didn't appear to be breathing. But... *Little fraud.*

"Oh God. How am I going to explain this to the police?" Devan whined. "It might be better to let the sea take him and give the fish a tasty meal."

Jonty coughed and opened his eyes. "You saved me. Are you a merman? Can I see your tail? Is it huge? Did you know there's a fish that has a penis under its chin?"

Devan threw him back in.

Jonty caught up with him on the way to where they'd left their stuff. They were both shivering.

"We need to warm up," Jonty said. "More sex. Then back in the water. Then more sex. In out, in out, in out, then — "

Devan pulled Jonty round and put his hands on his throat, not tight, just held him firm enough to let him know who was in charge, then he kissed him. Jonty arched against him and their cocks began to harden.

"Good idea," Jonty whispered against Devan's mouth. "We should make each other come right here because we're much nearer the water."

Devan looked round in case a horde of visitors had arrived, but apart from an overhead gallery of squawking seabirds they were still alone. "We need to get warm."

187

"Sex makes me hot."

Devan groaned. "We're not going to—"

He gulped as Jonty slid to his knees in the middle of the beach, stared up at him and slowly licked up his cock, swirling his tongue over the head.

"Mmm extra salty." Jonty grinned. "Are the birds watching? I wonder if I can perform with an audience?"

Devan put his hand between Jonty's mouth and his dick. "This is probably the hardest thing I've ever had to say in my entire life, but stop, not in the middle of the beach." He pulled Jonty to his feet. "If we're seen, we'd be arrested."

"Good point. We wouldn't get put in the same cell so I'd worry when I had to bend over and pick up the soap in the shower. I'm guessing that might be apocryphal, but I don't want to risk it. Let's go to my place. That's the third wonder of Northumberland. But I want a ten second head start to get back to our clothes. Okay?"

"Why do you need a head start?"

"Only ten seconds." Jonty blinked and pouted.

"Does that normally work?"

Jonty's bottom lip wobbled.

Devan sighed. "Fine."

"I want to dry myself with your shirt."

Devan groaned. "Fine."

Jonty went up on his toes and kissed him. "When we get back, I want you to hold my face while I suck you off. That's another wonder of today. I've made a list of ten. I think that was number seven. Want to hear the others?"

"Yes." The word came out strangled by the lust surging through Devan's entire body.

"I'll drip feed them as you drive."

"Don't make me crash."

By the time he'd parked on Jonty's street, Devan was dry-mouthed with excitement. He couldn't remember when he'd been more desperate to get a guy into bed. Though anywhere behind closed doors with no sand around would work fine.

"I'm not pushing you into this, am I?" Jonty asked.

Was he serious? "Do you hear me complaining?"

"One of your alter-egos is Mr Difficult. Complaining is probably in your blood."

Devan smiled. "Your bed better be big enough. Do the sheets have a high thread count? Are you really as flexible as you've made out? If you can't get your entire dick in your mouth, I'm going to be seriously pissed off. I insist on seeing all ten wonders of Northumberland. See? I have lots of potential complaints."

Jonty laughed.

As they climbed out of the car, Devan's phone rang. If he hadn't been hoping for a call from Hamish McAllister, he wouldn't have looked at it, and when he saw who was calling, he wished he'd left the bloody thing in his pocket. But now he was torn. It was a matter of pride to see if he could talk to Ravi without anger surging from his gut. If being with Jonty didn't keep his rage at bay, then he wondered if he might actually need therapy. He shuddered.

But he and Jonty were about to get naked—again—and talking to Ravi was the last thing he wanted to do. The phone stopped ringing, then began again a moment later.

Jonty grabbed his jacket and backpack from the rear seat. "I'm going into the shop to buy something. Take your call."

As Jonty walked away, Devan answered it. "What do you want?" He assumed Ravi was ringing to plead with him to be Griff's best man.

"I have something to tell you. I'm waiting at the hotel."

What the fuck? So much for suppressing his rage. "Which hotel?" Though did he even need to ask?

189

"McAllister's. Where are you?"

Devan's heart sank. "What do you want, Ravi?"

"I need to see you, to tell you face to face. It's…really important."

Devan had to think fast. Christ knew what damage Ravi would do if he opened his mouth about what Devan did for a living. He could scupper the whole deal. "I'll be there in fifteen minutes. Keep your mouth shut."

He turned as Jonty emerged from the shop. *Oh fuck.*

Jonty took one look at him and his shoulders dropped. "You're not going to sample the fourth, fifth, sixth etcetera wonders of Northumberland, are you?"

"Someone's unexpectedly come to the hotel to see me. I'm sorry."

"Okay."

"You've really no idea how sorry I am."

"It's okay."

"Can I come back later?"

Jonty gave a little shrug. "If you like. I'll probably go and see Tay though."

A surge of jealousy blocked Devan's throat. He pulled Jonty into his arms. "The last thing I want to do is leave now."

"Then don't."

"It's not that simple."

Jonty wriggled free and stepped back. "Just answer one thing. The person who's come to see you, is it Ravi?"

Fuck. Lie!

Don't lie.

"Yes."

"Then you should go. Drive safe."

"I could have lied to you. I didn't. I have no interest in Ravi anymore, but I…"

Jonty headed for his door without saying another word.

When Devan looked in his mirror as he drove away, Jonty was staring after the car. No interest in Ravi, yet he was driving away from the person he wanted to be with—towards one he no longer cared about. That was all Jonty would see. But his job... He kept driving. It took four tortuous miles before he came to his senses and turned around. Ravi didn't matter. The hotel purchase didn't matter. He swallowed hard.

Jonty *did* matter.

There was no answer when Devan banged on Jonty's door though that didn't mean he wasn't there, unless he'd already gone to see his friend. Devan called him, but the phone went straight to voicemail.

"I'm sorry," Devan said. "I came back. Call me."

The pain in his chest alarmed him. He sat in his car for a while, texted Stan the names of Jonty's parents, then gave a heavy sigh. There was little point sitting waiting when he had no idea when Jonty would return. He set off for the hotel. The sooner he got rid of Ravi, the better.

Chapter Twelve

Devan's car disappeared into the distance with his final words echoing in Jonty's head. *I have no interest in Ravi anymore, but…* It was the *but* that did it for Jonty. They'd been going to have fantastic sex—and one call from his ex had sent Devan running in his direction. *No interest.* Right.

Jonty huffed, kicked at some imaginary rock on the pavement and jarred his toes—*shit.* Well, that was it with Devan or it wasn't. Nothing he could do about it. Maybe it was for the best, because he was growing increasingly attached to Mr Difficult. Jonty was enjoying making him smile and laugh. They'd had fun today and he'd planned for that fun to… *Fuck it.* Everyone walked away. Or was pulled away. Devan was no different.

Let it go! He unlocked his door, stepped inside and froze for a split second, before going into a lightning-fast reverse back onto the street, just retaining enough presence of mind to slam the door. *Oh my God. OH MY GOD!* What he'd seen couldn't be right. *Couldn't, couldn't, couldn't.*

He felt as chilled as if he'd been thrown into the sea. His entire body prickled with goose bumps. He really didn't want to open the door and take another peek, but he had to, because if he didn't check and called for help and he was wrong about what he'd seen, he'd look such a prat.

You hear about the idiot who couldn't tell the difference between a rubber snake and a real one?

Jonty gulped. *Shit.* Maybe he'd just go with being that idiot because he didn't want to open the door. Devan was a prick, but he wished he was there because somehow Jonty knew he *would* open the door. He stared at his letterbox. He could peek through that and make absolutely sure it was a real snake wrapped around his bike, except… What if the snake had slithered across the floor and up the door and was

192

currently waiting on the other side of the letterbox flap, poised to shoot out and bite him on the nose?

In the end, Jonty opened the door again, took a quick look and closed it. The shiver that ran through him was like a personal seismic shock. He almost expected his knees to give way and the ground to crack. Though with his luck, he'd fall into a pit of snakes. He wasn't wrong about what he'd seen. That was most definitely a snake. A stripy grey and yellow thing. And not rubber, because it was moving.

I need help.

He put his hand in his jacket pocket for his phone, didn't find it, and tried the other pocket. No phone. *What the hell?* He checked his backpack, though he was certain he hadn't put it in there, and he hadn't. So it was either lost in the sand or in Devan's car. *Damn.*

Jonty went into the hair salon next to his door.

"Hi, Jonty!" Miriam, the owner, sat behind the reception desk, filing her nails.

Her dog Snoopy, came up to Jonty and flopped on his back with his feet in the air. Despite Jonty's anxiety, he managed a smile. "Snoopy, you are such a tart." He bent to tickle the dog's stomach, and looked up at Miriam. "I need a favour. I've mislaid my phone and I need to call the police."

She paled and handed him her mobile. "Are you okay?"

Jonty stood up. "Don't freak out, but I opened my door…" He lowered his voice. "…and I saw a snake."

Miriam shuddered. "Oh my God. Go into the back room. Don't let anyone hear you say that."

Jonty went through and pressed 1-0-1 even though it was a *fucking* emergency. What bigger emergency could there be than him being confronted by a snake? Okay, there might be a few other things that would qualify. A zombie would have been worse but…

"Alnwick police. How can I help you?"

He took a deep breath. "Oh hi. My name's Jonty Bloom. I live at 5A Hayton Street. I just came home and opened my door to find a snake on the stairs that go up to my flat."

"Your snake?"

Are you mad? "No, I'm scared to death of snakes. I think it was posted through my letterbox by a guy who's been harassing me. You have the information about him on file."

"Hold on a moment…"

What the hell was Brad thinking?

"Okay," the policeman said. "I see your details. Is the snake venomous?"

"I have no idea."

"How big is it?"

"It was curled around my bike, but maybe three-foot long."

"Someone will come out, but call the RSPCA. We can't handle snakes."

"I've misplaced my phone. I'm on one belonging to the lady who runs the hair salon next to my place. Miriam Hall."

"I'll make a note."

"Thank you."

Miriam stood at the door, clutching Snoopy and gawping at him.

"I need to call the RSPCA now," he told her.

"Go ahead," she told him.

"Can you find me the number?"

He handed her the phone with shaking fingers and a moment later, he was telling them what had happened.

Jonty returned Miriam's phone. "The police and the RSPCA are coming. They asked if anyone either side kept a snake."

"I don't." She peeked at the two elderly ladies who were having their hair styled. "I don't see them with pet snakes

194

tucked in their handbags. And how would it get from here to you?"

Jonty left the shop and stood staring at his door. *Fucking Brad.* It had to be him. There was no way in from either side up the stairs. No cracks in the steps, no holes in the walls. At least, there hadn't been. *Had* it escaped from a neighbouring property? This was a row of terraces, houses with a shared roof space. Jonty had never been up in the attic, though he supposed it was possible a snake had decided to go walkabout. Yet he thought not.

Why was Brad doing all this? The increasingly bizarre gifts? None of it was going to make Jonty want to go out with him again. Brad knew he was scared of snakes, so this had been done to frighten him. Maybe because Brad had seen him with Devan, but he'd gone too far now. Jonty wished he had his phone, but it was possible it was lost in the sand rather than in the Aston Martin. *And I can't fucking call Devan. I can't remember his number.*

The policeman arrived first. Jonty handed him his keys, but the guy stayed next to Jonty, well away from the door. It was a relief that he seemed as nervous as Jonty. It made him feel less pathetic.

"What makes you think Brad Greene is responsible?" the policeman asked.

Jonty gave him a potted history of *him and Brad* and added that Brad had confronted him outside the flat that morning, and that he knew how Jonty felt about things that hissed and slithered.

"Maybe it escaped from someone who lives in this row of houses," the policeman said. "I remember reading about a woman who woke to find she was sharing her bed with a three-foot-long python. Turned out to be an escaped pet."

For fuck's sake! Jonty could feel his anxiety starting to choke him. "I asked in the hair salon and there's no one in the laundrette. Those businesses own the floor above their premises, so there's no one living either side of me."

"Could be from several houses along if it moved through the roof space."

Which was what Jonty had considered, and yes, it was possible, but he really thought it was Brad.

"You're not making me feel better. Can you dust snakes for fingerprints?"

The policeman smothered a chuckle. "I doubt it."

"Will you google?"

The guy rolled his eyes, but a short time later, he gaped at Jonty. "Hey, you *can* take prints off a snake. That's amazing."

"Good. That will show you it's my ex." Assuming Brad had handled it.

The guy paled. "Not sure how I'm going to request we get fingerprints off a snake."

The RSPCA van pulled up in front of the police car. Jonty wanted to watch, but a part of him didn't want to see the snake again. The policeman spoke to the two RSPCA guys and gave them Jonty's key.

"We might need to dust the snake for prints," the policeman told them. "Try not to touch it."

The guys looked as if they were trying not to laugh. *It isn't fucking funny!*

Once they'd taken a peek, they shut the door again and went to get a plastic container and a sack from their van, along with gloves and a sort of metal grabber, before letting themselves back inside and closing the door.

A few minutes later, they emerged carrying the plastic box with the sack inside. Jonty didn't breathe until it was in the van and the van door was shut. He'd have preferred it locked, chained, welded, but...

"We're not sure what it is," said one of the guys. "We'll need to ask an expert. It's not native to the UK, so it likely needs to be in a heated tank."

"Would you check my flat too, please," Jonty asked. "Just in case."

The policeman raised his eyebrows. "You think your ex-boyfriend has a key?"

"I never gave him one, but what if he took one of mine and had a copy made?" *Oh fuck.*

The animal guys went up the stairs and Jonty's heart pounded. When they came back and said they'd found nothing, Jonty thought he'd feel better. He didn't.

"We checked in all your cupboards and under the furniture," one of the men said.

Still not enough. Jonty wanted floorboards ripped up, walls knocked down, toilet pulled out. "Thank you."

When they'd left, the policeman turned to Jonty. "I'll go and speak to Greene."

"Okay."

"If he admits he put the snake there, we won't need to dust for prints and we might be able to charge him with animal cruelty."

It seemed an irony that charging Brad with that was easier than trying to stop him being a pest.

The policeman drove off and Jonty stood staring at his open door. *I can't go in.*

There's nothing there. They looked.

Tay was leaning against the window of the laundrette.

Even so. Would you want to live there now?

No.

Jonty stayed on the pavement and pulled the door shut. He'd brought Tay back because Devan had gone.

Way to make me feel loved!

Sorry.

So what happened to Mr Impossible?

Jonty finally allowed himself to think about Devan. And Ravi. *I could have gone to the hotel with him if he'd asked.* But he hadn't asked. No use pretending that he wasn't disappointed because he was. Bitterly. So much for the packet of Flakes he'd bought from the shop. So much for his plans for the rest of the day. But that was what life had dealt him, and he'd get over it. Worse things happened.

Yep.

Though he still had the problem of what to do now. What if there was a snake that the guys hadn't found? What if Brad or one of his mates put another through the letterbox while Jonty was upstairs? Anxiety was toxic. He couldn't stop shivering.

He went back into the salon.

"They got it?" Miriam asked.

"Yep. Could I use your phone again please?"

She handed it to him and Jonty moved out of her hearing. He could have called the hotel and asked to speak to Devan, but he called Mike instead.

"Hi mate, what's up?"

"I need a favour." Jonty kept his voice low. "I've had a…bit of an issue with my flat. I need somewhere to stay, just for a little while, and a place to store my stuff while I sort out new accommodation. No more than a couple of days. I'm back on nights on Saturday so I wouldn't be around in the evenings. Could I kip on your couch until I get a room? You'd hardly know I was there. But if I can't, and it's fine if that's the case, if you could keep my stuff, I can find somewhere to sleep in the hotel. Probably."

"What the hell's happened? Is there a leak? Did you get thrown out?"

"There was a snake."

"What the hell?"

198

"It's gone. I called the police. The RSPCA came and got it. But I don't want to stay here."

"I'll come now. Lee's in the shop. He can close up for me."

"Thanks."

When Mike turned up, he had Willis with him. Mike pulled Jonty into his arms and gave him a hug. Jonty found it really hard not to cling to him, but he didn't want to upset Willis so he let Mike go.

"We can take your stuff now," Mike said. "I thought the faster we do this, the better."

"Thank you, both of you."

Willis lifted a pile of flattened boxes out of the back of the van along with rolls of tape and bubble wrap and they shared the load between the three of them.

"I'm sorry to be a bother," Jonty told Willis.

"It's fine," Willis said. "I wouldn't want to stay here either."

Jonty led them up the stairs, trying not to shudder. "The animal guys checked the flat too, but they didn't find anything."

"Still be careful," Mike said. "Don't either of you go reaching into spaces when you can't see what's there."

Jonty unlocked his door and tried to ignore the fact that his heart was beating out of his chest.

"Do they know what type of snake it was?" Willis asked.

"Only that it's not native to the UK."

"It must have escaped from someone's flat," Willis said.

"It was in the stairwell, wrapped around my bike. There's no way in except through the door or the letterbox."

"You mean someone deliberately put it through your letterbox?" Willis gaped at him.

"Yep."

"Who?" Mike snapped. "That fuckhead Brad?"

199

"I think so."

"Who's he?" Willis asked.

"A guy I went out with on a few dates. He wasn't…my type. He's sent me other stuff. Handcuffs, a dildo, a bag full of used condoms."

"Eww." Willis mock-wretched.

"I think the police will charge him now. If he gets put under a restraining order, it should make him leave me alone."

"Fucking hell, Jonty," Mike said. "You told me he was pestering you, but why didn't you tell me how bad things were?"

"Because it was my problem." *And you have Willis now.* Jonty was sort of surprised Mike hadn't told him.

"Right," Mike said. "Let's get to work. And be careful. I'm Australian. I know more than I want to about snakes."

They had everything packed within an hour. Jonty didn't have much, but by the time his furniture and bike were in the vehicle, there was barely enough room for the boxes and for him. He crawled over the passenger seat to the place where Devan had sat what seemed like weeks ago.

"Everything can stay in the van," Mike said as they set off. "While we're not busy, I can use the other one. If you don't find a place quickly, we'll store your things in our garage. So what happened to your posh guy, Jonty?"

Jonty's heart twanged like a tight violin string. "*My* posh guy? He's not mine."

"You didn't bond over your near-death experience?" Willis asked.

"That's about all we had in common."

"You can sleep in our guest room," Willis said. "Don't leap at the first place you find."

"Thanks." He hadn't expected that.

200

"Leap at the second." Willis turned and smiled.

Which Jonty thought was the true indicator of what Willis wanted even though he was smiling, but he wouldn't be staying any longer than he needed to.

"Damn it, Mike," Jonty said. "You told me Willis was up for a threesome."

Mike laughed. Willis didn't.

That was the only humorous comment that Jonty could manage. When both Mike and Willis said nice things about his sea glass art, Jonty barely responded. He was shocked by how quickly everything had fallen apart.

Once he was in the guys' house with his bag of essentials, he refused an offer of food and went straight to the guest room. It might be early, but he wanted to curl up somewhere safe.

Devan seethed all the way back to the hotel. He'd finally found a reason to smile and now he was angry again. Though Jonty had made him see sense. Ravi and Griff were welcome to each other. Let Griff put up with Ravi's moods and strange habits! They were both as spoilt as one another. Interesting to see how that would pan out.

He was still torn over whether he should have stayed outside Jonty's place, but there was no knowing how long he'd have had to sit there waiting, and the sooner he got rid of Ravi, the better. If Ravi accidentally or deliberately blabbed about what Devan did for a living, the whole deal could come unstuck. McAllister had asked for it to be kept quiet, and Devan wanted to work something out for Jonty before he told him he'd soon be minus a job, assuming it came to that.

There'd also been something in Ravi's tone that had worried him. Bad news about Griff? But wouldn't his parents or one of his siblings have been in touch if that was the case? Unless they didn't know.

His phone rang as he headed into the hotel and he stopped to answer it. This *was* the call he'd wanted to get. Well, one of them. He'd have preferred it to be a call from Jonty.

"Devan Smith."

"I was going to let you stew for a couple of days," McAllister said. "But my family are all for me selling, so get your people in and make me an offer."

"That's great. Thanks."

"I'd like to emphasise that I want this kept strictly confidential. If the deal goes ahead, I'd want to tell the staff and permanent residents myself."

"Of course."

Devan texted Alan that McAllister had said yes, and to put people in place, but keep everything under wraps, then slipped his phone back in his pocket. He should have been feeling pleased and instead he felt guilty. He wanted to tell Jonty and he shouldn't, but... He took out his phone and called him again. He wasn't entirely surprised when Jonty didn't pick up so he left a message.

"Hi, it's me. The me you were going to introduce to the fourth wonder of Northumberland. The me who can't wait to marvel at it and all the other wonders. As soon as I've spoken to Ravi and found out what he wants, I'll come back. I did come back after I'd driven a couple of miles, but you weren't there. If I wasn't anxious that something bad had happened to bring Ravi up here, I wouldn't have left. I should have brought you with me. I'm sorry I didn't. See you soon. There's something I need to tell you."

Devan went into the hotel to find Ravi sitting in the lounge. He was by the window, messing with his phone, a wine glass in front of him, and an overnight bag at his feet. Devan sucked in his cheeks. That was *not* going to happen. He wanted Ravi gone.

As Devan walked towards the guy who, once upon a time, had made his world turn, there wasn't a single pang of sadness, not even one of regret for having gotten involved with him in the first place. They *had* been good together. Devan was angry with himself for leaving Jonty, but in a wash of awareness, no longer angry with Ravi or Griff. The rage he'd felt as he'd driven back to the hotel evaporated. Jonty was right. Why waste time and energy on people who didn't matter? Though disappointment with his brother remained.

Ravi stood and smiled when he saw him. Devan didn't smile. He sidestepped Ravi's embrace. So it wasn't bad news he was here to deliver.

"You're looking good," Ravi said.

"What do you want?"

"Glass of wine?"

"No thanks." Because he was shortly going to be driving back to Jonty. "What do you want to say that couldn't have been said in a phone call?"

"Can we go to your room?"

Devan laughed.

Ravi settled back in the chair. "At least sit down."

Devan dropped into the seat opposite.

Ravi glanced around as if he didn't want to look Devan in the eyes. "This place is a bit of dump."

"It has character." *Which is more than can be said for you.*

"Brilliant position though. The view is fantastic."

"What do you want?"

"This hotel was Griff's. He's a bit pissed off you've taken it."

The irony of that was clearly lost on Ravi.

"Griff and I were going to have a few days up here together. I've been doing a shoot for Dior at The Angel of the North. The big—"

"I know what it is," Devan spoke quietly. "I really hope you've not said anything about what I'm doing here. If you fuck up this deal…"

Ravi rolled his eyes. "Bloody hell, you're not MI5."

Devan bit back his irritation. "In these early days, everything needs to be kept quiet. I need you to keep quiet. Tell me what you've brought me here to say, then fuck off."

"There's no need to be so mean."

Ravi always took his time to get to the point. Once it was cute, now it was not.

"Griff's really upset."

"Why? What have you done?" *Christ, is sarcasm catching?*

"He really wants you to be his best man."

Devan heaved a sigh of disbelief. "Is that it? Is that why you're here? He's not been injured in a car crash? Finally realised you're never going to rim him?"

Ravi pulled his sulky face. No longer adorable but aggravating. *How could I ever have thought this guy was the one for me?*

"We have another brother," Devan said. "Why can't he ask Cato?"

"Because Cato… Griff wants you."

"Cato what?"

"Griff wants you," Ravi repeated.

Cato said no?

"Please, Devan."

"Could this be because if I stand at Griff's side, he thinks I'll have forgiven him? That there are no bad feelings between us? That everyone watching won't be thinking—isn't it odd that Griff is marrying the guy that Devan was supposed to marry? But if Devan's here at his brother's side, then they must be okay about it. Is that it?"

"He doesn't like conflict."

Who fucking does? Take a deep breath. Count to ten.

He made it to five. "You're welcome to each other. I really don't care. But I am not standing at his side at your wedding. It's asking too much. I won't change my mind. You've had a wasted trip."

"I love him," Ravi whispered. "I loved you, but along the way, I fell in love with Griff too. He needed me more than you ever did. You were wrong for me. I see that now. All my life I've had people controlling me, telling me what to wear, what to say, what to do, and it made life easy, but not the life I wanted. I got paid a lot of money for pretending to be something I'm not. I want to be needed, Devan. Really needed — and you didn't need anyone."

That wasn't true. Devan *had* needed him. If Ravi thought Griff needed him, he was mistaken. Griff was fiercely independent. How long before his brother tired of Ravi? And Devan suddenly felt sorry for both of them. They were marrying too quickly.

"Neither of us set out to hurt you," Ravi whispered.

Was that true? Maybe Ravi had known Devan would come to the bedroom. Known what Devan would find. If not them actually fucking, then the pair in bed together. Was that easier than Ravi telling him to his face he wouldn't marry him? He was still finding it hard to believe that Ravi would come all this way for this discussion. Even if he'd been working in Newcastle, Ravi thought the North was full of Wildlings, White Walkers and flat-capped sheep shaggers.

"I wanted to see you," Ravi whispered.

"You have. Now you can drive away."

"I got an Uber from Newcastle."

Devan pushed to his feet. "Well, get an Uber back."

"I thought I could stay here."

"Think again."

"I miss you."

Devan gaped at him. "What the fuck?"

205

Ravi stood. "I do." He put his hand on Devan's arm. "You were always good to me."

Devan lifted Ravi's hand off by pinching the sleeve of his sweater. "You're unbelievable." After all Ravi had just told him?

"He'd never know. I wouldn't say anything."

So much for banishing his anger. It came roaring back. But Devan was aware that others had come into the lounge and he didn't want to make a scene. He stepped right into Ravi's space and kept his voice low. "If you can't keep your dick in your pants, leave my brother alone. You've done enough damage to our family."

"Let me sleep in your room tonight. I don't have anywhere to stay. Everyone else has gone back to London."

"That's not going to happen."

Devan walked away. On his way back to his car, he checked his phone, but there'd been no response from Jonty.

He called Cato who was currently studying for a PhD in astrophysics at Cambridge University.

"Hi, Devan."

"Am I interrupting?"

"Put your clothes on, Cindy. Leave my dick alone, Jamie. Stop licking my arse, Julian." Cato moaned dramatically. "Okay. I'm all yours. I was deep in the study of the dispersal of protoplanetary discs by energetic radiation from the central star and by planet formation."

Devan smiled. "Did Griff ask you to be his best man?"

"I said no."

"Why?"

"Because he's a git, because I'm not to going stand there and support what he did to you, and because he only asked me because you said no. At least you have some brains. Not as many as me, but still..."

Devan's heart thumped. "What do you mean—what he did to me?"

There was silence from the other end of the phone.

"Do you know why the wedding didn't go ahead?" Devan asked.

"Not hard to guess. Everything stops at literally the last minute with no good explanation? You don't spend two years with someone, pay a fortune to get married, and then decide there are too many differences between you. Weak excuse, brother mine. Why you didn't see he wasn't right for you way before then, escapes me. Not long before Griff is being all secretive about his new guy. I saw them together in London—and thanks to my amazing powers of deduction—figured Griff was the reason the wedding didn't go ahead. I had a quiet word with Griff and got the truth out of him."

"Does anyone else know?"

"Venice and Ellen. And probably their husbands. Christ knows who else because our sisters can't keep their mouths shut. But not Mum and Dad. Griff begged us not to tell them. You know how much they liked Ravi. They didn't see anything suspicious in a friendship between Ravi and Griff. They were already friends. So why shouldn't it develop into something more? Mum and Dad should have been told why you and Ravi didn't marry. It wasn't fair on you."

There was another long silence.

"So why the call?" Cato asked.

"I'm up in the north-east on business. Ravi just turned up to try and persuade me to be Griff's best man."

"The little fucker. Is that all he tried to persuade you to do?"

"I'm not sure."

"What does that mean?"

"He offered. He said *He'd never know. I wouldn't tell him.* But I'm not sure he was actually offering. Something felt off. I don't know what to do. If I tell Griff, it looks like I'm trying to cause trouble. You think it could be some sort of test?"

"I'd keep quiet. It serves Griff right. A lot of the family have said they won't go to the wedding."

"I thought holding it in the Caribbean would ensure that anyway. An excuse for not many to accept the invite."

"People are upset for you, Dev. Your marriage slams to a halt and eight months later your brother is marrying your ex? Not hard for people to wonder and come to the right conclusion. Maybe that's what has Griff worried, that people know the truth and blame him."

Devan swallowed hard.

"I'll tell Mum what Ravi said. That should stir things up. Other than being pestered by Ravi, how are you?"

"I'm okay. More than okay."

"Ah. Do I need to buy another dress?"

Devan laughed. "I'm still in the *I keep pissing him off* stage. Thanks, Cato. I'll let you get back to your stars."

He sat in his car and tried Jonty again. Still no response so he left another message. "I'm on my way back to your place. Give me a call. Please."

But no call came.

When there was still no response to knocking at Jonty's door, Devan was disappointed and a little anxious. He looked through the letterbox and didn't see Jonty's bike.

"Get away from there," a woman shouted.

Devan turned in time to have a shopping bag whacked into his side.

"What the—?" he gasped.

"Attack, Snoopy!" The woman let go of her dog's lead. The dog stayed where it was.

"I'm looking for Jonty," Devan said quickly, before the small black and white dog decided it was a Rottweiler.

208

"I'm going to call the police." The woman glared at him.

Devan felt as if he'd slipped into another dimension.

"What have I done?"

"Where's your snake?" she snapped.

"Er…"

When she lifted her bag again, Devan retreated to his car and drove away. What the hell had that been about? When he saw a place to park, he pulled in. If Jonty's bike wasn't there, then maybe Jonty was still at his friend's. But why wasn't his phone on? He had a nagging concern that Jonty was in trouble. Devan looked up the number for Mike's shop, but an automated message said it was closed until tomorrow. He left a message, saying he was worried about Jonty and asking Mike to call him. Devan tried Jonty again, then gave up and went back to the hotel.

He went straight up to his suite, then ordered room service. If he'd fucked things up with Jonty, anger was going to make a reappearance in his life. He could only in part blame Ravi. It was his own stupid fault.

The following morning, when Ravi settled into the seat opposite at breakfast, Devan regretted not having eaten in his room again.

"Don't mind, do you?" Ravi asked.

"Yes. Sit somewhere else."

"Don't be mean." Ravi smiled up at the waitress. "Black coffee, freshly squeezed orange juice, and avocado on toast. Thank you."

Devan ate faster. When his phone rang, he pulled it out of his pocket so quickly, he almost knocked over his coffee. He was ready to leave if it was Jonty, but it wasn't.

"Morning," he said to Alan.

"Good morning. I have Roger and Clara on their way north. I've read your report and I'm thinking a million to a million and a quarter. Any thoughts?"

Devan left his half-eaten breakfast and moved away from the table so Ravi couldn't hear. "The position is stunning. I think he'll want more. I'd go another quarter."

"Hmm, well there are a couple of properties coming up for auction that might work better. I'll send you details. Let the dynamic duo take a look at McAllister's and we'll come up with an offer. I'm not sure how quiet we're going to be able to keep this once they start measuring and asking questions. McAllister can say there are plans for renovations, which wouldn't be a lie. Tell him he needs to speak to his staff sooner rather than later."

"Okay. I'll be in touch." Devan went back to the table, reached for his coffee cup and once he'd emptied it, he walked away from the table.

"Hey," Ravi called.

Devan ignored him, which was what he should have done yesterday.

Chapter Thirteen

First thing on Friday morning, Jonty tried to creep out of Mike and Willis's place before they woke, only to find them having breakfast in the kitchen, smiling at each other and laughing. He hesitated at the door. They looked happy, settled…in love, and Jonty felt a surge of longing powerful enough to make him wobble. He wished he had someone to have breakfast with, someone happy to see him, someone who wouldn't let him down.

"Get in here and have something to eat," Mike said.

"It's fine. I can buy — "

"It's toast and marmalade we're offering, not scrambled eggs and smoked salmon." Willis beckoned him. "Coffee?"

"Thanks. Black." Jonty slid onto a chair.

"What are you going to do about your phone?" Mike put a plate and a knife in front of him, then sat opposite.

"If it's in the sand, it's gone. No way I'd find it. I hope it's in Devan's car. Could I use your phone to call the hotel? I can ask him to check. If it's not in there, then I need to buy a new one."

"Not insured?" Willis asked. "Your household insurance might cover it."

Jonty heaved a sigh. "If I had any. I didn't figure I owned anything worth the cost of insurance. The phone's six years old so…"

"But how much is it going to cost you to buy a new one?" Willis asked.

No need to sound so fucking smug, you git. "I'll get another used one."

Mike handed him his phone and Willis slid a mug of coffee in front of him. "Thanks."

Jonty called the hotel.

211

"McAllister's Hotel. How can I help you?"

Jonty winced. He hadn't thought this through. Vincent had answered, the last person he wanted to know about him and Devan. "Could ya put me through to Devan Smith in Wave, please mate?" *Shit.* That was a terrible Australian accent.

Mike and Willis gaped at him. Jonty shrugged and kept quiet as he waited for Vincent to get back to him.

"No response, sorry," Vincent said.

"Okay, cobber, thanks."

Mike slapped a hand over his mouth as he struggled not to laugh.

"Do you want to leave a message?" Vincent asked.

"No, no message."

"I could do with you here this afternoon, Jonty. Lisa has called in sick."

Shit, fuck, bugger. "Okay." Jonty used his normal voice.

"Two o'clock."

"Right." Jonty put the phone down.

"What the hell?" Mike asked. "Was that supposed to be an Australian accent, *cobber*?"

"I should have asked you to do it. I didn't think. My boss answered. I didn't fool him."

"I'm not surprised." Willis guffawed.

"I have to go to work this afternoon," Jonty said. "I don't know when I'll be back."

"I'm so going to miss you." Willis clutched his chest.

Bitch. Jonty jumped to his feet and flung his arms around Willis, holding him as tightly as he could. "You'll miss me? You really like me? You've no idea how happy I am. I thought you hated me because I'd ruined Mike for other men. Have you tried doing that thing with your toes? Or the kinky thing with bacon? He'll love you forever."

212

Willis shoved him away. Mike was creased up laughing. The toast popped up and Mike slid the two slices onto Jonty's plate.

"Don't worry." Jonty buttered his toast. "If your toes aren't long enough, I can show you other ways to please your man."

Willis's growl drowned out Mike's guffaw.

"Ignore him, babe." Mike put two keys on the table in front of Jonty. "Until you find somewhere. One for the house, one for the van in case you have to take anything out of it."

"I will, thank you. I'll need my bike."

"Right," Willis said. "We're off to work. Don't burn the house down."

"Shall I let the cat out?" Jonty asked.

Willis widened his eyes. "We don't have a cat."

"He's pulling your leg." Mike ushered Willis from the kitchen.

When Jonty had finished his breakfast, he washed up and put everything away. There was no point going anywhere until the letting agencies were open, so he sat and made a list of everyone he'd need to inform that he was no longer at his former address. Electricity provider, post office, council, bank, water authority, work… But most would have to wait until he had a new address to give them.

By the time he set off for work that afternoon, he'd told his current landlord why he'd left, reluctantly accepted he'd have to pay for a month when he wouldn't be staying there, and he'd been to see three rooms. He'd said no to them all. The first because the area seemed dicey—a guy pissing into a bush in broad daylight had put him off. The second was no good because the shared bathroom was clearly occupied by the spirit of a dead skunk. Or two. The smell made him gag. He discovered why the last was so cheap when the over-friendly guy with a comb over showing him the room made it clear he expected Jonty to be *nice* to him a couple of times a week. *Yuk.*

As he cycled, he wondered what to say to Vincent who was bound to ask him why he wanted to speak to Devan and why Jonty had pretended to be someone else. He decided to tell the truth, that he'd been showing Devan around the area and thought he'd lost his phone in the guy's car. That sounded perfectly innocent. Which begged the question as to why he hadn't wanted Vincent to know. *Damn.* He'd have to go with saying he thought Vincent might get the wrong idea.

And then there was Devan, who'd probably tried to call him, had maybe even gone back to the bedsit, and was likely thinking Jonty was sulking. He wasn't. Though he hadn't forgotten the choice Devan had made when Ravi had called him. *Not me.* Nor had he dismissed the fact that Ravi had been with Devan for two years and Jonty not even a week, and *been with* was a bit of an exaggeration in Jonty's case.

Jonty got off his bike in the hotel car park, and saw no sign of Devan's growly car. He wheeled his bike to the rail at the back and secured it. Once he'd changed into his suit in the staffroom, he headed for the front desk. Vincent was dealing with a couple checking in who were telling him they were attending the wedding the next day.

"Get Mr and Mrs Jessop's bags, please, Jonty," Vincent said.

Jonty nodded and collected the cart. The couple had suit hangers and a hat box as well as two cases. He took them and their luggage up to their room—a pound coin tip—and went back downstairs. He wanted to call Devan's room, in case he'd parked his car elsewhere, but he didn't get the chance. More bags to carry. Once he'd delivered them—no tip—he slipped up to Wave and knocked on the door. There was no answer, though he hadn't expected one, except maybe from Ravi. So no answer was good news.

But as he came down the stairs from the top floor to the next with a bounce in his step, he bumped into Vincent.

"What were you doing up there?" Vincent asked.

"I wanted to speak to Mr Smith."

"Why?"

"I think I left my phone in his car."

"You did what?" Vincent snapped.

Jonty thought he heard a door open down the corridor, but before he could warn Vincent, the hotel manager was off again. "Do I need to remind you of our rules? You've worked here long enough to know that you do not associate with guests outside the hotel."

"But I was —"

"There are no *buts,* Jonty. Devan Smith is a guest and you work here. How could you leave your phone in his car?"

"He asked me to show him the area." Though that wasn't true. He was the one who'd offered.

"Did he?" Vincent raised his eyebrows.

"Well, I might have offered."

"And did you show him your flat too?" Vincent spoke through clenched teeth.

"I've moved out. I'm staying with friends."

"You're on thin ice, Jonty. Do not bother Mr Smith, you understand?"

Jonty nodded.

"Go back to the desk."

Jonty checked in two more couples before he got a chance to use the computer. He googled *Ravi supermodel.* Ravi Mohnish was the only one he could find. He searched images and kept his finger ready to shut the page if anyone came.

The Asian guy was tall and slim with beautiful long dark hair and big brown eyes, his cheekbones sharp enough to cut cheese. He modelled for a lot of big names. Jonty sighed. *What did I expect?* He closed the page, deleted his browsing history and looked up to see Ravi Mohnish walking down the stairs towards the desk. Jonty wanted to laugh at the coincidence, but he couldn't. *Where did you spend the night, Ravi?*

Jonty put a smile on his face. "How can I help you?"

Ravi held out his hand, palm up, his gaze rising from Jonty's name badge to his face. "The key to Wave, please. I've lost mine."

Like fuck you have. "I'm sorry, but Mr Smith will have to ask for it himself."

Ravi rolled his rather lovely chocolate eyes. *Bastard.* "I stepped out for a moment and the door closed behind me."

"That is…unfortunate. But sorry. I have to follow hotel rules. How do I know you're not a thief or an assassin or a vampire? Or a thieving vampire assassin?"

Ravi gaped at him, then shrugged. "Fine. I want earplugs put in my room. The noise the seagulls make is appalling."

"I'll arrange for them to be shot." *Or you.*

"Good." He stalked off towards the stairs that led to the pool and the gym.

Jonty didn't want to believe Ravi had been in Devan's room. Wouldn't he have answered the knock on the door? Jonty thought about it. While Vincent had been telling him off when he'd come down from Wave, he'd thought he heard a door open. He checked which room Ravi was in. Second floor, so had Ravi heard what had been said?

He headed for the kitchen and was reaching for the packet of mini marshmallows when Wayne caught him.

"What the fuck do you think you're doing?"

Jonty took two marshmallows from the packet. "For a guest."

"And does the guest want fucking hot chocolate to go with them?"

216

"No. Coffee. Weird, isn't it?"

Jonty fled upstairs, went into the cleaning supply cupboard and found a tiny plastic bag that he could put the *ear plugs* in and left them by the side of Ravi's bed. He'd just returned to the front desk when Vincent reappeared.

"A guest in the hot tub has placed a drinks order." He handed Jonty a slip of paper. "I'll take over here and you deal with it."

Jonty went to the bar in the lounge, currently manned by Sophia. There were a lot of people in there and a group of young men congregating around the bar, so Jonty decided he'd handle the order himself. *Bottle of Laurent Perrier. Four glasses. A mojito.* The champagne was no problem, but he had to guess at how to make the mojito without his phone to give him the quantities of the ingredients.

He made more than he needed to in the cocktail shaker and taste-tested it a few times before he decided it was fine, just minty enough. With everything loaded onto a tray, including plastic glasses, he went downstairs, and out through the back of the pool area onto the terrace. Ravi was in the bubbling hot tub with four women.

"Ah our drinks," Ravi said. "What took you so long? We're dying of thirst here."

"Sorry." Jonty smiled. Sorry cost him nothing. "Would you like me to pour?"

"Go ahead."

Jonty opened the champagne, shivered as a blast of cold wind came straight off the sea. "Who wants the mojito?" he asked.

"That's for me." Ravi held out his hand.

Jonty distributed the champagne first. All of the women were young. He wasn't sure that a couple of them were old enough to drink, but Ravi wasn't going to be ravishing them.

Jonty wondered if they knew he was gay. It seemed obvious to him but…

He handed Ravi his mojito.

"Wait while I taste it." Ravi sipped through the straw and screwed up his face. "What did you put in this?"

"Limes, mint, sugar, ice, rum, soda water." *And I wish I'd spat in it.*

"Not enough mint. Go and make me another."

"Of course, sir." Jonty went back to the bar, muttering under his breath.

While he was unobserved on the stairs, he pushed the straw aside and drank from the glass. It was plenty minty enough. Before he reached the bar, he'd drunk the rest. No point wasting it. It was delicious. He made another cocktail, doubled the amount of mint, smashed it all together, topped it with a sprig of mint and took it back.

The women had gone and Ravi was alone in the tub. As Jonty bent to hand him the drink, Ravi looked straight at him and yanked hard at his arm. No amount of flailing could stop Jonty falling head first into the water. He hit his head as he went under, swallowed water and thrashed around as he panicked. It took a moment before he could find his footing and stand up. Ravi sat on the side, holding his nose, blood all over his fingers.

"What the fuck?" Jonty glared at him. "Why did you pull me in?"

"What are you talking about? You slipped, you clumsy twat. If you've broken my nose, I'll fucking sue the arse off you and this hotel. You won't have a job by the end of the day. None of you will by the end of the year."

"What?"

"Shit! My nose. Get me a towel."

Jonty stepped out of the hot tub and shivered. He was dripping water everywhere. His suit was ruined. So were his shoes probably. *Fucking hell!* He glanced around to see if anyone had seen what Ravi had done, but there was no one nearby. He picked up a towel from a lounger and dropped it at the edge of the tub.

"Did Devan talk about me?" Ravi asked.

Jonty didn't even try to avoid the question. "Yes, while he was listing the five things he hates most in the world. You came between boiled cabbage and maggots."

Jonty squelched away and grabbed a towel for himself. He stood by the door back into the hotel, getting colder and colder as he waited for the water to drain from his clothes so he wouldn't trail it all over the building. What had Ravi meant about none of them having jobs by the end of the year?

He was too cold to stand still for long. He made straight for the staffroom and his locker and was down to his wet boxers when Vincent came in.

"What the hell, Jonty?"

"A guest pulled me into the hot tub." Jonty wrapped the towel around his waist and struggled out of his last item of clothing.

"He says you fell in as you punched him. You broke his nose. What were you thinking? He's a top model and he's furious, talking about suing us, going to the press and putting it all over social media."

Jonty touched his head. What he'd thought was water dripping from his hair was blood. "I didn't punch him. As I handed him the drink, he pulled me and the mojito in, my head hit the step under the water and as I panicked, some part of me must have collided with his nose. I didn't do it deliberately. Why would I?"

"He has a witness that said you did."

Jonty's heart sank. "I didn't. And there was no one around."

"Let me check your head." Vincent grabbed a handful of paper towels and dabbed at Jonty's wound. "Keep the pressure on. It doesn't look bad. More a graze than a cut. Get dressed. Warm up. Put your own clothes on. I think it would be better if you were out of the hotel."

"Are you sacking me?" Jonty bit his lip.

"A guest claims you hit him. Another guest has backed him up."

"It was an accident," Jonty whispered. "You believe me, don't you?"

"You've broken the rule about associating with guests. You've assaulted a guest who is well within his rights to call the police. Is it a coincidence that the two guests are acquainted? I don't believe so. Go and ask the major if he wants Dottie walking while I'll consider this further."

Vincent didn't believe him. The pain of that forced Jonty to sit down. Vincent walked away and Jonty slumped on a bench with paper towels pressed against his head, his eyes squeezed tight shut. How could Vincent not believe him?

Because guests were always right. Except everyone, including Vincent, knew that wasn't true. Some guests might *think* they were right and that was sort of okay if they'd made a genuine mistake, but there were a bunch, including the whale trip duo, who knew they weren't right. What the words really meant was that it was better to assume customers were always right and let them have what they wanted, rather than lose them as customers. So who was more valuable? Jonty or Ravi? Who could cause the most problems?

Ravi.

Fucking Ravi! What a dickhead. Jonty regretted the marshmallows now. Almost.

Was Vincent going to sack him? Jonty gulped. He might have no choice. Jonty was still thinking about that comment about no one having a job by the end of the year. The hotel wouldn't shut down if Jonty was found guilty of assaulting a guest. Would it?

He checked his head and it had stopped bleeding, so he got dressed. No dry underwear so he had to go commando. Luckily, he had a spare pair of socks. He pulled on a beanie, zipped up his jacket and made his way to the major's room.

The major answered after one knock. "Hello, Jonty."

"Vincent asked me to ask you if you'd like me to walk Dottie."

"Are you okay?" The major frowned. "You're a bit pale."

"I took a nosedive into the hot tub with my clothes on. Banged my head. Managed to accidentally give a guest a nosebleed."

"Never a dull day for you, young man." He turned and called, "Dottie! Walk."

Dottie came running up. The major lifted her lead from a hook next to the door, clipped one end onto Dottie's collar and handed the other to Jonty. "There are three bags wrapped around the handle, just in case."

"Thanks."

"How did you manage to fall into the hot tub?"

"The guest pulled me in, though that's not what he claims."

"Ah. Are you in trouble?"

Jonty made himself smile. "I'm always in trouble, but maybe more trouble than usual this time."

The major smiled. "You remind me of me when I was your age."

Jonty raised his eyebrows. "As bad as that?"

He laughed, then sighed. "By the way, Jonty… That guest in Wave you had an issue with when he checked in…"

Jonty's heart did a complicated thumpity-thump-trip-thump. "Yes?"

The major checked up and down the corridor. "You mustn't tell anyone what I'm going to tell you, right? Confidential." He tapped his nose twice.

"Okay."

"Hamish is proposing to sell the hotel."

Jonty sucked in a breath. "To Devan Smith?"

"To the company he works for. I'm going to have to move out. As are all the permanent residents. I think it's very likely you'll be out of a job. They want to do extensive renovations. Hamish is going to tell the staff once a price has been agreed, but I wanted to give you a heads-up. I'm very fond of you, Jonty. You're a kind-hearted young man and you've made my days cheery. I thought if you knew a few days in advance, it might give you the chance to find a job in another hotel before the others start looking."

"Thank you." He swallowed hard.

Jonty wasn't sure how he managed to get out of the hotel without breaking down and sobbing. When was Devan planning to tell him? Today, tomorrow, sometime, never? It started to rain and Jonty pulled up his hood over the beanie.

"Okay with the rain, Dottie?"

The dachshund looked up at him and wagged her tail.

As they made their way across the car park, Devan's noisy Aston Martin drew up and the window slid down.

"So you're still alive?" Devan said. "I've been worried about you. Why didn't you answer any of my calls or texts?"

Jonty so nearly yelled at him, but managed to rein himself in. "Because my phone has either been swallowed by a sand dune, probably by a giant scary worm, or it's in your car."

Devan gaped at him. "What? Let me park and I'll check."

Moments later, he got out of the car and handed Jonty the phone. "It had slipped under the front passenger seat."

"Thank you." Jonty took it from him.

Ask him what the fuck he's been playing at.

Shut up, Tay. He might tell me. Please let him tell me. Jonty found it hard to remember when he'd felt as disappointed. Why hadn't Devan told him the truth about why he'd come up here?

"I didn't think you were working until tonight."

"Someone's sick."

"There will be a number of increasingly desperate messages on your phone," Devan said.

"Oh good, I've been waiting for a call from Matt Bomer. Hope he wasn't too pissed off I didn't answer." Jonty was trying to be normal, but it took a lot of effort. How long was he supposed to wait for Devan to tell him about the hotel?

"Are you taking Dottie for a walk?"

"We're going on a dinosaur hunt. She has an amazing sense of smell." *Stop being sarcastic.*

"Can I come?"

He should have said *no, I need to worry about whether I've lost my job and if you're a complete arsehole among a whole lot of other stuff,* but "If you like," came out of his mouth.

Devan pulled on his jacket and locked his car. They headed down onto the sand. Sheets of grey rain swept across an almost deserted beach. The tide was in and lace-fringed waves rolled onto the shore. Jonty let Dottie off the lead. She raced away, but she wouldn't go too far and definitely not into the water.

"Delete the messages," Devan said.

Be normal! "You have to be kidding. I'll play them right now. I hope there are a few dick pics too." He scrolled to the first one.

"I'm sorry. I came back. Call me."

"I drove four miles," Devan said. "Four miles too many."

Jonty forced a smile onto his face.

Hi, it's me. The me you were going to introduce to the fourth wonder of Northumberland. The me who can't wait to marvel at it

223

and all the other wonders. As soon as I've spoken to Ravi and found out what he wants, I'll come back. I did come back before, but you weren't there. If I wasn't anxious that something bad had happened to bring Ravi up here, I wouldn't have left. I should have brought you with me. I'm sorry I didn't. See you soon. There's something I need to tell you.

"Still no dick pic?"

"I'm an idiot." Devan reached for Jonty's fingers and held onto his hand.

Jonty pulled away. Was there anything Devan could say that would put this right? Anything that would let Jonty hope, when hope seemed pointless?

Jonty please let me know you're all right.

Call me.

Where the fuck are you? I'm sitting outside your place. It's eleven at night and your bike isn't there.

I don't want Ravi. I want you. Please be okay.

"I felt more desperate than I sound," Devan said. "I also got attacked by a woman this morning. Getting hit with a handbag hurts and she tried to sic her dog on me. That didn't work."

"What were you doing?"

"Looking through your letterbox."

"I'm guessing that was Miriam and Snoopy. You were in no danger. Snoopy's so lazy he drinks from his water bowl without getting up off the floor." Jonty chuckled. "Now there's no battery's left. I'm so disappointed. I assume the dick pics are at the end as an incentive to call you." *Tell me what you're doing up here!*

"I'm really sorry. I should never have left you."

"I wish you hadn't. Brad put a snake through my letterbox."

"He what?"

As they walked along the beach, Jonty ran through what had happened and how he'd moved out to stay with Mike and Willis until he found a new place.

"You sure it was Brad?"

"Yep."

"The police will do something now, surely."

"They went to see him, but I don't know what he told them. That's not all though. There was a bit of an incident at the hotel." *The major told me what you're really doing up here.* "I met Ravi." *He told me too, in his way.*

Jonty could almost taste the tension pouring off Devan. He wished Devan could sense the grief pouring off him.

"Whatever he said was a lie," Devan said.

You're the biggest liar. "Really? He said you were the most honest guy he'd ever met, the most fantastic lover, the most gorgeous, the most skilled with his tongue, the most talented with his dick, the most—"

"I think that's enough. He wouldn't have said any of that."

"He wouldn't? That's a bit of a disappointment. So why did he come up here?"

"He had a Dior shoot at The Angel of the North. The business I came here to do was supposed to have been done by my brother."

Jonty's lungs locked for a moment. Was Devan going to tell him?

"He and Ravi had planned a few days here together."

Jonty frowned. "But Ravi knew Griff hadn't come up, so why did he still come to the hotel?"

"To beg me to reconsider being Griff's best man and ask if maybe I'd like to fuck him for old time's sake."

Jonty gasped. "Bloody hell."

"Thank you for not saying *Did you?* I wished I didn't have to say that I wouldn't touch him with a pole of any description, but I do need to tell you that. Ravi and I are done. I can't tell Griff what he said, but I did tell my other brother who will tell our mother. She might believe it. Maybe it will filter back to Griff. But I don't even care and it's likely that Griff won't believe it anyway."

"Ravi asked me for the key to your room. He said he'd accidentally locked himself out. I said no because he might be a vampire."

"Out in daylight?"

"Do you know nothing? Vampires have mastered the ability to walk in the sun."

Devan laughed.

"But I'm pretty sure he overheard me telling my boss that I thought I might have left my phone in your car because Ravi then went on the attack. He complained about the mojito I made him, but there was nothing wrong with it. When I brought him another, he yanked me into the hot tub. He's wrecked my only suit. Maybe my shoes. I somehow clonked him on the nose when I fell in and made it bleed. He's saying I thumped him. I didn't."

"I thought you were going to kick him in the arse."

"I'm full of talk. So is Ravi. He's talking about suing me and the hotel. When he realises the ear plugs I left in his room are actually mini marshmallows, I think I'm doomed."

"Oh God. I don't know whether I dare laugh."

"Vincent sent me out of the way to walk Dottie. I don't think he believes I didn't thump Ravi. Another guest is backing Ravi's version. I'm pretty sure I'm going to get the sack."

"I'll talk to Vincent, tell him what Ravi's like."

I give up. You're not going to tell me. The disappointment was crippling. Jonty's stomach churned. He took a deep breath. "Do you need to bother? I'm not going to have a job soon anyway, am I?"

226

Devan stopped walking and stared straight at him. Jonty watched it gradually dawn on Devan that he knew exactly why he was in Northumberland.

"Were you going to *fuck* me, then *fuck* off, and let me find out what a real *fucker* you are?" Jonty clenched his fingers around Dottie's lead.

"What did Ravi say?"

"That I'd be out of a job by the end of the day and all of us would be by Christmas. I might have dismissed that as spiteful bluster, but Major Bagshott told me Hamish wants to sell the hotel to the group you work for. He said it was a secret, but because he likes me, he wanted me to know early so that I could look for a job before the others. That was really nice of him. The sort of thing a friend would do." *The sort of thing you should have done.* "Though I don't think the major was thinking I'd need a new job today."

Devan groaned. "McAllister swore me to secrecy. No deal has been agreed, but he wanted it kept quiet, because he preferred to let the staff know himself. Once he'd agreed in principle to sell, I wasn't going to keep you in the dark. I was going to tell you last night."

"Before or after I'd shown you the fourth wonder of Northumberland?" Jonty didn't try to keep the bitterness out of his voice and started walking again. Dottie was sniffing seaweed a little way ahead and jumping away from it before going back for another sniff. *No sense, just like me.*

"Jonty! I was. I swear. I've been working on a way to keep you employed if the deal is made."

"Me and no one else?"

"I want to keep Marcus, the head chef. Possibly Wayne. But I can't pay the staff to hang around until the hotel reopens. Anyone who's been working here longer than two years will be entitled to redundancy pay. I might be able to find some of them work in our other hotels."

"But not around here."

"No."

Jonty kicked at the sand. "I thought you were here for a break because of your brother and Ravi, and all the time, you've been planning to destroy us, destroy this." He gestured at the beach. "Because you know what the price will be for modernisation. More traffic, more visitors. Northumberland's secret will be out."

"This will be an exclusive resort. Fewer rooms, not more."

"So you can't stay here unless you're rich enough? Great." Jonty kicked again at the sand.

"There are plenty of other places for people to stay. The hotel needs updating. We have the money to do it. This is a special place and we'd like to keep it special. I want you to work for me…with me. I can arrange for you to learn more about the hospitality business. If a deal is agreed, I'll rent a place to stay up here. I'd like to be more hands on with this development than I usually am. You could live with me."

Jonty sucked in a breath.

"Too fast?" Devan asked.

Yes, but no.

"Shit. It *is* too fast, but I think this is the start of something special and I don't want it to end."

But if a deal wasn't agreed? Jonty's poor heart kept swapping places with his stomach. Did Devan just expect him to forgive him for his deceit, for leaving him to go to Ravi?

"I'm pissed off," Jonty muttered.

"I'd noticed. I'm sorry. I'm sorry I left you yesterday. I'm sorry I couldn't tell you about the hotel before you learned from someone else. I would have told you last night. I swear."

"Before or after you'd fucked me?"

"Ah shit." Devan sighed. "I'm not looking good, am I?"

"You look too good." *That's my problem.*

228

"That's not all I wanted to tell you. I have a friend who's a private investigator. I asked Stan to look for your father."

Jonty jolted. "What the hell?"

"I guess I jumped the gun there too. But I wanted to make something right in your life. I know you don't want to see your father, but he might know where your mother is. Anyway, Stan found him. He lives in Berwick. I have an address and phone number."

Dottie jumped up at Jonty as if she understood his turmoil. Jonty picked her up and cuddled her. How easy it was to be a dog. No need to be worried about anything more than when your next meal would arrive. A walk, a ball to chase, a piece of grass to sniff, an occasional stroke or tummy tickle, a quick fuck…all enough to make you happy. Jonty had been happy—in his way. Devan had turned his world upside down.

About time.

Is it?

Yes. Don't wreck this.

"I won't let Vincent sack you. I'm going to find somewhere for us to live. Whether the deal goes through or not, I'm staying up here for a month."

There was the answer to one of Jonty's questions.

"Whether the deal goes through or not, I want you in my life. Give me a chance. Give *us* a chance. You've made me smile again. I don't want to let you go."

Jonty pressed his face into Dottie's soft fur.

Give him a chance.

Take a risk.

You know there's something special between you.

"What's going through your mind?" Devan whispered.

"I'm wondering if you're going to break my heart."

"If you don't give me another chance, you're going to break mine."

229

Chapter Fourteen

Devan blinked rain from his eyes as he stared at Jonty. This was too fast. He was an idiot for thinking Jonty would want to move in with him. An idiot to look for his father without asking him. He'd let Jonty down so badly. *If he asked me to walk away from this deal… If the choice was between him and the hotel… Oh God. How the fuck am I even considering that?*

"Do you like dogs?" Jonty asked.

Er… Jonty's change of direction threw him for a moment. "Yes, if they're not stopping me kissing you. They do seem to make a habit of that."

Devan thought Jonty might put the dog down, but he didn't. He carried on walking, though he was smiling.

"Tell me what you hate," Jonty said.

Was this Jonty's way of forgiving him? Offering giving him another chance?

"Snakes, particularly ones that live in sand dunes, my ex, chewing gum stuck to my shoe, my ex, popcorn, new year resolutions, fizzy water that's lost its fizz, did I mention my ex? Pistachios that won't open, beards, having my hair cut, filing my nails, having to drink wine I don't like, wasps bothering me, flies even when they're not bothering me, sitting in heavy traffic in London, vultures, drama queens, cashews, people who hum for no reason, reality TV, noisy pens, paper cuts, football, TV soaps. I better stop there."

"You were just getting going."

"I'm not sure that *hate* is the right word. It's too strong."

"Unless we're talking about snakes that live in sand dunes and your ex."

"Goes without saying." The weight on Devan's heart began to lift. He hadn't added Griff to that list. Maybe that indicated there was hope. Everyone makes mistakes in their life. The last thing that remains was family. Devan didn't want his family broken.

"What do you love?" Jonty put Dottie down and the dog ran on ahead.

"I love listening to music turned up loud, but I like reading in silence. I love skiing in fresh snow, looking at the stars, mist in the morning, sunshine at any time, my family — mostly, unusual *how to* books, the beauty of mathematics, crisp smoky bacon, trees, unexpected things happening, riding on the beach, the realisation that something was worth the wait, second chances, Cadbury's Flakes, you making me smile, you holding my hand." *Maybe just you, and your mixed-up crazy life that I find myself wanting to be part of.*

"What do you think I hate?" Jonty asked.

Devan didn't hesitate. "Rude hotel guests, being interrupted when you're eating a Flake, your stalker, your father, snakes, sharks, being accused of something you didn't do, promises being broken, hospitals, people being sad, people letting you down, dogs that interrupt kisses, unfinished business."

Jonty gaped at him.

"I don't think there's a whole lot that you hate," Devan said. "You're not that type of guy. There's a whole lot more that you love. Northumberland with all its secrets and amazing scenery, Cadbury's Flakes, surfing, fish and chips, cooking, your job, riding on the beach, running down the dunes, doing crazy things, changing the subject, your friend Tay, collecting sea glass and turning it into something even more incredible, sunshine, making people smile, pictures of big dicks. Damn, I forgot to add that to mine."

Jonty chuckled and even in the driving rain, Devan felt the warmth of relief seeping through him.

"I came up here for two reasons. To escape from my brother's joy and the pain that caused me, and to look for a hotel to buy. Now I have a far more important reason to be here because you've shown me that second chances exist. Please…" He took a deep breath. "This is all wrong and yet at the same time, it's completely right. I've never felt more sure of anything in my life. Spend a month with me and we'll see if this is going to go where I hope it's going to go. If you ask me to tell Hamish I'm no longer interested in buying, I will. I still want that month."

Jonty glanced at him, his dark eyes wide. "You'd do that?"

"Yes." *Alan will kill me, but yes.* He wasn't going to let this chance slip through his fingers. He nearly had.

Jonty picked up a piece of driftwood and threw it for Dottie, who ignored it. He knew she would. He needed a moment to think. "Now the idea is in Hamish's head, he could sell to someone else. I'm not really surprised about him wanting to sell. If I had the money, I'd make this place as spectacular as the view."

"If the price isn't right, he won't sell and we won't buy."

"And you'd really still want your month?"

"Yes."

"You want to take that chance?"

"Yes. What's the worst that can happen?"

"I might be hopeless in bed."

Devan laughed.

"*You* might be hopeless in bed." Jonty grinned.

Devan laughed harder.

"We might run out of lube and condoms."

"I'll bulk buy."

"I've waited so long to find a guy who's into pony play." Jonty gave a sly grin. "The saddle will fit you, though I'm not sure about the hooves or the head gear. Never mind, we can always go with Daddy play."

"Oh, are you still talking?"

Jonty slid his hand into Devan's. "Let's head back now. Dottie's a bit bedraggled. Come on, Dottie. Home! Oh, home for now anyway."

"Those who live in the hotel aren't just going to get tossed out."

"Are you going to help them find somewhere?"

"I'll do what I can. There's an organisation called *Helper* that provides live-in care by putting active people into the homes of older, less active ones. The older ones get the level of support they need without it being overwhelming. I wondered if those from the hotel could live together in a couple of houses, with a support worker in one of the bedrooms? That person could still work in another job, as long as they were there to help with meals, cleaning, laundry and provide company."

"Like a very small care home?"

"Yes, sort of, but with no medical help, just domestic and social. Like living with your grandparents. Major Bagshott seems fit and well. He enjoys the comfort and convenience of having his meals provided, his room cleaned, his laundry done, and he has company when he needs it. I don't know if he gets on with the other residents, but he wouldn't even need to see that much of them. Well, it's just an idea."

"Who'd buy the houses?"

"They could be rented. Maybe my company could buy them. I don't know. I haven't thought through all the details. Assuming we do buy the hotel, we won't start work on it until after Christmas. There's plenty of time to sort things out for residents and for staff to find other jobs."

"Off-season's not a good time of year to be looking."

"I know, but I suspect once Hamish announces the sale, the staff will gradually leave and temporary staff will be brought in to cover reservations until the building work starts."

"Right."

"When do you get off work?"

"Tomorrow morning. Assuming I still have a job. I don't think I do."

"You're not going to get sacked. I won't let it happen." He squeezed Jonty's fingers.

"Hmm. You don't own the place yet."

"Do you want to talk about your father?" Devan asked.

"Living thirty minutes away from here?" Jonty huffed a laugh. "I thought he'd have moved back to Surrey. Did your investigator find out anything about him? If he was married? Does he have kids?"

"A partner. No kids. He's also sick."

"What sort of sick?"

"Terminal cancer."

"Oh… I guess the sooner I see him the better, then."

"I could drive you to Berwick tomorrow."

"What a fun day that sounds."

Devan slung his arm over Jonty's shoulders and gave him a hug. "I'll find something fun to do afterwards."

"As long as it has nothing to do with the beauty of maths." Jonty sucked in a breath. "Well, unless it's timing how long it takes you to come and how many times you can come in the space of one hour."

"Hmm. Do you *want* to go and see your father tomorrow? I feel like I bulldozed you into it."

"If seeing him is the way I might get to find my mother and my sister, then yes. And I mean, we can't fuck *all* day, can we? Well, I could, but you're getting on a bit."

Devan took out his phone. "I'll call him now, shall I?"

Jonty nodded.

A woman answered. "Hello?"

"Could I speak to Mr Bloom, please?"

"Who shall I say is calling?"

234

"My name's Devan Smith. He doesn't know me. It's a private matter."

Devan winced. He needed to be careful. Whoever the woman was, she might not know about Jonty. He didn't want to cause problems that might stop Jonty's father agreeing to see him.

"Hello?" a man croaked.

"Mr. Bloom?"

"What do you want?"

"Jonty would like to see you."

Jonty clutched Devan's sleeve.

"Would he?" Jonty's father muttered.

"Tomorrow okay?"

"I'm not going anywhere."

The call ended abruptly and Devan huffed.

"Let me guess," Jonty said. "He was thrilled to know I wanted to see him. He can't wait to see me. Right?"

The guy hadn't even asked Devan if he knew his address. Devan had the uncomfortable feeling he'd made a mistake.

When they walked back into the hotel with Dottie, Ravi was standing in reception talking to Vincent. Jonty swore under his breath and Devan sighed.

"Jonty, take Dottie to the major," Vincent said.

Jonty picked up the dog and headed for the stairs.

"I want him sacked," Ravi snapped.

"I want you gone," Devan snapped back.

"Would you both please come into the office." Vincent beckoned them.

Devan took off his wet jacket.

"Do you know what that jumped up little shit did?" Ravi demanded as Devan pushed the door closed. "Look at my nose!"

235

"It's no bigger than it usually is." Devan had chosen his words carefully and saw from the expression on Ravi's face that he'd hit his target.

"Yes. It. Is." Ravi glared at him.

Ravi had often talked about having a nose-job because he thought his nose was too large, but he didn't want to lose income by not being able to work for the several months it took to heal, so he'd moaned a lot, but never done anything about it.

"It's fine," Devan said.

"Are you blind?" Ravi gasped. "It's probably broken."

"Then why aren't you at a hospital?"

"I want the idiot who did it punished. It hurts." Ravi gingerly touched his nose. "I want him sacked."

"Not going to happen." Devan shrugged. "You pulled him into the hot tub."

Ravi widened his eyes. "You believe him over me? We've known each other for over two years and you've known him less than a week."

"Amazing, isn't it?" Devan stared straight at him.

"Let's see if we can settle this amicably," Vincent said.

"Sack him." Ravi's lips quirked in a semi-smile. "Or I'll call the police and open my mouth. You don't want that, do you?"

Devan knew exactly what Ravi was threatening to do. Open his mouth about the hotel sale. *You are such a fucking bastard.* Devan felt as if he'd never known Ravi at all.

"Look," Vincent said. "I'm very sorry about what happened. I've not been able to speak to the guest who you say saw what happened. She's checked out. But I find it difficult to understand why Jonty would want to hit you and why he'd risk falling into the hot tub. He has one suit. It's ruined. His shoes too. He cut his head. Why would he punch you on the nose? Jonty's not a violent person. I don't think I've ever seen him lose his temper. He probably slipped."

"He cut his head?" Devan swallowed.

"Not badly," Vincent said. "It bled a lot, but head wounds do."

"Nowhere near as bad as my nose. He was pissed off because the first mojito he made me was undrinkable and I made him go and make me another. He was also angry with me because Devan and I are close. He's jealous and lashed out."

"Ravi." Devan gritted his teeth in exasperation. "You're embarrassing yourself. Go home."

"I'm booked in here tonight and tomorrow."

"We'll refund the whole of your stay," Vincent said quickly.

"Sack him or this will be all over Twitter and Instagram. I have more than a million followers."

"And I'll upload my version of events," Devan said. Though he had an account on neither. "You won't look good."

The door swung open and Jonty stood there. Devan wondered how much he'd heard.

Jonty looked from Devan to Vincent. "I resign."

Ravi had the nerve to smile. He nudged Devan. "Drive me to Newcastle."

"No." Devan didn't take his eyes off Jonty.

"Please." Ravi wrapped his hand around Devan's wrist.

Devan shook it off. "No. You got an Uber here. Get an Uber back."

"You'll be fucking sorry." Ravi stamped out of the room, shoving Jonty aside as he went.

"I think it's for the best," Vincent said. "We can't afford the bad publicity this would bring."

"But—" Devan shut up when Jonty nudged him.

237

"Bye, Vincent." Jonty walked out and Devan followed him.

"Let me look at your head."

Jonty touched the place where he'd collided with the step.

"Do you have a headache?"

"No."

"Did you lose consciousness?"

"No. I'm fine."

"I'd like to kill him."

Jonty smiled. "It's enough that he's on your *hate* list. More than once."

"Right. We have things to do. Come on." He set off toward his car. When Jonty didn't go with him, he turned.

"I need my backpack and my bike's here."

"Get the bag, leave the bike. Maybe Mike will collect it for you. Meet me back here in a couple of minutes." Devan raced up the stairs to the suite. He packed up all his stuff, double checked he'd not missed anything and came back down with his luggage.

"Are you checking out?" Jonty asked.

"No, in case we can't find anywhere to stay tonight and I have to sneak you in."

"Ooh, I could wear a disguise."

"Saddle and hooves?"

Jonty barked out a laugh. Devan pulled his jacket back on, then they hurried through the rain across to the car and climbed in.

"What things do we have to do?" Jonty asked.

"Buy you a suit and shoes for work."

"But—"

"I'm going to smooth things over with Vincent. I want to find somewhere I can rent for a month that you'll like as much as me, that you'll share with me, preferably somewhere that's available now."

"Is that all?"

Devan frowned. "Have I forgotten something?"

Jonty leaned over and kissed him. Hard. When Jonty pulled back, Devan smiled.

"Oh yeah," Devan said. "I need to buy a big pack of Flakes."

"So what's first?"

"Look on the internet for a place to rent as I'm driving. If we have to go to a rental agency, we're running out of time today." Devan pulled out of the car park. "I'm going to call Hamish and warn him about Ravi."

"Okay. Can I charge my phone?"

"Yep. Do you have a charger?"

"In my pocket."

Devan made the voice activated call.

"Mr Smith," Hamish said. "What can I do for you?"

"Just giving you a heads-up that news you might sell could come out sooner than you'd hoped. There's been an incident at the hotel between my ex-fiancé and Jonty. Not Jonty's fault in the slightest but Ravi Mohnish, my ex, knows why I'm up here and might decide to cause trouble."

"I didn't want to say anything until we'd agreed a price."

"I know."

McAllister huffed. "I'll arrange to talk to the staff on Sunday morning."

"I'll try to have an offer in place by then. Two of my people will be here tomorrow. I'll come in on Sunday morning. I want to speak to Marcus about his future."

"Eleven o'clock. I hope you're going to make me an acceptable offer or all this will have done is unsettle my workforce."

The call disconnected.

"Do you think you'll be able to make an acceptable offer?" Jonty asked.

"Depends on whether McAllister has an inflated idea of how much the hotel is worth. While I'm driving, use my phone to search for a rental property. Yours will charge faster if you're not using it. Somewhere close to the beach. And isolated."

"Good idea. I don't want anyone to hear you screaming."

Devan laughed so hard he had a coughing fit.

"You do realise I'm taking that as a challenge," Jonty said. "So furnished, yeh?"

"Probably easier, though we could use your stuff."

"Most places are going to be furnished. What price range? Do you want me to try Airbnb?" Jonty hissed and made the sign of the cross with his fingers.

"I'd prefer not to use them, but look just in case. A lightning bolt next to the entry means it's immediately available."

"I guess Airbnb has put most hotels under pressure."

"It's an unfair market. It's particularly hard for hotels to fill key dates and weekends. Airbnb fills up first before the public turns to us. It's annoying that we have to conform to all sort of checks and regulations while a house can just be let out. We pay twenty percent VAT, have high business rates and heavy overheads, while people who let out their homes don't have those to deal with. The upsurge of Airbnb will have affected McAllister's too."

"So how do you compete?"

"In our corner of the market, people are looking for experiences. They want more than a room. They want to be a local for the time that they're in the area and cookie-cutter hotels don't give them that. We need to offer something different. We're known for excellent service, a high level of cleanliness, top class security, first class comfort and ease of use. A pool is important, as is a spa and gym. Room service has to be exceptional. Expert knowledge on the local area is essential."

"Local BDSM clubs and things like that?"

"That's not as farfetched as you might think."

"Oh God. Okay. I'll try agencies first. What's the budget?"

"A thousand a week? More, if the place is really special."

Now Jonty was the one choking. "I hope you're not thinking we can go halves because I've been paying eighty pounds a week for my place. Roughly eleven pounds a day as opposed to…a hundred and forty-three between the two of us. Seventy-two each."

"So you do see the beauty of maths."

"When you're continually stretching your wages—yes and I no longer have a job."

"I'll pay. See what you can find."

Jonty kept giving long and heavy sighs, which Devan took to mean he wasn't having much luck, and punctuated the journey with random comments.

"Who the hell would buy curtains that colour? They'd give me a headache."

"Couch isn't washable. That's not going to work."

"TV is too small. Watching porn wouldn't be anywhere near as much fun."

"Bed is too small. Though, since I'd be sleeping on top of you…"

"A vomit-green kitchen with no room to swing a dick."

"Not enough room for two people in the shower. How would you wash my important bits?"

"Bloody liars. The beach is not a hop, skip and a jump away, even if you're a rabbit."

"A bus stops right outside the door. People would get an eyeful of your arse. Though you might be into that."

"Next to a tattoo parlour. If we got drunk, it might prove too tempting."

Jonty groaned. "I'm being too picky, aren't I? But no compromising over the TV, right? Big is better. Always. Unless it's too big. Then it's not better."

"What search terms are you using?"

"Isolated beach-front, short-term rental property with heated outdoor pool, lazy river, hot tub, and stabling for one large and sometimes cantankerous horse. There's a surprising lack of properties in that price range."

Devan chuckled as he pulled into a car park in the centre of Alnwick. The rain had stopped falling. "Keep looking. I'll go and pay for parking."

When Devan got back in the car, Jonty handed him his phone. "I think I might have found somewhere."

Devan checked it out. A two-bedroom property at Shennan Sands, between Seahouses and Bamburgh.

"What's Shennan Sands like?"

"Quiet. No shop, no pub, no church. An isolated, unspoiled gem. Superb beach. For once, the online description is pretty accurate."

The two-storey property was right on the beach, one of a handful of dwellings dotted along that stretch of coastline, all accessed by a single-track road.

He scrolled through the pictures. "No pool. No lazy river. No stable. Bad luck. Otherwise it's perfect. Sea view from upstairs and downstairs. I'll give the agent a call." Devan tapped in the number and put the mobile on speakerphone.

"Good afternoon. Ganstone Lettings. Kristan speaking. How can I help you?"

"Hi. My name's Devan Smith. I'm interested in renting the two-bed property at Shennan Sands. One thousand four hundred a week. Is it currently available?"

"It is, but how long would you want to rent it for? The shortest period is one month."

"That would be perfect."

"Great. Are you in the area? Can you come to the office?"

"We're about ten minutes away."

"See you soon."

Jonty unplugged his phone, slotted it into his pocket, and they set off on foot.

Thirty minutes later, Devan had signed the agreement, proved who he was, handed over his credit card, and now had the keys to the property in his pocket along with the address. He checked the time. "Where can we buy you a suit?"

Jonty widened his eyes. "We?"

"It's my fault Ravi ruined yours."

"I'm not going to let you pay—and why do I need a suit?"

"Because you look hot in one."

"I'm going to pay," Jonty croaked.

Devan knew when to step back. Flaunting his wealth in front of Jonty was not going to impress him. Jonty was the opposite of Ravi, who loved Devan to spend money on him. Jonty led him to a small men's clothing shop. The bell rang when they went inside.

A guy younger than Jonty with a mop of curly hair and a lot of freckles smiled at them from behind the counter. "Can I help you?"

"I need a suit," Jonty said. "Pink or purple."

Devan laughed. The sales assistant gawped.

"He's colour-blind. Blue or grey," Devan said.

There was a choice of four in Jonty's size, which was quickly whittled down to one. Pale grey and Jonty looked so hot in it, even with his T-shirt underneath the jacket, that the breath caught in Devan's throat and his cock perked up.

"Does my bum look big in this?" Jonty asked.

"No."

"Damn."

Devan spotted the assistant smiling.

"Is it washable?" Jonty asked.

"Wa…wa…no." The assistant's smile had gone.

Jonty turned to Devan and pouted. "We'll have to spot clean the blood out of it then. Sorry, master."

"That will be your job," Devan said.

Jonty inclined his head. "Of course."

They walked out less than fifteen minutes after they'd walked in, with a hundred-and twenty-pound suit and a thirty-pound pair of black shoes that Jonty had wrangled down from thirty-five, because there was a scuff on the heel, though Devan thought the assistant was desperate to get rid of them. Devan would have laughed if anyone had suggested he look for a suit or shoes that cost so little, laughed even harder at the idea of bargaining. This was a reminder of how fortunate he was. If he'd been shopping for a suit with Ravi, not that Ravi would have set foot in a shop that didn't sell designer gear, they'd have been hours while Ravi made up his mind. Devan had hated shopping with him. With Jonty, it had been fun.

"I saw the way you looked at me in that suit," Jonty said.

"Like I wanted to eat you?"

Jonty widened his eyes. "No. Like you wished they had one in your size."

"You looked so sexy, I had a hard time not giving the guy fifty quid to lock us in the shop for fifteen minutes."

"Fifty quid? He'd have locked us in and watched for that. Though not after I'd mentioned the blood. But fifteen minutes is a bit disappointing."

"Hmm," Devan said. "I bet if I wrapped my hand around your cock, you'd come within three minutes."

Jonty stared at him and Devan could have sworn his eyes darkened. "Do it now."

"We're in the middle of Alnwick."

"No one will notice." Jonty smirked.

"Let's go back to the car," Devan croaked out.

"You want to do it in the car park?"

"Yes, but that's not going to happen. I'm not going to do anything that risks either of us getting arrested. I have plans for later. We need to buy food."

"This house has lots of board games. I saw them piled up in one of the pictures. We're not going to be short of something to do."

"Right."

"And my favourite TV programme is on tonight."

"What's that?"

"*Naked and Afraid.*"

"Don't they pixel out all the good bits?"

"Not backsides." Jonty grinned.

Buying the food was fun too, though Jonty had a bit of freak out when they'd walked in, because he thought he'd seen Brad. Devan kept his eyes peeled, but there was no sign of the guy. Even so, it was a reminder that they needed to be careful.

"This…and this…and these," Jonty said.

Devan had to keep taking out stuff that Jonty put in the trolley.

"We don't need three large bags of garlic," Devan said.

"But what about vampires?"

"I'll protect you."

Am I forgiven? Jonty seemed almost his normal bouncy self, despite the worry about Brad, but that didn't take away the fact that Devan had let him down and he'd probably lost his job. Devan was going to sort that, though he'd have to talk to Jonty about what he wanted to happen in the long term.

"Want pizza tonight?" Devan asked.

"Can I cook? Is there anything you don't like?"

"Liver, Brussels sprouts and sardines."

Jonty gaped at him. "On a pizza?"

245

"On or off a pizza."

"Is that all?"

"You want the list of everything I won't eat? Why don't you tell me what you're going to cook and I can tell you if I'll eat it?"

"Florentine tripe?"

"No."

"Brain masala?"

"No. Is that a real thing?"

Jonty smiled. "Brawn on toast?"

"What's that? No don't tell me. I'm not going to like it."

"You should know in case you're ever offered it. An economical dish made from all the bits of meat that can be salvaged from a pig's head. The trotters are used to make it set into a jelly. Even Marcus thinks that's revolting and he cooks with offal a lot."

Devan pressed his lips together and swallowed hard. "Pizza."

"How about fettucine alfredo?"

"Does that contain the remains of Alfred?"

Jonty's laugh made Devan smile.

They were still laughing and smiling as they left the supermarket, right until Jonty froze as they were loading the car.

"Oh God, it *was* Brad," Jonty whispered.

"Where is he?"

"Walking this way."

"Get in the car."

Jonty frowned. "No."

"Then keep putting the groceries in the boot." Devan looked around and saw the guy heading in their direction.

"Can I have a word, Jonty?" Brad called.

"Leave him the fuck alone," Devan said quietly.

"Shut up, you wanker. Jonty? Come here. I want to talk to you."

Devan's heart was beating faster. "Go away or I'll call the police."

Brad shrugged. "I'm doing nothing wrong. I want a word with Jonty."

Devan heard Jonty slam the boot behind him. "Get in the car, Jonty."

Brad laughed. "Be a good little boy and do as you're told." He mimicked Devan's voice. "Just like he did for me." He took a step closer so he was right in Devan's face. Devan held his ground.

"Go back to where you came from," Brad snarled.

"I'm not going anywhere."

"Then you might be having a little accident," Brad whispered.

"Go on then," Devan said. "Hit me. Plenty of witnesses. I'll have your arse in jail before you can—"

"Stop it." Jonty pulled at Devan's arm. "Brad, go away. Give this up. Stop pestering me."

"All I have to do is wait for this pathetic twat to fuck off home. You're mine."

"No, I am not," Jonty snapped. "You had your chance and you fucked up. You hurt me. I'm not into that shit."

"I put photos of us online."

Oh God.

"And I wouldn't have been smiling in any of them. Take them off and let this go."

Brad shook his head and walked away.

"Oh-God-oh-God-oh-God-oh-God." Jonty shuddered by Devan's side.

Devan held him tight. "Call the police."

"What's the point?"

"They need to know that he's still bothering you. You should have told them exactly what he did to you five months ago. Then they'd see how serious it is."

Jonty pulled away and Devan tugged him back.

"Sorry," Devan whispered. "Fuck it. I'm sorry. The guy is freaking me out. I'm worried for you. I don't know how to protect you."

Jonty nestled into Devan's side, pressing his face into Devan's chest. "I want to get out of here. Please."

"What car does he drive?"

"A silver Audi. Why?"

"I want to be sure he doesn't follow us to the house."

"Shit." Jonty took off his jacket and got into the car.

In London, it would have been fairly easy to lose someone tailing you — unless it was the police — because there was as much chance of it happening by accident as by design. But in Alnwick, there wasn't enough traffic to hide in, nor enough lights to nip through, or one-way streets to quickly turn down. Nor did Devan know the roads well enough. *As if I know anything about evasive manoeuvring.* He drove around aimlessly while keeping an eye on the mirror. Every silver car he saw made his pulse jump.

"Pity he doesn't drive an orange Beetle," Jonty mumbled.

"Yep. I think we're okay. We need to go and get your stuff from Mike's. Want to give him a call?"

"He gave me a key, but I'd like my board and wetsuit from the shop. I'm going to give them one of the bottles of wine as a thank you."

"Good idea."

"Take the second road on the right. Then left at the next traffic lights." Jonty tapped into his phone. "Hi Mike. You at home or the shop…? Okay, then can you bring my board and wetsuit back to your place? I've got somewhere to stay so I'm

going to collect my stuff and get out of your hair…
No…Yep… About fifteen minutes… See you."

"We're not going to get the surfboard in the car."

"What a crap car."

Devan laughed.

"I'll try to persuade Mike to drive out with it. But really, what a crap car! It sounds like it's coughing up a hairball when you start it."

"Don't criticise my car. She's temperamental."

By the time they parked outside a small house on a leafy street, and Jonty had grabbed one of the bottles of wine from their shopping to give his friends, Devan was positive they weren't being followed. He was relieved. Even so, he doubted Brad was going to let this go, so he had to find a way to keep Jonty safe.

Chapter Fifteen

Jonty knocked on the door to Willis and Mike's place, in case Willis was in, but no one answered so he used one of the keys they'd given him. Seeing Brad in the car park had shaken him. Looking back, he realised he'd made a mistake. Not just the big one of ever saying yes to a date with the guy. All those times he thought he was being watched, all those *gifts* he didn't want, and now Brad threatening Devan too… It had all stemmed from Jonty not telling the police the truth. Devan had been right. He should have revealed everything that Brad had done five months ago. Now it was too late. There was little to no evidence. Why would anyone believe him? Jonty *knew* Brad was dangerous and he'd tried to convince himself that he wasn't. *Stupid.*

I told you.

I know.

That Brad had been so jealous of Tay should have made every warning bell ring. They had and yet Jonty had ignored them, because Brad had flattered him, said what Jonty had wanted to hear. Tay had just started going out with Matilda and Jonty wanted someone of his own.

He was pissed off that Brad had made him feel unsafe today when he and Devan had been having such a good time. Jonty had just about gotten over the fucker-that-was-Ravi, and was sort of coming to terms with the not minor detail that he'd lost his job, and Brad had sent him scurrying back down the rabbit hole. Was it just coincidence that he'd been in the supermarket? What else could it be?

Maybe he *should* phone the police, but what were they going to do? Talking to someone wasn't against the law. If Jonty reported him, he might make things worse.

He handed Devan the bottle of wine. "You want to wait in the kitchen while I go up and get my bag? I didn't bring much into the house. Most of my stuff is in the van out front."

"Okay."

Jonty ran up the stairs to the guest bedroom and gathered his things. As he headed back downstairs with his belongings, the front door opened and Willis came in.

"Hi." Jonty jumped down the last few steps. "Did Mike call you?"

"No, what's happened?"

"I've got somewhere to stay, so I've come to get my stuff."

"And everything in the van?"

"No, I…I can't take that yet. The rental is only for a month."

Devan appeared at the kitchen door and Willis jolted. "Who are you?"

"Willis, this is Devan."

Devan held out his hand and Willis shook it.

"You were the one caught in the rip with Jonty," Willis said.

"Yes."

"Mike's bringing my board and wetsuit so we need to wait."

"Want a coffee?" Willis put down a pile of exercise books on the hall table and headed into the kitchen.

Jonty followed him. "The wine's for you and Mike for letting me stay."

"That's good of you, thanks." Willis looked at Devan. "I thought Mike said you weren't up here for long."

"A month, maybe more."

There was a clatter as the front door opened and Mike strode into the kitchen. "Hi, baby."

"Hi, Daddy," Jonty quipped.

251

Mike rolled his eyes, kissed a glaring Willis on the cheek, then turned to Devan. "How the hell are you going to get a surfboard in an Aston Martin?"

"Do you have any foam and straps?" Jonty asked. "Or a circular saw?"

"No to the straps and what the hell would you do with a circular saw?" Willis asked.

"Don't encourage him," Mike said. "Whereabouts are you staying?"

"Devan's rented a place on the beach road at Shennan Sands. Sunshine Cottage."

Mike raised his eyebrows. "Very nice. It's exclusive up there. I'll drop the board off with your wetsuit tomorrow before I go to work, okay?"

"Thanks, Mike. Could I ask a huge favour?"

"No," Willis said.

"My bike's locked up at the back of the hotel. That's something else that won't fit in Devan's pathetic car and I… I'm not working there anymore."

"You lost your job? What the hell happened?" Mike took the key to the bike lock Jonty offered him.

"A guest is claiming I punched him in the nose. I didn't. I must have accidentally kicked him when he pulled me into the hot tub, but another guest has backed him up and the hotel doesn't want the bad publicity."

"Jesus, Jonty. You loved that job."

"I'm going to sort it out," Devan said.

"What about all your stuff?" Willis asked Jonty.

"I'd like a few things, more of my clothes, but can we help put the rest in your garage to free up the van?"

"Me and Willis will do that. Just take what you need."

Jonty wrapped his arms around Mike. "Thanks for helping me out."

Mike gave him a tight hug. "That's what friends are for."

252

Jonty didn't miss the look that Mike shot Devan. *One that reminded him not to mess me around.*

When he and Devan were finally on their way to the house, Jonty heaved a sigh of relief.

"Nothing is going to stand in the way of sex, right?" Jonty asked. "Oh except, we need to empty the car, put the food away, unpack our clothes, make something to eat, eat it, wash up, have something to drink, watch the news in case aliens have invaded, take off our clothes, shower, I need to find a new job...then your lovely arse is all mine."

"Er..."

"Which bit of that didn't you like the sound of?"

"Er..."

"You want me to unpack everything? *And* put the food away? I can't rely on you to tell me whether aliens have invaded? I suppose not. You've too much on your mind. Oh, don't tell me your arse isn't lovely. I've seen it. I'm really worried that I'm going to disappoint you. That's why I'm talking so much."

"You always talk a lot. I like it. I like you." Devan glanced across and smiled at him.

"Even when I'm being sarcastic?"

Devan laughed. "Yes, even then."

"I need you to stop the car," Jonty whispered.

"Why?"

"I just do. There's an entrance to a farm coming up on the left. Please."

Devan pulled off. Jonty guessed Devan was thinking he wanted to take a leak or maybe throw up, but it wasn't that.

"Are you okay?" Devan switched off the engine.

Jonty unclicked his seatbelt, leaned over and pressed his lips to Devan's.

"Wha — ?" Devan managed before Jonty wrapped his arms around him and almost climbed into his lap.

Their tongues tangled and Jonty sucked on Devan's as he fought the steering wheel and the constricted space to get as close to Devan as he could. It had to mean something, not just the kiss, but…being with Devan. If all he'd get was a month, it would break him, but he had to hope it would be more. Devan had talked about a job, but if the deal didn't go through, what then?

Stop thinking. Just kiss him. Make him want you more than he wants to breathe.

But Devan pushed him away, gently, but it was still a push. "Jesus, Jonty. Can't you wait?"

I've waited all my life for one thing or another. I want you inside me. But he moved back onto his seat and pressed his hand against his aching cock, trying to relieve the pressure.

Devan stared at Jonty's lap, then looked into his face. "If we didn't have all your gear on the back seat… If it wasn't still light enough to be seen by anyone driving past… If there wasn't a chance a farmer could suddenly appear in his tractor… Or that aliens might get an eyeful…"

Jonty laughed. "You worry too much."

"I know." The way Devan looked at him then, made Jonty shudder. "I think too much as well. My life is risk assessment. What I'm thinking about doing to you requires us to be somewhere we won't be interrupted." He released a shaky breath. "Now, if you don't need to piss or throw up?"

Jonty shook his head and Devan started up and pulled back onto the road.

Ten minutes later, they were turning off the road onto a gravelled lane, made another left at a T-junction and finally they pulled up in front of Sunshine Cottage, a pretty white house with blue shutters. The house nestled in a gap in the dunes like some exotic white bird.

"We better check to make sure it's okay," Devan said.

"What are we going to do if it's not?" Jonty's voice was croaky.

"Go back to McAllister's or find another hotel."

God, no. I can't wait.

"I can't either," Devan said.

Jonty laughed. "Did I say that out loud or are you reading my mind."

Devan grinned.

"It looks lovely." Jonty got out of the car. "Unless there's a dead body in the shower, it'll be fine."

He could barely believe how expensive it was, yet Devan hadn't flinched when he'd handed over his card. Jonty had paid for the groceries despite Devan protesting, but Jonty wanted to at least pay part of his share. Devan headed for the door with the key in his hand. Jonty could hear the sea, and knowing it was a stone's throw away made his heart leap in excitement. Well, it was either that or thinking about what was to come.

Devan fumbled with the key and dropped it. Maybe Jonty wasn't the only one who was nervous. He'd talked too much, made this into too big a deal. It was just sex. It didn't have to be perfect. It was definitely going to be a lot better than the last time Jonty had been fucked. *Don't think about Brad.* All that needed to happen was that they both came. And still he felt his big mouth opening.

"We should have checked to see if we're sexually compatible before we moved in together."

Devan chuckled. "You like cock. So do I. I think we're fine."

"Do you always top?" Jonty whispered.

Devan hesitated. "Usually, but not always."

"I'll tick that off the list then." Not that Jonty had actually topped anyone but…

255

Devan pushed open the door. "After you."

As Jonty stepped into the house, Devan slammed the door behind him. He thrust Jonty against the wall and leaned into him, his hard cock pressing into Jonty's arse. Jonty could feel him panting against his neck, feel the groan surging up Devan's chest. Then Jonty was spun round and Devan kissed him so hard that Jonty's knees gave way. Not that he'd have fallen, because he was pinned in place by a long hard body. Devan slid his fingers to the back of Jonty's neck and held him tight as he kissed him.

Kiss him back!

Fuck off, Tay, but yeah, thanks for the reminder.

Jonty opened his mouth and Devan's tongue twisted with his.

The kiss…

The taste…

This kiss…

Oh fuck…

They kissed as if they were the last people in the world, as if they *had* to do this now, because if they didn't, something bad would happen and the chance would be taken from them. Jonty's heart raced so fast he almost worried, then *almost* slipped into *did* worry. *Fuck! How fast is too fast for a heart to beat?* Devan had him pressed against the wall as if they were welded to each other, and they rubbed, rocked, rolled and rutted until Jonty's cock hurt.

He wished their clothes would dissolve. He wished he was Harry Potter and could make lube and a condom magically appear. He wished most of all that he wasn't going to come in his jeans unless Devan did too. And if that happened, then he really hoped Devan came first.

Devan caught Jonty's hands in his and pulled them over his head, stretching them up and forcing Jonty onto the tips of his toes. Their fingers were entwined, and Devan still kissed him, only not just his mouth, but his ears—running the tip of his tongue over Jonty's piercings, then his eyebrow, sucking on the piercing there. *Oh fuck, that is so knee-tremblingly hot.* Then his chin—*Christ, that was hot too.* His neck… *Shiiiit.*

"I can feel your pulse under my tongue," Devan whispered. "Fluttering like a little bird."

Devan sucked his Adam's apple and Jonty couldn't breathe. He had the horrible, wonderful, petrifying sensation that he could actually come—first time ever—just from being kissed.

When Devan pulled back and gulped air, Jonty remembered he was supposed to breathe too, so he did, a shuddering inhale and stuttering exhale that proved he'd forgotten the most basic of life's lessons. Breathe or you die. Devan smiled at him and it was…perfect, so open, so melting and knowing, yet somehow a bit shy and vulnerable, that Jonty understood at some level the significance of this moment was more than it might have seemed.

He wanted Devan.

Only Devan.

For ever and ever and…

Oh God, too deep, too fast.

He wanted to be fucked hard and fast with Devan's teeth in his neck. He wanted to come so hard he forgot his name, though not the name of the guy who was making him see stars.

"Sexually compatible or not?" Devan asked.

Jonty mustered a sad sigh from the remnants of control he still possessed. "Well…"

Devan kissed him again, holding both of Jonty's hands with one of his while the other hand tried to worm its way into the back of Jonty's jeans. Not easy. Worse than that. Impossible.

"Your jeans are so bloody tight," Devan muttered. "Why don't you buy them in a bigger size?"

"Because you like the way my arse looks in these."

Devan laughed. "Fuck it." He switched his attention to Jonty's button, flipped it open, lowered his zip, then tugged at his waistband.

The jeans hardly budged, but enough that when Devan's fingers settled on the skin above the seam of Jonty's arse, and stroked, Jonty's entire body vibrated and he groaned into Devan's mouth. Devan let go of his hands to clutch Jonty's arse cheeks, his fingers sinking into his crack, and Jonty was spoiled for choice. *What shall I touch first?* His fingers fluttered over Devan's back in indecision like a nervous shoplifter, before he found himself pulling Devan's shirt out of his trousers. He'd only just begun to explore when Devan stepped out of reach, his pupils blown. "Clothes off. Now."

Jonty had to push down on his cock, which was pressing uncomfortably against the opening of his jeans. Continuing to kiss while stripping wasn't easy, but the only time their lips parted was when Jonty's T-shirt came over his head.

And when Devan spoke. "You are so fucking gorgeous."

Devan dropped to his knees, licked Jonty's cock from root to tip, and Jonty fell back, caught by the wall. Devan slid the flat of his tongue over the head of Jonty's dick as he looked up at him, curled it around the crest, then sucked.

Jonty said something, but wasn't sure what. Incomprehensible words fell from his mouth, punctuated by moans and cries. He wanted to watch, but the sensation was so intense, his eyelids kept fluttering closed.

"Have I actually discovered a way to shut you up?" Devan slid one hand up Jonty's chest and squeezed the undamaged nipple.

Jonty opened his mouth and closed it without saying anything. He grabbed Devan's hand, and sucked then kissed each fingertip in turn.

Devan fluttered his tongue over the head of Jonty's dick. "You taste so good," he whispered.

"You're not allowed to talk if I can't," Jonty blurted.

As Devan teased more precome from his slit, he wrapped his hand around Jonty's balls and pressed down. When he put his lips around the head of Jonty's cock and swallowed him down to the root in one go, Jonty shook, his balance shot as if he were being tumbled by the sea. He tried to shove his hips forward, tried to persuade Devan to *move*, but Devan took his time.

Jonty threaded his fingers in Devan's hair as Devan moved his mouth up and down, lips shielding his teeth, then using his teeth very gently, biting, kissing, sucking, up and down, on and on, while he maintained the pressure on Jonty's balls and held his orgasm at bay. While his cock was in Devan's mouth, Jonty touched Devan's cheek, felt his dick move against his fingers, and gasped. Then Devan swallowed him down again and took hold of Jonty's hand to let him feel his cock in his throat.

"I give in," Jonty blurted. "It was me who covered the chemistry teacher's car in shaving foam and wrecked the paint work. I mean, what do they put in that stuff? I lied to the police, but I'm not lying to you. It was me who did it."

Devan released his hold on Jonty's balls and Jonty knew he was going to lose it any moment.

"Devan! Please. Oh God."

Devan jacked him off and sucked at the same time. Lightning flickered down Jonty's spine, and the need to come began to overwhelm him. There was a tightening sensation in his gut that he managed to cling onto for a moment, the slight discomfort morphing to goose-bumped bliss as fire exploded

259

in his balls. Jonty wailed as his shaft pulsed and jerked, filling Devan's mouth with come.

Oh God, I'll drown him. Could he actually do that? Had that ever happened?

Devan kept him in his mouth as he came down, licked him through the aftershocks, cleaning his cock with soft laps of his tongue until the overstimulation grew too much and Jonty could have cried. But before he could beg Devan to stop, Devan licked his way back up his chest, over each nipple until he stood in front of him.

"Sexually compatible?" Devan asked looking too smug.

"I feel like crying. It's such a shame."

Devan laughed and leaned forward to brush his lips over Jonty's.

"I do taste good though," Jonty said. "That's a plus."

Devan bent down to his trousers and stood up with a condom and a sachet of lube.

"Were you a boy scout?" Jonty whispered. "Did you get a badge for this? Always prepared?"

"I was never in the scouts." Devan ran his finger down Jonty's chest. "I want to fuck you through the wall."

Jonty whimpered. "And lose your deposit?"

"Turn around."

"Are you always this bossy?" Jonty faced the wall.

"I'm amazed you're doing as you're told."

"I'm still worrying about the sexual compatibility thing."

Jonty heard the snap of latex, then the rip of Devan opening the lube. He widened his stance and pressed his face into his bent arm. Slick wet fingers stroked down the seam of his backside, then one finger pushed, and they both groaned. Well, Jonty yelped but… *Oh God.* The curl of a finger over his prostate and his dick was miraculously resurrected. He was going to call his cock Lazarus.

Devan pressed his mouth to Jonty's neck and nipped with his teeth as he finger-fucked him. When one finger became two, Jonty whimpered.

"Fuck me," Jonty pleaded. "Oh God. I need you inside me. Do you need me to talk dirty? Because I'm not good at that."

Devan's stubble rubbed across his shoulders and he added a third finger. "Try."

"Please, please." Jonty moaned. "Now. Stop messing around. You'll try and get your whole hand in there in a minute to get me ready and you don't need to, your cock's not that big."

He felt Devan shake as he laughed, then the fingers were gone and Jonty had his back against the wall instead of his chest. He wasn't sure how Devan did it, but Jonty found himself off the ground, wrapped around Devan, arms around his neck, legs around his waist, pressed back against the wall with Devan's cock nudging his hole.

"You didn't tell me you were Superman," Jonty blurted. "Now I'm glad you did all that weight training in the gym."

"From the moment you stood up with that Flake in your mouth…" Devan's breathing was noisy and unsteady. "I thought about doing this." Devan pushed inside him, one long, hard yet slow drive that brought a long wail from Jonty's throat.

"Je…sus," Devan gasped.

The pressure and burn stopped Jonty breathing for a long moment. The discomfort morphed to pleasure so quickly it was hard to convince himself it had ever hurt.

"Okay?" Devan grunted.

"Let me just finish praying for world peace."

Devan shot him one of his looks, slid his hands further under Jonty's thighs and supported him as he started to move, shunting his cock in and out, hitting his prostate every *perfect* time. Jonty felt like a plane accelerating down a runway, not that he'd ever been in a plane but… The quickening stream of pleasure was so intense that his world disappeared for a moment. All he was aware of was this. And *this* was getting better and better.

"Oh fuck, fuck." Devan groaned as he pulled back, moaned as he pushed forward.

Jonty squeezed around Devan's cock and his reward was a wild look in Devan's eyes and a grip on his arse that was tight enough to leave bruises. Jonty did his best to sink down into Devan's up thrust as Devan began to move faster, his heavy panting mingling with Jonty's gasps and cries. Fast, hard, dirty and beautiful. Jonty came in a shower of sparks. *I can't believe I came again!* Devan rammed into him hard, then shuddered, groaning as he filled the condom. Jonty clutched him tightly and Devan rested his head alongside Jonty's, his breath juddering into Jonty's ear.

As Jonty finally slid his legs to the floor, Devan pulled out of him and grabbed the condom before it could fall off. He knotted and dropped it, then pressed his forearms against the wall either side of Jonty's head.

He stared at Jonty as if he were the most amazing thing he'd ever seen, his gaze moving over Jonty's face before settling on his mouth. One gentle kiss almost undid Jonty.

Devan lifted his head and smiled. "What to say after a fuck like that?"

"Are you certain we're in the right house and the occupants aren't hiding upstairs, freaked out?"

Devan laughed. "Tell me you're not still fretting about sexual compatibility."

"An ongoing concern. I think we need to keep trying until it's clear one way or the other."

Devan smiled and took his hand. "Let's find the shower."

"But that will throw us right off schedule. We're supposed to empty the car and I've got wet clothes and shoes in a plastic bag."

"Shower," Devan repeated. "Everything else can wait. The rental agency better be right about the water being hot on demand."

Jonty had never been taken care of like this before. He'd once showered with a guy who'd fucked him, but he hadn't looked at or touched him like this. Jonty leaned against Devan as he caressed him with soapy hands. For once, Jonty didn't want to say anything, he just wanted to feel. Devan cleaned every part of him, every inch of his skin, then brought him off with his hand while he kissed him, Jonty shaking in his arms, wanting to dissolve into him.

"Three times," Jonty gasped. "Bloody hell."

"We need an even number."

"Eight then. I like that number."

Devan chuckled.

But even as Jonty fell deeper into lust, doubt crept in.

What if Hamish wouldn't sell the hotel?

What would happen when the month was up?

How was he going to earn a living?

Where would he live?

Devan already knew he didn't want to leave Northumberland. Did he think that finding his mother living happily in London might make him change his mind? There was no surety that his father would know where she was. Plus Jonty and Devan were worlds apart in so many ways, no matter how much Jonty might want to convince himself otherwise. Devan was wealthy, Jonty was not. That might turn into an issue.

Enjoy it while it lasts.

It's not going to.

Maybe you're wrong.
Maybe I'm not.

Once they were dressed, Devan and Jonty explored the house. Jonty had to keep reminding himself to shut his mouth. The place was amazing: spotlessly clean, beautifully furnished…awesome. The sort of place he'd never dreamed he'd set foot in, let alone be able to stay in for a month. *With a hot guy!* The kitchen was part of one large living area that ran across the rear, and the island unit that held the hob, was a slab of glittering brown granite with flecks of cobalt, silver and turquoise. A bank of floor-to-ceiling bi-fold doors opened onto decking with an outdoor living area and a hot tub, the sea fifty yards beyond.

"Everything seems to be brand new." Devan picked up a yellow cushion off the cream couch, then tossed it down.

Jonty reached out and put it in the exact position it was before.

Devan chuckled.

"I'm anal."

Devan groaned. "Don't…" He took a deep breath. "Want to go down to the sea before it's dark or look upstairs?"

Jonty turned toward the stairs and Devan followed. There were two large bedrooms, one at the front, and one at the rear with a balcony that stretched the width of the house holding two sun loungers, a table and chairs. Devan unfastened the catch on the glass doors, slid them open and stepped out.

"We can have coffee and croissants up here tomorrow." Devan came back in and locked the doors again. "Are you okay? You're uncharacteristically quiet and it's worrying me."

"I can't believe how much has changed in less than a week," Jonty whispered. *I had a job and now I don't. And yet…* "What did I do to be so lucky?"

Devan pulled him into his arms and kissed him. "I'm the lucky one."

Jonty pulled back. "I want the bedroom at the rear."

For a moment, he *had* Devan, then the familiar smile crept over his face. "That's tough. So do I."

They brought everything in out of the car, hung up their clothes, sorted out the wet stuff, though Jonty had no hope his old suit could be revived, but maybe his shoes would live again.

He took the ingredients out of the fridge to make dinner. "This place would be perfect if it had a lazy river."

"Do you have a thing about lazy rivers? Where is there one up here?"

"North Shields. I went once with Tay. Do any of your hotels have them?"

"One of them. In Kent." Devan looked around. "You know what would take this place to a level higher? And not a lazy river."

"What?"

"Your sea glass pictures."

Jonty rolled his eyes, yet the idea made his stomach flutter, and a lump formed in his throat.

"You could sell them. They'd look great on the walls in here."

Could I make and sell them?

I told you that!

Tay had tried on several occasions to persuade Jonty to approach some of the art galleries in the area. He'd never been able to pluck up the courage.

"It takes a long while to find the pieces of glass," Jonty said.

Devan took out his phone and a moment later, held it up to show him. "Buy the glass online."

"That's cheating."

"If you're making it for yourself maybe, but not if you're making it to sell. If we get the hotel, I want you to make some pictures for it. And maybe the names of the rooms."

Jonty gaped at him.

"Like a glass of wine?" Devan asked.

Did he have no idea that he'd made Jonty's world turn so much faster? "Yes please." Maybe getting a bit drunk would stop him feeling so...overwhelmed.

Devan put a glass of red wine in front of him. Jonty took two large swallows, then began to work. He'd watched Marcus cook fettucine alfredo, though Marcus had made his own pasta. Jonty filled a pan with water and set it to boil, then took another gulp of wine.

"How did you learn to cook?" Devan asked. "Using a recipe book for alcoholics?"

Jonty laughed. "Sometimes you're really funny." He took another drink of wine.

"Are you drunk already?"

"No. Not quite. I learnt to cook from a book my mum had. It was a tall, thin recipe book from the Be-Ro flour company. She used it all the time and when she'd...gone, I tried to make the things she'd baked. It was cakes and biscuits and scones mostly. When I was older, I progressed to things like spaghetti and stew and when my dad realised what I'd made tasted okay, he expected me to cook for us both. Sometimes, we had nice meals together. It wasn't all bad."

Jonty put the clotted cream, butter and cornflour into a pan and stirred it over a low heat.

"Is there anything I can do?"

"Just admire my amazing technique."

"I'm admiring the way you've polished off a large glass of wine."

266

"Fuck!" Jonty stared at the empty glass. "I didn't notice I was doing that." Not true.

He tipped the cheese and nutmeg into a bowl, added a couple of grinds of black pepper and mixed it before returning to stir the creamy mixture on the hob.

"It's going to be ready five minutes after I put the pasta in. Want to see if you can find some bowls and forks."

Devan poured him another glass of wine, then started to check the cupboards.

By the time they sat at the table, half of Jonty's wine was gone. Devan gave him a look but didn't say anything.

"You might like more pepper." Jonty turned the grinder over his bowl.

"It's delicious."

Since Devan had finished long before Jonty, Jonty guessed he was telling the truth. When Jonty finally put his fork down, Devan reached across the table and caught hold of his hand. "What's the matter?"

What do we have here?

Am I hoping for the impossible?

"Worried about seeing my father tomorrow." Not a lie, though not his greatest concern.

"You don't have to see him if you don't want to. I could ask him for your mother's address. It's possible that Stan could still find her without his help."

"I want to see him. I want to see if he's sorry."

"I wouldn't get your hopes up." Devan pushed to his feet and cleared the table.

Jonty couldn't sleep. Fantastic, exhausting sex and he still couldn't sleep. All he could think about was visiting his father the next day, or more to the point, whether he should or not. He didn't want to be weighed down with grief about a man who'd never really been a father to him, but this was their last chance.

Devan lay sleeping at his side and Jonty wanted so much to believe this was real, that they had a future. Maybe if he could find out where his mother was, he'd finally accept he could leave Northumberland. He should have accepted it long ago, but where would he have gone?

Then there was Tay.

Don't stay here because of me. I'm not here anyway.

Jonty rolled over. Devan slid his arm around him and tugged him close. Devan's breathing pattern didn't change and Jonty thought he was still asleep. *I'm safe.*

Yes, you are. He'll keep you safe.

And finally, Jonty slept.

Only to be woken by a violent banging at the door.

Devan jerked awake beside him. "What the hell?"

Jonty rolled out of bed and reached for one of the robes.

"Stay here." Devan pulled on the other one.

"No."

Devan gave a heavy sigh but didn't argue. They both hurried down. Lights were flashing outside and when Devan opened the door, two policemen stood there.

"We've had a report of an assault. Which of you is Jonty Bloom?"

"I am."

"You called to say you were being attacked."

"No, I didn't. We were asleep."

"What the hell's happened to my car?" Devan stalked out of the house.

Jonty gulped. There was a long scratch all the way down the side of the Aston.

"I think someone's made a malicious call," Jonty said. Probably Brad, though should he say that?

"Mind if we have a look round?" the policeman asked.

"No, go ahead."

Devan came back into the house. "Brad?"

"How would he know where we were living? No one followed us. We'd have seen them."

The policemen came back to the door.

"Any idea who might want to cause trouble for you?" one asked.

"Brad Greene. If you look up my details, you'll see I've reported him a few times. I can't think of anyone else who'd do this."

"We'll have a word with him."

The policemen left and Devan closed the door.

"I'm sorry," Jonty whispered.

Devan wrapped his arms around him. "It's only a car."

"Did it hurt when you said that?"

"Yes, but not as much as it would have hurt if it had been you."

Chapter Sixteen

Jonty's anxiety ramped up the closer they drew to Berwick. His gaze kept sliding to the sat nav counting down the time and distance from their destination. Devan had followed his lead on everything until they left the house, and even when Jonty had snapped at him for overcooking the croissants, he'd not reacted. Well, Jonty had got all stroppy and Devan had hugged him, stroked the stars in his ears, then stuffed a croissant in his mouth which made Jonty laugh. Every time Jonty felt himself on the verge of imploding, Devan grounded him.

"You can change your mind," Devan said. "You don't have to do this."

"Now I've put on my best sweater? The one I can only wear once without having to wash it?" Jonty chewed his lip. "I want to see my mother. I want answers from her so I think I *do* have to do this."

"You're still saying *think*."

"I know I am."

"Do you want me with you?" Devan asked.

Jonty glanced at him. "Yes, inside the house, but maybe outside the door of the room. Just in case I get all stabby and need stopping."

"Okay."

Mike had delivered Jonty's board and bike before they set off, and they'd put them in the garage only to find there were already a couple of surfboards in there, and other equipment for the beach along with two bikes. Mike had also delivered a warning to Devan, a quiet word when he thought Jonty couldn't hear. "You're making this harder for him. Don't fuck him around." Devan hadn't answered. Jonty wasn't sure whether he wanted to thump Mike or hug him.

270

"What would you like to eat tonight?" Jonty asked.

Devan laughed. "God, your changes of direction make my head spin. I'm happy with anything. But not brawn. I feel sick thinking about that."

"Pizza then. I'll make it. Pizza, then hot tub."

"I need to go to the hotel later today to talk to my guys and work out how much to offer for the hotel."

"Maybe I'll be able to afford to buy it. I've been saving up. I have a *This is going to change my life* fund. I'm counting on my new suit and shoes helping towards that change."

"No one could resist you in that suit. You want to come with me to the hotel?"

"I'll stay here and get the pizza ready. I like to cook pizza naked. *Shiiit.* I shouldn't have told you that. Don't rush back and crash. I can't eat two pizzas."

Devan smiled.

Jonty gave a shaky exhalation. "What if he's not in?"

"He'll be in. He's sick, remember?"

"Doesn't mean he can't go out."

"I suppose. But he knows you're coming."

"Maybe that's an incentive not to be in."

Devan's phone rang and he accepted the call. "Hi, Clara."

"Morning, Devan. Roger and I are about fifteen minutes away from McAllister's."

"Great. I'll meet you there late this afternoon. There's a wedding in the hotel today, so it's going to be busy. That works to your advantage. With so many people milling about, you're less likely to be noticed. I've left a message at reception that they're to give you a key to my room. Any problems call me. Hamish McAllister knows I have people coming up, so you can speak to him if you need to. If anyone asks, you're building inspectors called in by McAllister. He's going to talk to his staff tomorrow, so we need to give him a price as soon as possible. Sorry to press you."

271

"No problem," Roger said.

"We'll get right on it," Clara added. "See you later."

Devan pressed a button on the wheel to end the call.

"I had a text from Hamish saying there was a meeting for all staff at eleven tomorrow," Jonty told him. "So he didn't know at that point that Vincent had sacked me."

"I'm going to sort that out."

"Oh."

Devan glanced at him. "What does *oh* mean?"

"You said you'd give me a job." Jonty wished his voice didn't sound so…little. "I have enough money to wait until you can sort it out."

"I will. I just didn't want you to have been sacked for something you didn't do. But if you don't want to go back, that suits me fine."

Relief flooded Jonty's chest and he smiled. "We can spend our time making sure about that sexual compatibility thing. Right?"

Devan laughed. "Right."

"I feel a bit as if I've stepped onto a train that's going faster and faster. I had my life under control and now it's not."

"Does that bother you?"

Jonty swallowed hard. "Yes and no. I've been hiding all my life, protecting myself any way I could. Keeping quiet. Curling up in small places. When I learned that humour worked as a deflection, I used that. If I could laugh when I was hurt at school, then it made me the powerful one. But I have places inside me that barely need to be touched before I'm in pain. Sometimes, when it gets too much, I have panic attacks."

Devan grabbed his hand and squeezed his fingers. "You verged on one when we were rescued and you didn't want to go to hospital."

"Hospitals bring back memories of being beaten, memories of how scared I was, awareness that I could tell no

272

one, and I had no one who loved me. I didn't belong anywhere. I couldn't risk being gay and that hurt. I think people guessed, but I never admitted it. I laughed it off. I was too frightened of losing the one person who was there for me.

"Tay was my anchor. He held me firm, kept me in place. Without him, I'd have been washed away. He even tried to get his parents to adopt me when my father was put in jail. But his sisters kicked up a fuss, so that was that. When I got the job at the hotel, I was so happy. It was like I had a family of my own, people to look after. Marcus taught me how to cook basic stuff and I watched him work whenever I could. That's how I knew how to make your meal. Though if you'd picked something difficult, I'd have struggled."

"It was delicious."

"The problem with the hotel is that staff come and go. I've been there longer than almost everyone. The manager before Vincent liked me a lot more than Vincent does. Vincent isn't going to like me at all if he loses his job."

"Do you want the hotel sold?"

Jonty thought about it. "Are you asking me if I wish you hadn't caught me with that Flake in my mouth? That you'd never come up here and confirmed the hotel was something you wanted? If the first thing I'd known about it was Hamish telling me and the rest of the staff tomorrow that we'd be out of a job after Christmas? If I wanted to lose my job and everyone else to lose theirs? Or would I rather everything had stayed the same, that I'd never met you and selling the hotel had never even come into Hamish's mind?"

"I got lost somewhere in that, but all of that, yes."

Jonty shrugged. "I can't pretend none of it's happened. We are where we are. Hamish wants to sell. You want to buy. I'm happy I met you. That's the one thing that's…" He swallowed hard. "Hey, no one knows what the future holds, whether tomorrow's waves will be good surfing ones or not. You take what you can, while you can."

Devan put both hands on the wheel to negotiate a tight bend. Jonty missed their hands being together.

"I'm glad I caught you with that Flake in your mouth. I'm glad I got to be the one who came up here. I'm glad the hotel impressed me. Almost as much as you. I'm glad I could tell you before you heard it from Hamish what I was doing up here. I wish I could have told you before you found out from Ravi and the major. Meeting you has been the best thing…" For a moment, Devan choked up. "I'd walk away from this deal, but I won't walk away from you. Stop worrying that I might."

Jonty's heart did a jig on his stomach. He put his hand on Devan's knee. "Want a blowjob?"

Devan laughed. "Yes, but not right now. Your best sweater, remember?"

"You're turning me down? I knew we were sexually incompatible."

"We need at least a year to be sure of that."

"Only a year?" But Jonty was glad Devan hadn't said a month.

Devan pulled up in a parking bay in front of a line of houses that were part of a small housing estate, and turned off the engine. "You okay?

No. Jonty nodded. "God! Do you know how hard it is to nod and think no at the same time? Does it work better with thinking yes and shaking your head?" Jonty tried it. "Damn. I can't do it. Can you make a clockwise circle with your right foot, while drawing a number 6 with your right hand?"

Jonty was flailing and his breathing turned shaky.

Devan caught hold of both of his hands. "You're okay. Stop worrying. I'm not going to let him hurt you."

You can't protect me from his words. But Jonty leaned over and kissed him.

"You don't need to go in."

"I know. Is it okay to be angry with him?" Jonty asked.

"I'd be shocked if you weren't."

"Hmm."

As they got out of the car, they both shivered in the bitter wind. It bit at the back of Jonty's neck and he shuddered. It was a cloudy day, the sea a dull grey line in the distance. Devan locked the car and Jonty took a deep breath. He strode down the path and up to the door with a confidence he didn't feel, then pressed the buzzer. He put his hands behind his back, his fists clenching and unclenching. Devan wrapped his hands around Jonty's and eased his fingers apart. As the door opened, Jonty straightened his spine. Devan stroked his palms, then let him go. A woman in her forties stood there in jeans and a tight-fitting green top. For a crazy moment, Jonty imagined she was his mum.

"Hi. I'm Jonty. This is Devan. I'm here to see my father."

"You look a bit like him." Her lips curved in a slight smile revealing crooked teeth. She moved aside to let them in, and closed the door. "I'm Tamsin, Gary's partner."

Jonty offered her his hand and she shook it, then Devan's.

"He's in there. We had to move a bed downstairs." She pushed open the door of a room on the left. "It's your wee lad, Gary," she called and moved back.

"I'll be right here," Devan mouthed and squeezed Jonty's fingers once before letting go.

Jonty took a deep breath before he walked into the room, but even before he crossed the threshold, he was hit by the cloying scent of sickness. Inside the room, it wrapped around him and slithered into his lungs—stale air, sweat, piss, decay… *I don't want to take another breath.* His father lay propped against a heap of pillows in a hospital bed, the side

275

rails up and a tray table loaded with medical paraphernalia at his side. His eyes were closed, his arms lay motionless on top of the blue and green checked cover.

Is it my father? Jonty had to work hard to recognise him. He was thinner, paler, his skin almost transparent. His hair was grey now and wispy, though he had the same hard mouth.

His father opened his eyes. After a moment, the glazed expression cleared. "I didn't know eyebrows could fall off," he muttered. "A fucking safety pin?"

"Hello, Dad." Last night, Jonty had gone through a whole range of *what to say when I meet him* and these two words were the best he'd come up with.

"I'm sorry you're sick," Jonty said.

Plus those words.

"Are you?"

"Of course I am."

"Where's this sudden interest in caring about me come from?"

Well, I didn't fucking learn it from you! "I'd be sorry if anyone was sick. Well, maybe not evil dictators or mass murderers or whoever thought brawn was a good idea." *Or someone who beat his wife until she had to make a decision that fucked up my life.*

His father chuckled, which brought on a coughing fit. Jonty waited until the spasm had passed.

"How long have you lived here?" Jonty asked.

"What does it matter?"

I'm trying to make fucking conversation before I ask you the *question.* "It doesn't." Jonty shrugged.

"So what are you doing these days?"

"I work in a hotel."

"Carrying people's suitcases?"

276

"Among other things. I'm the night manager." *Shit.* Had that sounded defensive? *What if it did?* For some reason, Jonty thought his father already knew what he did.

"What do you want? Think we can be pals again now I'm dying? That you'll get my money?"

"Obviously that's why I'm here. Leave your ten million to me." Jonty rolled his eyes. "I don't want your money."

"Then what do you want?"

"An apology," he blurted. *Damn, damn, damn.*

"An apology? You sent me to fucking prison. Because of you I lost my job, my friends, my pension. The powers-that-be decided I'd abused my position as a police officer and brought the service into disrepute…" He coughed again. "All because I gave my kid a good hiding for being a liar and a thief."

And gay. Jonty curled his toes in his shoes.

"You going to deny it?"

"I lied every time my teachers asked how I'd got those marks on my legs or arms. I lied when I said I couldn't have anyone round to play because my non-existent gran was sick. I lied when I told people you were a good dad. I stole stuff you wouldn't buy me. Sweets, crisps, pencils. I wanted what everyone else had, but you wouldn't even do that for me."

"If I hadn't been a copper, you'd have been in serious trouble for your thieving."

Jonty almost wanted to laugh. "Did you ever wonder whether that was part of the reason I did it? I wanted someone to see what you were doing to me. You nearly killed me that last time. It was a lot more than a good hiding. You kicked me unconscious. Broke my arm, two ribs and a bone in my back. Dislocated my shoulder. Fractured my jaw. When I came round, you'd gone to work and left me lying on the living room floor. I lay there for twenty-four hours and you never came back so I had to force myself up and somehow, I made it to school. When I did, they called social services."

"You could have lied."

Jonty snorted in disbelief. "That I was attacked *again*? I finally saw sense, saw that you were never going to stop, that you couldn't stop because something inside you was broken. You drank to stop it hurting you and hurt me instead. I wanted to feel sorry for you, but you were so vicious. When you got pissed and angry, you didn't even see that you were hitting a kid. I kept thinking you'd change and you never did."

"Huh."

"I needed medical help that last time you hit me. Getting to school was the hardest thing I've ever done. If I hadn't already been in my uniform, there was no way I could have put it on."

"I was drunk. You got in my way. You always got in my way. I would have come back sooner, but I got caught up in something at work."

Jonty hadn't really thought his father would be sorry, but to hear him still try to excuse what he'd done, made him feel sick.

"They spoke to your mother when they arrested me. Did they tell you?"

"They said they couldn't find her."

His father choked out a laugh. "She said she didn't want you. Her new family didn't know about you and she wasn't prepared to disrupt their lives for a teenager with issues."

A cold sensation crept up Jonty's spine as if he were sinking in icy water.

"She didn't want you when you were eight and she fucking definitely didn't want you when you were fifteen. Just like I didn't want a son who wouldn't kick a ball or watch rugby. One who freaked out when he had to go to hospital."

278

"Because more often than not, *you* were the reason I had to go to hospital and you made it clear if I didn't lie, I'd be in even worse trouble."

"You were such a fucking baby. You cried for your mother night after night."

Jonty screwed his hands together. "And you came in and hit me until I shut up."

"It worked. You learned not to cry."

Jonty turned to Tamsin who was leaning against the door, her face pale. "Does he hit you? Well, not now he's confined to bed, I guess."

"Want to know where your mother is?"

Jonty turned back to his father. "No."

He thought his knees would buckle at the lie, only it wasn't a lie. It struck him with the force of an avalanche that he didn't care. She could have helped him and she hadn't. If his father was telling the truth. *If...* He was. Jonty felt it.

"You've two half-brothers. And your sister. Yeah. Denny. She's grown into quite a beauty. I keep tabs on them. Wouldn't you like to see them?"

Jonty couldn't bring himself to say no. A family who didn't even know about him. He wasn't sure he could stand the disappointment of them rejecting him too.

"I know where she lives. Your mother. Just like I know you live in Alnwick."

Jonty kept telling himself not to react, but he lost the battle. "I thought you'd no longer have the capacity to hurt me. I thought—he's dying, he won't want to die without saying he's sorry. What a fool I was. You were a terrible father and nothing's changed."

"And you think you were some perfect son?"

"I tried," Jonty snapped. "I tried to make you happy. You did your best to make me unhappy. You punished me for nothing."

279

"I thought it would harden you up. Everything I did for you was for your own good."

Jonty gaped at him. "Like shutting me in that old coal shed? You knew how scared I was of dark places. How petrified I was of spiders and bugs, let alone the dark. I was ten years old and you locked me in there on a Friday night and didn't let me out until Sunday morning. I screamed until I had no voice. I was convinced I was going to die. I thought you'd left me in there forever."

"You weren't frightened of the dark when I let you out."

"I didn't speak for a week after you opened the door."

"Seven blissful days." His father smiled. "You never did shut your fucking mouth. *What's this? How does that work? Why does that happen?* On and on."

Jonty seethed. He wasn't going to let his father win what would be their last battle.

"Well, my boyfriend rather likes my mouth."

"Yes, I do." Devan walked into the room and slung his arm around Jonty's shoulder.

The appearance of Devan silenced his father in a way Jonty had never managed, and comforted him in a way he'd not anticipated.

"Rosie Henley. Oaklands, Burton Road, Newcastle. She didn't go far, but I kept my word. I never followed her, never pushed her to come back. Now fuck off." His father rolled onto his side.

"You are such a piece of shit." Devan's eyes glittered. "It seems miraculous to me that a decent, kind and sensitive guy like Jonty could have a father like you."

His father turned to face Devan. "I put clothes on his back, food in his stomach, a roof over his head."

"But you never loved him. He was your kid and you never loved him."

"He's pathetic. A weak, cock-sucking excuse for a man. A shit-eating, shirt-lifting faggot." His eyes glittered and Jonty knew his father was enjoying this.

Jonty pulled at Devan's sleeve. He wanted to leave. Now.

"You're on your death bed," Devan said. "You're pretending what you did was right, but you know it wasn't. He was a kid. You were his father. You drank because you were unhappy with your shitty life. What happened? Did you marry too early? Have kids too soon? Not get that promotion at work you thought you deserved? Drink because your dreams didn't come true? Then took out your frustration on your wife first, then your son? What a specimen of manhood you are."

"What the fuck do you know?"

"Try and say something nice to him. There must be a memory that could make you both smile. This is your last chance. Don't waste it."

Devan wasn't talking to Jonty, but it was his last chance too.

"You used to do me fried mushrooms on a Sunday morning before Mum got up," Jonty whispered. "Just for me. You showed me how to use a drill. We watched TV together. Life wasn't all bad. I was so proud that you were a policeman. I wanted to make you proud of me, but you just got so angry sometimes, and I could never do or say the right thing to make you happy."

"You were a pain in the neck. You still are. Fuck off."

Jonty bristled. "Well, at least I *can* fuck off. I'm not lying in bed being a miserable sod. I almost wish I believed in hell because that's where you deserve to be. Bye, *Dad*."

Jonty tugged Devan out past Tamsin, then he stopped and went back to her. "Thank you for taking care of him."

281

"He's not been bad to me," she whispered. "We were good together until he got sick. I think he feels guilty he wasn't a better dad."

You are fucking delusional.

"Did you know about Pete?" she asked.

Jonty shook his head. Tamsin tugged him outside and closed the door. She shivered in the bitter wind and wrapped her arms around herself.

"Pete was his first partner in the police. Sure he never mentioned him?"

"I don't think so."

"Pete died. Run over by a guy they were trying to arrest and dragged under the car. Your dad blamed himself. He saw the car coming and threw himself aside and… Pete died in his arms and it screwed up your dad's head. He drank. Didn't think he deserved to be happy."

"And that I didn't either?"

"He never told me he'd hit you. He *did* tell me he hit your mother. He's damaged, Jonty. His head's not right. I'm sorry he wasn't a better dad. I'm sorry you came all this way for him to lash out at you like that. There isn't any money, by the way."

"If there was, I wouldn't take it. Thank you for looking after him."

Jonty didn't say another word until they were back in the car. "Well, that was fun."

"I'm fucking speechless."

"You think he had PTSD after his partner died?"

"It's not an excuse, Jonty."

"He bottled it all up and lost it when his shell cracked. I don't know whether I'm glad Tamsin told me or not."

"Don't you dare feel guilty. You were a kid. He failed as a father. I can't believe you came out so…intact."

Jonty smiled. "I'm decent, kind and sensitive, am I? You couldn't have added sexy and hot with a beautiful arse?"

"I should have done, sorry."

"Good."

"I don't think you should believe what he said about your mother not wanting to take you in after he was arrested."

"Except if she didn't want me at eight, why would she want me at fifteen?"

"He gave us her address anyway."

"Only because he knows I'm not going to like what I find. He gave it up too easily."

"You don't have to do anything. But turning up on her doorstep isn't a good idea. Let's go back."

"It's okay," Jonty said.

"What's okay?"

"You're feeling bad that you ever gave me a stick and told me to poke that hole. You couldn't have known what would slither out. A stinking shower of shit."

Devan glanced at him and gave a short laugh. "Maybe it should have stayed unfinished business."

"No, it needed ending. I already knew my father despised me. Him knowing he's dying hasn't changed his mind. Why would it? He'll never see what a prick he's been. That's fine. I don't need to give him another thought and I won't. Well, it was never about him but about my mother. Even though I said I didn't want to know where she lived, he knew I did. Except now I'm not sure I do."

"Have I made matters worse? Are you wondering if she *did* refuse to take you?"

"You don't think I questioned whether Social Services had told me the truth when they took me away from my father? Easier to tell a damaged boy a kind lie, that they couldn't find his mother, than tell him she didn't want him, even for the single year he'd need to be in care. One year and I would have

283

been able to live on my own. That was all I wanted. One fucking year somewhere safe and I'd work hard at school, take my exams and have someone to go back home to who cared how my day had gone."

"Would you have liked to do A levels? Go to college or uni?"

"No point thinking about something I couldn't make happen."

Jonty wanted to ask more about the job that Devan had mentioned, but he wanted Devan to bring it up. He wasn't sure he could afford to not look for work for the month Devan had rented the cottage, then end up with nothing if—when he fucked off back to London.

Devan slid his hand onto Jonty's knee. "When you're quiet for any length of time, I imagine your mind darting from one thought to another. What are you worrying about now?"

"How long my money's going to last."

"I'll pay you."

"I don't want you to give me money." Jonty pushed Devan's hand off his knee.

"You'll work for me for nothing? That's very generous. Not sure HR would approve. Nor my boss."

Jonty sighed, but hope flared in his chest.

"I'm going to work something out. I promise. Don't worry about money."

Words that could only come from someone with money.

"I'm going to call my friend and get your mother's number," Devan said.

Jonty's pulse jumped. "I don't want to talk to her on the phone."

"I will. Okay?"

"Okay."

Devan called his friend and Jonty curled his fists under his thighs.

"Good morning, Devan."

"Morning Stan. I have a name and an address. I need the telephone number. Rosie Henley, Oaklands, Burton Road, Newcastle."

"I'll get back to you."

"Thanks, Stan."

Jonty huffed. "As easy as that."

"Stan has his ways."

By the time they were back at Shennan Sands, Stan had texted Devan with the number.

"You tell me when or if you want me to call her," Devan said. "And what you want me to say."

As Devan started to get out of the car, Jonty caught his arm. "Call her now. Let's get it all done in one day. Not the seeing her but…" He took a deep breath. "Tell her you're calling on my behalf and I want to see her, that I don't want to cause any trouble, but I'd like to speak to her. See what she says. Do it on speaker. I'll keep quiet."

"Sure?"

"That I can keep quiet?"

Devan bit his lip. "I know you can't keep quiet. I mean do you want me to call her?"

Jonty nodded. As he watched Devan tap in the number, he held his breath.

"Hello?" *My mother's voice?*

"Hi. Is that Rosie Henley?"

"Yes. Who is this?"

"My name's Devan Smith. You don't know me, but you know a friend of mine. Jonty Bloom."

There was no answer. Jonty pressed his lips together so tightly that it hurt.

"Jonty wants to see you. He doesn't intend to cause trouble, but he'd really like to meet you."

285

Jonty exhaled as he heard her give a heavy sigh. "Is he with you now?"

Jonty shook his head.

"No," Devan said.

"Tell him I'm sorry, but I don't think it's a good idea."

Something crumpled inside him then. The last tiny hope... He'd thought... *Oh God.*

"You might think it isn't a good idea for you." Devan cupped Jonty's chin and stared into his eyes as he stroked his face, running his finger over his bitten lip. "You don't need to see him. He gets that. Otherwise you'd have been to see him before now or made some effort to contact him. He's not been hiding. This isn't for you. It's for him. He's waited seventeen years for you to come back for him. He's still waiting... Please let him have this."

There was such a long pause, Jonty wondered if she was still there.

"Ten o'clock on Monday. The Grand Hotel in Gosforth Park, Newcastle. I'll be sitting in the lobby."

She ended the call.

Jonty collapsed like a deflating balloon. Devan got out of the car, came round to his side, pulled him out and hugged him.

"Shouldn't she have said what she'd be wearing?" Jonty blurted. "A pillbox hat or a veil? I could have worn my Darth Vader mask. I still could."

"It's okay." Devan held him tight.

Devan was breaking his world, but that was fine as long as he helped rebuild it. Bed would be a good start. Once they were naked and entwined with each other, Jonty would have trouble remembering his own name. He tugged Devan towards the door. But the moment they were inside, Jonty stopped dead.

"Someone's been in here."

"How do you know?" Devan looked around.

"There's sand on the floor. Right there." Not a foot print, but as if sand had come off the bottom of a shoe.

"Maybe we did it. We were in and out carrying stuff."

"No," Jonty whispered. "I'd have noticed. I notice things like that. Vincent's anal about sand in the hotel reception. And after last night…"

"Should we call the police?"

"And tell them there's sand in a beachfront property?" Jonty shook his head. "Let's see if anything's been disturbed."

He took one step and Devan pulled him back. "We stay together, but you can walk in front of me."

Jonty laughed. He knew Devan thought the sand had been there when they left, but it hadn't. It didn't take them long to check every room and all their belongings.

"Oh God, did they take your Victoria's Secret Banded Brazilian panties? Or the very sexy sheer cut-out thong?" Jonty mock-wailed, then yipped as he opened the drawer next to the bed. "Ooh, they've left lube and condoms! What if they pricked holes in them? I might get pregnant."

"I thought you were worried?"

"I am. Humour is my defence mechanism."

Neither of them thought anything was missing or disturbed. There was no sign that anyone had found a way into the house, no open windows, no more sand, no odd scent, nothing. And yet…

"I'm not wrong," Jonty whispered.

"I'll call the letting agent and you can listen in." Devan took out his phone. "Hi. This is Devan Smith. We're renting the house at Shennan Sands."

"Oh yes, Mr Smith. How can I help you?"

"Has anyone been out to the house today and been inside?"

"Is there something wrong?"

287

"Just a small sign of disturbance when we came back."

"No one's been out there from here. I can speak to the owners. It's possible our message about renting it out didn't…"

"No, don't bother."

"Have you called the police?"

"No, nothing's missing. It could be our imagination. Thanks. Bye."

"It isn't." But Jonty was less sure than he had been. After last night, he was on edge and more likely to make nothing into something. Although…

"I'm not leaving you here on your own when I go to the hotel."

Jonty didn't want to be left on his own. "Can you take me to Tay's and then collect me when you're done? And…you can meet him."

"Will he be okay with you dropping in on a Saturday night?"

"He never goes anywhere." Jonty headed for the kitchen. "Lunch and then we surf, okay?"

"Okay."

Chapter Seventeen

Devan was still thinking what a bastard Jonty's father was as he tugged on his wetsuit. Jonty seemed to have gotten over this morning already and was back to his normal bouncy self, Devan's personal ray of sunshine. Devan felt as if he'd had his eyes opened onto a different world. He wasn't naïve; he knew some kids had terrible lives, but he'd never met anyone who'd been through what Jonty had.

It brought out his protective instincts. If Gary Bloom hadn't been lying in bed, Devan would have grabbed him by the throat, pushed him up against the wall and... No one had ever stood up for Jonty when he was a boy, apart from Tay, and it broke Devan's heart. He didn't want Jonty hurt ever again and that included being hurt by him.

He was going to find him a role in the company. After he'd made the offer to McAllister, he'd talk to Alan. If they weren't going to get the hotel, then he had a month to persuade Jonty to move south with him. Devan wasn't impulsive, though he did sometimes act on his instincts. Jonty wasn't a rebound. He was tender and warm-hearted despite the crap life had thrown at him.

Jonty was currently wriggling into his wetsuit and turning Devan on. But then everything he did turned Devan on. A smile aimed in Devan's direction, a cheeky glance, a pout, an inhalation...

"Bloody hell," Jonty panted as he finally zipped up. "Good thing it's worth the effort of putting this on. You need a hand?" Jonty glanced at the bulge in Devan's suit and laughed. "You *do* need a hand."

"I can hardly be in the same room as you and not need a hand." But Devan yanked the suit over his shoulders and zipped it up, the hard outline of his cock clearly visible.

"When I buy my next wetsuit, I'm going to go for one of those that deters sharks." Jonty picked up his surfboard.

"Is there such a thing?"

"Yep. Unlike most fish, sharks are colour blind and only see shades of grey, so if you wear a suit that blends in, it makes you difficult to spot."

"Tricky to test whether it works without making sharks see that wetsuits contain food." Devan picked up one of the two boards leaning against the garage wall and Jonty took it out of his hand and gave him the other.

"This one's better."

"One plus of surfing in the UK," Devan pointed out. "Sharks aren't a problem."

He pulled down the garage door, locked it and when they went around the back of the house, he hid the keys under a rock near the hot tub.

"Because no one will look there," Jonty said.

Devan laughed. "Better than losing them on the beach or in the sea."

Jonty hesitated. "What if that sand was left by Brad?"

"I really don't think it was, but even if it was him, he must have a key so it doesn't matter that I'm leaving these here."

"That sand wasn't there," Jonty whispered.

"You want me to ask the agents to change the locks?"

Jonty hesitated, then nodded.

"Then I will. Want me to ask then now?"

Jonty sighed. "No. Later will do. Thank you. Sure you wouldn't rather use your kite?"

"I'd rather surf with you."

"Even though there's a lot of hanging around?"

"You can entertain me. But not by talking about sharks."

"Piranhas, then." Jonty grinned.

"There are no piranhas in the North Sea, but I really don't want hear about any flesh-eating animals or viruses."

290

They headed down over the sand. "Anything to worry about in the water?" Devan asked.

"You're not going to let me talk about flesh-eating fish, so no."

"I was thinking of rocks, rips, underwater volcanos."

Jonty laughed. "We're fine. All sand."

They waded out into the water and paddled out.

"The waves are pretty good today." Jonty heaved himself onto his board. "And only us out here. Need me to show you how it's done?"

Devan glanced over to see him grinning. "I think I can remember."

He shouldn't have been so confident. He grabbed the next wave, but wiped out a few seconds later and came up spluttering.

"Has dementia set in?" Jonty shouted. "Look and learn, Grandpa."

As Devan sat on his board, Jonty caught a perfect wave perfectly. *Perfect, perfect, perfect. Yeah, he is.* Devan watched Jonty ride all the way to the beach and felt like a lump in comparison. As Jonty paddled back out, Devan was so desperate not to fuck up the next run that he mistimed the catch and had to paddle hard, then didn't cut left as fast as he should have, and was pushed under. *Shiiit!*

When he surfaced, Jonty was there, holding onto his board. "Okay?"

"Show me how it's done."

"My rates are forty pounds an hour. Fifty for friends."

Devan floated and watched for a while. He'd not surfed since he'd taken up kiteboarding and he'd never been as good as Jonty. He made it seem effortless.

When Devan finally spotted a wave worth going for, he saw Jonty point at it.

"Ride that fucker, cowboy," Jonty yelled.

291

Devan lay flat, looked round and waited.

"Now, now, now!" Jonty's voice came over the roar of the surf and Devan paddled furiously.

He had to time this right, get on his feet in one smooth movement, plant himself in the perfect spot on the board. Then he was up and riding. It felt good as he cut through the water, the wave rising up behind and around him. He didn't get all the way in, but far enough to make him whoop. He paddled back out to where Jonty was waiting, his white hair sticking out, looking darker than usual at the roots, a broad smile on his face.

"I am such a brilliant teacher," he said.

Devan laughed. "I'm paying fifty quid for *Ride that fucker, cowboy?* And—*Now, now, now?*"

"What more did you need to know?"

The surfing had been what they both needed. Well, what Jonty needed. Devan could probably have done without the seawater he swallowed and the pummelling the waves gave him, but Jonty had enjoyed himself, especially teasing him every time he wiped out and celebrating by dancing on the board whenever Devan got a good ride. And those moments of waiting for the right wave that Devan had used to find tedious? Not anymore. Jonty was…everything.

"What time do you need to go to the hotel?" Jonty asked.

"About four."

"What time is it now?"

"Three."

Jonty whined. "I was hoping for slow and tortuous and I'm going to get fast and furious—*again*—aren't I?"

Devan sniggered.

They rode the last wave in and walked back to the house, Jonty grumbling, telling him to hurry. Devan was only half-listening. He was too busy staring at Jonty's backside, which made him think all sorts of bad things. He retrieved the keys from under the rock and opened the garage.

Jonty wriggled out of his suit faster than Devan and took it outside to hose down. "Hang mine up and pass me yours," he called.

Devan finally peeled himself out of his and took it to Jonty. As he turned to take Jonty's to the garage, a blast of freezing cold water hit him in the middle of the back.

"You little shit!" Devan spun round only to get another blast on his chest.

"Oops. Sorry!" Jonty went back to spraying Devan's suit.

Devan shook the water from his hair and hung up Jonty's wetsuit.

"Yours is done," Jonty shouted.

Devan knew what was going to happen, but he walked through the spray, grabbed the hose and turned it on Jonty.

"Help! There's a man with a huge hose squirting me!" Jonty was darting around, holding Devan's wetsuit in front of him, trying to deflect the water but failing.

Jonty could have moved out of range, but he didn't, probably because beyond the small paved area they stood on, was an ocean of sandy pea gravel. Jonty smiled, pulled off his swimming trunks and stood there stark naked. Devan took his finger off the trigger on the hose and the water dribbled to a stop. Jonty walked past him, hung up Devan's wetsuit, then turned for the house.

Devan shut the garage and followed. When they were inside, Devan pushed the door closed and, without Jonty noticing, checked the lock was in place, because even if Devan thought one of them had walked that sand in, there was always a chance he was wrong.

"You are so slow," Jonty moaned.

"I thought you wanted slow."

293

Jonty heaved a sigh. "You haven't even taken your trunks off." He pressed wet, cold lips to Devan's and pouted. "Now I want fast."

"Ever awkward." But the kiss was like lighting touch paper. Devan pulled off his swimming trunks. "Bedroom," he whispered. "I like to chase my food. Run, little prey!"

Jonty gulped and fled with Devan on his heels. The moment Jonty was near enough to the bed, Devan leapt and brought him down, pinning him in place. Jonty laughed and groaned at the same time, then fell silent and immobile as Devan nipped the junction of his neck and shoulder, before slowly licking down his spine. Devan could feel Jonty shivering, but he doubted it was because he was cold. He trailed his tongue over the crease of Jonty's backside, spreading his cheeks and finally fluttering his tongue over his tightly puckered hole. Jonty still was neither moving nor speaking.

"Have I killed you?" Devan asked.

"You expect speech? I can barely breathe."

Devan licked him again, exactly as before, but this time Jonty pushed his arse against Devan's face.

"Fuuuuck," Jonty gasped. "Oh, that feels so…bloody…good."

Devan curled his tongue, worked it into Jonty's body and the room filled with ragged sounds, Jonty's short cries and longer groans, and Devan's dirty sucking and slurping. He held Jonty's arse cheeks further apart, pressed his face into his backside and fucked him with his tongue. Only when he'd turned Jonty into a quivering, gasping heap, did he reach for the supplies from the bedside drawer.

"Roll over," Devan ordered.

"No. Do it like this. I've temporarily lost feeling in my legs, arms… Oh God."

Devan was too desperate to argue. He slid on a condom, applied lube to his cock with one pass of his hand, then pressed the head of his dick against Jonty's arsehole. He knew he should have prepped him better than this. Jonty needed a couple of fingers to stretch him, not just a tongue, but he had to keep going now, keep pressing, not rushing, but not stopping, carefully pushing in until he bottomed out. *Fuuuuck!* Then he took a breath.

"Your fingers are getting fatter," Jonty mumbled into the bed.

Devan smiled. "Are you okay?"

"No, you promised fast."

He pulled back and pushed in slowly. "Better?" he asked and did it again.

"No! Look, this is me topping from the bottom. Have you never had anyone do that before? Just fuck me. Hard. I need you to fuck me. Or do you want me show you how it's done?"

The sounds in the room changed as Devan began to shunt in and out of him. Jonty felt so good—hot, tight… *Fucking squeezing me!* Devan moved faster, sliding his hands under Jonty, pulling him up so that they were both kneeling on the bed.

Jonty cried out every time Devan thrust into him. Devan shifted his hold so one arm held Jonty across the chest and he put the fingers of his other hand into Jonty's mouth. Jonty bit him.

"Jesus! Don't do that. Wet my fingers."

Jonty's tongue was all over his hand, but he was still biting and even in the midst of raw pleasure, Devan found himself smiling. He wasn't going to come until he'd brought Jonty off. When his hand was wet enough, he brought it down to Jonty's cock and jacked in the same rhythm that he was fucking him.

"Please, please," Jonty begged.

Devan's hand was soaked with precome and saliva. Jonty was arching back against him and when his hands settled around Devan's hands, one across Jonty's chest, the other around his cock, he felt the change in Jonty's body, the tension, the knowledge that in a moment, they would both fall.

One last forceful shunt and Jonty let out a long wail as his shaft jerked and covered their fingers with streaks of come. The moment Jonty had finished, Devan's hips shifted into short fast drives and he flung back his head as his world exploded.

They were late setting off. The only reason they were leaving the house at all was because he needed to get the hotel situation sorted, otherwise they'd have been in bed.

"I'll put Tay's address into the sat nav so you can find your way back," Jonty said. "Works better than breadcrumbs."

"Don't come back to the cottage without me. If Tay's had enough of you, call and I'll come and get you."

Jonty blinked at him. "You think someone was in the house?"

Devan had hoped Jonty wouldn't make that leap. "You were the one who was sure."

"Yeah, I know, but I needed you to say *You're a fucking idiot, Jonty.* Not tell me you'll get the locks changed."

"If Brad wasn't around, maybe, but I'm not taking any chances. Don't come back on your own."

"Not had enough of my lovely arse yet then?"

Jonty was smiling, but Devan heard vulnerability in his question.

"No."

"Are you going to make Hamish an offer today?"

"Probably."

"How much is the hotel worth?"

"Not as much as it would be in the south."

"But you don't get those views in the south."

"Which will be reflected in the price."

Devan pulled up outside Tay's house. "I'll try to be as quick as I can. I'm looking forward to that pizza you promised. Tay could come and eat with us if he wanted to."

"He won't be able to. When you get back, I'll introduce you to him, as long as his mum's okay with that." Jonty pecked him on the cheek and climbed out of the car.

What was wrong with Tay? Devan couldn't figure it out. He carried on toward McAllister's hoping this was all going to be straightforward.

The wedding hit him before he'd even walked across the car park, loud music and guests milling around outside, even though it was cold. Inside, the bride and groom were having pictures taken on the stairs, which had been draped with flowers. *Thank God I didn't marry Ravi.* Devan didn't have one single pang of regret. One week with Jonty and his head had finally cleared.

Clara and Roger were waiting in his room. Clara sat at the desk while Roger was on the bed with his drawing pad.

"Hi guys." Devan closed the door.

"Hi, Devan." Clara smiled at him. "This site is amazing. The beach is fabulous. We went for a quick walk. I've never been to Northumberland before."

"I have," Roger said. "It's bloody cold up here."

Devan sat on one of the chairs. "So what's the verdict?"

"I love it." Roger passed him his sketch pad. "There's so much potential."

Devan went through the drawings the architect had done. A magnificent new entrance, much larger. Extended glass fronted balconies for each room. A new build at the side of the hotel that would contain the spa and have additional guest rooms above. Meeting rooms. A way of making a large ballroom. Roger hadn't been short of ideas. Including a helipad.

"That could go nearby," Roger said. "A field a couple of miles away if necessary. As long as the council gives planning consent."

"You know it's an area of outstanding natural beauty?" Devan asked.

"Yes, but developing this place would give a bump to local businesses and provide more jobs. Our hotel would draw people who've never come up here before which in turn draws even more."

"The growth potential is huge." Clara talked about revenue streams and income projection. Her figures looked good and were in line with Devan's.

"A state-of-the-art spa with qualified therapeutic staff would be a big draw," Roger said. "Having sports facilities as part of what we'd offer as well is brilliant. Padi diving, fishing, surfing, sightseeing, sea kayaking. Any filming being done up here, then this hotel would be the place where the stars would stay. It has everything but the sunshine."

"Which is a big disadvantage," Clara said.

"But celebrities and wealthy people don't go to a hotel to sunbathe. Not in the UK anyway," Roger pointed out.

"True." Clara put her laptop on the table between her and Devan. "The rough costs for renovation, but they are very rough."

"Eight hundred thousand." Devan thought that was at the low end.

"Not enough?"

"No. Let's have another look. Did you check out the places coming up for auction that Alan found?" Devan asked.

"Yes, but this offers the best potential by far," Roger said which was what Devan had thought.

The discussion didn't take as long as Devan had expected. He didn't need Alan's go ahead to make the offer, all he needed was Hamish to say yes. Devan made the call and put it on speaker phone.

"Hamish McAllister."

"Hi, it's Devan Smith. I'm calling with an offer."

"Go ahead."

"One point two million." Devan expected to be pushed up, but he'd had to pitch it at a point that wasn't insulting.

"I was expecting to hear two million."

Devan wasn't surprised, but the figure was unrealistic. "If you'd been in Cornwall, maybe, but not up here. I'll go up another hundred thousand. We'd hope to take over at the beginning of next year to allow you to honour your bookings over Christmas and give your long-term residents a chance to find alternative accommodation."

"One point seven."

Devan sighed — silently. "No. That's not going to happen. One point three is as high as I can go."

"One point four and it's yours."

Devan smiled. "One point three-five."

"Okay."

Roger and Clara gave him the thumbs up.

"I'll be here tomorrow morning," Devan said.

He ended the call and blew out a breath.

"Congratulations," Clara said. "How high would you have gone?"

"One point six maybe, and it would still have been a good deal. I can't believe how cheap property is in this area."

"We have a reservation in the restaurant tonight. Want to eat with us?" Clara asked.

"I can't. I've made other arrangements. Thanks for all your help, guys. We'll get together next week and go over things in more detail. You should be able to get rooms here now the wedding is over."

On his way back to Tay's, Devan called his boss. "Hi, Alan. Sorry to disturb your evening."

"No problem. I take it you have good news."

"I hope you'll think so."

"You wouldn't be ringing me with bad. So what's the damage?"

"One point three-five."

"That's okay."

"I want to retain their chef. He has family in the area which I suspect is the only reason he's stayed. He's really good. I'd like to pay him from the day we complete on the basis that he'll spend time in the kitchens of several of our hotels until we're ready to open. I'm hoping his family will put up with him being away every other week if his job remains in place, particularly at a higher salary."

"He's that good?"

"Yes. Michelin star good. Some of our chefs could learn from him. Imaginative menus, beautifully presented food, much of it locally sourced." Devan mentally crossed his fingers. "Maybe even keep the sous-chef too. I also offered to help with sorting out long-term accommodation for those guests for whom the hotel is a permanent residence. I thought we could rent or buy a couple of houses and use a company called *Helper* to provide people as companions."

"We don't usually go to those lengths."

"I know. But we've never bought anywhere like this. We've never bought a place with long term residents, one of whom is a relative of the owner. Property up here is cheap and an act of goodwill can show we're a caring organisation. It might not be necessary to do anything, but I'd like to have that option to suggest."

"Look into it. Get me some pricings."

"One more thing. I'd like to offer one other staff member a job." Devan's mouth went dry.

"What does he currently do?"

Nothing because he's been sacked. "Night manager, receptionist, bell boy, concierge. But he's capable of far more."

"What qualifications does he have?"

"I'm not sure."

"You already have an assistant. We're not looking for more staff."

"Then I'll pay him, but I want him on the payroll from now."

Alan went quiet. Devan could guess what he was thinking. He just hoped Alan didn't voice it.

"He's on minimum wage here," Devan said. "It's not going to break us or me. He'd be an asset."

"I don't really think employing this man is the right thing to do."

"Then you're not going to be employing me either." The words came out without passing a sense check, but Devan meant it.

"Devan!" Alan barked out a laugh. "Just stop right there. Think about this. You approach me with a half-cocked idea of asking me to employ some young man you've taken a fancy to. Is his name Jonty, by any chance?"

What the fuck? But Devan wasn't going to deny it. "Yes."

"Griff had a phone call that he shared with the office. I wasn't best pleased, but nothing I could do once it had been said. Get your private life sorted out. I told you to take time off. Take it now. Have your fun and leave this guy behind, because —"

Devan cut his boss off. He was furious with both Ravi and his brother and he wasn't best pleased with Alan. But he needed Alan on his side. He pulled off the road as soon as he could and called Alan back.

"Sorry. I lost the signal," Devan lied. "I've pulled off the road now so we don't get cut off again. Will you please consider what I asked? Putting Jonty on the payroll now?"

Alan *tsked*.

"He'd make a brilliant concierge. He knows this area so well."

"Then we'll interview him when we're ready to start taking on staff."

Devan could feel himself losing the argument. "I want to manage this hotel. I want Jonty on the payroll."

"You'd be wasted going back to hotel management."

"I'm only talking about six months. It'll do me good to be back on the front line. If you need me at head office, with a good assistant manager in place, I can split my time. I want to supervise the build, stay up here and commute."

There was a long pause. "Are you thinking with your head or your dick?"

Devan cut him off again and called Griff.

"Hi, Devan."

"You are such a fucking piece of shit."

"You've already made that clear. And you're right. I am. I fucked your husband-to-be the day before your wedding. I couldn't do much worse than that and I'm sorry, but it didn't mean you had to try and get your own back by attempting to pull Ravi out of my arms."

Devan fought to damp down his fury. "Is that what he told you? He didn't have to come and stay at the hotel the company were thinking of buying. He could have easily found a hotel in Newcastle, but he got an Uber up here when he knew you were in London. I didn't tell you jack shit, but I'll tell you now. He offered me a fuck, said you'd never find out and I told him no."

"You told Cato that lie and he told our mother."

"Why the fuck would I lie, Griff?"

"Because you want the two of us to split up."

"I don't give a shit about either of you. Have I caused you any trouble since the wedding-that-didn't-happen? I kept quiet because that was what we agreed. I assumed, because you let me, that it was an aberration, a one-off fuck and there was nothing between you. But you carried on seeing each other."

"I love him. Ravi loves me."

"I'd wish you a happy life, but I doubt it will be. If you choose to believe Ravi over me, then believe him, but you stay out of my business. Whatever Ravi told you about Jonty that you repeated to the office, you had no right to do that. What happened to Ravi at the hotel was an accident. Jonty says he didn't thump him and I believe him. Ravi was pissed off and jealous. He pulled Jonty into the hot tub and ended up with his nose being hit *by accident*. Jonty's been sacked for Ravi's lie. I like Jonty. There isn't a dishonest bone in his body. If it comes to a choice between him and you, I choose him. If it comes to a choice between my job and him, I choose him. So fuck off and believe what you want, but don't spread Ravi's lies."

Devan ended the call and powered down his phone. He took a few deep breaths before he carried on to his destination.

When he knocked on the door, a pretty middle-aged woman opened it.

"You must be Devan. I'm Tay's mother, Philippa."

Devan shook her hand. "Pleased to meet you."

303

"Come and meet Tay. Ionty says you don't know anything about my son other than him being Jonty's best friend."

"No." What was she getting at? What hadn't Jonty told him?

She led Devan to a door on the left and pushed it open. As Devan took in the hospital bed, he registered that somewhere in his subconscious he'd suspected it would be something like this. Jonty lay on the bed next to Tay. They were both asleep.

"Oh Jonty," Tay's mother whispered. She went over and gently shook Jonty's arm. "Devan's here."

Jonty jerked awake, then smiled when he saw Devan. He pushed to his feet and walked over.

"Would you like a drink?" she asked Devan.

"A black coffee, one sugar, would be lovely, thank you."

After she'd left, Jonty wrapped his arms around Devan. "Did Hamish say yes?"

Devan nodded.

Jonty smiled. "Of course he did. How could he resist your talented silver tongue?"

"While you're thinking that… Will you come and live with me in London?"

Jonty's eyes widened. Tay groaned and Jonty spun round to the bed. "Come and meet Tay." He took Devan's hand and pulled him over. "Tay, this is Devan. Mr Impossible, remember? Open your eyes and look at him. He's got his suit on and he looks so sexy and sophisticated. He doesn't mind when I annoy him. You always said I needed someone like that. I wish—"

The door opened. Tay's mother came in with two coffees and put them on a side table. "Yours is on the left, Jonty."

"Thank you," Devan said. "Jonty was just introducing me." He turned to the bed, guessing he should behave as if the guy was conscious and upright. "Hello, Tay."

304

Devan hadn't expected him to open his eyes, but he did. Bright blue eyes that focused on him for a long moment before they closed again.

"Oh my God," Tay's mother gasped. "Did you see that? He stared right at you."

"He did!" Jonty hugged her.

"Does he...not do that?" Devan asked.

She let out a tremulous sigh. "Sometimes he opens his eyes and looks as though he understands what he's seeing. Other times there's a blankness there. I cling to everything that gives me hope." She turned to her son. "Tay, open your eyes again, sweetheart and look at Jonty's friend."

Tay didn't respond.

Devan stared at the pale young man in the bed. "Is he in a coma?"

She shook her head. "He was at first after his accident, but then he recovered a little."

"What happened?"

Jonty sat on the chair next to the bed and took hold of Tay's hand. "He was up a ladder at the back of the house, cleaning a gutter. The ladder slipped and he fell."

"No one was in," his mum whispered. "I came home and found him lying on the ground unconscious, blood everywhere, the ladder next to him. I don't know how long he'd been there. I called for an ambulance and I held his hand and talked to him and told him he was going to be all right." She gave a quiet sob. "I promised him that he'd be all right."

Tay groaned, but didn't open his eyes.

"His bones mended, but not his head," she whispered.

"When did it happen?" Devan asked.

"Five months ago." She and Jonty spoke at the same time.

Oh God. Five months ago, Devan had thought his world had ended when he'd opened the door on his brother and Ravi. Looking at Tay put that right in perspective. Devan

305

didn't need telling to get over it, but now he really was over it. Five months just lying here unable to do anything for himself. He hoped Tay wasn't aware of his situation.

Devan didn't want to ask the obvious question, so he didn't.

"Open your eyes, Tay," his mother said. "Meet Jonty's friend."

Tay still didn't respond.

She straightened up and put a smile on his face. "He's going to get better."

"Listen to your mother, Tay." Jonty's voice broke. "Stop messing around and come back to us. We miss you. I miss surfing with you, sharing chips, telling jokes. I miss annoying you."

You love him. An ache started up in Devan's chest.

"Do the doctors know what's wrong?" Devan asked.

"There's a disagreement as to whether Tay's in a minimally conscious state or a vegetative state," she said.

Neither sounded good. "What's the difference?" Devan watched as Jonty stroked Tay's hand.

"Minimally conscious means the person shows a very small amount of awareness, but it's not consistent. Tay sometimes moves a finger when I ask him to, don't you, darling? Or squeezes my hand. Or opens his eyes and seems to be aware of what he's looking at, as he just did with you."

"A vegetative state is when a person's awake but shows no signs of awareness," Jonty said. "They might open their eyes or blink when they're startled or pull back if you press on them too hard. But they don't respond to voices or follow objects with their eyes. Tay's responded to my voice and to his mum's. And to yours now."

"He's *not* vegetative," his mother said. "I won't accept that. It's a horrible term."

Devan agreed. It had to be awful hearing doctors compare someone you loved to a vegetable.

She turned to Devan. "Jonty has been wonderful. He comes two or three times a week and talks to him, reads to him, listens to music with him. He *will* get better. We promised him, didn't we Jonty?"

"Yes." Jonty's voice was quiet. "Are you listening, Tay? This is getting annoying now, mate. You're missing some great waves. I rode a double header the other day. I'm going to be better than you, all the practice I've had. I know that will piss you off."

Tay opened his eyes again and looked at Jonty, then turned his head a little to look at Devan before he closed them.

"Tracking," Philippa whispered. "Oh sweetheart."

Devan swallowed hard. Had jealousy achieved what love had failed to accomplish? But further comments by Jonty produced no response.

Jonty pushed to his feet. "We have to go now, Philippa. I told Devan I'd make him one of my famous pizzas." He turned to Tay. "Like anchovies on yours, Tay?"

Tay groaned and both Jonty and Tay's mother froze.

"Lots and lots of anchovies. I know how much you adore them," Jonty said. "Those little fishy heads and bones."

Tay groaned again. But although Jonty kept talking, Tay was still again.

His mother showed them out. "Thanks for coming. I don't know how I'd manage without you, Jonty."

Jonty hugged her and Devan's heart sank. How was he supposed to persuade Jonty to go to London now?

Chapter Eighteen

Devan clicked open the car and he and Jonty climbed in.

"I should have told you about Tay," Jonty blurted.

"Why didn't you?" Devan pulled out of Tay's parents' drive. He wanted to ask if he'd been Jonty's boyfriend, but he was afraid of the answer, afraid of how he'd feel about Tay's recovery. *Fuck it. I'm not a good guy. Jonty deserves better.*

Jonty sighed. "I guess I didn't say anything because I like to pretend Tay's fine, still my friend and still around. I talk to him in my head sometimes. He'd already had his accident by the time Brad went nuts with me. I can't tell you how much I missed him. Still miss him. He was lying there in his hospital bed and no one knew if he'd survive and I needed him to hug me and tell me what to do about Brad and he couldn't. Somehow, I started to talk to him in my head, imagine him standing next to me, cycling with me. He was sort of there when you arrived at the hotel."

Oh God. Devan swallowed hard.

"I know that sounds crazy, but he's my best friend and I miss him so much… It was comforting imagining what he'd say back to me and I could hear him so clearly, the exact sound of his voice, as if he was really there. I know it was just me."

"Did he like me?"

Jonty chuckled. "He knew how much I liked you. He kept telling me to apologise. Course, I rarely did anything he told me to."

"You did apologise."

"After a fashion. I know I wasn't very professional."

"Very?"

"You *did* catch my sarcasm virus. Sorry. I know I shouldn't have spoken to a guest like that. But you had all the charm of a pissed-off hungry polar bear who'd realised penguins lived at the opposite pole. You just…irritated me and make my cock twitch at the same time. That's quite a skill."

Devan shot him a smile.

"Are you going to ask me about Tay?"

Not whether or not he was…is gay. "What are his chances of recovery?"

"Depends who you talk to. If someone's in a vegetative state for a long time, in Tay's case, that would be another seven months on top of the five, because he had a traumatic brain injury, then it's called permanent and recovery is extremely unlikely, but not impossible. He might move from minimally conscious to vegetative, but his mother is convinced he can come back. I suspect his father is less hopeful, but he goes along with whatever his wife wants."

Jonty took a deep breath. "It breaks my heart to see him like that. I wouldn't want to keep living if that was all I had, fragments of consciousness that might not even be real, but even though he's been like this for five months, while there's still a chance, I'm with his mother and I hope he'll get better. When he reaches that twelve-month point… Then it will get harder. She loves him so much that she can't see any end to this other than him recovering. Each time he moves or groans or appears as though he's responding, she… Well, you saw. I don't want to talk about it anymore."

"Is Tay talking to you now?"

"No, but if he was, he'd be saying *shut the fuck up and live the life you have while you can.*"

Devan did one of Jonty's swift direction changes. "While you make the pizza, I'm going to sit in the hot tub."

"No, you are not," Jonty said. "You're going to help me, then we'll both sit in the hot tub."

"I've never made a pizza."

"Then you're fortunate to have someone with incredible pizza making skills to show you how. There is so much you can learn from me. My hands are skilled at kneading and pulling and stretching and teasing and…" Jonty made a strange sound then, a sort of choked whimper, and Devan glanced across at him.

"Are you okay?"

"I just turned myself on."

Devan laughed.

"I feel happy," Jonty whispered, "and guilty for feeling happy, which isn't fair. I like being with you. I like us doing things together. I like thinking about you, talking to you, making you laugh. I like that you make me laugh too and I love that thing you did with your… Too much, too soon, yeah? Sorry." He coughed. "I should carry duct tape or a ball gag with me at all times. Hmm, maybe not the ball gag because that reminds me of the guy I'm not going to mention anymore."

Devan put his hand on Jonty's knee and kept it there until they got back. He wished things were less complicated, but Tay was right. You had to live the life you'd been given. One life, one chance and don't fuck it up. He was relieved Jonty could switch moods so easily. For a guy with so many problems, he was more upbeat than anyone Devan had ever met. But Devan wasn't sure how he felt about being a replacement for Tay. What happened if Tay woke up?

They climbed out of the car and "Is he gay?" came from Devan's mouth before he could stop it.

"No," Jonty said. "I used to wish so hard that he was. You'd think I'd know that wishes don't come true." Jonty stared at the door of the cottage. "We should have sellotaped a hair across the door."

Devan opened it. He was relieved Tay was straight. "I think tape might have given it away. You're not still worried that someone got in, are you? Nothing was taken if they did, and there was a lot that could have been. My laptop for a start."

"You're probably right. They'd definitely have taken my collection of butt plugs."

"You have a —" Devan rolled his eyes when Jonty sniggered. "I'll turn up the hot tub. It won't take long to reach temperature. Fortunately, it's one of those that's left on permanently or it would have been days before we could use it. I might have had to keep dipping part of you in and out to test whether it was warm enough."

By the time Devan came back inside, Jonty was naked and there were ingredients all over the work surface. Devan's cock reacted instantly.

"*Bonjour, mon petit.*" Jonty's French accent was terrible.

"Not so much of the little." Devan's gaze honed in on Jonty's trim arse and he found himself licking his lips. As he stripped, he stared at Jonty's face. Jonty's eyes fluttered from Devan's face to his cock and back to his face, over and over.

"You're giving my eyes whiplash." Jonty moaned.

Devan laughed. He came up behind and pressed himself against him.

"I've forgotten how to make pizza," Jonty wailed. "My mind has gone blank. What do I need? Seaweed? Cornflakes? Chocolate?"

"The sooner we eat, the sooner we get in the hot tub."

"Okay. Wash your important parts."

"My hands, right?" Devan moved to the sink.

"Head, shoulders, knees and toes, knees and toes," Jonty sang. "Mouth, cock and balls and nose, balls and nose — ouch!"

Devan had flicked him with the tea towel. "Good voice but a terrible choice of song. Now what?"

"The oven's on. That's a beginner's mistake. We need it nice and hot." He waved a pair of scissors.

"These…are…called…scissors. See? They snap. I'm using them to cut open the packets of pizza base mix. Now you add them to the bowl. Not the scissors."

Devan tipped in the mixture.

Jonty gasped. "How can you miss the bowl?"

"Only a bit missed."

Jonty growled.

Eventually, they had two balls of dough on a floured surface and Jonty had flour handprints all over him.

"I'm a mess." Jonty sighed.

"And I haven't touched you."

"This place must be haunted."

"It's flour not ectoplasm."

"How do you know?"

Devan licked Jonty's shoulder. "Definitely not ectoplasm. Not sweet enough."

Jonty laughed. "Now you have to shape the dough and put it on one of these greased trays."

"There doesn't seem to be very much."

"It swells up when it's put somewhere warm and cosy."

Jonty waggled his eyebrows and Devan almost choked. He concentrated on trying to form the dough into a circle, but it was harder than it looked. Thin in the middle and too thick at the edges. When he glanced at Jonty, his jaw dropped. His was already on the tray, an erect cock and balls complete with a thick vein running down the length of the dick.

"What's that?" Devan kept the smile off his face.

"A tiger and two cubs. Why is your base full of holes?"

"Worms."

Devan tried to stretch dough over the biggest hole and made another one.

"Stop poking it, Mr Worm." Jonty elbowed him.

"Should I try tossing it?"

"Are you good at tossing?"

"I like to think so. I've had many years' practice."

"Don't toss it," Jonty said. "You'll drop it and you're not eating my tiger. I might let you have a cub if you can get it in your mouth at one go."

Jonty helped him lift his mess onto the tray. "We cover it with protective film, then watch it get bigger. Hmm, why does that sound familiar? Is it my dirty mind?"

"You have a dirty mind? Shall I wash it for you?"

"You're getting too mouthy. That's my job."

"You want a glass of wine, or a beer?"

"Beer would be good."

Devan took two bottles from the fridge and knocked the tops off. "How long do we need to wait before we put the topping on?"

"Long enough."

Jonty dropped to his knees, took a mouthful of cold beer *and* Devan's cock and Devan almost levitated. "Fucking hell."

"Not fucking heaven? Can you come in the next ten minutes?" Jonty grinned up at him.

The answer turned out to be *yes*. All over Jonty's face. And although Devan had planned to keep his cock in Jonty's mouth and let him swallow, seeing his come all over Jonty's cheeks and lips and throat somehow intensified his orgasm.

"We should do porn." Jonty stood up licking his lips, a smile on his face.

Devan wet a couple of sheets of kitchen roll and wiped off the mess, though somehow, he wiped Jonty's smile away too.

"What did I do?" Devan asked.

"You were kind. You don't only think about yourself."

That's because of you.

Jonty brought the trays over. "They've swollen so much, we don't know whose is whose."

Devan laughed. "I think we do. That one's mine." He pointed to Jonty's. "Life-size."

313

"In your dreams. No, I mean in *my* dreams."

The pizzas were given their toppings. Jonty managed to make his look even more like a cock and balls before they were put in the oven.

"They won't take long," Jonty said. "Ten minutes."

"Plenty of time." Devan lifted Jonty onto the island unit. Can you come in ten minutes?"

"No way."

Devan bent to take his cock in his mouth.

"Oh right, you're going to do that. Yes, then."

Devan fluttered his tongue over the head, lapping up precome.

Jonty gasped as Devan swallowed him down. "You're going to ruin your appetite."

That was all he said. All that was coherent. His fingers threaded Devan's hair and held tight. Devan let him take control and Jonty's ragged breathing echoed around the room. But Devan pulled back, took control again and strung Jonty out even as Jonty pleaded with him.

"Please. Ah God. I need to come. Now. Bastard. No, kind, lovely guy. Now. I can't… I really can't…"

The buzzer on the oven went off as Jonty exploded into Devan's mouth.

"Fucking hell," Jonty gasped. "Was that perfect timing or what?"

The pizza was so good, even with the holes, that Devan wondered why he'd never made one before. But then, it was making them with Jonty that made the difference. They sat on a rug with their backs to the couch and Jonty kept up a running commentary on how his tasted.

"Juicy, fruity — which is a shock because there's no pineapple on this. Yum yum. Look how it oozes. Cave-aged cheddar is much better than mozzarella. This tastes of diamonds and stalactites… And meat! Which is even more amazing. I could write menus, right?"

"No. You smothered yours with Parma ham. That's meat."

Jonty gaped at him. "Is it?"

"Hurry up and finish. That hot tub is calling."

It was dark by the time they went outside, but the lights were on beneath the bubbling water. Devan grabbed a couple of towels and Jonty carried two more bottles of beer.

"I read the house rules," Jonty said. "No eating or drinking in the bedrooms. No cooking tripe. No entertaining aliens. No glass in the hot tub. So be careful. No lurching at me and dragging me underwater. Well, not until the bottles are safe."

Jonty sighed as he climbed in. "Oh my God, this is bliss."

Devan left the towels within reach and joined him. Jonty was right. It *was* bliss. He took the bottle Jonty offered and took a swallow of cold beer.

"Look up," Jonty said.

The stars were clear and bright. "Northumberland skies are incredible. Too much light pollution in London."

"Look left. That's the International Space Station crossing the sky."

"Not that incredible," Devan pointed out. "It's a plane."

"Oh." Jonty shuffled round until he was next to Devan and Devan put his arm over Jonty's shoulder.

"This is a first for me," Jonty said. "I've never been in a hot tub before. I can't remember the last time I had a bath." He paused. "Obviously, I do shower regularly. At least once a month. Can you fuck in water? I've not done that either. I am such an innocent."

"Is that a question you actually want an answer to?"

Jonty nodded.

315

"Out of the water, sitting on the edge or a step—yes, but not under the water. I'm not saying it's impossible, but no lubricant."

"Unless you're a merman. They have self-lubricating bits."

Devan hesitated. "You do know there's no such thing?"

Jonty clutched his heart. "But I read a book… *Mermen Rising*. There's like a double meaning to that. Right? Clever author. Rising through the water and—"

"I get it." Devan laughed. "Since we're not mermen, we'll sit here and groan for a while as the jets caress our backs and any other parts we can get in front of them, then go inside and fuck like bunnies."

"Okay."

"You're not adding anything to that?"

"Well…do you know anything about bunnies? I'm not sure we want to fuck just like them. The male and female perform a sort of dance where the buck chases the doe until the doe decides to stop before the buck's too exhausted to fuck her. Then the doe turns round and boxes the buck with her front paws which I assume is like saying *you better clean that burrow before you even think about making me pregnant again, mister.* Anyway, then they do the deed. Lasts a few seconds. Literally. Barely longer than you."

"Watch it!"

Jonty grinned. "When they've done, the male squeaks and falls off to the side like he's been shot. A few minutes and they're at it again." Jonty gasped. "Wow, that *does* sound like you."

"Hurry up and finish your beer."

"Has that erotic romance about bunnies got you excited? You want me to box you? Okay, but only if you squeak and fall over when you've done. Promise?"

"Jonty!" Devan lifted the bottle from Jonty's fingers and stood up. "Out."

Jonty climbed out and grabbed a towel. "Are you going to chase me?"

"Not if you're going to turn round and thump me." Devan got out of the hot tub, wrapped a towel around his waist and pulled the cover over the top. When he turned round, Jonty was right in front of him. Jonty went up on his toes and kissed him.

Devan groaned into Jonty's mouth and wrapped his arms around him. Why did he always feel so desperate around Jonty? A hand slid into his and Jonty tugged him back towards the house. Devan reached around and locked the door before he let himself be pulled to the stairs. Despite the fact that his head was fogged with lust, Brad was still an unresolved issue.

In the bedroom, they lost the towels and Devan let his gaze travel over every inch of Jonty's body, from his spiky wet hair, his beautiful dark eyes, that safety pin in his eyebrow, down over his chest with his tight copper nipples, down to his rigid cock. Devan slid to his knees and laid his hands on Jonty's thighs.

"Can you stay on your feet?" Devan asked.

"Probably not."

"Try."

Devan wrapped his hand around the bottom of Jonty's dick and slowly licked from crown to root. He was hoping to give himself time to pull back from the edge, but the breathy pants and moans and instructions slipping from Jonty's mouth, plus the way Jonty curled his fingers in his hair, kept him hanging on to control by his fingertips. He had to fight the urge to push Jonty onto his back and drive into him.

He slid a hand around the back of Jonty's thigh and into the seam of his arse while he wrapped his lips around his

317

balls. Jonty gasped and stiffened. Devan wondered how he could ever have imagined this would calm him down. There was as much pleasure in doing this as there was in receiving it. The way Jonty's balls felt in his mouth, the way he could separate them with his tongue, the musky scent, the salty-sweet taste, the way he was driving Jonty wild…

"Devan!"

Devan brought his mouth back to the tip of Jonty's cock, and licked over the precome sliding from the slit before taking just the tip between his lips. One drag up with his hand made Jonty cry out and Devan's mouth was so full of come, it spilled from the sides. He pushed to his feet and kissed Jonty. He shouldn't have even wasted that split second wondering if Jonty would mind, the two of them were plastered together head to toe and Jonty was kissing him as if he were starving.

When they finally pulled apart, Jonty looked so beautifully debauched, his pupils blown, his cheeks flushed, his hair a mess, that Devan's heart stuttered.

"I can last longer than a bunny normally," Jonty said. "Actually, now I think about it, I wonder if I can. You need to make me wait next time."

"I thought the fist around your cock might work."

"You were too gentle. I need a grip of iron. I need Ironman. Damn. He's not gay. Now it's my turn. Lie down. I'm going to get something."

Devan pulled the covers off the bed and lay on his back with his head on the pillow. Jonty dropped lube and condom next to him, but he also had one of Devan's ties in his hand.

"What are you going to do with that?"

"You look really sexy wearing it."

"Round my neck or my eyes?"

Jonty tied it around his eyes. "Can you see?"

"No."

"Open your mouth?"

"Why?"

"I want to see if you can tell the difference between Coke and Pepsi."

Devan laughed and opened his mouth.

"Damn," Jonty muttered. "Now I want to play that game where you have lots of different foods and you have to guess what they are. I suppose I could look around the room and see what I can find."

"No food in the bedroom, remember? And apart from food, there's only one thing I want in my mouth."

"My foot?"

"No."

"Your foot?"

"I'm not that flexible." He felt Jonty settle on the bed beside him. A moment later, a condom was carefully rolled down Devan's cock, followed by a covering of lube.

"Now you have to count to ten before you take off the blindfold. Out loud."

"One, two—"

"In Japanese."

"*Ichi, ni, san, shi…*"

"Oh, fuck right off."

"*Go, rok, shichi, hachi, kyuu, juu.*"

Devan pulled the tie off and his heart stopped. Jonty lay curled up beside him, his legs over his shoulders, his semi-hard cock in his mouth.

"I can't stay this way for long… Hard to breathe… Be quick… Hey, you know how to do that." Jonty hooked his arms tighter under his thighs and fluttered his tongue over his dick.

"Jesus, Jonty." Devan squirted lube onto his fingers, all over his hand and the bed, God knew where else, and pressed his index finger against Jonty's hole. One finger, two, and… Devan couldn't wait any longer. He knelt behind Jonty, tucked up close and slid in, all the way in, counted to three, not in Japanese, then fucked him.

He was doing fine, holding on, holding back, until Jonty looked at him, his cock in his mouth, his eyes black. Devan's vision wavered and his balls tingled as if he'd been wired up to some battery powered circuit board. Muscles tightened as he tried to hold back his orgasm.

For a while.

A moment.

Several seconds.

Or two. "Arrggh." Fire raced down his spine to ignite his balls. He jetted into the condom and wished there was nothing between them, wished…

He pulled back, worried he was crushing Jonty, and as Jonty let his legs fall away a little, he watched a trickle of come spurt from Jonty's cock to hit his face. It was the kinkiest thing he'd ever seen, ever done. He hadn't even known it was possible. He straightened Jonty's legs and leaned over to kiss him.

"You…" Kiss. "Are…" Kiss. "One hot fuck." Then he remembered what the male rabbit did, and he yipped and fell on his side.

Jonty's laugh lit up his world.

By the time Devan was ready to leave for the meeting at McAllister's the next morning, he'd tried several times to persuade Jonty to go with him. There was no way that Jonty was going to go, even when Brad was mentioned, and he wished Devan would just give up.

"I've been sacked. I'd feel awkward." Jonty picked at the hem of his T-shirt.

"I'm not going to let you get sacked because of Ravi's lies."

320

What does it matter if you're going to give me a job? Except Devan hadn't said anymore about that job, other than asking him to go to London and Jonty worried.

"Please come."

"I'd rather stay here. If the surf's up, I—"

"Don't you dare go in the water on your own."

Jonty took a step back. "Okay, Dad."

Devan pulled him into his arms. "Sorry. But don't."

"I won't. I promise."

"I need to go or I'll be late. How would you like to stay in Newcastle tomorrow night and go to a club?"

"You can pole dance? I'm excited thinking about it."

Devan laughed. "I'm off. Be good."

Jonty pushed the door closed and made sure it was locked. Because...

There was a whole bookcase full of paperbacks at the far end of the room and Jonty went over to browse the titles. After the sex marathon they'd had last night—he ached, but in a good way—he planned nothing more strenuous than making a cup of coffee, lying on the couch, eating biscuits and reading. He chose a thriller by Jo Nesbo, dropped it on the cushion as he passed, and poured the last mug of coffee from the jug.

Do not take more than one biscuit.

Piss off, Tay.

He's not going to love you if you get a fat arse.

You know nothing about what gay men like.

But Jonty only took one biscuit.

Love. What a fucking monstrosity of a word. It caused more anguish than almost any other, in Jonty's life at least. He'd known Devan for one week. It wasn't love. It was lust and overwhelming attraction and friendship and fun and... But could it grow into love? When did delusion turn into hope? How long for hope to turn into reality?

321

Jonty took the coffee and biscuit to the couch, put the coffee on the floor, the biscuit in his mouth and lay back. Then sat up and took his phone out of his pocket and put it next to his coffee in case he called Devan with his arse. He stretched out his legs and wriggled his bare toes under the cushion at the far end to keep them warm.

He didn't have a good record in the love department. He'd thought his mother loved him and obviously she hadn't, but he'd loved her until she'd left him. *After* she'd left him too, for a long while, and then he didn't. He wasn't going to love her tomorrow no matter what excuse she gave for deserting him. There was no excuse she could give that would make him love her again.

The truth was, he was wobbling about seeing her. Did he really want to? How much more rejection could he take? It would be like ripping open a scar that had long healed but occasionally ached. Jonty knew his father didn't love him. Well, maybe when he'd been a baby or a cute little kid, but Jonty's memories of that far back were unreliable. He clung so hard to the good stuff that it warped his perceptions. He wanted to believe he'd been loved at some point in his childhood and yet he wondered if that was true. He'd never loved any of his very small number of—fingers on one hand— boyfriends. He'd never had a pet to love. Just a memory of his mother and sister until his heart finally broke.

Do I even know what love is? Wanting to be with someone, to look after them, be looked after *by* them. Putting someone before yourself. Having great sex. Wanting more great sex. Though it wasn't all about sex.

You love me.

That was true. He did love Tay. No sex involved. *Not quite true.* Tay had meant the world to him. He couldn't have asked for a better friend. He'd had a bit of a crush on Tay at one time, wanked off thinking about him more than one time, but he was so petrified of losing the only good friend he had that he'd never said anything, never given any hint of his attraction and when Tay had asked a girl in his class out on a date, after a few tearful nights, Jonty had let the crush go. That sounded a lot easier than it'd been.

He sipped his coffee and opened the book. A few pages in and he was hooked.

A hundred pages later, his phone rang and Jonty scooped it off the floor. "Hi, Mr I've-used-all-the-lube. Oh, are you on speakerphone?"

"No…fortunately. I've finished at the hotel and I'm heading for the car. All went well. Is there anything you need me to pick up?"

"More lube? A sex swing? Marlon Teixeira? I want to practise my I-can-turn-anyone-gay skills."

Devan's laugh sent a rush of pleasure through Jonty. "See you soon."

As the call ended, Jonty heard the front door open. He thought Devan had tricked him with the call and was already home, but there was a tingling down his spine that made him cautious. He stayed where he was and called Devan back.

"Changed your mind about—?"

Oh God. Jonty whispered, "Help!" and put the phone by the side of the cushion, hidden by the book.

He sat up and as he turned, he saw Brad. *Shiiit. Talk so that Devan knows what's happening!*

"What are you doing in here?" Jonty shouted. *Oh God that was too loud.* "How did you get in? You've been in here before, haven't you? You've bloody big feet, Brad. You left sand on the floor." *Please hear me!*

Brad laughed. "Not just the sand I left, though that was an accident. I didn't know I'd done that."

What? Jonty's mind raced as he tried to think what to do, how he could get away. The bathrooms had locks on the door, but Brad was a big guy and he'd not come out here to be deterred by a flimsy lock. How had he got through the front door?

"Accepted there's nothing you can do?" Brad smirked.

"There's plenty I can do. Would you like a coffee?" *Delay!*

"No."

"Have you taken your medicine?"

"I don't need it."

Shiiit! "What do you want?" Jonty swallowed to try and bring moisture back to his dry mouth.

"I love you."

Oh fuck right off.

"I want things the way they were."

"What do you mean?"

"Me as your boyfriend."

"We only had six dates."

"Enough to know I love you. I want more. I sent you presents while I was away working so you'd remember me."

"Brad. Don't you remember what happened the last time I was at your place? What you did? How I reacted?"

"Overreacted. You don't know what you want." Brad's tone harshened. "I do. Now pack your bag. Then you're going to write a letter to the arsehole with the Aston Martin."

Even if Jonty could get to his bike without being caught, it wouldn't take Brad long to catch him in his car. But one advantage Jonty had over Brad was speed. He hoped. Jonty was wiry and fast. Brad wasn't. The other thing Brad couldn't do was swim.

"Stop thinking and go and get your stuff packed. I'm taking you on holiday."

"I don't have a passport. And you can't swim. Learn to swim first and we'll talk about it."

The longer Jonty delayed, the more time it gave Devan to get here. Or the police.

"We're not going abroad. We're going to Scotland. Now shut up and pack."

"I don't want to go anywhere with you."

As Brad reached for him, Jonty threw himself over the back of the couch. He sprang to his feet, ran for the bi-fold doors, but only managed to pull one partly open before Brad wrapped his arms around him and dragged him back to the couch. Jonty's heart sank when he saw the phone had slid from under the book. Brad picked it up, looked at it and switched it off. Jonty tried to wriggle free, but one thump in his stomach and he doubled over, no air in his lungs.

Brad hauled him upright and cupped his face, his mouth inches from Jonty's. "You know how I like it when you fight, baby. Feel how much it turns me on."

As he grabbed Jonty's wrist and pulled it down, Jonty brought his knee up hard into Brad's balls. Brad cried out, Jonty wrenched free and darted across to the part-open bi-fold door which was wide enough for him to slide through, but would delay Brad. He bolted straight down the path to the beach, hoping someone would be there, policemen out training, someone walking a bad-tempered dog… The beach was empty.

"Get back here, you little bastard," Brad yelled.

Jonty didn't stop, didn't look back. He should have gone upstairs and packed. That would have delayed things, but he'd panicked. The tide was most of the way in and he ran over the beach, straight into the sea and kept running until he had to wade, then he swam until he couldn't put his feet down. The cold stole his breath, chilled his body until his teeth were chattering, but he hadn't been able to think of anywhere to go that Brad wouldn't follow. He kept swimming until he could pluck up the courage to turn and check behind him. He groaned with relief when he saw Brad standing at the edge of the surf. *Thank fuck for that.*

"Bet you wish you'd forked out for those swimming lessons," Jonty yelled. *Idiot!*

"I did. I just don't want to get wet."

Jonty gulped. He'd been shocked when Brad had told him he couldn't swim. *But you work on an oil rig,* he'd said. Brad's response had been *Assuming I survived the fall, you think I could swim back to shore?* Jonty remembered pointing out that if he *had* fallen in, at least he'd be able to keep himself afloat long enough for help to arrive.

So had he learned or not? Jonty thought not, but he couldn't be sure.

"Get back here!" Brad yelled. "Stop fucking about."

You can't swim. Jonty was pretty sure that while he stayed in the water, he was safe. Not that he felt safe and even he was safe from Brad, he wasn't safe from the cold. Brad was screaming at him to come back in. *Oh yeah. I really want to do that.* He lay on his back and kicked his legs only enough to keep himself afloat. *I'm so cold. Shit.*

"What the fuck are you playing at?" Brad paced along the wet sand. "Swim back before you get hypothermia."

A difficult choice. *Hypothermia or you?* Except, how long could he stay out before he became too tired and cold to keep himself afloat? September had been unseasonably warm, so the sea temperature was maybe a little higher than it usually was, but it was still too cold to stay in for long without a wetsuit. Jonty knew the way to conserve body heat was to use as little energy as possible. So even though he felt as if moving his arms and legs would help him get warm, it wouldn't. So he floated, rising and falling on the waves, ignoring Brad yelling at him, doing just enough to keep himself on the surface, waiting for Devan to come, until a wave broke over him and he realised too late what had happened.

He'd carelessly let himself drift back in on the tide and Brad was in the water up to his waist about to grab him. He screamed as Brad grabbed him and struggled to get free, but Brad dragged him out of the water by his neck, threw him on the sand and knelt on his back.

"Now I'm all wet too," Brad snapped.

Wracked with shivers, fighting to breathe, Jonty could do nothing while Brad had him pinned. Even if he got free, he was too cold to go back in the water. Too cold to run down the beach, but he had to do something to give Devan time to get here. All he had was running which should warm him up. But first he had to get free.

"Can't…breathe," Jonty gasped. Not a lie.

The moment the pressure was off his back, he pushed to his feet and sprinted away.

He felt Brad grab for him, but the touch was fleeting. Brad was faster than he remembered, or maybe Jonty was slower because his muscles were sluggish. He kept telling himself to go faster, faster… Then he crashed to the sand as Brad brought him down. He pressed on the back of Jonty's head and Jonty only just managed to turn his head to one side or he'd have had a mouthful of sand. Brad sat on his back and the pain was unbearable. Jonty groaned, but no noise came out of his mouth and no air went in. Black dots danced in his vision. He couldn't move any part of his body. He had just enough time to feel sorry that he'd lost chance of the future he'd hoped for before everything went black.

Jonty came round but didn't move. The weight on his back had gone.

Brad hauled him into a sitting position. "I'm beginning to think you're more trouble than you're worth."

Jonty struggled to suck air into lungs that felt crushed. "I am," he choked out. "A lot of trouble… Everyone says." He had to get his breath back, knee Brad in the nuts and run back into the sea. That was his plan. His only hope.

"Get up." Brad pulled at his arm.

"Just give me a minute. I can't get my breath."

"I nearly went too far there." Brad stood up and sneered. "You look like a drowned rat."

"I don't understand…why you're doing this."

"Because you're beautiful. You were all mine. I liked that. Liked having something just for me. But you were always going on about your pal and I wanted to be important to you like that. I needed you and you needed me. I've done so much for you." Brad booted him in the side and Jonty keeled over. "You don't need anyone else but me." He kicked him again and Jonty cried out and curled up. "I thought I'd made you see that. But no. You don't deserve me."

"I don't." *Oh God.* "I'm sorry. I can try harder. Let's go and get dry. I'll pack my bag and—"

Brad reached down and grabbed hold of his throat. "Do you think I'm stupid?"

"No." Jonty came up on his knees and grabbed at Brad's fingers, trying to pull them off.

"I cocked up with your fucking pal, but I won't make the same mistake with you."

"What?" Jonty was only sucking tiny amounts of air into his mouth.

"That ladder didn't exactly slip."

Jonty's dawning horror immobilised him for a moment, then all the seawater he'd swallowed surged up his throat and he threw up over Brad's arm and hand. As Brad made a sound of disgust and released him, Jonty scrambled backwards. *Run or die.*

He ran.

328

Chapter Nineteen

Devan caught up with the police about three miles away from Shennan Sands. The car was speeding, its lights flashing, yet it wasn't moving anywhere near fast enough for Devan. But at least the police had acted quickly after his call. It had been the hardest thing Devan had ever done, ending the call between him and Jonty so he could contact the police. He didn't have time to stop and ask for someone else's phone. Every second counted.

His car was more powerful than the police vehicle, and if it hadn't been a narrow road, he'd have overtaken, but it *was* a narrow road and an accident would delay both him and the police—and Jonty needed help *now!* He'd kept trying to call Jonty back as he drove, but there was no answer. If anything had happened to him, he'd fucking beat the shit out of Brad Greene. *I'll kill him.*

Hang on, Jonty.

Devan skidded onto the drive behind the police car, blocked in a silver Audi—*so the bastard is still here.*

"I'm Devan Smith, I'm the one who called you," Devan shouted as he ran to the front door with his keys.

"Stand back, please sir." One of the cops pushed the door open while the other headed round the side of the house.

When Devan saw the open bi-fold door, he guessed Jonty had gone into the sea. He'd given him a clue when he'd made the comment about Brad not being able to swim. He pushed past the policeman who was entering through the back of the house. "They're on the beach."

Devan raced down the path and onto the sand, ignoring calls for him to wait. There were two figures a couple of hundred yards away. Jonty and Brad. They were both running. *Thank God, he's still alive.*

The two policemen came up behind him.

329

"They're a long way down the beach," Devan said. "Is there a quicker way to get there?"

"We can drive, cut in closer," one of the policemen said.

"I'll go on foot. If I'm watching maybe…" Devan sprinted onto the beach, moving down to where the sand was firmer closer to the sea. He yelled Jonty's name as he ran. One of the policemen had followed him.

When he saw Jonty splash into the sea, Devan groaned. Brad threw what looked like phone and car keys onto the sand and went in after him. Devan's heart was beating out of his chest. He found another burst of speed from somewhere. The policeman was lagging behind. There was no sign of his colleague approaching over the dunes. Jonty was swimming straight out to sea.

Devan sensed the moment Jonty realised he was there, but when Jonty started to swim back, Devan realised Brad was moving to intercept him.

"Jonty, look out!" As soon as Devan was parallel with Jonty, he kicked off his shoes, tossed his wallet and phone aside and went into the water.

Brad launched himself at Jonty and pushed him under. Devan was swimming as fast as he could. When Jonty surfaced, Brad grabbed him again. By the time Devan reached them, the two of them were entwined and struggling.

"Let him go," Devan yelled and yanked at Brad's shoulder.

When Brad grabbed hold of him, Devan saw blind fear in the guy's eyes.

"He can't swim," Jonty gasped. "He's panicking."

"Jonty, swim away!" Devan shouted.

Brad's weight sent Devan under and the guy kicked him as he thrashed around. Devan stayed down and swam to Jonty, surfacing at his side.

"Get out of the water," Devan panted. "He'll drown us both."

As Jonty swam in, Devan saw both policemen were now on the beach and one was taking off his shoes. Brad was still thrashing around. As soon as Devan was sure Jonty was safe, he swam back to Brad. He ducked under the water to approach him from the rear and wrapped his arm around his chest. The bastard still fought and Devan considered letting him drown. But not with witnesses.

"Don't approach from the front," Devan yelled at the cop swimming towards them.

Devan managed to turn Brad so he was facing out to sea, then kicked to pull them both back to the beach. The policeman joined him and by the time they were able to walk, supporting Brad between them, Devan was exhausted and shivering violently. He dropped Brad on the sand—not gently—and Jonty flung himself into his arms.

"Thank you, thank you," Jonty sobbed.

"What the hell's happened here?" one of the policemen asked.

"He wanted me to go with him," Jonty gasped. "And he tried to kill my friend, Tay Robertson." Jonty was rigid in Devan's arms. "He pushed him off a ladder and Tay's still in a coma."

Devan stared wide-eyed at Jonty.

"Brad told me." Jonty turned to the policemen. "You have to arrest him for attempted murder."

Brad was coughing up water, but he lifted his head and glared at Jonty. "I fucking tried to save your life."

"You can't swim. I went into the sea to get away from you."

A paramedic came across the sand towards them carrying blankets and a kit box. Devan wrapped a blanket around Jonty's shoulders before he took one for himself.

"You need to arrest him." Jonty grew more agitated and Devan pulled the blanket tighter around him. "I was in the house reading and he broke in and threatened me. I left my phone on and Devan heard and called you."

"You have details on file of him harassing Jonty," Devan said. "He's reported him before. Please don't let him out of your sight."

One of the policemen moved away and spoke into his radio. The other, the one who was soaked, stood wrapped in a blanket next to the paramedic who was busy with Brad who was coughing up water. Devan didn't like the way Brad was staring at Jonty. The guy was dangerous. If the police didn't do something, he'd have to. Devan hugged Jonty to him and wrapped his own blanket around Jonty's back, but didn't take his eyes off Brad Greene.

"I'm so cold." Jonty shuddered against him.

The other policeman came back. "My colleague at the station has informed me of what was happening between you and Mr Greene. There's an ambulance on the way to take him to hospital. If the paramedic says you don't require treatment, then we'll drive you home. But we need you to come into Alnwick station this afternoon to give statements."

"Please don't let Greene out of your sight," Devan said.

"He'll be detained pending enquiries." The policeman walked over to where Brad had dumped his keys and wallet and picked them up.

Jonty gave a quiet moan and pressed harder against Devan. The paramedic checked them both out and Devan was relieved when he said they'd be fine. The ambulance crew arrived and took Brad to hospital accompanied by the policeman who'd helped pull him out of the sea. The other policeman gave Jonty and Devan a lift back to the house after Devan had retrieved his phone, keys and wallet.

"Sorry about wetting your car," Jonty said as they climbed out at the house.

"Don't worry about it. I'm PC Andrew Wells. My colleague's PC Steve Nelson. Ask for either of us this afternoon."

Devan hung back as PC Wells unlocked Brad's car. He clicked open the boot and when he looked inside, pressed his lips together.

"What?" Devan asked.

He and Jonty walked over. Rope, cable ties and duct tape.

"A kidnap kit?" Jonty blurted.

"It might be," the PC said. "Can I have a look around the house?"

"Sure." Devan opened the door.

"He must have had a key," Jonty said. "How would he get a key? When we came back yesterday, there was a small amount of sand on the floor. I was sure it hadn't been there when we left."

"You think he came in yesterday?" the policeman asked.

"Yes. He said something odd when I asked him about the sand. That it wasn't only the sand he'd left, but the sand had been an accident. So what did he leave on purpose?" Jonty moaned. "He put a snake through my letterbox where I lived before."

The policeman looked around the kitchen and the living area. Jonty pulled the bi-fold door closed.

"Tell me what happened?" the policeman asked as he continued to look around.

"I was reading a book on the couch. I'd just spoken to Devan on the phone and I heard the door open. I called Devan back and left the phone on. Brad appeared in front of me. He told me he hadn't finished with me, that I was to pack a bag and write a letter to Devan. I made a break for the door, we struggled, but I got away and went into the sea. He can't

333

swim. The first time I went in, I drifted closer to the beach without realising and Brad grabbed me. I struggled, ran again and when I saw Devan coming with a policeman, I went back into the water. Brad came after me, but he was drowning and close to drowning me. Devan and your colleague saved him."

"Do you know what that is?" The policeman pointed to a small black disc on the top bookshelf.

Devan ground his teeth. "It looks like a camera."

"A camera?" Jonty's eyes widened.

"I'll get our scene of crime officers out here. Be careful what you touch. Wait until they've been before you come into the station."

When he'd gone, Devan and Jonty took off their wet clothes in the utility room before they went upstairs. Devan checked for cameras and found one on top of the wardrobe.

"In our fucking bedroom?" Devan snapped.

"You shouldn't touch it," Jonty said.

Devan hung a T-shirt over it. He found nothing in the bathroom. He switched on the shower and they stood together under the hot water.

Jonty shuddered against him. "It's all my fault. He did that to Tay and it's my fault."

Devan wrapped his arms around him. "It's Brad's fault. Don't you dare blame yourself."

"Tay didn't like him. He only met him once and he told me to run. Why didn't I listen? If I had, Tay wouldn't be lying in that bed. Oh fuck."

Jonty slid to the floor of the shower in tears, and Devan crouched beside him and tugged him into his arms.

It took a while for Jonty to pull himself together, though he wasn't sure he'd got the pieces in the right place. The thought that he'd been in any way responsible for what had happened to Tay had taken root inside him like a cancer. He couldn't even talk to Tay inside his head now. He felt too ashamed.

Devan had tried to convince him to eat something, but he'd shaken his head and stayed curled up on the couch. The SOCO team had been and gone. They'd taken fingerprints from various surfaces and removed three cameras along with Brad's car.

"How are you feeling?" Devan asked.

"I'm okay." *I'm nowhere near okay.*

Devan settled next to him on the couch. "Shall we go to the police station and get it over with?"

Jonty nodded.

"I'm going to put that sandwich I made in a bag and I want you to eat it in the car."

"I haven't even asked how the meeting went."

"I'll tell you in the car."

Jonty grabbed his coat and followed Devan out of the house. "Oh God."

Devan spun round. "What?"

"If they let him go, how can I ever feel safe? And you won't be safe either. He tried to kill Tay because I was friends with him. He'll try to kill you because we're…we're fucking like bunnies."

Devan clicked open the car. "Is this the point where you tell me I'd be better off if I walked away from you, pretended I'd never met you? Because I won't do that."

"Not if I wailed and gnashed my teeth?"

"I might if you do that. How hard can you gnash them?"

A smile slid across Jonty's face, but Devan had read his mind. He ought to push Devan away, but he didn't want to. Jonty climbed into the car and clipped on the seatbelt. Even if the police arrested Brad and he was charged, would he be allowed out on bail? He shivered. *I have to go and tell Tay's mum. Oh God.*

"The meeting went well," Devan said. "I don't think anyone was shocked. I'd expected more of a reaction. Hamish had already told the residents so they weren't there. I spoke to Marcus and he's on board with what I proposed for him. He asked about the other kitchen staff, but I can't promise to do the same for them. Maybe for Wayne, but I'll have to look into that. They can apply for jobs next year closer to re-opening if they're still looking. I have contact details for everyone."

"What did Vincent say?"

"I explained about Ravi, what a little shit he was. Vincent said you can have your job back."

Jonty's already fragile world began to crumble. He didn't want his job back. He wanted the job that Devan had said he'd give him. "Right."

"Well, it's something to think about," Devan said.

No, it wasn't.

"I heard Vincent tell Hamish he'd retire when the hotel closed."

"So no one screamed abuse or fainted?"

"It was very civilised."

"I want to go and see Tay after we've spoken to the police."

"Okay."

"I'm not going to see my mother tomorrow."

This time, Devan's *okay* took longer to come. "Okay. Why not?"

"I changed my mind. She made her decision seventeen years ago. What does it matter now?"

"What about your sister, your half-brothers?"

"They don't know about me. It makes me seem needy to ask to see them. I'm fine."

336

Jonty curled up away from Devan and pressed the side of his face to the window. *Because that really screams I'm fine. Fuck!* But Devan just patted his hand. *He knows I'm not fine.*

It was seven at night before Jonty and Devan left the station. This time, Jonty told the police everything, exactly what Brad had done to him on that final date. It was easier without Devan next to him. He managed to utter the word *rape* without choking up, but felt something die inside him when he said it. He'd expected to be pressed about why he'd not spoken out before, but the guy interviewing him was kind and understanding, and that made Jonty cry.

All the tears he'd not shed started to fall. Guilt was eating him up. If he'd spoken out about what Brad had done… If… If…

Apparently, Brad had asked for a lawyer and was claiming he'd messed up his medication which had made him act irrationally. He had to be mentally ill. Obsessive behaviour that Brad thought was love. What an irony to be loved too much by a man he loathed. Jonty was relieved beyond words that Brad wouldn't be allowed bail.

When the police were done with him, for the time being at least, Jonty went to the bathroom. He threw up in the toilet, but it didn't make him feel any better. When he looked in the mirror after he washed his mouth out, he almost didn't recognise himself. Where had his tan gone? His face was as white as his hair. Add in his blood-shot eyes and he looked like a malnourished vampire. He felt empty—drained of everything except for a suffocating feeling of guilt. *Oh Tay, I'm so fucking sorry.*

Devan was waiting in the reception when Jonty emerged. Jonty needed the hug, but even as Devan wrapped his arms around him, he could feel himself pulling back behind his protective shell. If he was going to survive, he had to do what

337

he'd done before. Lock away everything, bin the key and move on. Except he wasn't sure that he could. Not this time. Devan was going to leave him. Maybe not for a month, but he'd still go because Jonty couldn't leave Tay and go to London. *If I rely on Devan now, it will hurt more when he's gone.* Jonty forced himself to pull away from Devan and wrapped his arms around himself.

"Don't," Devan whispered. "Please. I need you even if you're trying to persuade yourself you don't need me."

"You need a happy Jonty but I'm not him anymore."

Devan gripped his hand and tugged him out of the police station and back to where they'd parked. "After a day like today and seeing your father yesterday, it would be a miracle if you were happy. Give yourself time."

"What doesn't kill you, makes you stronger, right?"

"I don't know about that."

"Nor me. I don't believe it," Jonty whispered. "I don't like being shoved through hell to see what I'm made of, as if that will make me appreciate what I was doing wrong so I could do it right next time. If I was supposed to grow stronger, then I was doing something wrong because everything I went through made me feel weaker and sadder. How could there be anything empowering about being abandoned by my mother when I was a kid, being beaten by my father, being told I'm useless, worthless. I wasn't left stronger — I was left traumatised."

Devan stopped walking, pulled him in and held him tight. "But everything that's happened to you has made you into the person you are, which is kind and thoughtful and funny. You're strong in spite of your past, not because of it. You understand what it's like to be lonely, what it's like to be unloved by people who should have loved you more than their own lives. That you can rise above that and be the guy you are... I am in awe of you."

Jonty swallowed hard and hope flared in his chest. "I'm awesome?"

"Yes, you're awesome. One week with you and I know you're strong enough to get over what happened yesterday and today. You can deal with it. You look for help when you need it and it takes a strong man to accept when he needs help. I came up here with my ego battered and bruised. I didn't think I needed help, but I did. I'd lost sight of what I should have been thinking about and you saw that. It's not wrong to feel broken-hearted over things that have hurt you. It's not wrong to feel weakened by them. It's okay to feel glad those things are over."

"So...I'm awesome?"

Devan chuckled. He took Jonty's hand and they walked the rest of the way to the car.

"Still want to go to Tay's?" Devan asked as he sat behind the wheel.

"Yes. I have to tell them what I found out."

"Won't the police?"

"Not unless Brad confesses, I'm guessing. Though I don't know. Maybe they've already called Tay's parents."

"I'm not sure you're in a fit state to talk to them. You look shattered."

"I cried. I don't cry very often."

"Did you tell the police everything?"

"This time, yes. The guy was kind. He didn't say I should have told them before, but I should have."

"You think that would have saved Tay? When did Brad shove the ladder? Before or after he assaulted you?"

"Before," Jonty whispered. "But—"

"No buts."

Jonty stared out of the window. "Doesn't matter. Tay saw in Brad what I'd missed. He warned me and I ignored him and now Tay's life is shit. I'm not sure I can ever forgive myself."

Philippa was surprised to see them, so Jonty assumed the police hadn't yet been in touch. Should he have waited? Was it better or worse to tell her first?

"Back so soon?" she asked.

"I have something to tell you," Jonty said.

"Come in."

Jonty clung harder to Devan's hand as they walked through the door.

"Tell me or Tay or all of us?" she asked.

"Whoever's here and Tay."

"Go into Tay's room and I'll get Jeff. It's just the two of us."

Jonty let go of Devan's hand and went over to Tay. "I'm back again. I know what happened now and—"

Tay's parents came in, concern written on their faces.

"Hi Jonty," Tay's father said.

"Hi," Jonty mumbled.

"I'm Devan, Jonty's boyfriend." Devan shook Tay's father's hand.

"So…" Jonty took a deep breath. "I found out something today, and Tay, I need you to listen carefully. It's about Brad Greene."

Tay didn't react, not that Jonty had expected him to, but he heard Philippa let out a quiet sigh.

"You didn't like him." Jonty pulled free of Devan and took Tay's hand in his. "You told your mother there was something wrong about him and you were right. I saw the truth too late and you paid the price." He couldn't bear to look at Tay's parents. "Brad attacked me…raped me, and obviously, I dumped him. I reported him for assault, but not rape. He's been pestering me and I kept persuading myself he'd give up eventually, but it got worse. Today, Brad suddenly turned up at the cottage where I'm staying at

340

Shennan Sands. I ran away and he ended up nearly drowning."

Tay's mother let out a gasp of shock.

"The police have Brad in custody, but there's something he told me in the house before I ran that...that...broke my heart." Jonty bit back his sob.

Devan moved behind him and wrapped his arms around him.

Jonty took a deep breath. "Brad said he'd cocked up with my pal, that the ladder didn't exactly slip."

"Oh my God," Tay's mother whispered. "Oh no, no..."

Jonty swallowed hard and turned to Tay's parents. "Brad wanted me all to himself. He was jealous of my friendship with Tay. He wanted him gone."

It had to be Jonty's imagination but it felt as if Tay was squeezing his fingers, letting go, then squeezing them again.

"What are you saying?" croaked Tay's dad.

"That Brad tried to kill Tay." Jonty could barely say the words.

Tay's father gasped and hugged his wife.

Are you squeezing my fingers?

Yes, you dipstick.

"Tay, if you remember Brad pushing the ladder, squeeze my hand once," Jonty said.

One squeeze.

"Oh shit. He squeezed my hand." Jonty began to shake. "If you like tomatoes squeeze my hand once. Twice if you don't."

Two squeezes.

"He did it twice."

Tay's mother rushed to Tay's side and Jonty passed Tay's hand to her.

"Tay, darling, we're here. Try to wake up. Open your eyes, sweetheart."

341

"Ask him something!" her husband urged.

"Is your horse called Mungo?" she asked, then turned to her husband. "Two squeezes. Tay, is your horse called Blue?" She gasped. "One squeeze."

Tears were rolling down her cheeks. Even when Tay stopped responding, they were still excited.

"I'm sorry," Jonty blurted.

Tay's parents turned to him.

Jonty felt Devan's hand stroking his back. "If it hadn't been for me, this wouldn't have happened to Tay."

"Don't you dare say that." Philippa tugged him into her arms. "Don't you dare blame yourself for what that man did. You couldn't have known what he'd do. He hurt you too." She held him by the shoulders and stared into his eyes. "You worked a miracle here, Jonty. They were genuine responses from Tay. No one can argue they weren't. If he can do it once, he can do it again. We owe you thanks, Jonty. Nothing else."

Now Jonty was crying. He could feel tears trickling down his cheeks.

"All these times you've come to see him, it's maintained that connection between you and made a difference, will continue to make a difference. I love you for being such a good friend to Tay. You kept faith when others fell away, even his girlfriend and his sisters." She let Jonty go and hugged her husband. "If we get him back and we will, it will be because of you."

"But—"

"No guilt, Jonty," she said. "I won't allow it."

That wasn't going to make a difference, but he kept his feelings hidden for the moment.

"The police will probably call you," Jonty said. "I guess they might be able to get fingerprints off the ladder, unless Brad was wearing gloves."

"It's hanging in the garage," Tay's father said. "It's not been touched since that day. I was going to get rid of it, but…"

"If there's no evidence other than what Brad said to me, and if he now denies it, it's possible the police won't be able to do anything. They might say I had a motive to lie, to get Brad into more trouble."

"When Tay wakes up, he'll tell them the truth," his mother said.

Jonty nodded.

"We should go now," Devan said. "It's been a really long day. Jonty's had quite an ordeal."

"Of course." Philippa hugged Jonty again.

"I'm sorry I ever met Brad," he whispered. "I'm sorry I didn't listen to Tay when he told me Brad wasn't right for me. Please forgive me."

"Jonty, there is nothing to forgive," she said.

Jonty exhaled deeply when he and Devan left the house. The fragments of energy he'd had left had finally gone. He climbed into the car and slumped in the seat. "I'm so tired," he muttered. He closed his eyes and rested his head against the glass. No matter what anyone said, he blamed himself for what had happened to Tay and he wasn't sure how he could cope with the guilt.

"You made Tay's parents happy tonight," Devan said.

Jonty spun round and gaped at him. "Happy?"

"They had their son back, just for a while, but he was in their world, fully responding."

"What if he doesn't do it again?"

"He will. He did it once, he'll do it again."

"I know it sounds crazy, but now I feel worse about him than I did before because I'd sort of convinced myself he didn't really know what was happening around him, but what if he did? What if he's been fighting all this time to make us see that he's still there? He must feel so lost, so fucking…" Jonty bit his lip to keep the tears at bay.

Devan's hand settled on Jonty's knee. "That's guilt talking. Ignore it. This was not your fault."

Yes, it was and guilt was going to keep him in Northumberland, going to see Tay two or three times a week. Guilt was going to stop him going to London with Devan. Guilt was going to destroy his life.

"I haven't changed my mind about seeing my mother tomorrow. I don't want to. Will you tell her for me, please?"

"What do you want me to say?"

"That I've waited for her long enough. That I've finally realised the person I was waiting for doesn't exist. I know she felt pressured into meeting me and that wasn't what I wanted. So it's okay, I don't need to meet her anymore. She isn't going to tell me she loves me, that she thought of me every day. There's going to be no bundle of cards and letters that she wrote and never sent. She's not what I need. Not now. She hurt me and nothing she says can make that right."

He sucked in a breath. "And add that she's a selfish bitch and I wish I hadn't wasted seventeen years thinking she might feel bad about abandoning me."

"Er…"

"Fine. Don't tell her that bit, but call her. Now, please. Then delete her number from your phone. And block her. If she wants to find me, not that I think she does, let it be a bit harder than just calling you."

"Okay. Keep quiet then and she won't know you're there."

Why do I feel better? Meeting her had been supposed to be what he'd wanted and he'd realised it didn't matter anymore. Even if she'd met him with tears in her eyes and sobbed out an apology, there was nothing she could say that would make things right. Denny didn't need to know he even existed.

"Hi, is that Rosie?"

"Yes."

"This is Devan Smith. Are you okay to talk?"

"One moment." There was a faint noise of conversation, then a door closing before she spoke again. "Okay. I'm glad you've called. I've been having second thoughts about meeting Jonty, I don't think it's a good idea."

Fuck you! "Hello, mum." The words lodged in Jonty's throat. He'd waited so long to say that. And the *fuck you,* but still…

There was such a long pause, Jonty wondered if she'd put the phone down and wasn't listening. He wanted to yell that *he* was walking away from *her,* but instead he kept quiet and waited.

"Jonty."

He heard everything in that one word. No sorrow, no longing, just resignation. Someone who'd maybe been waiting seventeen years to be contacted, knowing that one day it would come to this and they'd feel…not happy, not sad, just resigned.

"Don't worry." His blood rushed around his body, setting him alight with fury. "You don't need to meet me. You don't need to speak to me after this call. Seventeen years spent wanting to know why you never came back to get me like you promised, and all I needed to understand was that you didn't love me enough. Just as you didn't when I was taken into care by the local authorities. You *were* asked to take me, weren't you?"

His heart was beating in his throat, fluttering like a trapped bird.

"I couldn't. When I left, I needed a new beginning. I had to hide from your father. I had to cut all links. You needed to

345

go to school. If I'd come back for you, he'd have found us. Then I met a man who wanted to take care of me and my first thought was I could get you, but then I realised how it would look that I'd left you behind, so I never told him I had a son. My husband still doesn't know about you."

Jonty had wanted his father to have lied, though his guess that he hadn't turned out to be right. There were harsh things he could have said to her. Had she wondered after she'd left if Jonty would be beaten instead of her? He could have asked if she slept easy at night, if she ever wondered what he was doing, if he was all right, if he was happy, but what was the point? She'd made her decision seventeen years ago and he guessed they'd both paid for it. Jonty in a desperate longing to know the truth. His mother by sticking her head in the sand.

"I'm sorry," she whispered and ended the call.

Devan pulled into the drive of Sunshine Cottage and turned off the engine.

"Delete the number. Block her," Jonty said. "Do it now. Don't ask me if I'm sure. I am."

Devan took out his phone and Jonty climbed from the car. He took a deep breath, but the air was thick and hard to inhale. *She doesn't love me. She doesn't want to see me. She doesn't care what sort of man I am. Maybe she loved me when I was little, but she doesn't now.* It hurt. And was he even remembering the truth of those early years? Had she ever loved him?

Arms wrapped around him and Devan pressed his face into Jonty's hair. "It's done."

"Promise?"

"Yes, but she could still leave a voicemail."

"Which you never need to open." Jonty turned in his arms.

"Are you okay? Stupid question. Sorry."

"Despite my fucked-up life, I like to think the best of people. I figured it wasn't healthy to go through life

346

distrusting everyone. I've always hoped for too much. That my father would change, that my mother would come for me, that Brad would leave me alone, that Tay would get better, that I'd win the lottery, which wasn't going to happen because I've never bought a ticket." He huffed. "Hope kept me going. Hope put a smile on my face. No point being miserable when things might get better that day or the next or the one after."

"You smile in your sleep. I've never known anyone who does that."

Jonty grinned. "Sexy dreams."

"Maybe, but I think it's you. You have sunshine in your soul."

"And a lump in my throat that I can't seem to swallow."

"Are you sorry I looked for her?"

"No. Seventeen years is long enough. I can let go now." *I have someone more important in my life.* But maybe not for long.

Devan pulled Jonty into the house and closed the door. "I feel slightly anxious about saying this, bearing in mind Brad's behaviour, but I'm not going to let you go. You're going to try and push me away and I don't want that to happen. This isn't the day to talk about the future, but we will talk about it. Okay?"

"Okay."

Chapter Twenty

When Devan woke the next morning, it was almost ten and Jonty was still sleeping, curled up like a comma though not smiling. Devan snuck out of bed, pulled on one of the towelling robes provided by the house, picked up his phone and went down to make coffee. Once it was brewing, he slid open the bi-fold doors and stepped outside. The blast of chilly air made him shiver, but he didn't want to make this call with a risk of Jonty hearing. He closed the door.

"Morning," Alan said.

Devan grimaced at Alan's sharp tone. "Morning. I thought you might like to know that the meeting McAllister had with his staff yesterday went well. No knives thrown."

"I'd already heard. I expected to hear from you."

He had no chance of explaining yesterday in a few words, nor did he want to. "Sorry. I got tied up with something."

"And the chef?"

"He was up for the idea of moving around a few of our hotels in the new year. As long as he gets to come home at the weekend and doesn't have to be away every week, he'll sign with us. His wife is pregnant and they already have three young kids. He needs job security."

"Fine. I've seen Roger's ideas and Clara's figures. They're staying up there for a week to speak to planners and get more detail into their reports. I've engaged a surveyor and I have our lawyers working on the contract. I thought I'd take some of the weight off you, so that you can have your break, get things…out of your system."

Devan counted to three. Nowhere near enough. He made a superhuman effort to keep his voice level. "By things, you mean Jonty? That's not going to happen. If you won't put Jonty on the payroll, you can take me off it."

"Devan! Don't be ridiculous. You're a large part of this company. You own a chunk of it. You know what a terrible idea it is to work alongside people you're involved with. You have enough trouble working in the same place as your brother."

Fuck you! But Devan kept his mouth shut.

"What happens when you tire of this man? We'd be stuck with a belligerent employee, one who could easily claim sexual harassment."

"I won't tire of him."

"You've known him a week!"

A day was long enough to know! "He can move from hotel to hotel like the chef, maybe *with* the chef and learn more about the hospitality business. I told you I'd pay his wages."

"You can't do that. We wouldn't be insured. It would be too complicated."

"Then you pay him out of a cut in my wages, and the company gets the benefit. I was serious when I told you I want to project manage the renovations and run the hotel for six months."

Alan made a sound of exasperation. "And what happens if you're needed elsewhere?"

"Then I'll catch a train or fly. At least think about it."

"Fine."

This time Alan hung up on him. *I probably deserved it.*

Devan took a shaky breath. If it came to it, would he give up his job for a guy he'd only just met? Where was his rational decision making now? His logical brain? His measured response? He didn't need the money, but that wasn't the point. He *did* need to be doing something, but he wanted Jonty in his life in a way that Jonty would accept. He went back into the house. The coffee had finished brewing so he poured two mugs and carried them upstairs.

Jonty was still a punctuation mark in the bed, so Devan left his drink on the side table and went onto the balcony. As he sat on the chair, he registered the door he'd just opened hadn't been locked, and he sighed. Had Jonty been out here and heard what he'd said? Or hopefully one of them or the police had forgotten to lock it in all the drama of yesterday.

He stared out at the sea; waves were pounding the shore. If the conditions had been like this yesterday, the outcome could have been very different. If he'd been a couple of minutes later arriving, Brad might have drowned Jonty trying to save himself, then drowned anyway. Devan was all logic and numbers. He gave little credence to luck, but his heart stuttered at the thought of what might have happened.

Pressing Alan to give Jonty a job might be moot because he was sure Jonty wouldn't want to leave Tay or Northumberland, even for six months. And while Devan liked the idea of managing a hotel for a while, he wouldn't want to do it long-term. He and Alan might part ways. Devan was good at what he did, but no one was indispensable, even someone with part-ownership of the company.

The door slid open behind him and Jonty came out carrying his coffee. He was wearing a robe, but he hadn't fastened it and was naked beneath. He put his coffee down, took Devan's from his hand, then unfastened Devan's robe and straddled his lap before pulling his own robe around them both and cuddling against him.

"How are you feeling?" Devan wrapped his arms around him.

"I'm okay."

"Said by someone who doesn't sound okay."

"I had a difficult day yesterday."

"Yeah, you did."

"We need to talk."

Shit. Devan felt as if he had his head on the block, waiting for the axe to fall. "I don't think I've ever heard those words followed by something I wanted to hear."

"We need to talk, I've won the lottery. We need to talk, I've had a penis extension. We—"

"Shush. Just tell me."

"Tell me what you want!"

"Right now?"

"Yep. What you really, really want." Jonty pressed his head into the crook of Devan's neck.

"Why don't you tell me what you really, really want, Sexy Spice?"

Jonty's chuckle reassured him. "I asked you first and I'm not talking about me sitting on your cock in the next five minutes. That's definitely happening." Jonty slid lube and a condom onto the table from his pocket.

Devan moaned. His cock had perked up the moment he saw Jonty and was currently wedged against Jonty's erection.

"The quicker you answer, the faster you get one small bit of you very warm," Jonty said.

"Small?"

"Well, it's not the size of your leg, is it? Or your arm. In comparison, it's small."

"Fine, it's small. I'm not going to waste time arguing."

"So I can tell people you have a small dick?"

Devan laughed. "No."

"But you said it was small."

"Jonty! Shut up."

"You're tired of my mouth already?"

"You know I'm not. But you asked me a question, then went off on one of your tangents."

"You don't have a small dick, in case you were worrying."

Devan laughed.

"I can tell everyone that, so really don't worry about it."

351

"Oh God. Right. What I really, really want. There are various options. One is that you go back to work at McAllister's until it closes down and I come up to see you or you come down to see me when you have time off. I can work from up here for short periods of time. I'd buy us a house to live in or rent one."

"Apart from the not-minor issue that I'd be Mr Unpopular at the hotel since I'm shacked up with the guy who's going to take away everyone's job, I work nights and most weekends. What's the point of you being up here if I'm not with you at night? I don't want you sharing your bed with anyone else. Though I *could* buy you a teddy. Or a blow-up doll? I looked them up on Amazon. There's a cheap one, but it doesn't have balls. And you do like balls. Maybe you were a dog in a previous life."

"Jonty?"

"Yes?"

"Shush. Another option is that when our month is up here, you come back to London with me and gain work experience in some of our hotels, then we'd return to Northumberland, be around as the hotel is renovated, and when it reopens, work in it for six months."

"What if the manager doesn't like me?"

"He already does."

"Your boss hasn't agreed."

So Jonty *had* overheard. "Little pigs have big ears."

"But aren't they the cutest ears you've ever seen?"

Devan nipped the nearest one and got a mouthful of piercing.

"Ouch." Jonty winced.

"Yeah, they are cute."

"That one's not cute now you've mangled it with your teeth."

Jonty rubbed it.

352

Devan kissed it.

Jonty melted against him and Devan's cock started getting bigger ideas. *Not yet. This is too important.*

"You'd be a brilliant concierge. You're an expert on the local area. Who else would have known you have to sing to the whales around here or feed them Maltesers? Though I don't want you showing anyone but me the fourth wonder of Northumberland. You get on really well with people of all types and ages. But you might need training on how to handle frustrated, difficult travellers and awkward celebs."

"You mean if they complain, I can't be sarcastic and tell them we treat all our guests equally badly?"

"No."

"Nor seduce them with my lovely arse?"

Devan laughed.

"Well, shit. I could take guests surfing, though, yeah? Well, the young and fit ones, guys with good bodies."

"A concierge doesn't get to do that."

"Oh." Jonty pouted. "What about the Harry Potter experience at Alnwick? Would I get to take guests to that?"

"You have to stay in the hotel."

"I could help guests out if they wanted a video of themselves in bed together."

"No, you couldn't."

"But I watch Pornhub all the time. I know just what to do."

"No."

"It's no fun at all being a concierge."

Devan smiled and kissed Jonty's head.

"Are they the only options?" Jonty asked.

"I…I sort of figured that you wouldn't want to leave Northumberland for long, if at all, because of Tay, and because of how much you love it up here."

"I got the impression your boss wasn't keen on employing me."

"I've never noticed how enormous your ears are. Bat more than pig."

"But still sexy and cute, right?"

"Yes."

"You threatened to resign if he didn't give me a job," Jonty whispered. "What if he calls your bluff?"

"It wasn't a bluff, bat boy."

Jonty gave a deep sigh. "So what could we do if we're both unemployed and need jobs?"

"Do you have any ideas?" Though the moment he'd said that, he sort of wished he hadn't because he could guess what was coming.

"Porn. Only with each other. We could make money and have fun at the same time. A win-win. Oh no, though. Your mother might see it."

Devan laughed. "Yeah because my mother watches gay porn all the time."

"I'm not surprised."

"Jonty, I was kidding. She—"

"Mum's the word. I get it. We could open a detective agency. From what I understand, most of their work is following cheating spouses and taking pictures to prove the infidelity. Imagine getting paid for taking pictures of big dicks. I'd love that."

"No."

"Run a gay bar?"

"No."

"Yoga instructors?"

"Can you do yoga?"

"No."

"Then no."

"Ghostbusters? Though if we actually found a ghost, you'd have to deal with it."

"No."

"Mr Negative!"

"Well, suggest something that's actually possible."

"Do you like your job?" Jonty whispered. "You told me you were a quantitative analyst."

"I was, I am, I stretched the truth."

"I know it has something to do with risks and money and computers, but what exactly is it? Short version. I have a terrible attention span."

"I hadn't noticed."

"Liar. What's for breakfast?"

Devan smiled. "A quant develops complex mathematical models used by financial firms to make decisions about investments, risk management and pricing. I went straight from studying maths and computer science at university into trading. But I was getting pigeonholed in the field I was in, plus it was stressful, and when I was offered the chance to work for and invest in the hotel group, I took it. What I do now is work out whether a potential purchase is a good investment."

"Can you do it freelance, not just with hotels, but anything?"

"Yes."

"So you could set up a business and I could be your sexy assistant."

"Doing what?"

"Making coffee, coming up with endless ways to de-stress you. You could train me to do what you do. I might have to conquer the nine times table first. Oh God, is it all computer code work? I'd be too tempted to flick onto Pornhub. I'd better stick to stress release." Jonty shifted against Devan's cock.

Devan clutched Jonty's hips and held him still. "You asked me what I wanted to happen. I want you. And I'll do whatever it takes to keep us together."

"Without using rope?"

"Only words."

"And sex."

"Fine. Words and sex."

"Dirty words?"

"Shush. If it means commuting, then I'll commute. If it means giving up my job, I'll give it up. But I'll have to travel because the demand for quants won't be high in this area. You want to stay here. I get that. In an ideal world, I'd like us working in London where opportunities are better for both of us, but I want to be wherever you are."

"But not like a stalker."

"Exactly like a stalker, though without the creepy part. And the rope."

Jonty laughed. "No more talking."

Devan didn't think they'd finished, but he'd let it go. He just had to be patient.

Jonty slid his hand between their bodies and wrapped his fingers around their cocks. "Ooh look what I found." Jonty gripped tightly, then moved his hand up a fraction, squeezed and did it again.

"What, apart from the obvious?" Devan clenched his arse cheeks, shuddering as precome pearled at his tip and overflowed.

"Another way to drive you wild."

Devan slipped his hands inside Jonty's robe and cupped his backside. "Only 1,497 to go."

"What? You're short-changing me. The average Brit has sex a total of 5,778 times before he dies and obviously you'd have to at least double that for a gay guy. So, there should be…"

"10,059 to go, minus the few you've already managed."

"I am so turned on. You're a human computer."

Devan shuddered again as Jonty moved his hand a little higher and squeezed.

"Being driven wild doesn't always lead to sex, so maybe that figure needs to be tripled," Jonty murmured.

"30,177."

"If I'd died yesterday, I'd have missed so much. The beauty of maths on the lips of a sexy guy, for a start." Jonty squeezed again, brought a finger to where his hand clutched their cocks and swiped up precome from both of them. He brought his finger to his mouth, licked, then sucked.

"We not sharing?"

Jonty smiled, dropped his hand and when he brought it to Devan's mouth, he gave him three fingers to suck.

"I forgot to say thank you," Jonty whispered and ran his thumb over the head of Devan's cock.

"What...did I do?" Devan was having trouble thinking straight.

"Saved my life."

Devan looked into his eyes and what he saw there wasn't just heat and lust, but something else, something deeper, something that made the breath catch in his throat and his heart race.

Jonty leaned in until his mouth was inches from Devan's. "Thank you for making me happy."

Devan scarcely had time to breathe in before their lips met. No gentle kiss, but a hard, forceful one, greedy and desperate. Jonty ate at him, consumed him, rocked and ground against him until Devan forgot about breathing. He clutched tighter at Jonty's backside, his fingers deep in the seam of his arse. He found the lube pushed, then forced, into his hand and laughed into the mouth plastered against his, laughed again when Jonty squealed as Devan hauled his robe up and squirted cold lubricant down his crease.

Jonty's groan when Devan eased a finger inside him dragged a groan from Devan too. When one finger became two, the sounds they were both making grew louder. Then Jonty was a writhing mess on his lap, gasping into Devan's mouth, his hands curled between their chests as Devan finger-fucked him.

"Oh God," Jonty groaned. "How come you know where *Eldorado* is?"

"Because I have an *Eldorado* of my own."

Jonty laughed. "You do?"

"Put the condom on me."

Jonty grabbed it, ripped it open and rolled it down Devan's cock. "It fits, Cinderella!"

"Let's see if it really does."

Devan lifted Jonty by the waist and Jonty settled his feet on the chair cushion either side of Devan's hips. Jonty crouched down, still supported, reached for Devan's cock and held it against the entrance to his body.

"Don't drop me," Jonty whispered. "I might break something. You can break cocks. I read—"

"Jonty!"

"I'll be careful. I'd hate to break—"

"If you keep talking about breaking a cock, there won't be anything to worry about in a moment."

Jonty smiled, and slowly sank down while he stared into Devan's eyes.

"Fuuuuck." Devan released a shaky breath. "That feels so good." He moved his hands from Jonty's waist to cup his backside, stroking his hips with his thumbs.

Jonty's hands were everywhere, caressing and teasing, fluttering over Devan's face, his mouth, his neck, his nipples.

When Jonty finally moved, lifting himself up before sinking back down, Devan's world shimmered out of focus.

He let Jonty set the pace for a while, knew from the keening sounds Jonty was making that he was hitting his prostate, then Devan took over, bucking up into Jonty's arse until they were moving together faster and faster. He managed to get one hand to Jonty's cock to jack him off, but every fibre in Devan's body was strung so tight, it was a fight to keep control.

Jonty came first, crying out, soaking Devan's fingers and his chest. The ache in Devan's head and gut felt so good, he wanted to string it out, stay in that blissful state of awareness of knowing even better was to come. He tried and tried to keep riding the wave, but every wave breaks and Devan finally tumbled, his body exploding into Jonty's, his cock pulsing, and he knew there would never be anyone else for him.

He pulled Jonty close and wrapped his robe around both of them.

"Don't leave me," Devan whispered. "Not ever."

"I won't. I want this so much."

"This?" Devan smiled.

"Not just this, but you and me and going on dates and doing stupid things and holidays and birthdays and chocolate and Christmas and you complaining about me burning the toast and me trying to add two and two faster than you and finding *Eldorado* time after time—"

Devan kissed him. "I want to give you everything."

"Even your Aston Martin?"

"Almost everything."

They spent a lazy twenty-four hours in bed, kissing, exploring each other's bodies, mapping trails, marking treasures, sleeping, laughing, eating. If it hadn't been for Tay, Jonty *would* have left Northumberland with Devan. Even if his mother had turned out to be what he'd hoped for, he'd still have left, because seventeen years was long enough to mourn. He knew it was too soon for either him or Devan to say *the L word* but… What Jonty felt was so all consuming, so powerful that he wanted to yell out his joy. They were from two different worlds, but they would make a planet of their own.

Jonty squirmed as something tickled his neck. *What?* Not a finger. *A feather.* "Tell me you took that off the seagull first."

Devan laughed. "I think it came out of a pillow."

"What are you going to tickle me with next? Not anything small and hard."

Devan growled. "I do not have a small cock."

Jonty rolled over to face him. "Of course, you don't." He patted Devan's cheek and just managed to move his fingers away from snapping teeth.

"I wonder if Tay's responded again," Jonty whispered.

"You do know he's not going to just get out of bed and resume his life as if nothing had happened?"

"I know. His mum told me what the doctors said in those early days, but I checked online, read everything I could, so I knew what to look out for and what might be in his future. If I didn't need to be near Tay, I'd follow you to the ends of the earth."

Jonty ran his finger over Devan's lips. "Where do you think that actually is? I don't mind cold, but not too cold. So not Antarctica or the Arctic. Or anywhere too hot like the Sahara or Dubai, or anywhere with snakes like Australia or the Amazon, or crocodiles so Africa is a no, and not France because they eat snails. And I have a phobia about monkeys so… I forgot to add them to my *don't like* list. Oh God, there's loads of places I'm not going to be able to follow you to. I'll make a list and if you go, you can send me postcards and pictures of your dick so I don't forget it."

Devan turned Jonty over and tucked up behind him, pulling him in close. "Why would I want to go anywhere without you? My role in life is to keep you warm and safe."

"You *are* one big hot water bottle. At least I'm *fairly* sure now that we're sexually compatible. Though it's going to take years until I'm certain. And I haven't yet introduced you to the tenth wonder of Northumberland."

"I'm not going to ask."

Jonty chuckled. "You will eventually."

"If not for Tay, would you really leave Northumberland?"

"Yes." Jonty didn't hesitate. "I never wanted to. I know I told you that. It wasn't just because of the possibility of my mother looking for me that I wanted to stay, but now, if not for Tay, I'd go in a heartbeat. Northumberland will always be here and I can come back anytime and nothing much will have changed. It hasn't over centuries. It'll still be the most beautiful and mysterious county in England. But Tay *is* here, and he needs me, and no matter how much everyone might tell me I'm not responsible for what happened, I feel that I am. Even if Brad hadn't been involved, I couldn't desert Tay. And I don't want you to feel that I'm choosing Tay over you. I'd hate you to think that."

"Your loyalty to your friend is one of things I admire about you."

Jonty squirmed round in Devan's embrace so he was facing him. "Another thing that isn't going to happen is you giving up your job because of me."

When Devan opened his mouth, Jonty pressed his hand on it.

"I've been thinking..." Jonty said.

Devan lifted Jonty's hand away from his mouth. "You were able to think while I've spent all this time blowing your mind? I'm so insulted."

Jonty laughed. "I had to do something in between the times you were doing that, when you needed to take a rest, Grandpa. What if I found a different job up here? One with reasonable hours. Maybe part time. There must be something I can do in Alnwick. Supermarket or a shop. I could ask Mike if he has any ideas. We'd need to rent a place, and I'd have to have help with the rent if I didn't work full time. Maybe even if I did. Ooh, I'd be your rent boy."

Devan groaned. "We're not going down that path."

"Every time I knew you were coming home, I'd take my clothes off and lie on the couch waiting for you, ready to be licked all over."

"Maybe we *are* going down that path."

"And if you wanted to get into pony play, I could buy some reins."

Devan whined.

"Was that a whinney?"

"No."

"If we rent a place up here, you can do your job in London and come up whenever you can, and sometimes I can get a train to London to stay with you. As long as you promise to meet me at the station. You know how easily distracted I am. An offer of chocolate and I'm off. If you're more involved with the renovation of McAllister's after Christmas, then that would be great, but if you don't really want to be dealing with the hotel and you only said it so we could be together, then don't do it.

"As soon as Tay is making progress, I won't need to be so close, though I don't know how long it will take for Tay to get better. I could come up from London to see him though. We can make it work, can't we? I mean, you spent a fortune on

362

this place, but we only need a room with a bed and kitchen and bathroom. Could you afford to help me rent somewhere up here as well as wherever you live in London?"

"This is where I tell you that you don't need to worry about money. I have plenty."

"You do? How much is plenty? A few thousand?"

"A few million."

Jonty sucked in a breath. "Wow. Are you a prince?"

"No."

Jonty pouted and dropped his shoulders. "Oh well."

Chapter Twenty-One

Jonty stayed curled up in bed while Devan showered and dressed. Devan wanted to go out and Jonty didn't want to move.

"No more lazing around." Devan yanked off the sheets.

Jonty groaned and curled up tighter, pressing his face into the pillow. "I'm never lazy in bed. Why do you think I'm so tired? You make me do all the work. Suck this, lick that, stroke this, kiss that. Your demands are never-ending."

Devan laughed. "So are your moans. Today I want to go on a trip. Get up, get dressed and I'll make breakfast."

"What if I want to lie in bed all day?"

"We've been doing that for the last four days. I want to go out."

"Go out then."

"I want to go out with you, because I see things differently through your eyes."

Jonty groaned when Devan breathed into his ear.

"I've been asleep too long in more ways than one," Devan said. "I've got your list. Let's pick something off it."

Jonty felt paper land next to his head.

"Choose or keep your eyes closed and point."

He reached out, and let his finger drop onto the paper.

"Knight and dragon at Dunstanburgh Castle," Devan said.

Jonty opened his eyes and beamed. "We might as well do the BDSM experience at Craster too. Forty ways to have fun with a kipper."

"I'm not a huge fan of kippers."

"Bet I can change your mind."

"Bet you can't. Uncurl, so I know you're not going to drop off again."

Jonty stretched into the shape of a starfish, lifted his hips and humped the bed.

"I'm not looking," Devan said, though Jonty suspected he was.

"Oooh, aaaah, mmmm," Jonty moaned.

"Not listening either. I'll make a start on breakfast."

Jonty wailed. "You've gone off me already."

"Just in case that's true, put those tight jeans on," Devan called as he headed downstairs.

"It's my job to be the funny one," Jonty called back.

They walked from the car park on the edge of Craster along a beautiful stretch of coastline to the castle. The sea was wild again today and the wind biting.

"It's not far," Jonty said. "We can have fun with kippers when we get back."

"Not going to happen."

The castle was in ruins, but the twin-towered keep was still impressive. The closer they drew to it, the more magnificent the ruins looked.

"It's amazing to have all these castles on your doorstep." Devan took a picture with his phone and Jonty took a picture of Devan taking a picture to add to the ones he'd already taken. He had a plan.

"There's been a fortification here since 3BC," Jonty told him. "This castle was built in 1313, and had bits added later. It was the biggest in Northumberland."

"To keep the Scots out?"

"No, which is unusual for this part of the country. It was built for protection by a guy who'd fallen out with the English king."

Jonty had a bit of battle with him over who'd pay to go in. Devan won, but only because he had his wallet out faster.

"Is that why you wanted me to wear these tight jeans?" Jonty asked loud enough for the woman on the desk to hear.

Devan rolled his eyes and ushered him inside.

"I don't want you to pay for everything," Jonty said.

"Then buy your own kippers." Devan slung his arm over Jonty's shoulder. "It makes me happy to spend money when I'm with you. I don't mean to be insensitive, nor do I want to undermine your independence, but until you're working again, you're eating into your *this is going to change my life* fund and you don't need to do that."

Jonty didn't need the fund anymore. His life had already been changed. He felt like pinching himself every time he woke with Devan lying at his side.

"Did you make your millions in your first job?"

"I didn't rob a bank as you so helpfully suggested to Tay's aunt. I was well paid, but I also made some good investments. I seem to have a knack for making money grow."

"And I can make it disappear." Jonty laughed and took hold of Devan's hand. "There's a story about this place. Want to hear it?"

"Yep."

"One dark and stormy night… a bit like today, but it was night and stormy… a knight, Sir Guy, took shelter in the castle and a wizard led him to the bedside of a princess. She was sleeping under a spell surrounded by sleeping knights, and guarded by two skeletons. One held a sword, the other a horn. The wizard told him the fate of the princess depended on the knight waking her. He had to choose the sword or horn. What would you have picked?"

"The sword."

"You chose wisely. The knight didn't. He picked the horn and it woke the knights. Sir Guy found himself outside the castle, and spent the rest of his life trying to find a way back in, haunted by the words *Shame on the coward who sounded a horn, when he might have unsheathed a sword.* Except if he was a knight, wouldn't he have already had a sword? I don't quite get it."

"Maybe it's to make the point that when faced with adversity, you need to be strong and prepared to fight for what you want."

Jonty pulled Devan out of sight of the only other couple who were looking round. When they were close to the wall, Jonty lay down on the grass and looked up at Devan. "Pretend I'm a sleeping princess."

"Oh God," Devan groaned.

"Make the right choice," Jonty said in a creepy voice. "Remember what those bad guys chose before Harrison Ford picked that crappy looking chalice."

"Fuck," Devan mumbled. "Fine."

He took a look round, and with his back to the direction anyone might come, he unzipped his jeans, knelt down and took out his cock. Jonty shut his eyes, opened his mouth and fluttered his tongue.

"Bloody hell," Devan croaked. "Be quick."

Jonty licked Devan's cock, opened his eyes and grinned. "Sir Guy, what a mighty sword you wield."

When Jonty went for another lick, Devan stuffed his cock back into his trousers and zipped up. He put out his hand, hauled Jonty to his feet and into his arms.

"Do not get any ideas about me wielding my sword against a dragon until we get back to the cottage."

"You are no fun at all. How is the BDSM with a kipper going to work if you don't get your cock out?"

There was little Jonty liked better than teasing Devan. But by the time they were back in Craster and looking for somewhere to have lunch, Devan had put his foot down several times about the kippers.

"I'll watch you eat one," Devan said.

Jonty hated them. "I'll go without."

Devan narrowed his eyes. "I'll buy you one and if you don't eat it, I won't buy you a sex swing."

Jonty gulped. "Okay."

Devan ordered fish and chips for himself and kippers for Jonty. He knew Devan didn't think he was going to eat it, but he was. Though when the plate was put in front of him, he almost gagged.

"Looks delicious." Devan grinned.

"It looks like the mummified remains of two fish. Why do they have to leave the tails on?"

Fifteen minutes later, Jonty had carefully separated a small amount of flesh from a large amount of bones and skin and tails and he wasn't convinced that he'd actually found all the bones. The fuckers were tiny. He knew Devan was trying not to laugh.

"Are you actually going to eat it now?" Devan had hoovered up his fish and chips without sharing. *The bastard.*

Jonty took the tiniest forkful and put it in his mouth. Chewed, swallowed and smiled. *God, it's awful.*

"I'm completely full," he said.

Devan laughed and let him leave the rest.

After Jonty had paid and they were back outside, he groaned. "I'm empty again now."

"Chips?"

"I could eat a few."

They sat on the sea wall while Jonty ate a large portion of chips, smothered with salt and vinegar.

"I was surprised you ate even a mouthful of those kippers," Devan said.

"They were vile. I mean I know some people love them, but ugh."

"I've never enjoyed watching anyone eat something as much. There's never a dull moment with you."

"I knew you'd be impressed by my forty fun things to do with a kipper. Looking at it, taking a picture, cutting it, finding every bone, then finding all the other bones and so on."

"Where's the BDSM in that?"

"I think you'll find the kipper thought that was BDSM."

Devan chuckled.

Not every day was filled with fun. There were more visits to the police. More questions to be answered. Brad was still claiming he was innocent, that he had nothing to do with Tay's fall, that he'd tried to save Jonty from drowning, but the cameras he'd put in the cottage condemned him, linked to his laptop. At least he was locked up and would be until the trial.

Devan went with Jonty to see Tay and there was some reaction from Tay each time they visited, particularly when Brad Greene was mentioned. Tay's mother made a point about Tay being more responsive with Jonty, which just added to the weight of guilt Jonty struggled under. Without Devan he would have crumbled, but the need to stay in Northumberland didn't lessen, even as Tay slowly made progress.

Jonty and Devan talked about what their future held, but had come to no decisions. For Jonty, his plans were clear. He had to stay, find a job and see Devan when he could. But getting down to London not only took a long time, it cost a lot of money. At the moment, Jonty had no home, no job and dwindling savings.

But they were working through Jonty's list of things to do and Jonty had never been happier. Every morning, Devan persuaded him out of bed. If not before he'd been for a run on the beach, then after.

"I'm off," Devan called up the stairs.

"Take something metal with you so if you get lost, I can find you using the metal detector. Do we have one?"

Devan hadn't been gone long when the doorbell rang. Jonty pulled on a robe and went into the front bedroom to check who was there before he went to open the door. It was the postman with a parcel addressed to him.

Jonty put it on the table and sighed. He couldn't think there was any way that Brad could get this delivered to him, but he wasn't going to open it until Devan was back.

He made himself a coffee and waited.

By the time Devan returned, he was bouncing. "A parcel's arrived for me. I'm frightened that Brad's sent it."

"It's a present from me."

"Oh God. Please tell me it's not all your filled condoms. Though the parcel's not big enough."

"That's your first thought?"

Jonty grabbed the scissors. "I'm so excited!"

"Don't get too excited. In one way, you won't approve of what's in there, but I've had an idea and you need what's inside for that idea to work."

"It's not a sex swing then?"

"No."

Jonty cut across the top of the packet and tipped the contents onto the table.

"Ooh. Sea glass. Wow." Each pack contained a different colour.

"Obviously, it's not sea glass. But it looks like sea glass. My idea is that you make things with these and sell them. You'll be less attached to them because you didn't find the glass yourself. I want you to make pieces for the new hotel. There'll be a shop inside and we can sell your work there too. There's a market for your art, Jonty."

"You think?"

"I know."

Jonty smiled. "I need frames."

"I've thought of that too. Ikea. Frames are not the only things we need. We have to buy furniture, kitchen equipment, a couch, bed…"

Jonty's heart leapt. "You're going to stay up here?"

Devan took his hand. "We're going to look for a place to rent for a year. You want to stay near Tay and it's easier for me to come to you. I can work remotely some of the time. If I need to travel, you can come too."

Jonty moved into his arms. "And I've been thinking that I'd come to London with you when our month here was done. I'd train in your hotels like you wanted or I'd find another job and every two weeks, we'd come up here for the weekend and I could see Tay."

"Which would you prefer?"

Oh God. It meant so much to Jonty that Devan was willing to disrupt his life to live up here. But he needed him to want a life in Northumberland, just for a while.

"I don't want to choose," he whispered.

"Then we'll stay here. You've still not shown me the tenth wonder of Northumberland."

I think that wonder is you!

They found a newly built rental property in Seahouses that faced the water. When Jonty had read that it had a hot tub, he didn't want to check out anything else and convinced Devan it was perfect. It was. Not that Jonty could have afforded it, but Devan didn't seem to think it was expensive.

On the last morning at Sunshine Cottage, they'd packed and had everywhere cleaned by ten. Mike was due in an hour to collect Jonty's board and the one Devan had purchased at Mike's shop. Mike would also take the things they'd not been able to wedge in Devan's car that they'd bought for their new place, and help them move in.

"I'm already worried about leaving you on Sunday," Devan said.

"We can have Skype sex three times a day. Four if you're desperate."

Devan laughed.

"You could keep looking to see if Brad *did* put pictures of me online."

"He didn't. Stop worrying."

"I keep telling myself it's only a week." Jonty sighed. "But it feels so long. You'll forget how funny I am. You'll forget how tight my jeans are."

Devan had asked Jonty to go with him, but he'd said no. He'd be a distraction and Devan had a lot to do. Devan had agreed with Alan that he'd work remotely as much as he could and when renovations started on the hotel, he'd take on the role of project manager, living full time in Northumberland, only travelling when Alan needed him to. Alan had agreed, that once the hotel opened, Devan could run the place for six months and Jonty could act as concierge, though he wanted Jonty to train in one of their hotels.

What Alan didn't yet know was that Devan wanted to take a sabbatical, and travel to the ends of the earth with Jonty, though Jonty *was* going to put his foot down about some places. Even if Tay wasn't better in a year's time, Jonty would accept he'd done what he could. Tay wouldn't have expected him to put his life on hold forever. It wasn't as if he was abandoning him, just going away for a while. But not yet. And Tay might be better by the time Jonty left. He hoped he was.

"Want to take a final walk?" Devan asked.

"Yep."

They stepped out of the cottage and as they headed down to the beach, Devan took Jonty's hand in his.

"I'll be back on Friday and we'll go to Ikea again on Saturday." Devan shuddered.

"You are the best boyfriend ever. You only lost me twice in there."

"I'm going to get one of those things parents use to keep kids with them."

"Reins! Yay! They can be multi-purpose." Jonty laughed and tugged Devan towards the sea. The wind was whipping foam off the surface and the waves were huge.

"Are you sure you want to work for Mike?" Devan asked.

Lee, who worked in Mike's Sports Shop, was leaving in a month for a winter job in a ski chalet in France and Mike had offered Jonty part time work.

"Willis kept asking me that. Mike's a grumpy dick at times, but I can do the job. I know the beach. I know the equipment—mostly. I'll enjoy it and it gives me time to work on the sea glass pieces."

"I thought Mike wanted to change his mind when he heard your idea to turn part of the shop into a café."

"He's still going to argue, but in the autumn and winter, people will be glad of somewhere to buy a drink. I can make biscuits and scones. If he puts chairs and tables in the lee of the building, people will have somewhere to sit, and dogs and all other animals apart from snakes will be most welcome."

"Just be careful in the water."

"I will."

Jonty got a shiver of pleasure when Devan worried about him.

He squeezed Devan's fingers. "We can make this work. We have a plan. This time next year we'll be looking forward to having vaccinations against cholera, yellow fever, TB, encephalitis..."

Devan chuckled. "Don't forget to apply for a passport in case I feel the urge to whisk you off to Paris. And don't forget you have a driving lesson on Sunday afternoon."

"I could drive to Seahouses to our new place." Jonty waited for Devan to shudder.

"My precious? I think not."

Devan had freaked out the first and only time Jonty sat behind the wheel of the Aston.

"You were hyperventilating before I got out of the drive. Every time a car came in the other direction you shut your eyes."

"You're supposed to start slowly. I hadn't expected you to ram your foot on the accelerator."

"Twenty miles an hour?"

Devan laughed. "It was more than that."

Devan had paid for Jonty to have twenty sessions with an instructor. He was leaving his resprayed car up in Northumberland and taking the train back to London because he didn't want to have to drive back and forth. Quicker to take the train or fly and use an Uber.

"Remember you promised to leave the Aston in the garage," Devan said.

"I might sit in it and pretend to be James Bond."

"Without moving it from the garage."

"A naked horny James Bond."

"Oh fuck. Take selfies."

Jonty laughed.

"Apart from a few difficult moments when I thought we were going to die and that includes you driving my Aston," Devan said, "this has been the best month of my life."

Jonty glanced at him. Devan was looking at him with that expression on his face that always made Jonty's cock jump. Like he'd never seen anyone like Jonty before, never wanted anyone as much.

"I came up here full of anger and bitterness…" Devan gave a short laugh. "As you accurately pointed out, I was sad, and you taught me how to smile again. You've not only shown me life was worth living, but worth living well. There's so much to see. So much to do and I want to do it with you. Every day has been an adventure. Every day you've made me laugh. I've done things with you that I would never have contemplated."

Devan stopped walking and pulled Jonty round to face him. He held his face with his hands and kissed him, a deep passionate kiss that warmed Jonty from head to toe. "Thank you for being there for me, Jonty Bloom. Thank you for changing my life."

"Are you thanking me for making you do the broomstick training at Alnwick Castle?"

"Thank you for making me look a prat, mounting and dismounting a broomstick, time after time, surrounded by a bunch of giggling kids."

"You're welcome."

"I still don't believe you had to keep taking pictures because you hadn't caught me in the air." Devan frowned. "And I still haven't forgiven you for sending *all* my contacts that shot of me leaping up with the broomstick between my legs and my mouth open. I mean, *all* my bloody contacts. *And* I was wearing a Slytherin scarf."

"Would it have been okay if it had been my Gryffindor one?"

"No, it wouldn't." But Devan was smiling.

"It's been the best month of my entire existence too," Jonty said. "Since you arrived, my life has tumbled like a piece of sea glass. All those sharp edges smoothed over, my true colours able to shine. My world has grown brighter and brighter. I feel…whole. I always thought it was my mother who was missing, but it wasn't. It was you." *Because you love me and I don't need to hear the words. I just know.*

They walked back to the dunes in front of the house and sat down out of the wind.

"I've got a present for you to take to London." Jonty pulled a photo book out of his jacket pocket. On the front cover, Devan was kite surfing. The sky was bright blue and Devan was miles above the water, flying high.

"I'd be careful who you show it to," Jonty said. "Your mother is fine, but maybe not your father."

Devan opened the book. The first page was a shot of Devan grinning and pointing at a seal on their boat trip to the Farne Islands. The next was Devan and Jonty at Hadrian's wall wearing Roman helmets and pretending to fight with plastic swords, taken by a bemused Japanese tourist. But the one after was Devan lying asleep in bed, sucking his thumb.

"When the hell did you take that? I don't suck my thumb."

"Your mouth was open, and your thumb was available so…"

Devan laughed.

Jonty stood up, and started to walk backwards in the direction of the house. As Devan turned the pages, Jonty knew exactly what he was seeing. His own bare arse, Devan's bare arse. Lots of shots of Devan laughing. None of him looking miserable. A few of him naked. A few of Jonty's cock. More of Devan's cock. The last picture in the book was of the crooked sea glass heart that Jonty had borrowed from Devan's pocket then replaced.

"It wasn't found on that beach," Jonty said. "I'd kept it with me until I found a guy who could make me happy."

Devan came to his side. "You knew then?"

"I took a risk. I could have taken it back if you'd turned out to be a wanker. But I hoped…"

Epilogue

Nine months later

Jonty was beside himself with excitement. After six months of construction and interior design work on the hotel, today was the day it reopened. Well, today was the party and The Dunes—not the name Jonty had chosen—was full of people, a lot of whom were celebrities, though not many Jonty had heard of. Champagne was flowing, not cheap stuff either, and the food prepared by Marcus and his team— Wayne was still around—looked almost too good to eat, but it wasn't, because Jonty had sneaked a few canapés when no one was looking, then rearranged the others to disguise what he'd done.

He and Devan were wearing new suits. On their last trip to London, Devan had bought them both Armani two pieces. Devan's was grey, Jonty's blue. Jonty's fit perfectly, though he'd tried to persuade Devan that he didn't need to pay so much, but Devan had insisted in a way that Jonty had learnt not to push against.

Devan was busy circulating, making sure everything was running smoothly, but he kept coming to find Jonty to check he was okay *and not eating all the canapés* which Devan asked every time. How the hell did he know? Jonty had no concierge duties today. His instructions were to circulate, tell people how wonderful Northumberland was, and help out where needed. Which Jonty took to include testing the food.

He was by the window in the lounge, when he spotted Mike and Willis walking across the car park. Jonty went into the lobby. They handed their invite to a man at the door and Jonty headed towards them.

"Welcome to The Dunes." Jonty grinned.

"Bloody hell, Jonty," Mike said. "This is fantastic. It's like one of those hotels in Dubai, all glass and glitter."

There was a waterfall feature in the lobby where the lift had once been. The stairs and lift had been moved around the corner and the former lounge doubled in size with a wraparound patio. The doors to the patio were open because Devan's desperation for good weather must have got through to someone, and the sun was shining in a cloudless sky. Jonty didn't think he'd ever seen a sky that was so consistently blue, the colour of forever.

A waiter came towards them with a tray of champagne and they each took a glass. Jonty was under strict instructions not to drink too much. He didn't think three was too many.

"You look good," Willis said.

"New suit. Primark."

Willis laughed. "I don't think so. But I wasn't just talking about the suit. *You* seem different."

Jonty pouted. "I didn't look good before? I thought you loved my arse, Willis. You were always looking at it."

Mike glared. "Stop provoking him. You do look different, mate. As if you belong."

A comment that made Jonty realise what Devan had done in buying him such an expensive suit. He'd tried to make him feel good about himself. It had worked. Jonty was sorry he'd made the Primark joke now.

"It's still me under the suit. I've not changed that much. Same amazing hair. Same dazzling intellect. Same delightful arse."

"Jesus, is that Lex Kenyon?" Mike whispered.

Jonty turned to look. The American film star was heading their way with Devan. Lex was in his early forties, the star of a series of hugely popular assassin movies. He and Devan had been to the cinema last month to see the latest. Jonty had spent the whole night—

"Jonty, this is Lex. He's an old friend of mine."

"You didn't tell me he was an old friend when I was drooling over him in the cinema." *Damn, I didn't mean to say that out loud. Well, not in a jealous tone.*

Lex laughed.

"Lex, this is Willis and his partner Mike who are friends of Jonty's. Mike runs a sports shop on the next beach along so when you come up here, he's the guy to go to for equipment. And if he's not got it, he'll get it for you."

Everyone shook hands.

"Devan tells me you're the concierge," Lex said to Jonty.

"Yes, would you like a back rub?" Jonty blurted.

Lex chucked.

"You might be laughing, but he's serious," Devan said. "He's still in training. I suspect it will be an ongoing process until he retires."

"He means as a concierge, not for back rubs," Jonty said.

"I might be up for a back rub." Lex's smile was…well, not as nice as Devan's. Plus, Devan had that hint of a glare on his face.

"I've been told no," Jonty said.

"Devan didn't say a word." Lex looked between them.

"He doesn't need to speak." Jonty shrugged. "We have a telepathic link. I just told him he doesn't have a small dick."

Devan groaned. "Jonty, what have I told you?"

"Don't let it out of my mouth?"

Another groan. "And?"

"The importance of appropriate conversation." Jonty held his hand out to Lex and put on his poshest voice. "It's so lovely to meet you, Mr Kenyon. I had no idea you were a friend of Devan's, so I do hope we see a lot more of you. A *lot* more. Maybe you'd like to come for supper. We have a hot tub."

Lex laughed and Devan groaned. When he moved on with Lex, the three of them sighed as they turned to watch the pair go.

"Think we could have an invite too?" Mike asked.

"The hot tub's not big enough," Jonty said. "Did you hear that Brad Greene finally changed his plea to guilty?"

"No. That's great." Mike squeezed his shoulder.

"The bastard's let me spend all this time worrying about having to go to court, when he could have confessed at the start. Now he'll just get sentenced. Not for stalking me though, but for trying to kill Tay."

"How is Tay?" Mike asked.

"Getting there. Very slowly. He's frustrated." Jonty really didn't want to talk about Tay. He'd hoped he'd come today but…

"Why didn't they charge Greene with what he tried to do to you?" Willis asked.

"The Crown Prosecution Service pursued the bigger offence and after Brad's fingerprints were found on the ladder, it was a sort of slam dunk for attempted murder."

"So harassing you, sticking a snake through your letterbox, breaking into your house, dragging you off, nearly drowning you in the sea… that didn't matter?" Mike gaped at him.

"Yeah it did, but not as much as what he did to Tay. Brad didn't break in. A friend of his sister's works at the rental agency and Brad had been following us and spotted us go in. It didn't take him long to find out where we'd rented, then *borrow* a key. The friend of his sister's was sacked. The police talked about charging her, but Brad was still denying everything. There's food in there." Jonty nodded toward the dining room, keen to get off the subject of Brad. "I'll see you later, okay?"

He exhaled when Mike and Willis walked off. He lifted another glass of champagne from the tray of a passing waiter, then turned to see Devan behind him.

"Do I need to gag you?"

"Before my first glass of champagne? That would be cruel and unnatural punishment."

"First glass? How many?"

"Two?"

"Your voice going up at the end of that sentence doesn't fill me with confidence. You're working. No more." He took the champagne from Jonty's hand and put it down.

"You said I wasn't working."

"You're still the face of The Dunes."

Jonty beamed. "Am I? Will I be on the publicity shots? Though I wished it'd been called the name I suggested."

"Sandy McSandface was never going to cut it."

Jonty pouted.

"I had a call from Griff wishing me luck," Devan said.

"Good luck or bad luck?"

Devan laughed. "I assumed it was good luck."

"He was lucky he didn't end up married to Ravi."

"I took a risk interfering."

Devan had asked Stan, his private investigator friend, to follow Ravi. It hadn't taken long to get pictures of Ravi in positions he had great difficulty explaining to Griff. Griff and Devan were less bristly with each other after last Christmas. Jonty thought it was only a matter of time before the two were friends again.

"I've heard a lot of compliments about your sea glass designs. The hotel shop has sold several today."

"Really?"

Devan narrowed his eyes. "So it wasn't you who kept going in to ask Dieter if any had been sold?"

Jonty put on his innocent face, even though it never fooled Devan. He'd made a number of sea glass signs in the hotel, including the names of the rooms and a larger piece featuring two seahorses with their tails entwined that was on the wall in the lounge.

"A couple of guests want to speak to the artist to discuss commissions."

Jonty widened his eyes, then smiled. "One of them you, by any chance?"

"Lex and Delia Drummond, the TV presenter."

Hands landed on the shoulders of both Jonty and Devan.

"Well done." Alan dropped his hands. "The place is fabulous. I've not heard one negative comment."

"We're not quite up and running," Devan said.

Jonty shrugged. "There still won't be a negative comment."

"We need future bookings from the people who are here, or from people they tell about the hotel," Devan said.

"We'll get them." Jonty smiled. "I think we'd drum up interest with my nude weekend idea." He turned to Alan. "It isn't only the guests who are naked but all staff members. I think it's a winner. Everyone here that I've asked has agreed with me."

Alan's jaw dropped.

Devan laughed. "Alan. Think whose mouth that came out of."

Alan let out a relieved huff and scurried off.

"You are an evil little shit," Devan said.

"Am I?"

"It's why I love you."

Every time Devan said that he loved him, the most enormous lump appeared in Jonty's throat. *Is that always going to happen?*

"Struck you dumb again?" Devan smiled. "If I'd have known…"

Jonty swallowed hard. Opened his mouth, then closed it again.

"I really *have* struck you dumb. Wow. Want me to say it again?"

Jonty nodded.

"I love you," Devan whispered.

Jonty bit his lip, grabbed Devan's hand and yanked him through the groups of people and into the office. He closed the door and leaned back against it.

"You're worrying me now," Devan said. "Say something."

"I'm still not sure we're sexually compatible, but I do love you. I love that you want to keep trying to make the sex work."

Devan growled.

"I feel so lucky," Jonty whispered. "You've said I love you four-hundred and eighty-nine times now. And every time you say it, I choke up."

"Sure it's as many as that?"

Jonty plastered a horrified expression on his face. "You haven't been counting, Mr Maths-is-beautiful?"

"I thought it was four-hundred and eighty-seven."

Jonty pulled Devan in and kissed him twice. "I love you. I've never had anyone of my own before and I love you so much. You've given me everything I never had. You stopped me hurting. You made me happy. Properly happy. Deep down inside happy. Just tell me Lex is coming to look at our hot tub and I'll be ecstatically happy."

"He's not coming to look at the hot tub."

Jonty whined. "I'm going to put up a blue plaque. Romance died here."

Devan laughed. "*This* is where romance came to life."

383

And Jonty kissed him.

The End

Tay's story will be told in **A Long Way Back** *(book 2 in the Unfinished Business series) All books will be stand-alones but with linked characters.*

Jonty's Christmas *will be released on December 1ˢᵗ 2020*

About the Author

Barbara Elsborg lives in Kent in the south of England. She always wanted to be a spy, but having confessed to everyone without them even resorting to torture, she decided it was not for her. Volcanology scorched her feet. A morbid fear of sharks put paid to marine biology. So instead, she spent several years successfully selling cyanide.

After dragging up two rotten, ungrateful children and frustrating her sexy, devoted, wonderful husband (who can now stop twisting her arm) she finally has time to conduct an affair with an electrifying plugged-in male, her laptop.

Her books feature quirky heroines and bad boys, and she hopes they are as much fun to read as they are to write.

She loves hearing from readers and can be contacted at bjelsborg@gmail.com If you'd like to hear about future releases please ask to be put on her mailing list.

Other books by Barbara Elsborg

Contemporary MMs
Whatever it Takes
The Story of Us
Edge of Forever
Cowboys Down
With or Without Him
Every Move He Makes
Give Yourself Away
With or Without Him
Falling (Fall and Break book 1)
Breaking (Fall and Break book 2)
Drawn In

385

Dirty Games

Paranormal MMs and MMMs
Archangel's Assassin
Dirty Angel
Bloodline (Norwoods book 2)
The Demon You Know (Norwoods book 3)
Second Chance
A Faerie Story - MMM

Short Stories (MM)
Zeke's Wood

Contemporary MMFs
Anna in the Middle
Susie's Choice
Girl Most Likely to
Talking Trouble
Just What She Wants (novella)
Starting Over (novella)

Contemporary MFs
Strangers
Summer Girl Winter Boy
Kiss a Falling Star
An Ordinary Girl
Perfect Timing (Bedlingham brothers book 1)
Something About Polly (Bedlingham brothers book 2)
Doing the Right Thing (Mansell brothers book 1)
Finding the Right One (Mansell brothers book 2)
Digging Deeper
The Princess and the Prepper (novella)
Snow Play (novella)
On the Right Track (novella)

Short Stories (MF)
Saying Yes
The Bad Widow
The Gift
Dragon Race
Two Birds, One Stone

Romantic Suspense (MF)
Chosen
Crossing the Line

Paranormal MFs and MMFs
Perfect Trouble MF
Power of Love MF
Kiss Interrupted MF
Jumping in Puddles MF (Norwoods book 1)
Rocked MMF
The Small Print MMF
Worlds Apart MMF
The Consolation Prize MF (Trueblood book 1)
Falling for You MF (Trueblood book 2)
Lightning in a Bottle MF ((Trueblood book 3)
The Misfits MMF(Trueblood book 4)
Fight to Remember MMF(Trueblood book 5)
Lucy in the Sky MF (sci fi)
Taking Stock MMF (sci fi)
Just One Bite MF novella

Milton Keynes UK
Ingram Content Group UK Ltd.
UKHW010703280424
441876UK00003B/96

9 798656 371674